The Woman in the Hall

G. B. STERN

First published in 1939

This edition published in 2025 by
The British Library
96 Euston Road
London NW1 2DB

Cataloguing in Publication Data
A catalogue record for this publication is available from the British Library

ISBN 978 0 7123 5523 0
e-ISBN 978 0 7123 6824 7

Text design and typesetting by JCS Publishing Services Ltd
Printed and bound by CPI Group (UK), Croydon, CR0 4YY

For product safety information, please visit
shop.bl.uk/pages/british-library-publishing,
or the Publishing pages on bl.uk.

Contents

←→

The 1930s

←→

←→ 1930: There are 3,621 deaf children of school age in England and Wales. By 1933, there are 81 dedicated schools for deaf pupils in the UK and Ireland.

←→ Between 1930 and 1935 unemployment rates in Britain average 18 per cent.

←→ 1930: Women comprise about 6 per cent of the prison population in England, down from 18 per cent a decade earlier.

←→ By the 1930s, a third of women in the UK do paid work outside their home, of whom about a third work in domestic service.

←→ 1933 (April): The Children and Young Persons Act 1933 sets a minimum working age of 14, among other laws.

←→ 1934 (June): In response to high levels of poverty in Britain, the Unemployment Act 1934 creates the Unemployment Assistance Board to provide means-tested benefits.

←→ 1934 (July): The Hays Code censorship guidelines for motion pictures become enforced, ending the period now known as 'pre-code Hollywood'.

←→ 1937 (May): The Coronation of King George VI, who ascended to the throne after the abdication of his brother Edward.

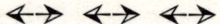

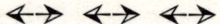 1939: *The Woman in the Hall* is published.

 1939 (September): The outbreak of the Second World War.

← → ← → ← →

G. B. Stern (1890–1973)

← →

G. B. Stern was born Gladys Bertha Stern in London on 17 June 1890, later changing her middle name to 'Bronwyn'. Her family was involved in the gemstone business and suffered financial ruin in an economic crash when Stern was 14 years old. At 16, Stern moved with her parents to study in Germany and Switzerland, including two years at the Swiss Academy of Dramatic Art.

Stern's first publication was a poem in a magazine, aged 17, and her first novel, *Pantomime*, was published in 1914. She went on to write more than forty novels, numerous short stories, plays and ten volumes of autobiography – which tended to take a starting point such as 'gratitude' or 'names' and then move in a non-linear fashion through various reminiscences and observations. Two of her most-loved books were co-written with Sheila Kaye-Smith: *Talking of Jane Austen* (1943) and *More Talk of Jane Austen* (1949), featuring essays about themes and characters in Jane Austen's novels. *The Rakonitz Chronicles*, a series of novels loosely based on her own family, were particularly popular during her lifetime. Her prodigious output was helped by the fact that her writing tended to be dictated to a secretary.

Noel Coward introduced Stern to Geoffrey Lisle Holdsworth, a journalist from New Zealand, with whom she embarked on a short-lived marriage in 1919. Stern was also friends with the novelist Rebecca West, who gave her the nickname 'Peter', which most of Stern's friends came to call her.

Several of Stern's novels were adapted into films, including *The Woman in the Hall* which was filmed under the same name in 1947, directed by Jack Lee and starring Ursula Jeans, Jean Simmons and Cecil Parker. Her final novel was published in 1964, and Stern died nine years later in Wallingford, Oxfordshire, at the age of 83.

Preface

The reader never manages to get very close to Lorna Blake. Deliberately targeting wealthy benefactors, she plumps up her meagre income by shamelessly manipulating money out of them; a task that seems thrilling to her and soon becomes an obsession. But even as her daughters grow up and we delve deeper into her past, she remains as enigmatic as she does when Visiting – a flattering mirror to the presumptions of the person addressing her. Lorna's ability to cloak herself in the respectable gender roles of 1930s society, turning them inside out and upside down in the process, makes her oddly endearing to the modern reader, even as her actions ripple out and cause profound damage to those around her.

The Woman in the Hall is a study of women more generally and of the expectations placed upon them. The story is dominated by flawed female characters: Lorna, of course, but also her promiscuous housemaid, Susan, who relishes other people's daily failures and distresses, and Lorna's friend Mrs. Anderson, who secretly looks down on her companion's dowdy sense of fashion. In contrast, the men in the story seem largely passive victims of the women's actions, their most notable flaw being their gullibility. Could this host of wicked women be Stern's deliberate challenge to the contemporary reader's gender biases? Without any concrete evidence to explain Lorna's actions, the reader is left to form their own judgement.

One wonders if the subject of familial monetary struggle stems

from the author's personal experience. Stern's parents worked in the gem industry and suffered financial ruin during an economic crash when Stern was just 14 years old. The remainder of her youth was marked by years of constant relocation for the family. Still, even if the roots of the narrative may be personal, themes of financial pressure, the complexities of parent-child relationships and gender inequalities will surely resonate just as strongly with contemporary readers as they did with Stern's original audience.

Catriona Gourlay
Curator of Printed Heritage Collections, 1701–1900
The British Library

Publisher's Note

The original novels reprinted in the British Library Women Writers series were written and published in a period ranging, for the most part, from the 1910s to the 1950s. There are many elements of these stories which continue to entertain modern readers, however in some cases there are also uses of language, instances of stereotyping and some attitudes expressed by narrators or characters which may not be endorsed by the publishing standards of today. We acknowledge therefore that some elements in the stories selected for reprinting may continue to make uncomfortable reading for some of our audience. With this series, British Library Publishing aims to offer a new readership a chance to read some of the rare books of the British Library's collections in an affordable paperback format, to enjoy their merits and to look back into the world of the twentieth century as portrayed by their writers. It is not possible to separate these stories from the history of their writing and as such the following novel is presented as it was originally published with minor edits only, to remove a few racist terms and one instance of ambiguous racist intent. We welcome feedback from our readers, which can be sent to the following address:

British Library Publishing
The British Library
96 Euston Road
London, NW1 2DB
United Kingdom

The Woman in the Hall

Part I

A Perfect Childhood

Chapter One

←→

"There's two nuns begging at the door," said Susan.

Mrs. Blake did not reply at once. Her fuzzy head was bent and concentrated. Susan stood for a few moments watching her struggle with glue and cardboard and grey flannelette, and then remarked: "A donkey's head is a thing you didn't ought never to have home-made. Fiddling the way you do—what are shops for? Two nuns. And the children coming along with another child in red I don't much like the look of. And here's a letter, though it's only the water-rate."

None of this was good news for Lorna Blake. Nuns at the door meant they were collecting subscriptions, and that "The Rhododendrons" and "Bloemfontein" and "Cosy Cot" had already contributed. She knew perfectly well that Bottom's head for Molly in the school play was not going to look anything like a head of an orthodox ass. The bill for water-rates (and Susan was well aware of the fact) had arrived two hours before, only Lorna had not picked it up from the mat, but looked at it lying there and said: "Oh dear!" and left it; and Molly and Jay, sociable little girls, never stopped making new friends at school who had to be asked to the house and provided with the sort of tea that would allow them to go home and say *what* a tea they had had at the Blakes'. It was not fair that Susan should have had these four small treats of announcement, all at once. Devoted to Lorna, quick at her work, with black eyes and white vixen teeth that flashed at some perpetual secret joke, no morals, a hangover once a week after her evening out, resourceful in emergencies and primly respectful in front of visitors, Susan had one fault which permeated all her good qualities and very nearly cancelled them: a relish for life which drew its sustenance from other people's daily failures and distresses. If something went right, if that dress of Jay's which Susan said would not wash, did wash, Susan nearly died of chagrin.

On this particular morning her tone was brisk, her eyes snapped and mocked; the sun was shining, and doubtless the weather would break when Mrs. Blake and the children went to the seaside next week: "Oh, and I forgot," concluded Susan, with an enchanting grin, "that new coal's no good, mostly stones. And we've got in twelve hundredweight."

Jay and Molly ran into the room.

"Jay's done frightfully well in the arithmetic paper"—that was Molly, Jay's trumpeter. But Jay always did well in arithmetic. Figures, for Jay, were clear-cut and agile, not those smeared and dragging symbols they appeared to most schoolgirls.

"Mummy," whispered Jay, in what her mother called her sweet-pea voice, putting out little soft coaxing tendrils, "if you come to the window, you'll be just in time to see Naomi. That's her, in red."

"Naomi?"

"Yes, she was new this term, only we thought she swanked until today, but now we like her terribly and she's coming to tea this afternoon if that's all right. Is it? Please, is it? We said it would be."

"But, darlings, Naomi what? and where does she live? and—wouldn't it be better to wait? We know nothing about this little girl, nor who her parents are, nor anything. And she oughtn't to be wearing red for school."

Mrs. Blake hated to disappoint them. But children were so undiscriminating; the last-but-two of these Naomis did not even come from the sort of home where curls were regularly shampooed.

"Well, but then she doesn't know anything about *us*," Jay pleaded. "And *we* might be anyone, but Naomi said her mother never minded a bit."

"Naomi's mother may not mind, Jay dear, but you see, your mother does. After all, they haven't been long in the neighbourhood."

"Well, but nor had we been long in the neighbourhood when we first came here." Jay began to be faintly dizzy with the charm of logic when it worked on her behalf; "and when we came to Barnes from Highgate we were only six weeks in the neighbourhood, and—"

"Shut up," shouted Molly, who was not even the eldest. And pushed against her, like an urchin in a crowd on Bank Holiday.

"We had to hunt for a house, naturally. It would have been too lucky to find at once anything round here to suit us so well as Benares Lodge."

Molly asked in such a casual voice that it hardly seemed worth while for her to be asking at all: "Are we here for ever and ever, now?"

"I hope so, my poppet. I don't like changing homes, any more than you. It's nice to settle down."

Susan, who through the archway was slapping down the knives and forks for lunch, suddenly laughed out loud.

Mrs. Blake gazed at her with gentle reproach. When she had been a girl of seventeen with ideas about noble works, she had adopted Susan, who was nineteen and the village tart and in trouble. She had made Susan her charge and responsibility. Susan, who had queer fires burning in her, had run away twice, and yet, drawn by some strange attachment, had each time returned to Lorna; seemingly unrepentant, sardonically amused at her own surrender, yet ready to work again and to prove herself house-trained. And Susan could be trusted, Lorna thought, not to talk in the wrong way in front of Jay and Molly, for whom she had a caustic affection. But she must not, no, she really must *not* laugh like that when she, Lorna, was delivering one of those plump little lectures wrapped in tolerance which were necessary for the children's guidance.

"Is that my ass's head?" Molly enquired, "because if it is—" she hesitated in search of politeness, for her mother had obviously taken a great deal of trouble, "if it is, mightn't it be better, Mummy, if we had a shop one?"

"I suppose it might," Lorna's inflection was rueful, but not fussy with offended feelings. She rejoiced in Molly's sturdy build and serenely executive dealings with life; in the child's deep sense which was nourishing as crusty bread and a hunk of cheese to the hungry. Holding the square, comic, charming little face between her hands, not regretting that Molly's hair would not curl, nor that she had a clown's wide smile and snub nose, she explained: "You see, darling, if we're to have lots of money to go to the seaside when you break up next week, I think you must try and make your acting so good that nobody in the audience will notice if Bottom's head isn't quite right. Money isn't elastic, is it?"

Susan reminded Lorna that the two nuns were still cluttering up the hall and couldn't stay there for ever, could they, looking holy? She thought a shilling would be enough to get rid of them.

Lorna put on her horn-rimmed spectacles, picked up the worn black notebook belonging to the nuns, and studied the entries: "Oh, I don't think I could give as little as that. No one else has."

"Two shillings; two shillings; two shillings; two, two, two" Jay pressed against her, reading aloud. "All two shillings. Oh, Mummy, do, *do* give ten; no, fifteen; give them seventeen shillings and sixpence, and look different from the rest of silly, mean old Huntingdon Terrace."

Molly was horrified at the showy suggestion, as any boy from a conventional English public-school: "Mummy *can't possibly* give more than two shillings, if not one other person hasn't."

"Molly's quite right." Lorna wrote her name in the book and handed it back to Susan with a florin from her bag.

"Mummy, isn't it wrong and awful to ask for money?"

Lorna replied gently: "It's quite different and not wrong at all, Jay darling, asking for others and not for ourselves. Nuns are Sisters of Charity."

"*Sisters of Charity*—" Jay's voice vibrated queerly, with a warm thrill. Gazing at an obstinate back belonging to her younger sister, she mischievously tried to compel her to turn round. But Molly picked up the ass's head from the table, clapped it over her own head and began a blundering dance, stamping and pawing the carpet, lifting her legs as though they were hoofs and knocking into the furniture because, she chuckled, the eyeholes were in the wrong place down by her ears, and she couldn't see with her ears.

"Sisters of Charity, like Molly and me are sisters?"

"No, darling. Nuns needn't be related at all."

Jay sighed and returned to a more locally interesting subject:

"It's all settled about tea this afternoon, then, isn't it? You see, we felt we *had* to ask her, because she's called Naomi."

"Because she's called Naomi?" Mrs. Blake was puzzled.

"Oh, it's such a lovely, heavenly, lovely name. We've never known a Naomi except in the Scripture lesson; 'Thy country shall be my country—'" Jay slightly over-acted the part of Ruth.

"You've got a lovely, heavenly, lovely name of your own, Miss Jasmine Blake," her mother teased her.

Jay considered that point in silence. Jasmine: a white starry flower with a drop of honey in its calyx if you squeezed it (or even if you didn't). And it smelt like heaven, especially when you were passing Bloemfontein's garden on a warm night. It shone on dark nights, no, more than shone, blazed like white fire: I'll have a park garden one day with all the jasmine and laburnum and lilac there is in all the gardens of Huntingdon Terrace, and a long terrace of my own, and fountains to bathe in. And they'll say: "Have you heard about Jasmine? She's a generous, gracious lady, and she has just given a whole Hundred Pounds to some nuns in the front hall."

Chapter Two

Mrs. Blake and Mrs. Anderson were always together, down at Clifford's Bay. They sat on the beach together and knitted, while the little girls played and paddled and dug in the sand. Together they organized picnics for the children, on the rocks; they sometimes went for a stroll together in the evenings on the Esplanade, to listen to the Band, when the children were safely in bed. And all the time they talked, earnestly or lightly gossiping. Their conversations might have been repeated in any drawing-room and would have caused offence to no one. Mrs. Anderson knitted a great deal better than Mrs. Blake, so that Mrs. Blake said frequently, her brown eyes full of humble admiration: "Oh, I do think you're so clever. I wish I could do that. I'm not good at anything much."

Mrs. Anderson laughed and told her she should not be so modest. "People ought to make the best of themselves," she said, "not the worst," and she looked longingly at Lorna Blake's fuzz of khaki-coloured hair and wondered whether her new friend would be offended if she asked whether she might experiment at arranging it. Her clothes too. In spite of their endless discussions of the fashions in *Woman's Choice* and *Penelope's Patterns*, Mrs. Blake always seemed to lose some of the right effect in transporting them from the coloured page on to her own person. She had no outstanding good points, thought Mrs. Anderson, appraising her, otherwise one could make much of them and tone down the bad points, as the wisdom of *Woman's Choice* taught with care and insight. Yet really she had no bad points either. Just a little bit dowdy. Perhaps if she used a touch of rouge and lipstick—everybody was using them now in 1928. Unless you could count as a good point her perpetual expression of eager amiability, rising from a long mid-Victorian neck. Her only skill in dressing was with scarves; not the sporting downright kind, but fairy airy scarves, Lilian scarves, Mrs. Anderson called them, remembering a poem by Tennyson, "Airy fairy Lilian" and so forth, that she had learned in her early youth. Lorna Blake's scarf floated round her shoulders with an effect of never touching her person anywhere, and looked pretty when she changed into something a little more festive for the evening and strolled up from the rooms she had taken in Granville Road to the Strathmore Private Hotel where Mrs. Anderson and her little daughter, Kathleen, were staying during the August holidays.

"Look at your painting," said Mrs. Anderson now, in reply to "you're so clever and I'm no good at anything."

"Oh, but I shouldn't have told you. It's only tinting Christmas cards that are there already; nothing original. I do it to eke out my little income. One wants to give the infants so many special treats, especially round Christmas, and, of course, one can't get into debt."

Mrs. Anderson agreed that of course one could not get into debt, and quoted Mr. Micawber to the effect that if you had twenty shillings— "spend nineteen-and-six, result happiness. Spend twenty-shillings-and-sixpence, result misery."

"Happiness," Lorna Blake mused, "I wonder exactly where happiness lies? Do you know, I once heard someone say that happiness was a boomerang: you throw it out and think no more about it, and back it comes, tap-tapping at the window. It sounds a little priggish, but I've proved it *is* true, over and over again." She laughed away any suggestion of abstract philosophy, and added: "I expect the journey out into the fresh air does it good."

You nice little soul, thought Mrs. Anderson.

Molly, Jay and Kathleen came dashing up to enquire if it were eleven o'clock yet and how soon could they bathe and need they wait till after bathing for their greengages?

"Another half-hour, darlings. It's too soon after breakfast. You *can't* be hungry yet. Why don't you build two beautiful thrones with your spades, and presently Mrs. Anderson and I will come and sit in them."

They pondered with a certain suspicion on this idea, and then accepted it. Kathy Anderson, a thin, tentative, bookish child, mentioned King Canute, and the three scampered off to build a throne where the tide could presently be trusted to lick round the king's feet.

"They're having a good time, I think, bless them. I wish we lived in London, too, so that Kathy could often see Jay and Molly. They're just what she needs."

Lorna smiled, and said, after the disparaging fashion of mothers of this generation: "They're not bad little crumpets!" It was her quaint habit always to follow up a serious remark with some light contribution, or vice versa, as though she found it too difficult, even at thirty, to be decisive as to whether her nature were grave or playful. So now she picked up a piece of chalk from the sand and stared at it absently, whilst in the manner of one taking a vow she declared: "Jay and Molly are to have a perfect childhood, or as nearly perfect as I can make it. I don't mind what sacrifices …"

Mrs. Anderson was used to mothers saying they never minded what sacrifices. She said it herself and meant it. But she realized an unusually steadfast quality in her nice, rather dullish Mrs. Blake just at this moment. As though she were consecrating herself.

"Perhaps," she ventured, "you weren't very happy yourself, when you were a child?"

"Miserable, most of the time. Mother and I were alone, you see, till I was fifteen. She was very pretty and very helpless, and then her deafness—"

"Oh, my dear!"

"Yes. And so most of it fell on me, long before I was old enough. People were kind, as they usually are if you give them a chance. I've learnt that if you're in trouble, you always find someone who is willing to help. But you have to ask. I've been surprised, over and over again, how kind people are, directly they *know*. But they never guess of their own accord."

"'There are more things in heaven and earth—'" But Mrs. Anderson was curious about the facts of Mrs. Blake's past, now she had got down to it without violating manners, and tried politely to steer her away from abstractions: "Did your poor mother ever marry again?"

"Yes, I'm glad to say. I was delighted at first; Mr. Inglefield was well-off, and I was so tired of responsibility—"

She paused. Mrs. Anderson made sympathetic sounds, but she was casting off at the neck of the jumper she was knitting, and so for a moment neither spoke. Then Lorna tossed away the piece of chalk and laughed and said:

"I expect I should manage better now. Step-relations have to be humoured. After all, one was there on sufferance."

"Was he unkind to you, your stepfather? What a shame!"

"Not he, no. But he had two sons, Marcus and Neil, and they, well, they were not exactly unkind, I suppose, but—Oh, I was wretched. Never mind, it's all past and forgotten, and life's going to be splendid for Jay and Molly."

She related nothing of her own marriage with Mr. Blake, whoever he was, and Mrs. Anderson felt that there, too, must have been disillusion and grief, better not spoken about. She did not feel that it would be too tactless, however, to enquire whether Jay and Molly took after their father's side of the family or their mother's. "They neither look like you."

"No, Molly takes after her father, bless her." (Not bless *him*, noted Mrs. Anderson in parenthesis.) "She's a plain little cub, though." (Then *he* was handsome, Mrs. Anderson noted again.) "Jay looks a little like my own mother, I always think."

"Jay's going to be a beauty," Mrs. Anderson came in on her cue.

"Do you really think so? Well, perhaps. It's an attractive little guinea-pig, even now."

Mrs. Anderson could not think that "guinea-pig" was the best description for Jay, with her delicate mobile face like something seen swiftly in a classical frieze, and her almond eyes tilted like a geisha's, except that they were blue, not Japanese brown; deep sea-blue. She suspected that Jay was her mother's favourite; that though Mrs. Blake would have asserted quickly and conventionally that she had no favourites and that both children were her favourites, "Jay" would have floating up from her heart like a small secret bubble.

"Molly tumbles about so; look at her now. And I shall have to comb all that sand out of her hair."

"I could never see the pleasure in somersaults, but children seem to like being upside down."

"I suppose they know they will have to spend the rest of their lives right side up."

"You do say the most original things." Though this was probably the first even mildly original thing Mrs. Blake had said to her.

"Me, my dear? Original? Why, you wouldn't find a more humdrum person than me anywhere! Pottering among my flower-beds, and cobbling up the kiddies' clothes on my sewing-machine—I haven't the knack of it like you; it's genius, the way you dress Kathy, even her little beach-suits, but Susan and I manage between us to keep our young horrors looking just respectable." She smiled, without martyrdom.

"She has a very sweety merry smile," thought Mrs. Anderson. "And a charming voice, too, though I suppose one hardly counts voices."

Aloud she said: "Susan must be a treasure, from what I hear of her."

"Oh, she's what I'd call a rough diamond. She was in trouble once— hush—-*you* know; that was before I married; and afterwards she literally followed me wherever I went. She's not a polished specimen, but very good for me, and keeps me from fussing too much over my two monkeys, and making too many ambitious plans for them. Molly and Jay are so independent."

"I think they all are, nowadays."

"I expect my maternal pride will have a fall, when I see my Molly an acrobat in a circus."

"And Jay?"

"Oh, there's no doubt about Jay's future. Jay, you wouldn't think it, it's so unromantic, but she's brilliant at anything to do with figures. Adds up like a streak of lightning. You should hear what her present headmistress says about her."

"They haven't always been at the same school, then?"

"No. No, they haven't. We moved to Huntingdon Terrace just over a year ago."

"Moving into a different neighbourhood is sometimes a little depressing and lonely, I always think. I cried for weeks when we first went to Cheltenham. Or did you already have friends in Huntingdon Terrace?"

Mrs. Blake shook her head: "A few people called on me when I first moved in, but I didn't return their calls. I'm afraid I'm not very good at visiting; so many questions, and so often nothing comes of it."

"Can't you possibly stay a few days longer than tomorrow? These holidays have flown so fast, and my young sardines are going to miss Kathy."

"Not so much as Kathy will miss them. They'll be going back to school."

"Yes, but we have another ten days at Clifford's Bay after you go. And Kathy goes to school too, doesn't she?"

Mrs. Anderson shook her head and looked worried.

"She did, but I'm afraid I shall have to take her away. Her chest. She really isn't strong enough, and Clifford's Bay hasn't done as much as I hoped for her."

"I'm so sorry. What will you do, then? Teach her yourself?"

"My goodness, no. I'm not nearly clever enough. Besides, I have my work cut out with the boys. My house is like a zoo and I never get a minute to myself. It's dreadful."

"I know," said Lorna, slyly smiling, "it's dreadful; and you'd much rather be without them. Still, does one ever mind how much one does for one's children?"

"No, that's true. I'd beg my bread from door to door," said Mrs. Anderson, "rather than let Billy and Tom and Kathy go without."

"Yes," said Mrs. Blake, "so would I—" She broke off to warn Jay, who had just run up from the sea to the bathing-cabin, to dry herself properly between the shoulders. "And where's Molly?"

"Here, Mummy."

"Lie quiet for a bit after your bathe, Molly. The greengages are over there, next to the rugs."

"In a sec." Molly dashed past, intent on some urgency of live crabs in a bucket.

"You have to let them run wild sometimes." Mrs. Blake and Mrs. Anderson resumed their chat.

"Yes, Kathy's been pampered at home. I really must force myself at last to send her old nanny away, now that I'm going to get a governess. You know what these old servants are, so absurdly jealous and bossy."

"Oh, my dear, yes. You should hear my Susan. I'm not sure, really, if I employ her or if she very kindly employs me." Lorna laughed at her little joke. Then, sliding into a serious mood, she asked: "But are you actually planning to have a *governess* in your house?"

"My dear, you said that as though you were asking if I intended to have a snake loose in my house."

"I'd rather have a snake. You know where you are, with snakes."

"I'm not so sure that you do." Mrs, Anderson twisted round and stared at the other woman, surprised at her passion. Only once before had she spoken in the least like that, when she had declared her intention of giving Molly and Jay a perfect childhood. "Some governesses are rather a trial, I believe, so plaintive and such ladies always, and of course servants hate to wait on them, but on the whole—"

Mrs. Blake interrupted: "I could put up with them being no more than plaintive," she was trying to control her voice, but it still shook with the same unnatural excitement. "I'm speaking for your Kathy's sake, and I know what I'm talking about. I'm not exaggerating. I had two dreadful experiences with governesses for Jay and Molly when they were younger. And if I hadn't been on the look-out with the last one—Gardiner, that was her name, Miss Gardiner—Luckily I think no real harm has been done, but if I had my way, I'd have every governess turned out of England."

"My *dear*!" Mrs. Anderson was still half-laughing, though she felt a trifle uncomfortable.

"Listen," said Lorna Blake …

Chapter Three

Kathy and Jay had been running too fast, down on the hard sand, and Kathy had fallen over and was crying loudly-Both mothers rose quickly and went to the rescue.

"I'll remember what you told me and think it over," Mrs. Anderson promised.

And Molly sat on in the sand-hole near by, where she had rolled comfortably a few minutes ago to eat her sun-warmed greengages. She looked dazed as though she had received a shock, her funny determined face white and strained.

So it was not over. It was all going to begin again. Visiting.

For they had never had any governesses, she and Jay.

But Molly remembered that strange excited voice when her mother made things up, so different from her usual indulgent comfortable voice, a little helpless, a little amused at its own helplessness. And Molly remembered, too, that there *had* been a governess, though not theirs. ("You'll be all right, then? Miss Gardiner will meet you at the station and put you on your train. I do hope you'll find that your husband …")

She had been eight, not ten as she was now. They were not living in Huntingdon Terrace, nor in Highgate, nor in Barnes, where they had moved after Highgate. It was before they had begun to move about. They had lived as long as Molly could remember at The Nook, Woodgrange Road, Putney. And Jay was terribly ill. They were afraid Jay would die, she and Mummy. So many children, when they were like Jay, died in one's stupider story-books. She was in a nursing-home not far away. Susan had said: "You're mad not to let her go into hospital. Much better looked after and much cheaper. They'll take the skin from your ears in those private homes and not say thank you." But Jay had screamed herself into a fit at the word hospital and clung to Mummy and prayed and pleaded not to be sent to one, as though it were as bad as prison and the same thing. "Must have read some nonsense somewhere," said Susan. "Or picked it up chattering with people she shouldn't have been."

Anyhow, Mummy had given in to Jay and sent her to this small nursing-home, which, she had assured Susan, could not make charges like the big West End places. Susan snapped: "You'll see." And now the account for the first three weeks had come in.

"It's those injections, more than anything else," Lorna had cried wildly, sharing her dismay with Susan, who as usual showed forbearance and tenderness, having been in the right. "She must have them, of course, but—"

"Wish I had it to lend you," Susan said. And Mummy had kissed her and had tried to be cheerful at lunch and to make a fuss of Molly, though once she had said, as though thinking aloud: "Money. How *does* one earn a lot of money quickly like that? It isn't as if I were clever—"

"Aren't you clever, Mummy?" in surprise.

"No, my pet," half-laughing, half-crying, and a kiss, and then a smother of kisses as though she were not only Molly but Jay as well.

All that long afternoon Mummy could settle down to nothing, not even for a nap, as Susan suggested, for she had not been sleeping at night. She tried to sew a little, and she tried reading.

Molly, at Susan's suggestion ("Take her mind off it"), had been allowed to paint the dolls'-house roof. She cared nothing about dolls; dolls were stuffed and silly; but roofs and walls and doors, building matters, achieved a certain solid status in Molly's play world. Every now and then she came and stood on tiptoe at Mummy's shoulder as she turned the pages, and saw that the book was full of photographs, and spelt out: "Lionel Lovett. De Reszke. Mrs. Patrick Campbell. John Barrymore—Do you know them all, Mummy? Was any of them your best boy?" Susan had a faded photograph in the kitchen, and always told grocers and butchers and people that it was her best boy who had been killed in the war.

"No, lambkin, I'm not as grand as that. And you're my best boy." So Molly had gone back to the dolls'-house, squatting there disconsolately and blobbing the paint listlessly over herself, the floor and the roof, for she had not been allowed to do this when she wanted to, while Jay was at home, and now it was no fun.

Suddenly her mother had slammed down the book and jumped up and cried in a loud voice which Molly hardly recognized: "I will. I will. I'll try it. She can't eat me." She picked up the book and swiftly read over a certain page as Molly and Jay used to have a last frantic early morning look at their history for the day, to make sure they knew it, before they got to school. Then she ran upstairs and came down again in a raincoat with her hat pulled on anyhow over her hair all untidy and no gloves; Mummy couldn't surely be going out without gloves? And she stared at Molly, her eyes screwed up like Miss Thompson in the junior drawing-class, getting what she told them was "a perspective" and "vanishing-point." How they had giggled over "vanishing-point"; when Nora was in the lavatory and Doris came in asking where she was—"She's at vanishing-point!" they chanted in chorus, triumphantly.

"Come on, Molly, leave that. You're coming out with Mummy. No, just as you are; you needn't go upstairs again. I'm in a hurry."

Molly was wearing an old gym tunic, very worn and shrunk and much too short for her now, but Susan had said it would be good enough to get smeared all over, with paint. And black wool stockings with holes in them. "But, Mummy, where are we going?"

"Visiting. Visiting a nice lady."

"Must *I* go?"

"Yes. Yes, it may help."

And when they were out in the street, she stood still, dropped Molly's hand and stared at her in the same frightening way she had done before. "She does look a pathetic little object," she murmured. And Molly had hard work not to cry. Her mother had never before called her "she" when there was no one else there.

A long jolting journey by bus, and then a wait in the rain, and another journey into a beautiful part of London, with flower-boxes, and big shining motor-cars in front of nearly every door. Molly wanted to stop every minute and admire something, but her mother pulled her along. They stood outside a front door and rang the bell. It wasn't a sort of Susan who opened it, but a stern man in a black coat.

"Is Baroness von Soll in?"

"Would her ladyship be expecting you?"

"No, but she'll see me. Please tell her Mrs. Blake is here and that it's very urgent."

The man stood like wood. "The Baroness only sees people by appointment."

"I must see her."

"She is engaged at the moment."

"Mummy," gasped Molly, tugging at an unresponsive hand, "let's go away. Let's."

"Will you tell the Baroness that I'm a friend of Mr. Lionel Lovett, the famous actor? I have a message from him."

The man hesitated; then, leaving them standing on the doorstep, he disappeared.

"Is it a new game?" Molly tried piteously, for the last time that day, to bring experience into familiar range.

"Hush, baby, hush. But no wonder," soothing her, "you're tired and hungry."

They had had lunch as usual, lunch and tea; and she had never been "baby" but "Molly" right back along her eight years of memory. Bewilderment thickened.

Yet now, two years after, squatting desolate in the sand-hole in the hot swimmy sunshine, a gritty half-eaten greengage tightly clenched, how surprisingly bits of cheerful ordinary school life provided an answer to what had then been all a choking fog: rehearsals for the *Midsummer Night's Dream* and Miss Collins drilling them in their parts, saying her emphatic stresses: "The *best* way to get integrity into your performance, indeed the *only* way, Molly Blake, is to think yourself *right into* Bottom. Be Bottom, even *before* your entrance. Do you see what I mean?"

"Oh yes, Miss Collins." That was easy. "Miss Collins, what is integrity? How do I get it?"

The headmistress twinkled. "You either have it or you haven't, child."

The manservant came back.

"The Baroness will see you."

They followed him through the hall, through a vast drawing-room grandly furnished all in white, with one enormous dark blue rug before the fireplace. Their steps clattered on the parquet. He opened the door for them into a smaller room, stood coldly aside for them to enter, then vanished.

At first it was not as bad as Molly had dreaded. The Baroness was quite an old lady, and listened with a kind and encouraging air while Mummy just quietly told her all about Jay's illness and the expensive treatment, and how her tiny income was at its lowest ebb just now because by the terms of her lease she had recently had to re-decorate and put their tiny house into repair. Molly heaved a sigh of relief. She could not define exactly what she had feared and expected; but there *had* been painters sitting on swings outside their windows and workmen hammering at their walls for weeks and weeks, and the Baroness, who spoke funny English, rolling her "r's," said yes, she had suffered from much the same thing in her own house last year: "a trremendous expense," and she enquired how old Jay was and how old Molly was, and would Molly like a piece of cake? No, thank you. And then Mummy said: "You can't imagine how I hate asking, I've never done it before, but when it's for the children—" "Yes, yes, when it is for our children—" "You do see? I knew you would. I've lost touch with dear Lionel ever since he settled in America, but he used to tell me you were the most golden-hearted woman he had ever met, and how wonderfully you had helped him that time in Rome when the tenor was jealous and wanted to get him out of the company. So when I didn't know which way to turn, I heard a voice speaking to me out of the blue: 'She'll help you. Go to her and quite simply tell her the truth. There's no shame in it, and you need never do it again, but just this once, for Jay's sake.' So I came."

Nothing about the book. And Molly had heard no voice saying all that, but perhaps Mummy had better ears. Anyhow, the Baroness had said: "Let her have the treatment and send the bills to me, I will see that they are paid."

Mummy said gently: "You are too good and generous to wish me to thank you, so I won't say anything more." And the Baroness said, "No, please, I understand." And Mummy said: "Yes. You understand." And as they could not keep on telling each other they understood, Molly hoped she and Mummy were soon going.

And then a dreadful thing happened. Her mother got terribly excited and began to laugh and cry all over the Baroness's hands with their sparkling rings, and poured out a further tale, messy and incoherent, which she said she had never told anyone before, but there was a hope now, just a hope, that if the Baroness would help her, and she could go up to Liverpool that very evening, her husband was sailing in the morning, they had been separated for years, she might never see him again, but his father and mother were rich, they would be seeing him off, they had never acknowledged her, that was the trouble, she was not a Roman Catholic, it wouldn't be fair to tell his real name; no, not Blake, Blake was only a name she used so as not to—yes, she would tell it, she could trust her kind, kind friend: Inglefield. Neil Inglefield …

Molly could hardly believe it was her own mother speaking; her nice, funny, unfussy mother; even her face had slipped out of its familiar cosiness; the lines were deeper, the eyes rounder and bulged a little. She used wide distraught gestures that did not seem to have anything to do with what she was saying. Once, when she told about showing them their grandchild, she drew Molly towards her in a suffocating embrace, then pushed back the hair from her forehead so that the Baroness could see her more clearly: "Isn't it a dear, innocent little face!" she exclaimed, and, not waiting for an answer, had rushed on with more and more about going to Liverpool: Surely if Neil's mother and father could see Molly, if she took Molly up with her, she might be just in time, just in time. If she could say: "This is your grandchild. And her sister, your other grandchild, is dying," perhaps it might mean a regular income, a help at least towards bringing up the children, educating them, giving them a chance—oh, it might mean everything, might make all the difference in the world if she had the fare for herself and Molly to set out this very evening. Tomorrow would be too late … "I could show you all the papers, only there isn't time."

And in the end, the Baroness sent for her bag and took out a lot of notes, actual money this time, not a promise, and gave them to Mummy. She said it was their return fare to Liverpool; but perhaps she just wanted them to leave, perhaps she hated this scene as much as Molly, and felt as helpless and hot.

Mummy, having got the money, became quiet again and said: "Thank you and God bless you. You don't know what you've done." And then they followed the manservant out, as they had followed him in, and Mummy, when they were out in the street once more, smiled at Molly and said, "Wasn't that a pretty room, Mollykins? The white one with the blue rug?"

Molly imagined that directly they got home they would pack all in a hurry and set off for Liverpool. But when they got home, there was no sense of hurry nor of a journey impending; no one brought out a rug-strap, nor started folding underwear. Her mother rang up the doctor, and Molly heard her say that it was all right about further injections; they were to be paid for. And then she had a long talk with Susan; Molly was shut out, but it all sounded gay and laughing. And Susan called back over her shoulder, coming out: "Well, I'd have done it myself, if I'd the nerve. It isn't as if they hadn't got plenty to spare." And seeing Molly huddled on the stairs, still in her shrunken gym tunic with smears of paint on it, and one of her stockings coming down, twisted and wrinkling, she remarked with a shade of compassion in her tone: "You do look a young scarecrow, I must say. Run along up to bed, now."

"I can't," explained Molly forlornly. "We're going to Liverpool."

"Oh, you are, are you?" Susan stood for a moment as though not quite knowing what to say. Then went on into the kitchen, and Mummy came out from the sitting-room and said she was going to put Molly to bed for a treat and tell her a story. "Cheer up, Jay will get well now."

"But aren't we going?"

"Going where?"

"To Liverpool."

"Not this time, pet."

Up till that moment, all that had happened had seemed a nightmare jumble, but at least a nightmare that no one could help. But now Molly knew that her mother herself had actually made it all happen, and could have stopped it, and didn't. Her mother had asked for their fare to Liverpool and got it, and they were not going to Liverpool. Perhaps she had never meant to go.

She tucked in the sheets and sat on the edge of Mollys bed and told her a fairy tale. She told nice fairy tales.

The next day Molly was hardly surprised when informed that Mummy was going to take her out again. Visiting. Mummy made it sound like a treat; but when Molly came downstairs in her prettiest frock, an embroidered tussore, and a floppy hat with buttercups round the crown, her mother looked at her critically, shook her head and commanded her to get back into the old gym tunic she had worn yesterday.

"But it's much too tight," whispered Molly, her throat dry with apprehension.

"Never mind. Put it on. And the same stockings." And in the hall, just before they started, she changed Molly's sailor-hat for an old green floppy tam belonging to herself, which hung on a peg and was usually worn for weeding in the garden in the rain.

They took a bus to another rich part of London, and this time there was a maid at the door who said no, they couldn't possibly see Miss Betty Phillimore herself, but Miss Phillimore's secretary. And Mummy said that would be no good, and could she write a note? "Well, really, I'm not sure," said the prim maid. "Please. It's terribly important." "Miss Phillimore isn't in." "Then I'll wait. But I have to see her; it's a matter of life and death."

The maid, perplexed, brought her an envelope and a pencil and a piece of paper, and admitted grudgingly that Miss Phillimore might have come in just a moment ago.

Molly, standing first on one leg and then on the other, watched while her mother scribbled about three frenzied pages. It was funny how soon you got used to a routine of awful things. Only yesterday morning she had known nothing about Visiting, and strange thresholds with antagonistic servants barring the way. But now she felt no surprise any more; it just had to be endured. At least Jay had been spared from doing this. If Molly could have used metaphor, but she never did, she might have expressed her belief that Jay was glass, brittle and thinly clear and lovely, and she herself a strong bit of clay, solid as a flower-pot. Mummy planted mignonette in flower-pots; they never got broken.

Once they were allowed to see Miss Phillimore, it was even easier than yesterday, and Mummy did not have to cry so much nor kiss Molly so wildly; she only said pathetically: "She's all I've got," and didn't mention Jay. She left out all the true part about treatment for Jay and the house-painters taking the money, but this time her wicked, cruel husband, Neil Inglefield, Molly's father, was plotting to kidnap Molly, and their only sanctuary lay with an uncle who lived in the wilds of Ireland, so that they had to cross from a place called Holyhead, a long way and a big fare. "I hardly dare ask you, only directly I read what you'd done for Oliver Bell, I knew you'd understand and be sympathetic. There are some people I'd rather die than ask."

As hope survives at the very bottom of the box, there remained a hope in Molly's heart that yesterday had been a mistake, and today they really would use the money to travel to a place called Holyhead to cross for the wilds of Ireland. She hoped and waited until she had to go to bed, and that was the end of it. She asked no questions, for she knew the answer: "Not this time, pet." And she was grateful when her mother made no offer of a bedtime fairy tale. Her mother was still wholly unfamiliar, in a mood abstracted yet jubilant, and wandered restlessly from room to room, humming an old tune: "Rhoda, Rhoda ran a pagoda, selling tea and syrup and soda." Jay and Molly had always liked the words of that tune with its suggestion of playing at shop.

Susan came in to switch off the light. She appeared ready to chat; curious, maybe, to hear Molly's point of view: "Your mother's struck oil," she remarked.

Molly remained reticent. And Susan departed after one or two more tries: "She's not half pleased, too; money for jam. Mind you, I think she'd better not have mixed you up in it. Not that I'm one to preach at anyone for liking a gamble. She's always been the best joke I know, Miss Lorna has. Always. And pulled it off every time—except Mr. Marcus; and then would have but for that there Young Neil—Well, you *are* a Miss Sleepyhead. Mind you don't forget Rabbits and Hares directly you wake up, for luck the first of the month."

You dreamt of someone called Young Neil. He was chasing you round and round the Baroness's white drawing-room, and when you slipped on the parquet and were caught, he kissed you and laughed: "Don't be afraid, we're going for a ride in a pagoda." And Susan, in the dream, rode in front of the Lord Mayor's chariot with the coachman whom she claimed as her best boy. And that-there-Young-Neil sat with you behind on all the custard cushions and he picked up a trumpet and shouted through it: "Isn't it a dear innocent little face" …

She woke slowly, her mouth sick with hate for the dawn. "Jay!"—And then a quick gabble: "Rabbits and hares! Oh, rabbits and hares!" But too late: she had already said "Jay."

Nothing happened on Wednesday or Thursday. Molly was not deceived; the lull did not mean that the good times had come back again. On the third day, when she was summoned with a jolly air to come out Visiting with Mummy, Molly put on her old gym tunic without being told.

The third visit, at the beginning, looked the easiest of all. The lady herself passed through the hall just as the words: "I couldn't say when she'll be back" sounded more obdurate than usual.

"Is it somebody for me, Robson?" wispy, peering, indecisive.

Mummy flung herself forward, and from the torrent of her appeal Molly picked up that Mrs. Flaxman was not herself famous like the Baroness or Miss Betty Phillimore, but had a little boy who played the violin so wonderfully that millions of people paid to hear him:

"And when I heard him last year doing the Concerto in G, we both cried and cried, my little daughter Jasmine and I—No, this isn't Jasmine, this is Molly; you don't like concerts, do you, my darling? And I thought his mother must be the proudest woman in the world. I thought he must have a sensitive, imaginative mother or he couldn't play like this. And today I was desperate, with Jasmine so terribly ill. She's not a genius, or perhaps she is, I don't know, I don't care, she's my little girl just as he's your little boy, even when the whole of the Albert Hall is cheering him. And suddenly I saw your name as clearly as though it were written up on a wall, and I knew there was just one chance …"

Molly's attention wandered, and she did not grasp what the one chance was, except that it was somehow connected with their fare to

Edinburgh and it had to be immediately, by the 10.50 that evening, or it would be too late to stop somebody and get him to do something to save them. No mention this time of dear old Lionel Lovett or the book. Molly couldn't remember that Jay had gone to hear a little boy playing the violin last year, and had cried and cried. But she was glad that this visit looked as though it were going to end very quickly, and that she hadn't been brought into it much. Already Tony Flaxman's mother, weakly apologizing for being able to do so little to help, had gone to a drawer in her desk and was taking out quite a lot of crackling notes. Miss Betty Phillimore had asked a few searching questions, but Mummy had given all the right answers. Mrs. Flaxman had asked none. She's stupid, thought Molly, unconsciously criticizing the lack of criticism.

And then the door opened and a tall woman strode in dressed in black, with big bones and shrewd eyes. She took in the scene at once. Perhaps she had been warned by the offended Robson.

"Can I help you, Mrs. Flaxman?"

And Mrs. Flaxman fumbled guiltily with the money which she had already been going to hand to Lorna, and dropped some of it, and looked as though she wanted to push back the rest into the drawer.

"Oh, Miss Gardiner. Yes … No … I thought you and Tony would—were still—isn't this Thursday? French and geography morning?"

"Friday. And Tony's with Signor Vecchione, practising." So that was disposed of. "What's the trouble? Do we know this lady?" She looked at Mummy hard and straight, and yet with a suspicion of a smile behind her eyes.

"Mrs. Flaxman has been so wonderfully kind," put in Molly's mother, speaking humbly and gratefully. Her voice trembled, her eyes supplicated, and never once did she look towards the handful of notes which Mrs. Flaxman had been about to pass her when Tony's governess had marched in. "Some instinct made me come to her. I've never before in my whole life asked anyone to help me in trouble. One has one's pride. And there are always things one can do for oneself in a crisis, aren't there?"

"There certainly are," Miss Gardiner agreed heartily.

"But this time I was at the end of everything." She went on to repeat what Mrs. Flaxman had already heard about the Concerto in G and Jay's illness, and the need for her and Molly to have their fares to Edinburgh, and to start that very evening or it was no good.

Miss Gardiner nodded once or twice. Molly wondered if she believed a single word of it, but she did not interrupt the sorrowful recital to turn round to Mrs, Flaxman and say: "I forbid you to give her a penny. She's not going to Edinburgh. She doesn't want to go. She didn't go to Liverpool, nor to Holyhead."

"… It's cruel when you're a woman alone. However hard you work, you're at the mercy of men who take advantage of you, men who have stones instead of hearts. Oh, I don't want Leonard back again, I just want this one chance to see him and get my five hundred pounds. It's now or never, for my little girl's health."

Miss Gardiner's eyes wandered to Molly.

"No, not Molly. Molly's strong and well, thank God." Mummy kissed her, pulled off her green tam-o'-shanter, smoothed her hair, kissed her again passionately. "I can't promise to pay it back to you. It wouldn't be fair to promise. But I swear that I'll try my utmost. It's no good saying thank-you, words are so empty …"

"Don't you think, Miss Gardiner," Mrs. Flaxman's quavering voice broke the silence, "with that poor little girl so ill—you remember when our Tony was ill in Austria and I nursed him—"

"I'll tell you what I think," said Miss Gardiner, firmly inserting a full-stop to the tentative sentences. "I think it's a very good idea to give Mrs Blake her fare to Edinburgh, and the child's. But she's not in a fit state to look after these practical matters. I expect she's had bad nights. Anyhow"—and she took the notes out of Mrs. Flaxman's hands, but kept hold of them—"I'll be at Euston myself tonight and take your tickets and put you on the train."

Molly was silently praying that Mummy would not exclaim: "Oh, that won't do at all!"

"Oh," gasped Lorna Blake, "but this is more than kindness. I couldn't ask it or expect it; I never dreamt—"

"I'm sure you didn't." Again that firm, hearty, reassuring voice. "But it's quite all right. I don't mind trouble of that sort. Ten minutes before the train starts, at the barrier. Will that suit you?"

"It couldn't be better. Thank you very very much," brown eyes swimming with gratitude raised first to Miss Gardiner, then to Mrs. Flaxman. "You've been an angel to me." Mrs. Flaxman's hand was snatched and kissed, while she stood shooting timid deprecating glances towards Tony s governess. "Molly, kiss Tony's mother. Give her two of your best big kisses," with a wan smile.

Miss Gardiner looked on at the adieux with grim satisfaction; Molly knew that both she and Mummy were perfectly well aware that tonight there would be no meeting at Euston. Her own exit beside Lorna had a certain childish dignity. She belonged to the defeated side. Somehow, she was a shade happier than on the other occasions when they had got away with it.

Her mother did not speak until they got home. Molly heard her burst forth to Susan: "It's my own damn fault for not keeping to the book. That book brought me luck. I should never go outside it."

"Why, whatever's happened?"

"We'll have to leave this house, that's all." She calmed down, took off her drab hat at the looking-glass and began patting her hair into place with ineffective yet pleasantly domestic movements. While she patted, she told Susan of their rout by the Flaxman governess.

Susan harangued her: "Seems to me you're panicking for nothing. What do we want to leave here for? That interfering bitch won't take the trouble to find you and prosecute. She'll just have her laugh about doing you out of the fare, and leave it at that."

Molly felt dimly that Susan was not altogether sorry that her mother had failed so ignominiously with Mrs. Flaxman; quite glad, in fact, though she loved Mummy and said "we" about leaving the house, meaning therefore to go with them.

"Too much of a compliment, letting her drive you out when you don't want to go. Look here, you didn't leave your address, did you, to make it all nice and convenient?"

Lorna's voice had regained its ladylike control; her lips even wore a rueful smile: "Yes, Susan dear, that's just what I did do. Left *this* address, nice and convenient. The Flaxman woman was going to send me a cheque: 'From Tony for his dear little unknown friend Jay.'"

"Um. Better give up this game, hadn't you?"

"Oh, how I wish I might. It's so humiliating. But for the children's sake, to give them a chance—"

"Don't waste all that," advised Susan, twinkling. "*I*'m no mug with more cash than's good for me. But it's working out a bit dangerous. Two or three blunders like this, and we'll have the police in."

"I don't make blunders," with an air of offended pride, as though she had been accused of choosing the wrong shade of blue for the curtains. "I can trust my instinct each time to pick out a really *nice* person. It's more than instinct, I've a gift: I know it, Susan, but I can't explain it; like clairvoyance or whatever it is men do with a hazel twig to find water. Was the Baroness a blunder, or Betty Phillimore, or least of all Mrs. Flaxman? You wouldn't believe, Susan, what kind hearts most people have if only you feel, as I do, what line to take from the moment you see them. You must have *faith* from the very outset; faith to move mountains—"

"You can move mountains all right. Make 'em dance a hornpipe. I've seen you at it. I supposed you'd given up your old games, that's all, since Jay and Molly were old enough."

"Games? Oh, Susan, life isn't a game. And my babies shall be given everything that rich people can do for their children. I'll sacrifice myself willingly. I'll take risks—You know, Susan, there *are* no risks except from the snarling suspicious ring of parasites that surround all wealthy people; their servants, secretaries, governesses—Oh, they're heartless, they're cruel. Fancy turning me out of my own home, just because I asked for a little help in a crisis."

"Now we're down to brass-tacks again. This is my advice. Take Molly and a suit-case and clear out this very night. They'll act quick on the address if they act at all. Though we can't reckon on that enough to skip for only a day or two. I'll stay and pack up and arrange with Mackenzie, the agent; give him a paper-shop address and say—Oh, well, I'll pitch him some tale."

"Say I've had money losses."

"True enough." Susan burst out laughing. It was evident that she got a lusty joy out of her mistress in this mood. "I'm sorry for 'em if they try to get where you are out of me. Better make it furnished rooms, though, not another house, or it'll come expensive to keep on moving till you've got all that talent out of your system."

"Susan," Mrs. Blake of The Nook, Woodgrange Road, Putney, uttered a mild reproach of her maid's exuberance: "Susan, please understand it's no question of my system. Or talent. I've no talents at all, I'm afraid, except for loving my children and respecting my fellow-creatures."

"Yes, and knowing directly what line to take with 'em."

Molly's mother looked a trifle disconcerted: "Who said that?"

"Why, you did yourself, not five minutes ago."

"I can't have meant what you mean. Come along, Molly my angel-bird, and help Mummy pack."

It was part of the new disorder of things, that her mother was so curiously oblivious, nowadays, of Molly's sentient presence and what she might chance to overhear. Formerly, it had been all the time: "Darlings, run away, Mummy has to talk with Susan," or "Hush, Susan, the children; they're not old enough yet—" "It does them harm to hear grown-ups discuss—" Or, if they inadvertently overheard what they shouldn't, a careful explanation tempered to their years: "You see, darlings, that was simply another way of saying—"

Now Molly was in the room during Visiting, and in the room while Susan spoke her mind, and while plans were formed, and everything was left lying about unexplained.

Panic—and then wisdom.

Of course they must leave the house, change their address, run away and never be found, especially not by Miss Gardiner, who knew about them and would tell Miss Betty Phillimore and the Baroness. "We must leave this house" enlightened Molly once and for all that Visiting was not only wrong, but mysteriously punishable.

She began to be afraid of policemen.

Chapter Four

The postman never came to their new address, which was Highgate and a little like the country. They had a big bedroom and two little ones, and a not very attractive sitting-room full of furniture and photographs. Presently Susan followed them there with a lot of trunks and boxes and bundles.

"Here we are, bag and baggage, and that pug-faced man at Mackenzie's said he'd get rid of the rest of your lease in no time. And I've stored the furniture. Pug-face said he was sorry to hear of your *money losses*."

Mummy did not respond to Susan's significant grimace. She said: "It's very kind of Mr. Mackenzie," and that Miss Adams at the children's school had been very kind too.

They had been to see Miss Adams yesterday, she and Mummy. It had been nearly the end of the term, and Miss Adams did her best, but in vain, to persuade Mummy at least to leave Molly there until the school performance. "I'm really sorry to lose her, Mrs. Blake: sorry to lose them both. Molly was to have played the Mock Turtle. We wanted her for Alice, but she's such a funny little thing, she preferred the Mock Turtle. And yet I always think she's not unlike Alice herself; both so reasonable. Ah well, it can't be helped; the best of luck, Mrs. Blake, as you have to move away from this neighbourhood, but don't let us lose sight of you altogether."

"Of course not, dear Miss Adams." Mummy's eyes filled as she promised. "The last thing I want to do is to cut myself off from my friends. If I may count you as one?"

"Indeed you may. And I wish all parents were as little trouble as you. You don't know what a headmistress goes through."

"I can imagine it," Lorna laughed through her tears.

"But I've never believed my ducklings are swans and I'm quite glad they're not; ducklings are so much more cuddle-some.

"I'm sure they will be a comfort to you."

"Oh, they are, they are; what I should do without them—Molly's the greatest comfort. And Jay's on the mend already."

"Have you broken it to her yet that she and Molly are leaving?"

"No. I ... It's so difficult. Not just yet. When she's stronger."

Six weeks later, Jay was fetched back from the nursing-home in a taxi. Her bobbed hair had grown long and fell in a pale, heavy mane down her back, making her look old-fashioned, like the illustrations of princesses in the sort of volume she and Molly had begun to despise. She was dismayed at first over their change of dwelling, but in a few moments began to be enthusiastic, because it was new and on top of a hill.

"Where shall we go to school now?"

"After the holidays, there's a nice little school quite near where I'll arrange for you and Molly—"

"Oh, please don't bother, Mummy," laughed Jay, in love with freedom and idleness.

Molly told her nothing about Visiting. There were no words to fit it. Besides, perhaps it was over. She had not been summoned to go out with Mummy since their flight from home. Nevertheless, now that Jay was back and available at any moment, Molly's fear swelled inside her till she thought it would crack her skin. She became wilder and noisier than she had ever been before. Noise was a sort of barricade. If you yelled enough, other things might not get through.

"Molly, I don't know what's come to you. ... Molly, don't racket about so; you might have a little consideration for your sister if not for me. ... Molly, if you look very closely you'll see that doors have handles and the only way to close them is not by a big bang. ... Molly, I don't know what that horrid game is, it sounds like a charge of cavalry. ... Molly, this isn't a home for hooligans. Why don't you act a nice little play for Mummy? You used to enjoy dressing-up."

But Molly did not enjoy dressing-up any more. She preferred jumping down the stairs, first three, then four, then-five-six-seven steps—thud, thud on to the linoleum in the hall. "Three cheers for the King and Queen! I'm a thousand people watching the king pass. I'm fifty thousand people! Hip—hip—hip—"

Jay still remained frail and delicate. She toyed with her food, pushed it round and round the plate. She became tired too easily. She was prettier than before, more appealing, more defenceless. Nobody would have taken her for nine.

One evening when their landlady, Mrs. Crockett, came in to clear away the tea and chicken-paste and radishes, she remarked to Lorna: "That child's looks would melt a heart of stone."

At once Molly knew that was not a good thing to have said.

When Mrs. Crockett waddled out with the tray, she put out her tongue after her.

"Molly!"

"She's dirty. She's awful. I hate her. I'd like to kick her fat bottom. I would. I hate her. This is how she walks."

Her mother did not continue the scolding. She was not really interested in Molly's excellent mimicry of Mrs. Crockett. Her eyes dwelt thoughtfully on Jay.

It came the very next afternoon:

"Jay darling, leave that and come along. Mummy wants you to go out with her."

"Oh, good!" Jay sprang up willingly. Anything for a change. "Where are we going?"

Molly shouted: "Me too," over and over again at the top of her voice, so that she might not have to hear the answer.

("Visiting. Visiting a nice lady.")

"No, Molly, not you today. Tell Susan she may give you an egg for your tea instead. You needn't go upstairs, Jay, my poppet; your coat and cap are in the hall!"

All through the hours after the last sight of Jay, innocent and pleased, chattering down the steps, Molly sat in a heap on the hearthrug, not a squeak left in her of all the turmoil and bravado with which she had fended off catastrophe. She sat as still as a crippled child.

Should she at least have warned Jay of the horrors ahead of her? Jay would get ill again, Jay might die, Jay might go mad. Miss Adams had said: "Molly is so reasonable." But who could be reasonable while Jay was Visiting with Mummy, seeing her for the first time wangle her way past servants into strange houses, crying and telling lies, and driving frantic fingers backwards through her hair.

(Other children, children with proper mothers, could rush to them for safety and protection ... Bulls, snorting with then-heads lowered, bad dreams, a cut knee with the blood flowing, scarecrows and bogeymen: "Mummy! Mummy!" "Hush, my sweet. Hush, my baby. You're all right with Mummy.")

Hours, while you waited to see what sort of a Jay would arrive back home again. You must think of a plan that wasn't childish and silly, to rescue Jay. Hours of growing older, growing up.

When they came at last into the hall and into the twilit room, Molly did not turn round.

"Not started your tea yet? That's nice. Now we can all have it together. Turn on the light, Susan."

Mummy's voice was gayer than it had been since Miss Betty Phillimore. Then this time there had been no governess to spoil it all? Her heart thumping, Molly forced herself to look at Jay.

She had a shock. Jay was not broken. Jay was excited and wide-awake, half-frightened certainly, but terror had a sort of secret dancing quality to it. Molly had seen that same elusive sparkle in her mother's eyes, though they were round and brownish and quite different from Jay's.

After tea, with boiled eggs for a treat, Molly and Jay were several times left alone in the sitting-room. But they did not speak of what had happened. They played card games, "Snap" and "Happy Families." And argued more meticulously than usual about the rules. They did not speak of it, either, while they undressed. Their mother tucked them in and warmly kissed them good-night and went downstairs, humming.

A silence so long that either might have dropped off to sleep. Then across the room through the dark came Jay's voice, on a queer, thrilled note: "Molly, are we beggars?"

As though by unspoken consent, they never discussed it again. Not after that one long talk in the dark. Jay had taken a far more lurid and frightening view of the danger than Molly, whose measurement fitted squarely over just what there was to deserve terror. Molly found that she had no need to produce her comforting improvisation, that all children whose mothers were alone and not rich had to go through something of the sort, for Jay obviously comforted herself by saying: "I'm an outlaw now, like Robin Hood."

"… The part I most hated was when the old gentleman gave us the money and Mummy thanked him and thanked him and I had to say thank you with Mummy lots of times, and throw my arms round him and kiss him. I didn't like that."

Molly chuckled: "I made my kisses wet on purpose. They couldn't dodge, in front of Mummy." "They" stood for the victims.

Jay babbled on: "He'd been a friend of Mr. Lionel Lovett who was famous and who Mummy knew too; it must have been before we were born. The old gentleman lives in a lovely flat with carpets your feet were sucked right down into, so that you have to drag them up. His seckerterry, he was angry when we arrived, and tried to keep us out. I simply quaked. But then Mummy managed him. Oh, Molly, *do* you think the police are on their way now? Do you think they're on the doorstep? I hear something knocking terribly loudly. If it's the police—"

"Course not. No one's on the doorstep. Besides, we haven't done anything wrong."

"Isn't it wicked to—to—We're going by train to Southampton early tomorrow, did you know?"

"No, we're not," Molly quietly contradicted her.

"Oh. I thought we were. Molly, the old gentleman, I forget his name, he said I looked dreadfully white and dellycate, and Mummy said 'Yes, I'm so afraid of losing her. She's all I've got.' She must have forgotten you. I'd been told to go and play with the dog on the rug on the other side of the room, but I heard. It was a bulldog. I'd like a bulldog. The old gentleman said: 'They make quite an old-fashioned picture together, with her pretty long hair.' Molly, *is* she going to lose me soon? Am I going to die?"

"No, you silly. That's part of it."

"Part of what?"

There was a pause. Both lay in the dark and waited for the other to speak first.

"Molly, I'm coming into your bed." A patter of feet, then Jay snuggling down. "It's funny about Mummy, isn't it?" in a scared whisper.

"I don't suppose"—Molly struggled to keep on an everyday note—"I don't suppose she'll always be like this."

"Don't you? I do. Do you mean she's like when Susan says we're feverish and they put a glass thing in our mouth and say 'It's gone up,' and next morning: 'It's gone down'?"

"We can't go and put a glass thing in Mummy's mouth."

They both giggled hysterically.

"Molly we've got a father. I bet you didn't know that, anyhow. His name's not Blake. He's an abanderer and isn't dead like she used to say. He 'bandoned his wife and children heartlessly before I was two. And I think, I'm not sure, he was going to be at Southampton if we'd gone but you say we're not going. Molly, are you crying, or is it hiccoughs?"

Molly gave in.

"Oh I don't know, I don't know. I don't know what to do. I want it to be last term and everything the same, and Mummy to *tell* us what to do. I want us to wake up and be back again at The Nook. Oh, don't cry, too, Jay, don't, don't"

But Jay, now that she had lost the idea that it was all exciting and fun, sobbed even more wildly than Molly:

"Oh my hair's all messy and long, it gets into my mouth. Oh, it's worse than being ill. Oh, suppose they find out when we go to our next school that we're objicks-of-charity and point at us and—"

"Shut up. Don't cry, darling, they needn't ever find out. And Mummy'll cut off your hair again short like before."

"She won't," sobbed Jay, disconsolate. "I asked her, coming home, and she answered, 'No, my pet, it's a g-g-godsend.'"

Even not seeing each other's faces, they sheered off asking in cold words what could have happened to their comfortable ordinary mother.

"Godsend" reminded Molly that she had not yet said her prayers. She felt too bewildered and sore to use the usual form, and consulted Jay, who was shocked at the omission: "You *must* say your prayers. It's being heathen not to. I said mine before I even spoke to you. Say them now," commanded the elder sister. "You know how strict Mummy is about it."

Chapter Five

School began, and they did not go Visiting again. Molly was sure her mother went without them at least two or three times a week, for she did not return to being the blessed familiar Mummy of The Nook. Even though she petted them, she did it with a remote air. She superintended their clothes and their health and asked all the conventional questions about their progress in lessons, but her eyes were too bright and prominent, and when she talked she threw her hands about more than she used to. And there were sudden exotic treats for her and Jay which must have cost Mummy pounds and pounds, such as hiring an electric launch with a striped red and white awning, for a whole day on the river, and a man with a peaked cap to drive it.

And another funny thing, not so nice as the launch, showing how Mummy was translated ("Bless thee, Bottom, thou art translated"). Jay was enthusiastically describing some school escapade: "… And Miss Lucas said how sorry she was for having been wrong and how glad that Jasmine Blake was brave enough to speak up, and thanked me, and Rosina thanked me for saving her, and everyone thanked me. And Miss Lucas said—"

But Lorna, who had been tapping her foot impatiently during the narrative, stopped her with a sharp: "That's not the way to tell a story, Jay. You want to watch the effect on your listeners; you're looking the whole time at yourself. But they must never notice you watching them. If you see you're on the wrong key, change it, gradually. And don't revel in silly, fussy detail. I'm not going to have any child of mine grow up to be a bore," she added, to justify her outburst to Susan.

Jay, taken unawares in full spate, burst into a nervous storm of crying, sprang up from the table and ran out of the room.

"I don't mind Mummy jumping on me if I've disobeyed or broken something or said 'I shan't,'" she wept to Molly afterwards. "But scolding me as if it was a lesson, just only for telling what really happened—"

"Did it really happen?" asked Molly, deeply impressed.

Jay made no direct reply, but went on sobbing.

They moved again, all in a hurry and a flurry, just like last time. First Mummy with both of them, and Susan following with the trunks. Furnished rooms at Barnes, more luxurious than the Highgate ones, more expensive, Susan said, but not on a hill. It meant starting yet once more at a different school. Mummy was terribly particular that their education should not be interrupted. She said to Susan: "I may be lax about some things, but I never stop worrying about my children's future. I don't care what I do myself, as long as they're not mixed up in it."

Susan remarked in her odd way, loving not what Mummy had said, but something on one side of it: "No, I must say you've been good about that lately. All the same, you're not letting Jay bob her hair. Never know, do you, when her long curls may come in useful?"

Lorna began to be more frequently at home when Molly and Jay returned from school in the late afternoon. Her face settled into placidity, like a restless cat who has prowled long enough and prefers the mat in front of the fire. She looked older, but tranquil. Her hands, when they were not busy with some pleasant sewing, lay quietly clasped in her lap. Molly felt as though a hot room were gradually growing cooler, doors and windows opening. Molly began to relax. Jay recounted long and not at all interesting anecdotes about school and the other girls; her pretty mischievous voice lilted on and on without once being pulled up.

One day Mummy said to Susan: "Susan, I'm sick to death of living in furnished rooms."

"You are, are you?"

"They were an economy, of course, while we were so hard up over Jay's illness; but now that things have improved, don't you think we might move again into a dear little house of our own?"

Susan grinned and said: "Don't ask me. You know best."

So they moved into Benares Lodge in Huntingdon Terrace. It had quaint gables and wavy wooden beams among the red brick; and two white pillars and an archway; it had laburnums in the tiny front garden, and a row of lime-trees down the terrace, one in front of each house, and lamp-posts between. Some of the houses were rough white plaster and some shingle and some half-white and half-red, but they all had quaint gables and either lilac or may or laburnum in their front gardens.

A road to be happy in, a house to be happy in. Every humdrum foolish day on which nothing happened except lessons and meals, the sound of the sewing-machine, a fresh kind of pudding, solid and not especially succulent, added to Molly's confidence. Until presently she forgot that there was any more need for confidence, and accepted their release, hers and Jay's, into the kingdom of normal heaven.

Quite soon after moving in, they went away by train for the summer holidays, and came home again, and it was still the same home; and at Christmas they were allowed to give a small party, though Mummy fussed over the credentials of every child they wanted to invite. And after Christmas, Mummy knitted her brows over the bills dropping into the letter-box, and kept adding them up and exclaiming: "Oh dear, how *is* one to manage with an absurd little income like mine? Sometimes I'm almost tempted to start accounts and settle up at the end of each month, but I don't know, I've always thought that was a dangerous style of living. It's more honest to pay one's way."

And spring was glorious in Huntingdon Terrace, and by summer the bees swung round the lime-trees. They were the nice little Blakes who lived half-way down the Terrace; had always lived there, more or less. Another family of Blakes, no relation, lived at Salisbury, almost opposite, *they* had only lately arrived with vans. The *real* Blakes, the settled ones, were themselves. Molly secretly jubilated in this important discovery.

During the next spring-cleaning, when she was ten and Jay eleven, Mummy discovered she had to buy fresh cretonne curtains and chair-covers to put all over the house, and grumbled a little: "These oughtn't to be worn out already. Why, good gracious, it seems only yesterday we moved in." Only yesterday? Yet they had surely always been there, always and always seen that pretty fading pattern of poppies and cornflowers?

Mummy allowed her and Jay to help choose the new cretonne, saying: "As it's your young knees and bottoms and shoes that have got to wear it out, it's more your affair than mine."

"Mummy!" primly, "we don't get on to the chairs with our shoes."

"Don't you? They look as if you spent all day rubbing your feet on them."

"We rub our feet properly on the door-mat."

"Do you know the difference? Oh, Jay, you goose—"

Lorna rumpled up Jay's hair, and sang in her shrill, merry voice:

"Teasing, teasing, I was only teasing you.
Teasing, teasing, just to see what you would do …"

"We shall have to change our butcher," said Lorna over the sirloin one Sunday. "There's not a bit of undercut with this, and I've asked him twenty times to keep me a sirloin with undercut. And that steak last Wednesday was full of gristle." She sighed deeply. "I do hate change, even when it's a butcher."

"I like it," laughed Jay, "even when it's a butcher."

"Mr. Gristle the Butcher," suggested Molly, after pondering for a few moments. "And Mr. Stale the Baker and Mr. Caterpillar the Greengrocer—"

This brought peals of laughter from Jay.

"Go in, Molly, go on."

"And—and Mr. Waters the Milkman," Molly brought out as a final triumphant effort. And then started giving imitations of this new band of Happy Families admonishing their wives and children round the Sunday dinner-table.

"Bless the child!" Lorna gazed at her proudly. "Would you like to go on the stage, Mollykins, when you're older?"

"I don't mind," said Molly indifferently. "I'd rather have a farm."

Jay broke in: "We're going to act a play by Shakespeare next term. I'm to be Titania, the Fairy Queen, because of my long hair, and because I'm so small and light for my age, Miss Collins says.

"And Molly, what's she going to be?"

"Oh, Molly's to be a donkey because she can act," explained Jay in faith and admiration.

And after the play the summer holidays yet again, for the second time in the same place. Fine weather on the sands, and Kathy to play with, and Mummy and Mrs. Anderson sitting in deck-chairs happily gossiping—

—Until Mrs. Anderson mentioned that she would have to send away old Nanny and get a governess for Kathy. Just as Molly, in a sand-hole near by, was biting into the warmest, plumpest, ripest greengage in the bag.

Chapter Six

They all three walked up to the station to see Kathy off. It was a seaside station with the crunchiness of shells on the gravel approach, and bright, salt-blown nasturtiums in beds along the platform. Mrs. Anderson said: "I've been thinking over your advice about a governess. I'm afraid I shall have to have one; I can't teach Kathy myself, and there's no other way to manage, but I'll remember your warning and not be satisfied with written references. It's so easy to trump up a reference."

"It's the easiest thing in the world," murmured Lorna.

They were early for the train, but they stood in a little group near the Andersons' heap of somewhat dishevelled luggage, Lorna was snappy and discontented, as though she resented the idea of even one governess getting a job in spite of her.

"I think you're making a grave mistake," she persisted crossly.

And Mrs. Anderson changed the subject. "It looks as though we were taking the fine weather with us. It's blowing from the south-west. Kathy's father was a sailor, and so we're all weather-wise in our family."

The weather blew up grey and chilly, and sitting on the sands was poor fun; you had to run about and play ball and dash quickly into the sea and out again while the wind lashed at your wet bathing-suits. Mummy complained that it was dull, there was nothing to do, and she would not come again another year. Strangely enough, Jay echoed her:

"It's dull, Every morning's the same sort of day. What are Molly and me to do? I'm getting too old to dig. What's digging for? You make a hole and then the tide comes in and washes it flat again."

"Then make a castle instead."

"It's the same thing."

"I can't have you mooching about, Jay, it gets on my nerves."

"I'm sorry, Mummy darling." Jay hugged her impulsively. "It's only that I wish something would happen." She did not even remember to stipulate for something nice.

Dull. They could actually find it dull. But Molly worshipped dullness. If only it could be dull for ever and ever; if only nothing need happen, for ever and ever.

Lorna talked perpetually about being short of cash: "I don't know where to turn." And: "We simply can't go on like this."

They went back to London, to Huntingdon Terrace.

One day they heard their mother calling them: "Come along, darlings. No, just as you are. You're going out with Mummy."

Jay shrank back. Now that it was here again at last, she was genuinely frightened. It was Molly who in a perfectly steady voice answered:

"Both of us? Not just me?"

"No, Both."

PART II

The Victims

Chapter One

←→

"Please, madam, there's a woman in the hall."

"Oh, Edith, not that woman *again*?"

"She won't go away, madam."

"Has she got the two little girls with her?"

"Yes, madam. Up all those stairs in this heat, and she's in dreadful trouble. I do feel sorry for her, really I do, madam. She says if she could just see you for five minutes, you'd understand."

"Yes, I expect I would. The personal touch to bowl me over."

"She sent these for you to look at, madam, and please could she have them back."

"They always send in some ghastly bogus bumph to prove their rectitude, all thumbed and stained and folded under their pillows for years."

Marian Sinclair's cousin, Betty Marshall, sitting on the bed and watching with amusement the minor predicaments of the famous, asked: "What sort of bumph?"

"Oh, marriage lines and their grandmother's birth certificate and a letter from the lawyer to say they should have had the estate, and perhaps cuttings from the *Evening Courier,* and a long letter to prove that they'll be in jobs the week after next with large salaries. Oh, and usually something from a doctor, too: 'My dear Mrs. Sapphira Ananias, it is absolutely essential that you should go away to the mountains for three years' cure or you will be dead tomorrow—' I get them in shoals; I'm so degradingly sentimental. All the same, I'd rather be swizzled by eleven crooks than send away one honest person. God, I shall be late! Is she still there, Edith?"

"Oh yes, madam," surprised that there should be any question about it.

"And those two helpless brats she drags about with her—"

"Oh, you've seen her, then?"

"Not this one, no, but Lucilla has. She got a fiver out of her. She only had one kid, that time. The other was supposed to be a boy in Switzerland with t.b. She wanted her fare to go out and see him before he died."

"You could prosecute, couldn't you? If you and Lucilla combined?"

"Oh, one could, but one doesn't. Why should I? It's such a ghastly life, no one would choose it; and I might be doing it myself, only I happen to be able to dance."

"Perhaps she enjoys it."

"She couldn't possibly. Besides, her tears are genuine enough. Lucilla said the studio was drenched for hours afterwards. Oh hell, that's to say the car's here. How am I to get past her if she's in the hall?"

"There's the back way, madam."

"I'm damned if I'm going to leave my own house by the tradesmen's entrance. Here, Edith, give her this and tell her it's no good coming here again. Then when she's gone I can go too."

But Edith came back with the pound still in her hand. "If you please, madam, she wouldn't take it. And she said she must see you personally, if only for a few minutes."

"Such a sad case, Jane. I'm sure you wouldn't blame me if you'd seen her. She had had one little boy, too, just like me, only he was killed in a road accident. Now she's alone. And when she saw the photograph of my Ronnie on his motor-bicycle, she cried and cried. I felt dreadful, just as though Ronnie were guilty."

"Did she tell you it was a road accident before she saw the picture of Ronnie on his motor-bike, or after?"

"Jane, though you're my own daughter, I'd hate to be as suspicious as you. I believe modern girls are cut out of tin, for all the feelings they have."

"Meaning we're two-dimensional. Darling mother, how clever of you."

Lady Manfield-Locke preened herself. For Jane to say: "How clever!"

"Well—"

"I suppose you'd say it's better to help eleven wrong 'uns on the off-chance that the twelfth may be a real down-and-out?"

"Certainly I would."

"Statistically that's bilge, darling. How much did this beauty rook you?"

"All she wanted was to get back to her sister, who's married to a planter in Kentucky, I think she said. Her sister is all she's got now."

"My sacred aunt, you didn't give her her fare to America, did you, to make whoopee on? That's a bit thick."

"I have just told you," retorted Lady Manfield-Locke with dignity, "that there was no question of whoopee. She showed me photographs of her little boy and her sister—"

"Picking cotton?"

"Jane, I'll never tell you anything any more. She desperately wanted to catch the *Berengaria* on the 15th. Tomorrow."

"Wouldn't the next boat have done?"

"No, that's just it, there was an excellent reason why it wouldn't—I forget what it was; otherwise I might have waited and sent her the money after I'd talked it over with you and convinced you that it was very real need."

"I believe you're mug enough to have handed this plausible lady her first-class fare across the Atlantic, and enough to live on for a year afterwards."

"I may have given her a couple of pounds, for Ronnie's sake."

"Oh well, it's your own money. I expect I wouldn't far out if I multiplied the couple of pounds by twenty."

Lady Manfield-Locke took up the *Tatler* and made no reply. Jane would not have been far out.

←→

"My dear, I *had* to ring up and tell you. It was a scream. She got so excited, I kept on expecting her to take out a revolver and shoot me. What did she look like? Oh, just nondescript, in a raincoat. Fairish, I think, with round light eyes. Typical English suburban. The children were the quaintest little objects; they actually wore sailor-suits; where *does* one get sailor-suits nowadays? The old-world braided kind with sort of whistles hiding under their collars?"

"Lanyards."

"Lanyards? Aren't those the ropes you pull on to get the sails up? Oh, and one of them, the pretty one, had long fair ringlets. It reminded me of the *Police Gazette* of fifty years ago, or back numbers of *The Keepsake*. And, my dear, black woollen stockings."

"What did she want? Was she a swindle or real?"

"Oh, she was real enough, no doubt about that. Her husband's done a bolt, been missing for years, and she just heard he was doing a spot of bigamy in Nice. She felt she had to nip off and prevent it 'for the sake of my babes' and so forth. It was all a bit complicated; a will came into it somewhere; she showed me a copy, and copies of the lawyer's letters, and her marriage lines; Leonard somebody to Lorna Mason. I gave her the cash and wished her luck. I've no sympathy with bigamists. And imagine what a lush scene when she turns up at the English Church with a chee-ild on either side, calling out 'I forbid the banns.'"

"You always had a taste for crude drama, Monica."

"Well, I've had to act in so much modern psychological stuff. There's nothing psychological about Lorna Mason and Leonard Blake—that's the name: Blake. I gave one of the brats, the pretty one with long curls, a five-pound box of *marrons glacés* to eat on the Channel."

"She'll be sick. And what about the other one?"

"The other one scowled and took hardly any interest in what was going on. She didn't look sensitive, rather a little tough, in fact. If you're not sensitive, you don't get *marrons glacés*. That's loife, that is. Are you going to be at Elsa's party at the Savoy tonight?"

←→

"Look here, Miss Garbo"—he had had several Swedish masseuses and called them all "Miss Garbo"; it always went well—"I wonder if you'd mind seeing who's at the front door. They've rung three times now, and I've sent Denby to the dentist."

"But certainly, Mr. Jefferies," amiably smiling as she drew the sheet over him.

"I say, there's no need to put pennies on my eyelids just while you're gone to answer the door."

But she had already left the room.

He heard a murmur of voices. Then she returned, her fresh, handsome features distressed, a little excited: "Oh please, Mr. Jefferies, there is a lady in the hall and two sweet little girls, Mrs. Blake, she said. And please, you don't know her, but she knew Mr. Lionel Lovett and he danced with her at her first ball—"

"Well, that wasn't very nice for her, but I can't help it. Send her away."

"Oh, but, Mr. Jefferies, she has read your books and your articles and she knows you are so kind—"

"That's where they all make the mistake."

His masseuse beamed at him incredulously. She, too, had read his books, especially *By the Rippling Stream*, so of course he was only pretending to be hard-hearted.

"Aren't you going to concentrate on my diaphragm?" he demanded, recumbent and exasperated.

"But, Mr. Jefferies, the lady in the hall? She waits."

"You don't expect me to interview her while I'm being massaged, do you? I know what's seemly."

"Ah, but here is your dressing-gown." She held it for him to insert his arms.

"No. Send them away."

The masseuse went, sorrowfully shaking her head. The conversation in the hall went on and on.

"Miss Garbo," he called impatiently, after a time.

She returned with a large stuffed envelope.

"Why the lugubrious expression and the portfolio?"

"She has told me the story. It is so sad, I had to cry. I do not know why God if He is good allows these things to happen to one who has done Him no harm."

"Did she say that, or you?"

"Her beautiful dark eyes are red with crying. She has dark hair and a thin white face. Her grandmother was a Russian Grand Duchess, and she has inherited the noble carriage. What she wears was once expensive, and even now it is unsuitable for your English weather today; a fine scarf like a rainbow, but she has no proof against the rain. Her little girl, she gave me a kiss, two, three kisses when her mother tells her. I could not help crying. That child, you know how it is when you lay a piece of linen, fine and delicate, on the fresh green grass to dry, but it is so light, that unless you put stones on the four corners, the air will lift it and carry it away from the earth. So it is with that child."

A. S. Jefferies scribbled a few lines in a notebook he kept beside the bed. "Thank you, Miss Garbo, and for your reward I'll examine this mass of forged evidence." He took up the envelope gingerly.

"And also she wrote for you just now in the hall. It will tell you about the typewriter."

"Typewriter?" He read the scrawl:

"Dear A. S. Jefferies: forgive me, I am in despair. If I could have seen you I know you would have sympathized and helped me. I did not want to go to anyone else, it is too like begging, but you were a friend of a friend of mine, Mr. Lionel Lovett. And 'Beside the Rippling Stream' made me feel as though you had written it *for* me and *to* me alone—" [He groaned aloud,] "I'll come straight to the point. Can you spare fourteen pounds for me to buy a typewriter, and a little extra so that I can take the two kiddies down to their grandmother in Penzance? If I have to be out at work all day I cannot look after them any more. I was very comfortably off until now, but it all went in that dreadful crash in steel. I do not mind how hard I work to keep myself and the kiddies. Work is wholesome and I have learned how to type. But I must have a typewriter of my own, then I can be independent like Deirdre in your book. Isn't it odd that she should have the same name as myself? Thank you a hundred times and again forgive

Deirdre Blake."

A. S. Jefferies looked up helplessly at the sole messenger between him and the outer world.

"Ach, Mr. Jefferies, she is as sincere as heaven. I have met many people and always I know the truth."

"Tell her to go away."

The masseuse shook her head: "I cannot."

Suddenly he had an inspiration: that very old clumsy machine of his which had not been used for at least a dozen years. It was in the box-room. Damn it, she asked for money to buy a typewriter, and a typewriter she should have. *And* Miss Garbo would have no more to say. Why were rosy, healthy, buxom people always so infernally sentimental? The riddle answered itself: they could afford to be.

He directed the masseuse to find his Rip van Winkle and take it out to Lorna with his kindest regards and five shillings to take it home in a taxi. "Now are you satisfied?"

"You are so good. I knew before, you were only making play with me. She will send you a blessing."

"I bet she will," chuckled Jefferies.

Five minutes later, when the front door had closed and massage was resumed, he shot out accusingly: "And how much did you give her out of your own pocket? Come on, confess."

"Oh, Mr. Jefferies, how did you guess? But it was so little, just for each of the children to buy a nice toy and perhaps to wear something new and warm and blue to travel to their grandmother. I can spare it well."

Chapter Two

Captain Alexander Muir-Leslie, M.C., strode along Hill Street with a military air and a fatuous expression. He was going to see Sylvia, and since he had become engaged to Sylvia, his eyes, his hearing, his mind, as well as his steps, all took one single route. The blessed little girl, and she lived in a blessed little white house with blue shutters like a Provençal farmhouse in a blessed little mews set plonk down in the middle of Mayfair, with a plane-tree stippling the wall with a pattern of sun and leaves, and the steady swish and hiss of cars being washed down on the cobbles outside, which she said was as good music as a mountain stream. Well, let her say all the damn-fool things she pleased, since for him she was so lovely and so beloved. While he was alive, nothing crude nor coarse nor evil need ever come near her. He was the high fence round the deer park; he was the thick yew hedge; he was the wall of brick and the bristling barrier of spears. And he was, moreover, a man of the world. And this, thought Captain Muir-Leslie, complacently, this was confoundedly important, for before she got engaged to him, Sylvia had let herself be gulled into some sort of tenderness for a sissy, a sissy with long hair, a dreamy sort of voice, and not a bean: "Don't know how he pays for his scent." No good for a girl like Sylvia, who needed a he-man. Every time he thought of the sissy-chap and how he had been defeated, Alexander's ugly weather-beaten face went a little redder with pride. Damn cheek in a fellow to believe he had a chance with a beauty like Sylvia, a girl who was always in the papers, doing this and that, charity balls, tableaux, pageants. If Sylvia had had a father or brothers they'd have hounded him out of the house long before he dared put his silly classical nose in at the front door. Not that he, Captain Alexander Muir-Leshe of the 17th Lancers, wasn't a reader himself, though fools supposed that being in the Army he was bound to be practically illiterate. How

– 54 –

they stared when he quoted Confucius at 'em: "Artful speech and an ingratiating demeanour rarely accompany Virtue." He was standing for Parliament, too, next time there was a reshuffling. A lot of reforms he was keen on. Sylvia would be no end of a help there, entertaining; a lot depends on who sits at the top of your table. He was a good speaker once he got started; at the opposite end of the pole, a first-rate gardener. That place of his down in Berkshire, couldn't run down there often, but he was breaking it in to be yet another tribute to Sylvia. Sylvia's gardener; Sylvia's crusader; Sylvia's philosopher; her sophisticated protector. And yet with all this, a never-ending wonder that he could have been found worthy to take up duty as Sylvia's bodyguard.

Her bodyguard. Odd, how he had never before thought of the word in two parts instead of one. Guard of her body, her slender girl's body. And he so leathery and tough and ugly. Sixteen years older, too. From complacence he could pass over in a moment to an utterly despondent outlook on his own claims; this was the mood which faintly bored Sylvia, all this ripe fruity talk about his own awfulness: "Look at me, Sylvia darling. Look at my frightful beaky nose and my sandy hair getting a bit grizzled. Most girls won't stand for sandy hair."

His forehead jutted over his eyes, hollowing a cave for their monkey sadness; but this he left out of his inventory, thinking: everyone has eyes, and mine are no worse than everyone's. "But the worst is, I've got a knack of putting people's backs up. I suppose it's no tact, or something. And I'm not subtle. Have you found that out yet? And, my God! I've got a hell of a temper. Not that I'd ever let you see it, but I know what people are, they'll come and tell you, blast 'em. 'Can't go marrying that bad-tempered brute,' they'll say; 'he'll make go you utterly miserable. I'd think twice about it, if I were you.'" And by this time, a bewildered Sylvia would have lost count as to whether he were pleading his own claims to be jilted or merely repeating in secret agony what he feared others might be saying to dissuade her.

But lately he had been a little calmer on the subject of himself, less peremptory in his demands that she should recognize all his horrible faults. Nice Alec. Kind Alec. She never doubted for a moment but that he was on the side of the angels in spite of the zest with which he kicked himself round the room. She could not plead with him to abandon that line, for, like all men with no reticence, he was unbelievably touchy.

He strode into the room, glowing with good-humour and a recent plunge into his club swimming-pool. When the preliminary embraces were over: "Sylvia, who was that female leading her young, whom I met on your doorstep?"

"I tried to keep her," said Sylvia, whose eyes were shadowy and troubled. "I wanted you to see her, but she couldn't wait. Oh, Alec, life's such a beast sometimes."

"Who's been a beast to you?" he demanded, his thunders gathering.

"Oh, not to me. I'm in clover. It's that poor soul who's just left. I gave her what I could, but of course you can do more—"

"Well, tell me the facts."

"She's a Mrs. Inglefield; she met her husband when she was quite a young girl living at Market St. Dunstan's. She was crazy about him, and so was he about her until he had what he wanted. She must have been very pretty once, don't you think?"

"I? My dear child, I hardly looked at her."

"They ran away together and got married. She showed me her marriage certificate; it was quite clear: Lorna Mason to Neil Inglefield at the Church of Market St. Dunstan's in — I forget the year. He began to ill-treat her almost at once—that's why the eldest little girl is so delicate. He used up all her money. And then he bolted; and left her penniless to have their second child quite alone. She didn't know where to look for him. She had to work like a slave to get those two children educated. That's what worries her most, their education. She's scraped together the most grotesque clothes for them to go to school in; the poor infants must have suffered agonies; I know what schoolgirls are, devils unless you're conventionally dressed and have an ordinary conventional home. Now, suddenly, through a newspaper, she's heard at last where he is. She'd torn it out and showed it to me: in California, opening a new hotel or managing it or something; his job was mixed up with hotels. But unless she can get there by the 18th, he'll be gone again. I hadn't enough in the house, but I sent Mary round to the bank; there was just time before it closed. But I wondered if you could do something? You've got influence. Do you know anybody over there? Just to keep him there till she arrives, in case he heard she was coming and bolted again. Could you, Alec? Could you? It's just the sort of thing you're so good at."

He sprawled back in the armchair, pulled his short moustache, smiled at her whimsically: "You've been had, my darling. And it sounds to me as though you'd been had by a pretty feeble tale. Usually they spin 'em better than that. It's a damn shame, taking your money."

Sylvia had been sitting on the arm of his chair, at intervals gently touching his cheek, his eyelids. Her finger-tips, more wanton than she was aware, thrilled him. Now, however, she moved away. No girl of twenty-two, credulous, a little foolish, illusion floating about her like a thin golden scarf, cares to be told that she's been had, after squandering so much enthusiastic pity.

"I'm afraid I haven't done her cause much good by telling it badly," she tried to laugh. "But if you had heard her yourself, Alec. Honestly, there was no question of being had. Every word of it was simply wrung out of her soul." Sylvia was pleased at having created this vivid phrase.

"'It's Gord's truth I'm telling yer, lidy,'" Alexander burlesqued a gipsy's whine. He did not realize how dangerous was the ground he trod. He felt, indeed, rather more than usually pleasant and lordly. Here was an additional service he could render her, out of his cynical experience: protect her from these swindling rogues who believed her to be solitary and fair game. And fair game she was, none fairer. They had not reckoned, he would remind them, with Captain Alexander Muir-Leslie, fire-eater and gentleman of the sword.

"I'm afraid it's hopeless trying to get your money back for you, angel. If she's left an address at all, it'll be a false one. I could put the police on to it, of course, but—"

"Alec, I think you're mad!" Sylvia's voice shook with passionate indignation. "The police! As though she hadn't had enough to bear. You're as cruel and callous as her swine of a husband."

This amused him immensely. "And what about *your* swine of a husband, Sylvia?" He heaved himself out of the armchair, towered above her (not as towering as he pictured it, for he was not a tall man) and captured her hands, though she tried to prevent him.

"Princess, you're wasting your lovely generosity. You must trust me to know; I've mucked about a lot. This creature had all the glib impudent patter—"

"She wasn't glib. She wasn't impudent. She wasn't even complaining. She was humble and gentle, almost divine. She said: 'Perhaps I showed my love too clearly. I should have been wiser, and then Neil might not have left me.' Oh, Alec, if you'd been there! Do you know, she made the youngest little girl, the solemn one, stand on her head for me to see how nicely she did it; she hoped it might give me a moment's pleasure. Can you imagine anything more touching? Doesn't that make you choke? doesn't it convince you?"

"I don't see why it should." He remained obstinate. And at the same time confident that this was the right hour and occasion to assert his manhood. Deep in her heart, Sylvia must be admiring him; deep in her heart, she must be impressed by the corrugated male texture of his scepticism. As usual, he compared himself with that sissy-chap who would have been all blubbering sympathy, and no doubt written a poem about it.

"Look here, Sylvia, it's suddenly occurred to me—California. You don't actually mean to say that you've forked out with a lump sum big enough to take her to California?"

"Why not? I can do as I like."

"Princess, I'm not blaming you. God, you can't imagine that. I think you're adorable. You'd give the shirt off your back. It's this bloody woman I'm after, who took advantage of you. I *will* go to the police. She deserves it. It's my duty to see that the next victim on her list doesn't get imposed on."

She said nothing, and Alexander fancied that at last she was feeling a little rueful at having been so easily duped.

"Princess—these gangsters—Look here, a fellow once told me, and he knew because he'd stayed with his uncle who was a vicar and gets no end of 'em. They work in together, and they've got a regular code: marks on the front gate or the wall, warning the others if there's a dog or a bad-tempered cook, or encouraging them if they're on to a soft thing: 'Got money here and a square meal' or 'Keep off, no good' … A whole code; done in chalk, usually, don't look as if it meant anything unless you're in on it—"

"I'm afraid I can't see that any of this is relevant." Her voice was the cool north wind.

Nonplussed, he ransacked invention for other ways to comfort her. "Tell me how much you gave her and I'll send that very sum in your name to a decently organized charity. Will that make you feel all right? The Great Ormond Street Hospital? Or—look—I know, of course, you'd rather not say the exact amount. I'll sign a cheque, and you can fill it up secretly."

Sylvia was touched by the inadequacy of what he deemed a triumphant solution.

"Alec, you're so sweet. That's why I love you. And please send the cheque to the hospital all the same, I couldn't bear to think that they so nearly had it and then lost it again because I was pettish about it. Send it as though it were nothing to do with me, but a gift in the name of Lorna Inglefield." Bland as cream was Sylvia, as she rippled forth her outrageous suggestion. Her fiancé strangled back an explosion of mighty wrath; but for the first time she considered that she had an original point of view about something, and was not following with the crowd, and it seemed to her that this entitled her to more respect than a jealous man was willing to produce. "You've too much consideration. Alec; the dauntless kind that used to wear armour and call itself chivalry. But you're Chivalry Limited; limited to me. You haven't one tiny shred for a woman who so desperately needs it."

"Sylvia, my darling, aren't you being a bit—"

"A bit of a prig? I don't care. I suppose I am."

She had done her best to communicate (was it her fault if he failed to understand?) how strangely she had been stirred by this visit and spontaneous appeal; how she had had a sense of assisting at a legend: not one of those expensive rose-and-gold legends put in a holy niche with a glittering crown for virtue; but a legend of a woman in mouse-grey, mole-brown, trudging burdened yet clear-hearted upon earth. Surely she, Sylvia, would be disqualified from among the enlightened and blessed had she failed to penetrate the disguise; failed to respond when the woman turned to her, just before going, and said so simply: "And isn't there something I can do for you?" Meaning: "I don't shut you out because you're rich. It's foolish to believe that the rich can't understand; only let us trust them enough, not always rail against them. See, I'm trusting you, though you are young and lovely and protected; I dared to break in—" Those were the words unspoken. Sylvia felt ashamed of all the condescending movements she had made in the past towards "helping the poor" without any visible impact on a daily life of the texture of satin and nectarine.

But what was she to do in atonement for this stranger woman with tragic eyes above the high slant of her cheekbones? This woman with the attractive husky voice, the long meek neck and sudden radiant smile, drab hat pulled on anyhow over her fuzz of hair, raincoat and worn-out shiny handbag? What swift generous thing could she do to rescue a child who stood on her head obediently, instead of by joyous impulse of childhood?

Remembering the little incident, Sylvia's eyes filled. Alexander instantly clasped her in his arms. "No, Alec, *no*. It isn't that. I don't need petting and patting." She pulled away from him: "I'm feeling too proud. After all, she chose me."

He stared, bewildered.

"My God, what's there to be proud about? You were simply a name on a list. One among hundreds. Probably she's been on that racket for years, and made a damn good thing out of it. Their dodge is to pick a well-known name, from the gossip columns, most likely, or from one of those chatty books of personal memoirs, and so get enough data to do their stuff convincingly—"

Sylvia tried once more to lift a spear against his obtuse point of view. "I'd far rather be taken in by nine frauds than refuse the tenth who's really in need."

Nobody, Sylvia was sure, could have summed up in such lucid, succinct style, though many must dimly feel the same. And she could hardly believe it, when she heard him, still unimpressed, indulgently chaff her for being "romantic."

"Romantic? But you, you're a sentimentalist. You can't see love unless it's wearing white in the moonlight with the nightingale turned on. But today I've met a woman who could die for love, painfully, and not boast of it as men always have, always must—Look at their poetry—"

"Women don't die of love, my sweet. Not they. They go to fortune-tellers and get promised another dark man from across the water. Let's return to our moutongs. You've been stung for quite a bit and naturally you're piqued. Well, I won't go to the police. We'll buy it. As you say," he soothed her, "it's your own money, and though it's a deuced odd way of having your fling with it, we'll not speak of it any more. There. Where shall we go for dinner?"

But he had to realize that his girl had been thoroughly upset by that charlatan ("Must have hypnotized her"). She refused to listen to reason. She refused to let him mop up her tears with his clean silk handkerchief. Gradually it dawned on him that it did not take two to make a quarrel; one was doing it all by herself, Perhaps he had better be supremely tactful and leave her alone for that evening, He kissed her several times on the nape of her delicious little neck; then went straight to the most expensive florist in Bond Street, and sent her a bouquet of the most articulate flowers that were on view: dark red roses and so forth.

What should he do now? Ring up old Seaforth and treat him to a bit of dinner and a revue? Old Seaforth was a bore, but he was down on his luck; it was up to Alec to see what could be done to cheer him.

Lulled by the choruses and the dancing, he looked forward happily to a reconciliation with Sylvia tomorrow. This had been their first quarrel. And what a damn funny thing for a man and a girl to quarrel about.

All the same, impossible to let Sylvia be mixed up in anything sordid. She was a heaven-sent victim. He must try to enlighten her a bit about what went on in the underworld; slums and brothels and police-courts—No, though, why should pretty Sylvia be worried? Much better hurry up their wedding-day; then he would always be there, more or less, and these begging pests would soon get to know it and keep off. Hurry up their wedding-day. ...

"What are you grinning at?" demanded old Seaforth. The curtain had fallen, and they buffeted their way to the bar.

By the first post he had a letter from her, breaking off their engagement.

Chapter Three

At first he refused to believe it. Had there been a substantial reason—but there was none; he had given in all along the line. She wrote in her letter that she could never live with a man (but he had asked her to marry him, not to live with him) who could even contemplate going to the police and asking for official assistance to hound down a woman already bankrupt in safety. He had appalled her by his attitude of persecution for persecution's sake. It was a revelation. She had thought him at least kind—

What did she mean by "at least"? And: "to hound down a woman already bankrupt in safety"? Alexander had a sense of humour, though Sylvia had none; he smiled wryly at the pompous, exaggerated phrases, and tenderly at her round careful handwriting.

But this letter. It winded him. Would he have to do his courtship all over again? ardently pelt her with telegrams and letters, gifts and flowers (she thanked him much too politely for his offering of last night)? Or could it all be righted in a single interview? He was inclined to think it could.

But Sylvia had gone away and left no address. She knew the persistent character of this soldier. And Alexander had to face the fact that he had lost her.

All owing to that blasted bitch. He was shaken by such a rage and such hatred for Lorna Inglefield that only strangling her would then have satisfied his lust for revenge. She had stolen his happiness as truly as though she had carried it away with her in an old sack, damn her.

Within three days of Sylvia's quittance, Alexander had become a monomaniac. He found it less agony to dwell on what he would like to do to the unknown woman, than on the curve and softness of Sylvia's mouth and the thrilling touch of her fingers as they had last strayed across his cheek and eyebrows.

Police? No. He would track her down himself.

It occurred to him thankfully that at least he knew her name. It must be the right one, or it would not have been in the marriage certificate, which is a difficult thing to fake. Besides, there was no reason why she should not have shown a genuine marriage certificate to Sylvia; it could do harm (so she had thought, not reckoning with him). Lorna Mason married to Neil Inglefield at Market St. Dunstan's. Good that his memory should have retained it.

Market St. Dunstan's was in Essex. There he could surely pick up some trace of her. Once get clear proof that he had been in the right, that here was the usual sort of crook on the begging lay, and bring his proofs to Sylvia, and lay them before her, and she would have no more case against him She would love him again. So argued the poor fool. Sylvia (he thought) had broken off their engagement because he had shown himself a cruel sceptic. Justify his scepticism, and Sylvia would as swiftly consent to a speedy marriage—

A surge of giddiness swept over him, so that he had to cling to the table. He had eaten hardly anything since the letter had arrived; his brick-red face did not look natural when it was pale. He rang for his man, and told him to pack a bag at once and to have the car brought round; he could drive it himself; "I have some business to see to, down in Essex. It's important. I don't know when I shall be back."

Market St. Dunstan's was a fair-sized village, with a war memorial in the middle of the Green, and several good houses with parks in the neighbourhood. Alexander put up at the Red Dragon, and began enquiries at the bar on the premises.

Inglefield? Yes, they dimly knew the name. But the Inglefields were all gone away. Plenty of graves, however, near by; plenty of tombstones testifying to the good qualities of the Inglefields, if the gentleman cared to take a stroll through the churchyard. And there was a memorial window. The sexton had the keys. The sexton lived over yonder in the cottage leaning against the church wall. They warned the Captain in in their broad Essex dialect that the sexton was deaf, deaf in the right ear. After he had thanked them and gone off, they winked at each other slowly and with ripe enjoyment; it was the sexton's left ear which was deaf.

Alexander had no particular fancy to read the inscriptions on the tombstones of noble Inglefields, pious upright Inglefields, charitable to the poor and faithful to their wives. One Inglefield had earned his profoundest pity by marriage to one Lorna Mason, and then merely deserted her instead of beating her and locking her up to keep her from insolent intrusion between a man and his happiness. That is to say, if any fragment of that woman's story were true. True or false, obstacles or no obstacles, she would not escape him now: he was moving relentlessly in her direction.

It gave his hatred a childlike pleasure to use all the phrases of sleuth fiction: relentless, wily, cunning, indefatigable, keen-eyed, biding-his-time.

Anyhow, there had been Inglefields at Market St. Dunstan's. Ah, but she might have picked the name at random from the churchyard. They often did.

But the marriage certificate?

In the wake of the toddling sexton, Alexander shouted questions. A late autumn wind hurled the tree-tops together and wrenched tattered leaves from the yellowing oaks. "Neil Inglefield? Do you know anything about Neil Inglefield?"

"Old Inglefield? Ay." The sexton remembered him well; twenty years ago or thereabouts it must have been that he died. Past his three-score-and-ten. Hadn't been married long neither. ... Most regrettably, for he too was past his three-score-and-ten, the sexton made a very lewd joke.

But his information only fitted crookedly with Alec's facts.

"Lorna Inglefield!" he shouted, to see what that would evoke.

"She be dead too, and pretty and good and patient she were. 'Joe,' I mind her saying to me, 'I can't hear you in this wind, Joe.' And her smiled then, same as to show it weren't no more than the wind. But we all on us knowed, poor soul, that she was a-losing her hearing, and worser every day. Of the two on 'em, she was the first to die, poor soul. In Monte Carlo, I did hear said, same as where they break the banks. Her ears be sharp enough now, I'll maintain, to hear the harps and the singin'. I was a young 'un at that time, and I didn't think I'd never have no trouble that way meself. 'Joe,' I mind her saying, 'it's that wind a-blowin' your words away.' Standing same as where we be standing now, where that's a-blowin' from the east. Old Mr. Inglefield, he allus treated her same as she were a queen, and after she were gone he fretted bad. 'That's three wives I've buried,' he'd say, 'and three's too many.' Master Marcus and Master Neil, the young gentlemen, after he were dead they sold up that place. They come down afterwards once or maybe twice but childer soon forget where they was born. They soon forget."

Alexander tipped him, and went for a walk to sort out all this jumble. "Master Neil." Put your finger on that. And Lorna Inglefield had died abroad, carefully leaving no tombstone in Essex. Could it be that she did not die, after all? Was that the mystery? Was her death a rumour spread about by her septuagenarian husband when he found her out in a betrayal which he would not be likely to confide in the sexton? Was she still wandering about, living on her wits? Yes, but then the two little girls. Who was their father? And if she were alive, after all, and had married a second husband, then what was the point in using her first and not her second marriage certificate?

And the age? did that tally? Sylvia had not mentioned, and probably had not noticed, the age of "Lorna Mason, Spinster," on the certificate. But could she have been young enough, some twenty years after the death of Neil Inglefield, to have two little girls of her own, one old enough to stand on her head when bidden? Sometimes they borrowed children, these people. If she had stolen the name, probably form a tombstone in Monte Carlo, and borrowed a couple of property children to create the right effect with soft-hearted angels like Sylvia, would that not be good enough to put Alexander right with his girl?

Proof. As yet, he had no proof; only theories and speculation. He decided to ask the vicar if he might look at the parish records. This much he thought he had established: that the real Lorna Inglefield was dead; she had been pale and pretty, and had gone to Heaven, according to the sexton; no hellish living woman to plague good men and shatter their dreams.

He worked it out to his own satisfaction that she had had no association whatever with the Inglefields, but had liked the name and forged the certificate. Then he veered round again: "Master Neil"? Could she be Master Neil's wife, and the old boy's daughter-in-law? But the sexton had agreed immediately that Lorna had indeed been the name of *old* Mr. Inglefield's wife. Might she have afterwards married the second Neil Inglefield? Alexander could not remember if that were legal or not. Still, if she had not worried over the legal aspect, why should he? Then Master Neil, even if he had deserted her (and how right he had been), would yet know where she could be found; a man in flight is always careful to locate the whereabouts of those who are trying to locate him.

Try the vicar.

The vicar had not been many years in Market St. Dunstan's and was bored by enquiries after the old families. Yes, he had heard of old Mr. Inglefield who had lived up at the Hall. Sir Valentine Sandys lived there now. A delightful family. No, he didn't believe any branch of the

Inglefields were still in the neighbourhood. Nowadays people were restless, they did not cling as their forefathers had done to the place of their birth. Captain Muir-Leslie might learn something in conversation with the older inhabitants, no doubt. Certainly he could examine the parish records. With pleasure.

The register of twenty years ago yielded nothing. Alexander plodded on, cursing. It was not the most entertaining type of literature, and all the detectives of whom he had read, employed a useful friend on such drudgery. He had to work his way through four years of marriages in the Parish of Market St. Dunstan's before with an exclamation of triumph he discovered what he wanted. Nineteen twelve. The sexton had been years out. "Neil Inglefield. Widower. Sixty-eight. To Lorna Mason—"

Here, what was this? "—To Lorna Mason. Widow. Aged forty-six."

Widow, not spinster. And forty-six in 1913. Then if she were alive now in 1928, she would have to be sixty-one. Hardly the mother of two *little* girls. And Sylvia had not described her as an elderly woman, grey-haired, lined, wearily anxious to support two granddaughters. No, the first, the *only* Lorna Mason must surely be dead. Who, then, was the pretender?

He remained down in Essex for about a week, plying the locals with drinks, making purchases at their shops, pretending to be ignorant of all that he already knew, in the hope they would enlighten him further. His quest was not wholly unsuccessful. All the legends and memories drifting about of the second Mrs. Inglefield, the real Lorna, Alec called her in his mind, confirmed what the sexton had said. She had been a sort of saint, pure and patient. She was a figure in a shrine. Whenever a shaft of light fell on her, it dazzled, Mr. Inglefield had doted on her, and offered thousands to whomever could cure her of her affliction. One daughter she had by her first marriage, not a patch on herself, a quiet little thing, devoted to her mother. But she married a war-hero and went away.

Had everyone gone away or died? Alexander demanded of the murky November air; he was exasperated by the tenuous the quality of the evidence. What, for instance, had become of Master Marcus and Master Neil?

"Master Neil" had a feudal sound, associated instantly with old servants; nurses, grooms, butlers. The grocer's wife, pressing tinned fruit on the Captain, extolling one variety which they had in stock at the expense of another, shook her head at first: as far as she knew, the staff at the Hall had been disbanded at the time and most of them gone up to take service in London. Reverting to business, she reminded him that tomorrow was the 11th, Armistice Day, when they would not open till the afternoon, so the gentleman had better lay in stock of whatever he might urgently want: rice, currants, biscuits, matches, soap, string—gentlemen were always running out of string; though now she came to think of it, there was Mrs Wright who had been cook up with the Inglefields before old Mr. Inglefield married the lady from Monte Carlo ("not in my time it wasn't. We began in Gloucestershire, me and my husband"). Mrs. Wright was now living with her married daughter, Florrie, over yonder.

Alexander thanked her gratefully, picked up his matches and ball of string, and went off primed with the address of Mrs. Wright's married daughter Florrie.

He could not see Ma just now. Ma's chest was awful bad again. Always was, in November. She might be better and up and seeing company in a day or two, or she might not.

It did not once occur to Alexander to throw over his mission and return to London, take up his life where he had dropped it, put Sylvia out of his mind. He could only forget Sylvia while he was actively occupied with his revenge on the woman who had cost him Sylvia. He was on his way to become a monomaniac.

He attended the village service round the war memorial the next morning, with the idea that it might impress Market St. Dunstan's more favourably than if he stayed away. His recollections of fiction prompted him that the popular detective with the ever-ready smile could always get his questions promptly answered, while the morose fellow met with suspicion and sulks. He could not be ready with his smile just now; at best it was a forced grin which stretched his mouth but did not lighten his eyes. Upright and military in his bearing, he stood to attention and remembered that a younger brother, Ray, had fallen at Verdun; it was a relief even for a few minutes to regret Raymond who was dead, instead of Sylvia, alive and lovely and scorning him.

Beside him was a wiry little woman with a humorous face in spite of the solemn occasion, and bright, inquisitive, black eyes. She joined loudly in "Abide with me," and seemed sorry when the Two Minutes' Silence was over and the National Anthem had been sung and the crowd began to disperse. "That was my best boy," she informed Alexander. "The second from the top out of thirty, though I expect that's because he began with an 'A'." His stare, however, was so unresponsive (indeed, he had not heard her) that she turned with the rest of her proud information to the District Nurse on the other side of her: "That's my best boy. The second from the top. Haven't seen you before, have I? Miss Dennison dead? I never miss a year; wherever I happen to be, down to the old Market on the 11th. What I say is, I like to show respect for the Fallen, same as others. Besides, he was a nice boy, though at the time it was me they called fallen and not much respect about it either!" She chuckled in a carefree manner.

The District Nurse was a little surprised, but polite. Susan was not shy. It amused her, on the annual occasion of revisiting her birthplace, to chat with everyone, those who remembered her and those who didn't; giving them a few sharp nips whenever an opening occurred for nips, and tantalizing their curiosity by refusing ever to reveal what she had done since she went up to London; whether she was in service, or if not, what she did instead; nor her address, nor the name of her employer, if she had an employer. She asked questions but answered none.

"Not that he was the first who got me in trouble. Nor third nor the fourth. More like the twentieth. Wasn't much competition then, in one-horse places like this. Now it looks as though I'd have my work cut out holding my own, if I wanted to. Who's Major-General Stick-in-the-mud?" nodding sideways at Alexander's back, "Holding himself like a poker and wouldn't answer when spoken to. What's *he* doing down here besides buying up the place and everyone in it?"

She learned that he was a Captain Muir-Leslie from London. That he had been staying for several days now at the Red Dragon and went about pumping everyone he met at Market St. Dunstan's about the Inglefield family that used to live up at the Hall, and especially about Lorna Inglefield, the second wife, her that died out in Monte Carlo.

Susan stared at Alexander, and learned him by heart.

Unconscious of his contact with the person who could have led him, so to speak, straight to where the body was buried, Alexander chafed and fretted through the interminable three days before Mrs. Wright's chest permitted her to receive visitors. Then, however, he was rewarded. Not long ago, not more than a month, or it may be two, she had received a picture-postcard from Master Neil, which she was perfectly willing to bring forth and boastfully display. It was really better than a postcard, a sort of coloured folder with the address on the outside, and when opened out showed a super-train called "The Chief" bound for Los Angeles with little pictures inset of all the places that "The Chief" roared through from Chicago to the Coast. Scrawled across the very small space for communication was the message: "I'm on this train. Love, Neil Inglefield."

"Every now and then he remembers his old Wright, and then I get a card from him travelling about wherever he is; and always at Christmas; ah, I expect he don't forget the puddings I used to make, black with richness my puddings were. And Master Neil was the one I liked best, though always up to his tricks. With most people, it was Master Marcus."

Alexander said to himself, gloating over the brief message signed Neil Inglefield; "I shall have to follow him to California." He did not mind. For love of Sylvia, for hate of the unknown woman whom he refused to call "Lorna Inglefield," he might just as well go to Los Angeles as to Margate. Life was very simple when you had one love and one hate.

Mrs. Wright could tell him no more. She had had a row with old Mr. Inglefield, and gone as cook to another part of Essex before he married again. So she only knew of the second Mrs. Inglefield by hearsay, who again appeared, though dressed in homely words, as a sort of Lady of Shalott, sorrowful, pure and pale.

"Have you no idea, Mrs. Wright, where I could find Mr. Neil Inglefield now?"

Mrs. Wright's forefinger pointed to what was the obvious reply.

"He's on that train."

"Not permanently," he barked, as he might have to a not very bright subaltern, and forgetting that detectives must always be amiable and smile pleasantly.

"He's on the train," repeated Mrs. Wright.

"He *was* on that train when he sent you the card.—But the train doesn't take nearly as long to reach its destination as that card took to reach you all the way back here in England."

"Ay," Mrs. Wright agreed. "Come all that way, it has. And Master Neil's on that train, or he wouldn't say so."

Alexander gave it up.

"And what's become of Marcus Inglefield?"

She was vague about Master Marcus. He had meant nothing to her. There might, of course, be some other retired cook in Essex who had preferred Master Marcus to Master Neil, and received his picture-postcards from a slightly more accessible country than California. But even if it were so, Alexander was unable to establish the contact. Never mind, Neil Inglefield would be undoubtedly the more useful, for he suddenly remembered with a thrill of satisfaction that the woman who had pretended to be Lorna Inglefield had asked for her fare to California on the grounds that her wicked husband was there. Hadn't Sylvia said something, too, about a newspaper cutting? If only he had listened more closely; but it had all seemed so unimportant apart from his determination that his blessed little girl should not be swindled while he was there to protect her. He could not now return to Sylvia and ask to see a newspaper cutting which had suddenly become a valuable clue; Sylvia must not hear of his campaign yet; not until the flame-coloured moment of reunion which he so often planned in a thousand shapes of setting and dialogue; his vindication and her adorable surrender.

Besides, for the present he could not endure thinking of Sylvia at all, in any connection with that fatal visit which had sundered them. There had been a catastrophe, over there in the distance, muffled since by a thick curtain swinging across. By and by it would be all right.

Still, a newspaper which stated, for whatever reason, that Neil Inglefield was in California, tallied with Mrs. Wright's picture-postcard in which he declared himself on his way there; and established, moreover, that his journey was on some errand of public interest which would make it easier to find him. Alexander was usually a man of military precision in his arrangements. But now, not bothering to make any, he hurled himself across the Atlantic like a stone from a catapult, in pursuit of Inglefield.

Chapter Four

Although Alexander did not himself recognize the name of Neil Inglefield as that of a film star, he assumed that as he was important enough for his photograph to be reproduced in an English newspaper, his name would at least be known in Hollywood. He made his first enquiry at the bureau at his hotel, the Chateau Maintenon, and struck lucky, though not in the way he had expected.

"Sure I know Neil Inglefield. A grand guy. He's the fellow they sent over from the Neptune Hotels Board to open up their new place on the Coast: the Neptune-Palisades. I was there and spoke to him. Knows his onions, I'll say. And I saw him again not a week ago at the Brown Derby. I expect he's staying on a bit, to watch how it makes out. A fine building, barrack or rococo, I'm not sure. And pure Looey all through, though of course it's not right here in Hollywood. The other end of

Sunset and then some. You want an automobile to drive out? All-righty. All-righty."

Arriving at the Neptune-Palisades Hotel, Alexander said he wanted a suite, he did not know for how long, but would like to discuss it with Mr. Inglefield.

"Mr. Inglefield himself?" The booking-clerk seemed a bit surprised. Apparently it was like dropping in at Buckingham Palace and without further palaver asking for the King. "I'll see."

While he was gone, Alexander considered what policy to pursue. He would not, naturally, mention his objective for the first day or two: one must advance warily, show cunning, bide one's time.

His ostensible reason, then, for an immediate interview with this man must be to create an impression from a business angle. Alexander was well off, and being now on a single-minded quest, did not care what he spent. Half his fortune would gladly be spent for the recapture of Sylvia, provided the other half were left for him to lavish on her afterwards. So he would demand the most expensive suite in this new hotel, yet prove courteously exacting over certain requirements. In two or three days it might do to ask him if by any chance Lorna Inglefield were a relation. Careful, though, careful was the word. Don't tackle him too suddenly.

"My name's Inglefield. You wanted to see me?"

("Yes, I've been chasing you since the fifth of November, Guy Fawkes' Day, when that woman who calls herself Lorna Inglefield made a bonfire of what I care about most. She's a professional swindler and you've got to help me prove it or I might as well be dead.")

"Yes, I must apologize if I'm a nuisance, but there are various conditions I have to have in my suite, and I've always found it pays to go straight to the man at the top, if he's handy."

"The company employs me as handyman," laughed Inglefield. "Come along. The clerk didn't tell me your name?"

He gave Inglefield a card showing his regiment and his club. His heart was beating a big drum, as it had beaten when he had first manoeuvred an introduction to Sylvia. But this, this mattered even more, now Sylvia must be won all over again.

So here was Mrs. Wright's Master Neil. How amazed he would be if the well-behaved military man with him in the elevator suddenly prodded him in the back and said: "How is Master Marcus?" Or, even more effective: "What price Lorna?" What price indeed? The price of his happiness, unless he managed to outwit her now.

He did not debate whether he liked Neil Inglefield or not. The man existed only as a means to an end. He would have to make friends with him, of course. Fortunately he did not appear at all forbidding. They were friends before they reached the eleventh floor. Alexander had to inspect several magnificent apartments and to invent eccentricities of taste to justify having sent for the managing director himself.

"I'm not really that, either, because I don't stay in one hotel for long. I'm their Flying Dutchman. The job was almost invented for me."

"What does it involve?"

"If one of their hotels goes wrong, or isn't paying as it should, or there's a rival too close that has to be cut out, then I get sent along and put the fear of God into everyone and find out the root of the trouble and get cursed all round, and go back and get told by the Board very graciously that I've done well. Or when they're opening up new places like this one. It's like launching a ship, not only breaking the bottle over the prow, but staying on till all the engines are running smoothly."

"Interestin'. Was"—he might allow himself just this—"was your father in the hotel line?" (Neil Inglefield, widower, and Lorna Mason, widow, at Market St. Dunstan's church in 1913—)

"Lord, no. The old man was a brewer, but he retired early into the country, and my brother took on the brewery. He put me into the law, but I got restless, waiting for briefs. One of the only successful jobs I had was as junior in the famous case of the Neptune Hotels versus the Bombay Steamship Company. They thought I was a bright boy, too bright for the Bar, so this was the final result. Not that my father would have approved—" with a swift grin. "After all, a hotel is just a glorified form of pub to people who don't stay in 'em. My brother doesn't mind, but his wife hardly knows how to pass me off at dinner-parties without blushing: 'This is my brother-in-law who sort of runs the Red Dragon, you know.'"

Yes, thought Alexander, I know the Red Dragon, thank you.

He moved into the Trianon Suite at once, and invited Neil Inglefield to dine as his guest that evening.

"No, you're the stranger here. You must dine with me."

Not a bad excuse, thought Inglefield, for getting out of his date with Mourne Fitzdarcy. Mourne was very appealing, with those enormous eyes and that heart-shaped little face and her not quite genuine Irish brogue, slurred like dropping rain. But he had not yet committed himself, and was not sure whether it would be altogether a good thing to start an idle affair with a synthetic colleen in a Spanish house in Beverley Hills. She was the adhesive type that almost literally grew on you. But for Mourne, he would have been off a week ago. Mourne my sweet, I have a business engagement to dine tonight with a rich client, Captain Muir-Leslie of the 17th Lancers; come, come, mavourneen, it was up to me not to rebuff Croesus himself when he happens along and when, without blinking, almost absent-mindedly, in fact, he agrees to the insane terms for our most elegant, Looeyest apartment; after all, I'm a shareholder.

That would do to damp down Mourne, for the moment.

Inglefield had seen to it that the cellar at the Neptune-Palisades was as good as any to be found in Continental cities. He wanted to try out a certain claret, to see how it had survived the long journey, two months ago, so he ordered a magnum to be decanted. They had sherry, Montrachet, a 1906 Château Haut-Brion, an excellent old cognac, and, after an interval, highballs. Alexander went straight through the drinks so carefully provided as though they were all water, without pleasure or pain. He did not even notice that his reticence, such as it was, was loosening, leaking, letting in draughts. He had enjoined on himself sternly, before dinner, that he must not mention Lorna; it was too soon: "First play your fish—" He kept to this resolution; but when they were half through the magnum, he began to talk of love, love in general terms; there was no detective rule against that, was there? He spoke of love in a disparaging, hoity-toity sort of way. He quoted Confucius. He asserted that a man married was a man marred. But presently, softly swayed by the claret, presently he was telling Inglefield about Sylvia. The sound of her name spoken aloud, even by himself, was like the bursting of a cork from a bottle of pent-up peroxide; a gasp of unutterable relief. For he was by nature gregarious and confidential. When they brought along the big tulip brandy-glasses and set the bottle down between the two men that they should help themselves, Alexander absently filled his glass to the brim as though it were a thimbleful. His spate of description became wild and feverish. Inglefield had to hear of every incident twice; once out of sequence, and then again when his guest exclaimed: "Look here, hadn't I better tell you the whole story from the beginning?" The first meeting with Sylvia, everything that Sylvia had ever done, worn, said, looked; what it felt like to love Sylvia passionately; appreciations of Sylvia from the four points of the compass; how rare she was; how unique; how she smiled; Sylvia with the sun in her hair; Sylvia and Sylvia and the glory and tenderness of Sylvia; plans he and Sylvia had woven for the future; her innocence and unworldliness, her need for a strong protector. The sissy-chap scornfully touched upon, and triumphantly flung away. Then, at last, the visit from a mystery woman who had cast a mesmeric spell on Alexander's darling. And out came their whole quarrel, and her letter breaking off the engagement: "Mind you, I'm not justifying myself." Until the dawn he went on not justifying himself. Yet, still exultant at his own self-control and craftiness, he did not mention the woman's name, nor even hint that the story might have any personal significance.

Inglefield never forgot that dinner. He realized then that boredom could be so intense as to approach a mystical experience. His brain went rigid. He felt as though he were powerless while the voice netted itself about him, tighter and tighter. He was in a mesh and he could not escape. He attempted to remove his soul and hearing from that voice, and only leave his body behind, but Alexander must have apprehended this plot against him, for he leant forward and fixed Inglefield with a bloodshot truculent stare, cutting off even spiritual retreat.

Sylvia and Sylvia and Sylvia. … The poor devil's a monomaniac, thought Inglefield. But after this bout comes to an end, I'm off before the next. Impossible to stop in the same hotel with the risk of such an encounter down every corridor. Obviously the man had to talk, but any other listener would serve his purpose equally well, so let him seek a fresh victim every time. For Inglefield knew that a monomaniac may unburden himself, but when he has finished he finds his burden still mysteriously restored to him, as heavy as before.

Love? God, if love turned a man into a pathological case and a public nuisance, better not give it a chance. This Sylvia was probably no more rare and no more attractive than Mourne Fitzdarcy. The hotel could stand on its own legs now so better to remove himself from Mourne's reach, and definitely out of Alexander's. "I'd have sworn till tonight that he was just the conventional British Army type; pleased with himself, a good sport: women all right in their proper place, God bless 'em. But now—he's like Don Quixote on an off day, seeing his Dulcinea to be rescued from every whirling windmill."

Alexander rambled on: the name "Sylvia" had been so often repeated that to Inglefield it was no longer a girl's name, but syllables which clicked like a wooden toy and had lost all meaning. Sylvia? Who is Sylvia, what is she?—and how this raving lunatic adores her!

He reached the conclusion that she must be a rather stupid young woman, or she would have handled the affair better than this. He was perfectly right.

Alexander woke late the next morning. In spite of a head that felt as though it were stuffed with cold porridge, and a mouth dry as leather, morally he was feeling decidedly better. It now appeared, in terms of clear sense, that he need not wait for three days more before telling Neil Inglefield about Sylvia's visit from the woman who professed to be Neil Inglefield's deserted wife. Such a nice ordinary chap; it was grotesque, the mere idea that he could desert anyone dependent on him, leave them derelict, stranded and penniless, a wife and two little children. A wicked slander which ought to be exposed without delay. Why, it might damage the man in his profession. It was therefore Alexander's duty, apart from any personal motive, to lay the whole matter before him this very morning. Then they could both pack up and start for England without further delay. And deal with it, not angrily, but stern and cold.

But when he telephoned down to the bureau and asked to be put through at once to Mr. Neil Inglefield, he was told that Mr. Inglefield had already left.

"Left? Left where? Where's he gone? Can't have left."

They could not say where he had gone, sir. They did not know themselves, sir.

They did, but Inglefield's orders had been imperative: not to anyone staying in this hotel; nor, if it comes to that, to anyone else, he added, remembering Mourne Fitzdarcy.

"But he'll be corning back?"

"No, sir, he said not."

The shock was hardly less than when Sylvia had broken off her engagement. He could not believe it. Unceasingly he badgered the executives and the staff of the Neptune-Palisades Hotel. And then he badgered every visitor in the hotel to whom he thought Inglefield might have confided his destination. They grew to dread the sight of him, and asked the management when that Englishman with the queer miserable eyes would be leaving? Alexander could imagine no reason why he should be treated like this, tormented and betrayed, except that an anthropomorphic God had suddenly taken to hating him.

Meanwhile, Mourne Fitzdarcy, as baffled as the fellow-victim of whose proximity she knew nothing, lay disconsolately in a gay striped hammock in her patio on Laurel Canyon Drive, and wondered what could have happened that she had lost her Broth-of-a-Neil so abruptly. She had never cared for any boy as much as she cared for her Neil. He was different from the rest. He never meant a word of the nonsense he spoke, but hell, the way he spoke it! Hell, his round black head and divvle-may-care walk (you got into the way of using brogue, and so you did). She would have slept with him, gladly, without any purity fuss, except that of course, this being Hollywood, they would have had to marry first, but you can't call that "fuss," with Reno so handy.

She refused to go out. Her usual companions, when they were not working at the Studios, dropped in at first to cheer her up, but it was rumoured that she had become a bore, and never talked of anything but Neil, Neil, Neil. She was not cast for a part in the next production; the metamorphosis from a bewitching Irish colleen brimming over with all the infectious laughter of the ould counthry, to an unhappy woman from the Middle West who glowered and moped and forgot her brogue, was not professionally helpful.

It happened that she cared more for Neil than he had noticed. She puzzled endlessly as to why he should have done this to her. She shredded every hour they had passed together into sixty fragments, and each of these into another sixty, to be conscientiously scrutinized to see if one might contain the black speck that could have started the trouble.

Lorna Mason. Lorna Blake. Lorna Inglefield. But Mourne, if offered the three names in answer to the recurring riddle, would have asked, surprised, and dropping the improvised brogue which was only another weariness: "Gosh, who *is* this darn Lorna, anyway?"

Chapter Five

Alexander left Santa Monica. There seemed no sense in remaining on. He travelled from one Neptune Company hotel to another, zigzagging to and fro across America in the wake of Neil Inglefield. Then even that coherence to his journeys broke down, and he wandered without purpose. What was the use of returning to England? He sent in his papers. He did not answer letters of natural expostulation from his friends and colleagues and relations, and from the constituency he had been nursing so tenderly. With a guilty feeling that he was of no use any more to others nor to himself, and must do something to atone, he gave orders to his lawyer to double the allowance to his various pensioners: a woebegone aunt and her children, his cousins; a bedridden servant; his father's ancient clerk; he added an anonymous present to old Seaforth, who was down on his luck. Twice a day and every day, he expected a miracle: a letter from Sylvia: "Darling Alec, I love you. I was wrong. Come home." Even in such places where the mail only came in once a day, the mental rhythm worked as it had worked when he was a child seeing an English postman morning and evening briskly marching up the avenue to the front door of the country house where he was born.

Now that the seal was off the stopper and he had talked about Sylvia all one evening, he could not stop talking of her. He talked of Sylvia from one end of the United States to the other. Quite a few bewildered Americans could have passed a gruelling examination on Sylvia.

He had been used to regular exercise, but he took none. Talking about Sylvia could hardly be called exercise. He never blamed her, but was merciless in accusing his own clumsiness and brutality. The unknown woman called Lorna he hardly mentioned any more; he hated her too terribly.

A complete fool of a girl who served him at a drug-store, in the Middle West, sorry for his plight, took him along to a fortune-teller, earnestly praising the perfectly wonderful talents of Madam Cassoapy ("because she sits in a chair, see? But Cassoapy's the goods all right"). Alexander pooh-poohed all fortune-tellers, but went along to please the girl because she had a look of Sylvia. His resistance had been brought very low. Madam Cassoapy, in a moment, promised him a blonde lady and hinted that there was also a brunette across water from whom dire trouble might be feared. She meant that his wife in England might not care for the drug-store cutie hanging on his arm, but Alexander found no difficulty in sorting out the characters as Sylvia and Mrs. Neil Inglefield ("She's with you right now"—did it not certainly mean that a spirit-Sylvia still loved him and hovered near?). After that, all went swimmingly. Confucius had been a dud, compared with Madam Cassoapy.

There were plenty of fortune-tellers in America. He always made it clear to them at once that he desired Sylvia to be provided for him, loving and forgiving. They were more than complaisant, except that they warned him they could give no exact guarantee of time; it might be this month, or it might be next. Or even longer.

PART III

Fare to Nowhere

Chapter One

Jay saw that Susan, on her return from the country on Armistice Day, had something special to say to Mummy. She hoped that it might come out while she was inconspicuous but present. For she, as well as Molly, had noticed the funny way in which during her Visiting times Mummy didn't mind what was discussed in front of the children. Susan never minded, anyhow, and Mummy had to check her during the nice but rather dull between-periods: "Hush, Susan; not now; afterwards." And Susan would snap back: "Ow, they've got to hear things some time and might as well hear 'em young."

What Susan reported now, after clearing away, was much more exciting than just "things." "Better look out," she advised brusquely. "There's a man snooping about down at the old Market, trying to find out what he can about you."

Lorna looked mildly surprised, and a little grieved that anyone should be so uselessly and unkindly employed: "Did he speak to you? Who can he be?"

"I asked. He's a Captain Muir-Leslie, staying at the old Dragon; hope he likes it; from what I remember—No, he didn't speak to me. Didn't know I'd anything to do with you, or he'd never have left me alone. None of 'em know, down there. They believe anything I tell 'em."

"Captain Muir-Leslie?" Lorna screwed up her eyes in an effort to remember.

"You haven't tried putting it over on him?"

"I don't put it over on anyone, Susan."

"Sorry I spoke."

"People are very sweet and generous to me when I'm in trouble. I've got the children to think of."

"They ought to do nicely."

"What sort of questions did he ask, Susan?"

"Mostly about Neil Inglefield, and you being married to him or not."

"*Neil!* The enemy boy."

"Won't be a boy now any longer. Your age, wasn't he?"

Jay was passionately interested. She and Molly never doubted but that a man called Neil Inglefield was their wicked parent. Mummy had a certificate to show she was married to him; and whenever she displayed it, she explained how he had run away when they were babies and left her to look after them with hardly any money. It sounded more real than any of her variations. But how could a wicked parent possibly be "the enemy boy"?

"Always Neil," Lorna murmured.

"Well, you needn't flash daggers. It isn't him that's after you, it's this other fellow."

"What does he look like?"

Susan told her. Alexander would have hated the portrait.

"I haven't seen anyone like that."

"Husband? Out at the time? You wouldn't have seen him, then."

"Muir-Leslie?" Lorna repeated. "No."

"Private detective for all we know; and put in a Captain to make it sound more stylish. Better lie low for a bit, or clear out."

Lorna ceased frowning and patting her hair. On a gay inspiration, she cried: "I'll take the children to Monte Carlo for a lovely holiday."

"Monte Carlo? Whatever do you want to take them there for? If it's gambling, you can do it cheaper at Belloyne."

"Who told you, Susan dear, that I wanted to do it cheaper?"

"Well, perhaps not, since that Miss Sylvia Mainwaring and the two after her. But Monte Carlo's a place where people don't go to hide, and if anyone's looking out for you—"

But Lorna laughed away all objections. She declared that Susan ought to trust to her diviner's twig by now, and the twig said Monte Carlo would be perfectly safe. She had a strong desire to see if she liked orthodox gambling, and whether she would be lucky at that too.

"Too," Susan echoed, with a flash of white teeth. Immediately Lorna lapsed into her previous mood of gentle seriousness: "And the children really ought to see their granny's grave."

"H'm, you say that as if you was taking them on to the merry-go-rounds. Ought to save your money; you won't find it so easy to go back to skimping on three-fifty a year less income tax, if the well runs dry."

"Susan, another word, and I'll take you along too and dump you down at the roulette-table."

"That you won't."

"I'll get the children some dainty French clothes. They'd pay for dressing."

"You mean other folk would."

"Oh, *Mummy!*"

Lorna turned with a merry smile towards Jay; and, ignoring Susan's last quip, held out her hand, not in the least disconcerted to find her elder daughter present in the room.

"You'll like that, won't you, pet? A long journey in a train, then the sea and lots of sunshine. More sun than you've ever seen before. And oranges growing by the road."

"Oh, *Mummy!* Can I tell Molly when she comes home from the elocution class?"

"If you like. No, we'll keep it secret for a day or two and let it be a surprise." She laid a warning finger against her lips; her eyes danced. Then she hugged Jay, swinging her off her feet. Jay adored this sort of Mummy. Susan said: "Laugh before seven, cry before eleven."

"It isn't before seven. It isn't. It's half-past three. And no one's going to cry."

"Remains to be seen."

"Susan, you're an old wet blanket. An ironing-blanket, scorched, with holes!" You could hardly tell the difference between Jay and her mother when they both teased Susan and made light of her fears.

"And now, my jasmine flower, run along and put on your things. You're coming out with Mummy."

Jay whirled upstairs. On the first landing she stopped and called out: "Mummy."

"Yes? Hurry up, lamb."

"If we go to Monte Carlo, shall we still be living within our income?"

Lorna laughed up at the serious face which peeped at her over the banisters. "Where did you pick that up, you funny little snipe?"

"From you, Mummy. You say it often: that whatever happens, we must live within our income. But if it's within our income, I'd like a yellow dress, please, not always white or blue. Yellow silk, now I'm eleven. With a belt, not a sash. And, of *course*, not the sailor kind of blouse."

"There'll be rows and rows of yellow silk dresses with belts in Monte Carlo. I'll buy you one."

Satisfied with the promise, Jay scrambled into the shabby sailor-suit which made her look even slighter and more babyish than she was; the old-fashioned green tam-o'-shanter which she knew wasn't the right wear with a sailor-suit, her long curls pulled well forward; the socks with a large hole in the heel above the shoe, not in the toes, where it couldn't be seen; the shoes with rubbed toecaps and the heels worn down on one side.

It was not worth while, now she knew so well, to ask afresh each time what clothes Mummy meant her to wear for each occasion. Clothes fell into sets, and she found it quite easy to keep one set distinct from the other. First, during the between-times, the simple "suitable" clothes worn by all little girls, Kathy Anderson and the others, from those coloured magazines with patterns that Mummy copied on the sewing-machine. And then the Visiting clothes, which were funny, like dressing-up. There had been a tacit row, one day, everything pressed down and not spoken right out, when Lorna discovered that a pair of their oldest socks, darned and lumpy, had been thrown away: "You children have no right to throw anything away without asking me first."

"But, Mummy, Susan said they were past praying for."

"What Susan says has nothing to do with it."

But now Jay had a vision of gleaming yellow silk to be worn in the sunshiny place where you "gambled" along the road by the sea, with yellow oranges growing on the trees; Jay had once played Titania in the *Midsummer Night's Dream:*

"Be kind and courteous to this gentleman,
Hop in his walks
And gambol in his eyes."

"Are you ready, darling? I'm waiting."

You could never be sure whether you were frightened or not, when one of those queer visits to strangers lay just ahead. Jay relished them in a different way from the romping enjoyment of children's parties where they gave you ice-cream and presents, but where the games had been slow, the other children too little to play properly, and the grown-ups not leaving out one of the usual tiresome things about her pretty hair and how was their mother, and what did she like doing best at school; and she must hurry up and grow taller or her little sister would be shooting up ahead of her and that would never do, would it? ("Yes, no, I don't know, I shouldn't mind.")

But on these expeditions, as now, you could not foretell what would happen, nor how it would happen. You wondered vividly what sort of a house it would be. Mummy never told you beforehand, she just let you wonder till you got out of the bus or the Underground and walked along—and suddenly she stopped and said: "This must be it." And then came the terribly hazardous game of getting past the servants. Sometimes it was a haughty butler and sometimes a cross parlourmaid, except once by accident when it had been a darling Swedish woman with eyes like a kind cow, who wasn't a servant and gave them money as well as a dreadful heavy old typewriter. But servants or secretaries were grim and incredulous, and always put up obstacles; you turned icy and held your breath and your legs trembled like water. But Mummy up till now had always somehow got past the sentinels. And then you began wondering with even more excitement whom you were going to see next? Would it be the important person who had the money? And what was Mummy going to say-first? and was Neil Inglefield their father this time? and to what place would the fare be? and who was ill? and would they get out alive and free? One day in the future (but Mummy did not know this, and not even Molly knew) Jay meant to plunge in and take an active share, instead of standing mute and wistful until the moment came to kiss and be kissed. She was sure that, like Mummy, she could guess in a moment, just as you had to guess things like lightning to win in games, what were the right words to use with each lady and gentleman in turn. Though she would never be so wonderful as Mummy. Yet even with Mummy in charge, something went wrong every now and then, and Jay would twist her hands behind her back, and pretend not to be listening while Mummy sort of curled backwards and came round again by a different way.

If only Visiting could be cut short before you had to help with the thank-yous. Thank-you could never be done in a hurry. Mummy spun it out with lots about the children's sake (or the child's sake, if you hadn't a sister that day) and was dreadfully humble during such long streaming sentences; and the lady or gentleman who had given her the money was uncomfortable too, Jay could see it; or, what was worse, smug and smiling with the pleasure of having helped a very Deserving Case.

Whenever she lay in bed in the dark, remembering, Jay always changed the game just before it reached the thank-yous, after the money had been given; and, instead, let her fancy declaim loftily that, after all, she and Mummy and Molly didn't want it. "As a matter of fact," Jay invented, in bed in the dark, and knowing less of fact and matters of fact than any child alive, "it's us who've come to give *you* a present. We wanted to see first if we could bring you up to scratch"—the expression was a favourite of Susan's. "Now that you have, here you are." And added with great sweetness and dignity: "Please don't thank us, because we'd rather not be thanked." Or, when even this was too tame for her racing blood, she let her mind escape into an imaginary place which she called "the house of jeopardy." Jeopardy meant danger, but it was more dangerous even than danger. This reverie was not all pleasure, though she could not always stop herself from doing it:

… She and Mummy and Molly had to live in the house of jeopardy. It had doors and windows, and when they were open, the view was lovely, but if they were all closed, it would be prison. Sometimes while they were Visiting, Mummy made an awful mistake and they were all nearly found out. But she, Jay, thought of something just in time to save them. Or, ultimate thrill, she did not succeed in saving them, and the doors and windows slowly swung and clanged, and they were shut up where there was no more light. Jay never told Molly that she enjoyed frightening herself, for she suspected, when put into words, that Molly knew about real plain fear, and played no tricks with it.

Was Visiting wrong? Mummy did it, and Mummy said it was for the sake of her children, and it was what you did things *for*, which made them right or wrong. If you didn't ask for yourself but for others, Mummy said, a blessing would be on it. She said so, not to Jay or Molly, but to Susan when Susan went too far. You took it for granted all your life that what Mummy did was right and that you would understand some day, though for years and years she had done nothing at all exciting. Yet now Jay knew without telling that her mother felt just as she did herself, that icy tingle of expectation waiting outside a strange front door, yet already committed by bell and knocker: What is it going to be like, this time? Can we manage it? Shall we get out safely? She believed that Mummy didn't mind the thanking part, but that was the only difference between them.

Chapter Two

Molly was out with Mummy. When they came back and Jay rushed down to the gate and welcomed them, just managing to hold back a jubilant "Any luck?", Lorna said: "Run and pack your things, babies. I'll send Susan up to you. We're going South. Jay, you may tell Molly now."

Jay raced ahead of Molly up to their bedroom, the same bedroom in Huntingdon Terrace looking over the oblong strips of their neighbours' gardens and their own. They had not been obliged to move this time, for Lorna gave a false address, when indeed she had to give an address at all. Usually she said she was afraid it was no good telling her benefactors where she lived, because they had to move out at once.

"Molly, we're going away. We're going South."

"Yes, I know. Southampton. But we shan't really be going."

"But, Molly, we are. We *are*, this time. It's different. It's a place where oranges grow on trees by the road, thousands of miles away. Monte Carlo."

Molly was bewildered.

"But we haven't asked for the fare to there."

"We're going all the same. It's for fun. It's for gambolling. It's within our income because of the last three times—and today, I suppose?"

There was no need for either of them to ask the other what was meant by "the last three times," and Molly's laconic "Southampton" explained today.

"And I'm going to have a yellow silk dress, made rather grown-up. What colour will you have?"

Molly was tugging off her sailor-suit. Her head was buried in dark blue serge and she could neither waggle it up or down because it was too tight. Her voice came through, saying "Orange."

"Oh, you can't; *I'm* having yellow because of the oranges."

"You could have lemon."

"I hate lemons. I never chose the lemon side, even when I was a baby. And if we're both dressed the same, it'll be like sailor-suits."

That, too, needed no explaining.

"Violet, then," said Molly slowly, after a long pause of deliberation.

"That'll do. Susan, have you come up to pack for us? Oh, Susan, I'm going to have a yellow dress and Molly violet. Shan't we look lovely? Silk, not cotton. Silk satin cotton rags. Look, the lock of the trunk's broken; you'll have to cord it. Coach carriage wheelbarrow walk—Oh, Susan, have you ever been to Monte Carlo? This year next year some time never—"

"Never," said Susan with emphasis, rapidly folding clothes and dumping them into the bottom of the trunk. "I've no use for hot places, thank you. A pretty sight you'll both look when you come back, your hair bleached white and your faces burned. Won't matter then, wearing yellow and violet."

Jay and Molly stared at her in horror. Their hair bleached white and their faces burned?

But, in spite of Susan, Monte Carlo proved a glorious paradise, enriched by their mother in a more enchanting mood than they had ever known before. In the old days she had allowed them, so she said, to run wild on holiday; but to run wild at Clifford's Bay had been really quite a restricted business, with little anxious prohibitions for ever bringing them up short: children they mustn't speak to and landladies they mustn't vex with too much noise, bunches of wet seaweed that might not be brought up home from the beach, doughnuts and greengages only to be eaten after bathing, not before; we mustn't catch cold; we mustn't be late for lunch; we mustn't spend too much (remember we're not rich, darlings); we mustn't sit on wet sand; you must keep your hats on all the time. But down here in the South, even though an unusually hot November sun shone with more brilliancy on their bare heads than any English summer sun could achieve, they were not bothered with hats; and until the chill of sunset, wore the minimum of clothing, only as much, in fact, as they themselves desired, so that their arms right up to the shoulder and their legs and their backs got burnt, not as Susan had viciously prophesied, but a glowing walnut-brown. Jay crooned over the smooth sunburn which lay not only outside but, she declared, gilded her warmly the whole way through, so that she felt more alive, more tireless and splendidly immortal than ever before. She had been used to being the delicate one, but now she and Molly were both strong and happy and wild. They were allowed to eat and drink whatever they pleased, and by a miracle whatever they pleased did them no harm; though the head waiter at their small but renowned hotel down on the sea-road delighted to indulge them with every French caprice of superb cooking, and capped their unsophisticated but greedy suggestions with the most fantastic embellishments.

Mummy allowed them to dash about alone wherever they liked, instead of herself trotting in the rear looking fussy; she did not enjoin punctuality in the exact hour of their return, nor question them in a worried way as to whether anyone had spoken to them, with the tiresome tag: "You must never answer strangers, you know, darlings, because one can't be sure who they are nor where they come from." All that motherish stuff and nonsense had melted in the sun. They were given full freedom, and money to spend on any bright rubbish which caught their eye. The sea was bluer than the bluest ultramarine in their paint-boxes, and oranges grew according to schedule except that they were still a little green and unripe: and strange flowers cascaded over walls; and they drove up into the hills in an open carriage with a horse; and a yellow silk dress was bought for Jay and a dress the shade of dim blue violets (not quite what she had meant) for Molly. This was Monte Carlo; a place indeed for riotous pagan gambollings, and certainly not to them what it apparently meant to most of the English people there, who talked unweariedly about "the tables."

"Have you been to the tables today?' people in the hotel asked Mummy. And once: "Have you been to the kitchen?"

Tables and a kitchen. Kitchen-table. What could be sillier?

Mummy answered indifferently: "Only twice, when I first arrived. I don't care about it much."

"My dear Mrs. Blake. But then why come to Monte Carlo?"

Why come to Monte Carlo? Jay and Molly could have told them. Idiots.

"I expect Mrs. Blake lost a packet," suggested a colonel (lots of colonels here), with a twinkle of understanding in his eyes. "Wise woman. I wish I had your self-control."

"No. The first day I went in, I came out even, and the second time I won. But it didn't amuse me. I suppose I'm not a gambler by nature."

"Then, my dear lady, I repeat, why Monte Carlo?"

Lorna said gently: "I chose it because my mother is buried here and I hadn't visited her grave for a very long time. Too long, I'm afraid."

Molly chuckled and nudged Jay: "Look at them all pulling down the blinds in their faces."

Granny's grave had been more or less of a side-show. They had been taken to see it, their only decorous expedition. Molly had had secret doubts as to whether it were there at all and not merely a sort of Liverpool or Southampton, the always invisible objective. But when they stopped at the florist's and their mother bought a huge wreath of beautiful white and dark red carnations, and two small bunches of anemones for her and Jay, doubt wavered, because a wreath was not a thing you could put in a vase. And here on the tombstone, clean and spruce among the other tombstones, she and Jay solemnly read the words: "Lorna, beloved wife of Neil Inglefield."

This was a surprise. Molly dropped her flowers over the name as though to cover something she wished to forget, and ran off quickly to examine other graves with their inset photographs and complicated beadwork: "Jay, come and look!" Just as though this were not an occasion to stand reverently and a little stiffly, heads bent, thinking of poor Grandmother. But Jay, in the relaxed atmosphere of this miraculous holiday, did not see why she should not ask her mother one or two pertinent questions: "'Wife of Neil Inglefield'? That's Granny, isn't it?"

"Yes, darling."

"Did you love her very much?"

"Yes, darling." But Lorna had bestowed the flamboyant wreath with the air of claiming a score against an adversary.

"But—Neil Inglefield, isn't he alive? Isn't he our father, mine and Molly's?"

Mummy was not angry, nor even puzzled how to answer. "Sometimes two people have the same name, my lamb. Now go with Molly. If you like, you can walk about quietly and look, but you mustn't shout to each other."

"Aren't you coming, Mummy?"

"No. I want to sit here alone for a few minutes."

"To cry?" sympathetically. "But, Mummy, she died in 1917. It says so there. And this is nineteen hundred and thirty, so it's an awfully long time ago. I wouldn't bother if I was you."

"Run away, you little pagan."

But that was their only conventional hour. The rest the time they were three truants laughing defiance at a far-away Susan who was now, since Mummy had crossed over to them from the side of authority, the only person left who might bark sharply at their goings-on.

Chapter Three

But already Lorna was beginning to muse: "We must be thinking of going home." And then: "We've spent far too much. It was wicked of me."

"Couldn't you paint some more Christmas cards?"

"Too late, in December, Mollikins."

"It's not Christmas yet."

"No, but the cards are prepared in the summer."

And, as though more to herself than to the children: "One ought to have begun by putting aside one's return fare. Nobody with children on their shoulders ought to spend as recklessly as I've been spending." Her gaiety was ebbing away fast. Jay had a premonition. She sobered down from her former hilarity, but tiny little tremors of excitement shot up from a different place; while Molly tore about even more wildly, shouted roughly, grasping every pleasure.

When the opportunity came this time, Jay believed she would have the courage to seize it. She felt so bold and brown, not white and wispy as she had felt in London, two years ago, for months after she came out of hospital.

"Come along, children, put your things on. You're going out with Mummy."

"We haven't got our things," said Molly, speaking very low. Mummy laughed.

"What are you whispering for, you brown little scrap? I packed some of your clothes in my trunk. Yours was full. And how we're going to pack your Riviera trousseau, yours and Jay's—I shall have to buy another trunk."

"When are we leaving, Mummy?"

"Tomorrow, I hope. I'm dreadfully worried."

She did not sound worried; she sounded rapt and excited, her eyes glistening, her voice young and eager.

They took a victoria part of the way, but when they were nearly at the top of the hill, Mummy stopped the driver and told him to wait for them here. "*Ça sera longtemps?*" "*Je ne sais pas,*" said Lorna. They walked round a corner and on for about ten minutes, Mummy holding their hands and not letting them race ahead along the dusty road. At last they came to the gates of a beautiful white villa.

They could hear the steps of someone coming to open the door from much further away than in London, because they slapped on the marble pavement. The servant who admitted them was dressed like a gondolier; Jay knew because she had seen *The Gondoliers*. He asked first in French and then in hesitating English whether they wanted to be shown the garden. Apparently he was used to visitors who wanted to be shown the garden. But Lorna said no, it was Madame herself whom she must see.

It seemed unnatural that here in Monte Carlo nobody tried to stop anybody from seeing anybody. Mummy did not have to struggle or plead. They were escorted to Madame as though the gondolier were certain that she would be delighted to see a shabby English lady and two children in frightful dark blue sailor-suits.

Jay recognised Madame instantly. She had been pointed out to Mummy by one of the colonels from the balcony, as she drove past their hotel very slowly in an open Hispano. The colonel called her an ex-mistress, English by birth, and sinking his rubicund voice, but not enough, he related that in her time she had been most expensive and fascinating He said it regretfully; he was a very tottery colonel. Some ex-mistresses, he added wittily, fell loosely apart in old age; others took to their pods and shrivelled.

Madame was the second kind, though ardent violet draperies were her pod, the colour that Molly had coveted for herself. She was not spongy and pliable like most of those chosen by the diviner's twig, but strident and overbearing. And she interrupted Mummy, grabbed at what she supposed was coming next, and brought it out all wrong:

"I know what you're here for. You needn't start with a lot of compliments. I haven't lived eighty years in the world and not picked up a thing or two. Such an old story, my dear: You never meant to, you were tempted, you thought you'd stop when you'd won a thousand francs but you went on till you lost all you had. And now here you are with the children and can't get home. What's the use of bringing me a story like that? I'm tough. I'm hard-hearted. Go to the Casino authorities, they'll give you your fare. Silly woman."

Yet Lorna managed to correct without offending her. No, she did not care for playing. No, the tables had no temptation for her. The actual story was pitiful and commonplace enough, but it had nothing to do with gambling.

"Well, out with it. Don't beat about the bush. But I warn you, tell me the truth. If it's just a trumped-up tale, you're wasting your time; I know too much about it."

The narrative continued as a duet: "An invalid husband who was a war-hero—H'm. They all say that."

"I've got his medals here—"

"Thank you, my good woman, you needn't show me. I know what a D.S.O. looks like. And if you're going to tell me that he wasn't able to provide for you, then you had no right to have children, and that's the end of it. Started a school, did he? a co-education school, of all the silly notions. And it failed last year. I'm surprised it ran on so long; share anything except education, that's what I believe. Is this story going to last till doomsday? For the life of me, I still can't see how co-education brought you to Monte Carlo."

"I wrote for advice—in fact, I'll confess the truth, I wrote for help—to a maiden lady living on the Riviera who had been a great friend of my mother's; my mother died out here; that was long ago." Mummy produced a little snapshot of the grave of Lorna Inglefield.

"You've managed to keep it furbished up in spite of all this rubbish about being so poor. … Oh, your stepfather left it to be paid for in his will, did he? And what did he leave you? Nothing? Can't have played your cards properly. You little mouse-coloured objects never know how to play your cards. Give me a red-head every time. And your maiden lady living on the Riviera, I can tell you what she said: she had a lot of nieces of her own and couldn't be bothered. You know, you oughtn't to trail round Europe on an off-chance, with a pair of infants, trusting to luck and to strangers to get you home again," with a shrewd glance over her spectacles. "Isn't good for 'em. That one's going to burst into tears in a moment, and I can't have her crying here. Upsets me. What is it, little girl? Hungry? Could you eat an éclair if you saw one, eh? Two éclairs?"

Jay never knew how it happened, but she found herself really crying, proper salt tears: "It's my violin," she sobbed, heart-broken. "Mummy had promised me I could have lessons if we lived abroad. She said it was cheaper. I've got a violin and I learned a little and I do practise, but I want lessons more than anything in the world. I can't give it up, I can't."

Silence. Was that her own heart beating, or Molly's? '

"Humph," exclaimed the ex-mistress, and then silence again. At last: "I'm a judge of character. I can tell humbugging a mile off. That child means what she says. She's got it in her to play. I'll pay for her to have the best lessons, and if I hear a word of thanks I'll ring for Luigi and have her put outside."

This, thought Jay happily, was the right sort of benefactress. In a moment she was going to produce a handbag or go to the drawer of her desk (they usually hadn't enough in a handbag) and take out lots of notes and give them to Mummy to pay for the lessons; yet she discouraged thanks and wanted no kisses. Jay felt intoxicated with success. The ease of it. That sort of inside tickling which had prompted her not only what to say, but how to say it, when to say it. She had helped Mummy. I'll always help her now, thought Jay, a worshipping disciple.

But she did just wish, a tiny aside in all this joy, that Molly need not have been present.

Meanwhile, the ex-mistress did not bring out her handbag nor go to the drawer of her escritoire. She made Lorna finish the pitiful story, still galloping just ahead of her so that instead of listening she had the superior pleasure of transmuting it all into her own jargon: "So your mother's friend ran a small select hotel, did she? and told you it was profitable. And sent you the figures. Ah, but you never thought of verifying them; consulting your lawyer? No. And the D.S.O. was duped as well? That's the worst of brave men, I always say. It's the cowards who have the brains. Now, now, you can leave out the rest. And stop dipping into your bag and bringing out those bits of newspaper and passports and nonsense, it fidgets me. You used up all your spare cash to come out here with the children, meant to send for the invalid husband directly you were settled, and found the maiden lady's hotel was on its last legs and you weren't on any legs at all, but being a fool you found it out too late. And now your mother's friend has taken to drink or sal volatile, and here you are with no money to stay and no money to get home. That other child's looking as if she don't like me. She's not musical. It's written all over them when they're musical." She hobbled across to her desk, and pulled out the expected pile of notes from a little drawer; gave Lorna enough for her fare back to England with Jay and Molly, and promised furthermore that she would write to Signor Ferranti, a very old friend of hers who lived in London, *il maestro*, she called him reverently, and arrange that he should charge her for a course of violin lessons for the child.

Two or three times, walking demurely along the road back to where the victoria was waiting, Jay slanted an appealing look towards her mother, not sure if she had earned warm praise or if she were cast out in disgrace.

"Mummy," she had never felt shy before with Lorna, but she did now, "It wasn't true, you know, that I wanted violin lessons."

"In that case it wasn't very honest of you to ask for them. Molly darling, don't lag behind. Look, there's our carriage at the corner. When we get back to the hotel, you shall give the horse a lump of sugar."

Jay's enterprise wilted after this bitter disappointment; a double disappointment, for she had been given no money and had failed to delight her mother. But a few weeks afterwards, back in London, something happened during Visiting which made her feel happy again: "bold and brown," she called this kind of happiness now, linking it with her sunburnt period of hot, leaping vitality in the South.

"… And it isn't only a question of their ordinary schooling," said Mummy wistfully to the young American writer in the Hampstead house; "it's Jay's violin lessons." She drew Jay closer with a caressing movement. "The child is passionately fond of music. I don't know where she gets it from; not from me, I have no ear at all. But ever since she was quite tiny—" And this time they got cash down.

Chapter Four

But the period when Mummy was strange and unholy and extravagant, and could not keep off Visiting, went on too long, even for Jay. It ran on for months and months; it ran on for years. Jay and Molly got infinitely, helplessly bored, having to stand by and listen to the perpetual sagas. You rubbed one leg with the other; you wandered round the room picking up what you dared to examine more closely; out of sheer boredom you even quarrelled with your sister, and once you rolled fighting on the carpet till Mummy pulled you apart: "Oh, children, how *can* you! How can you, when Mother's so wretched and worried?"

Yet she went on taking them with her.

There was the time when Molly had a cough, quite a spectacular cough. Jay could see her trying to force it back and pretend it was nothing; even, desperately, pretend she was pretending, so that the two elderly ladies should not be influenced by the hacking sound of it. "It's nothing, thank you. No, it isn't a bit chronic. I've never had one before, and it always goes away quite soon. I'm awfully healthy, really." Jay felt protective and nevertheless irritated. It was such a good cough that in a way it seemed a pity to waste it, and she sympathized with her mother for throwing her sister that quick worried look each time it happened in public, Yet Molly's earnest disavowals went down with more effect than if she had been plaintive. Lorna could never induce her to repeat the act.

There was the time, a departure from precedent, that Jay was sent upstairs to the schoolroom, to the lady's own nine-year-old niece, who treated the strange, shabby little girl with condescension, and displayed her presents from a recent birthday. When they were both sent for to come downstairs to the drawing-room, Marigold was still clasping the favourite gift of all, a painted musical-box with a repertoire of ten tunes. The lady was just closing her handbag of glossy leather with gold monogram. Mummy was just closing hers.

"Well, Goldilocks darling, and did you show the little girl all your lovely toys?"

"Yes, Auntie."

"And did she like them?"

"Yes, Auntie."

"Which did she like best?"

"The musical-box, Auntie. And so do I," added Marigold quickly; she had had experience of her aunt's vicarious philanthropy.

"Don't you think it would be nice, Goldilocks, if you gave the poor little girl your musical-box? just because it's the present you like best?"

"Oh!" cried Marigold in genuine anguish.

"Think how pleased she'd be, and think what a lot of beautiful things you've got, while she has nothing at all."

Jay turned scarlet. Yet the lady continued to regard her, not as a defenceless collection of nerves and agonies, but as a mere wooden block all in one piece on which to thump out object-lessons.

"I want to see you being unselfish. Go right up to her and say: 'Here, little girl, you can have this to keep. I'm glad to give it to you.'"

Until this moment, Jay felt that she had never known what it was to be humiliated. She looked at her mother: "You can stop this slow torture," her glance pleaded. "Won't you, just this, once? Won't you?"

But Lorna was no help. Rather the reverse. She played into Auntie's hands. She deprecated on Jay's behalf: "I couldn't let her accept such a valuable present. You mustn't dream of allowing your little niece to give it away, indeed you mustn't. My Jay must learn not to envy other little girls who are more fortunate than she is."

"Oh, but my Marigold has so many toys, she won't even miss it.

(They kept on saying "my Jay," "my Marigold," as though there were any doubt as to where each of them belonged.)

"Come on, Goldilocks, we're waiting. Auntie will be quite angry with you in a moment. Remember what we heard in church last week: 'It is more blessed to give than to receive.'"

Marigold protested, twisted her shoulders round, looked ready to cry, but still clung to the musical-box.

(If I were dead, thought Jay, this couldn't be happening. If I'd died in hospital ... Oh, I *hate* Mummy, she's making out as though I'd asked for it ... Remember all your life she brought you into this and could have helped and hasn't.)

"There you are!" cried Marigold suddenly in a passion, and flung the treasure with some force on to the parquet floor at Jay's feet.

It all worked out at an additional profit to Lorna. Someone had to be amply recompensed for the exhibition of temper; and the mother was obviously honest, proved by her distress, her apologies, her previous admonition not to accept presents. Auntie thought that Jay was in tears because the box was broken. Lorna said with a wan smile that her little daughter was rather highly strung but she mustn't be naughty: "Say thank you very much indeed, Jay darling, and kiss the little girl and tell her you're sorry."

Marigold also had to kiss the little girl and tell her she was sorry. The rich little girl and the poor little girl—And the two ladies smiled at each other, and smiled at the pretty tableau.

(Remember all your life.)

There was the time when Jay and Molly were playing with skipping-ropes up and down Huntingdon Terrace with the other Blake children who were no relations. Then the other Mrs. Blake opened the window and called out: "Come along, infants, and put on your things. Mummy's going to take you out."

Jay saw Molly avert her eyes from the joyous, squealing, scuttling response. They had often wondered if they were the only children in the world to whom going-out-with-Mother meant Visiting. As they walked back slowly to their own gate, trailing their skipping-ropes, they entered into a silent bond to find out. They did not consult aloud, for the subject was still all but taboo.

But at school in recreation-time they laid traps, childish, crude traps, only just not questions, to make Penelope and Joan and Sarah betray whether the other Mrs. Blake Visited.

Molly began. "Where did you go yesterday?" carelessly.

"Oh, we went to the Zoo. We saw—" a long catalogue. "Uncle Bert's a Fellow, so we had tea in his enclosure."

"D'you like going out with your mother?"

"Oh, ever so much better than with anyone. When it's summer, she rows us on the lake and lets us row too."

"Where does she take you when it isn't the Zoo?"

"You do ask a lot of questions. It isn't your business. Where does yours take you?"

Jay said in a low voice: "She can't take us anywhere very much. She's lame."

"Oh, I'm sorry."

Molly quickly and lightly sketched in a description of the electric launch with the awning, and a man in a white peaked cap holding the wheel, and lobster and ices.

"We've never been in a launch. I'd like to sit at the wheel and drive it."

"We've been to Monte Carlo too," boasted Jay, who had not learnt to leave well alone. "Mummy took us there. That's where I got so brown."

"What's it matter if you're brown or not?"

"It does matter."

"Why?" Joyce and Gladys Lloyd suspected her of vanity and affectation and the undue use of looking-glasses.

"Edna McCarthy has been to America," they reminded her.

"She hasn't *been*, she's only come back from. She was born in America."

The plot ended in a bragging competition.

But Penelope, the eldest other Blake, duly reported:

"Mummy," virtuously, "isn't Jasmine Blake naughty? She says her mother's lame, and her mother *isn't*. We've seen her often."

"Then Jasmine Blake tells lies, dear, and Grandpa and I wouldn't wish you to have anything more to do with her."

"Oh, but Mummy—" Penelope had not meant matters to go as far; she had an engagement with Jay, important from the schoolgirl point of view.

"You can quite easily say that Grandpa wants you to go to the optician to fetch his spectacles."

"But isn't that a lie too, Mummy?"

"No," said the other Mrs. Blake firmly.

But Grandpa added, with a regrettable twitch at the corners of his mouth: "It's a social necessity, my dear."

At the end of the term, Jay left. Not Molly. Frances Butler, the well-known explorer, deeply moved at hearing that Mrs. Inglefield was never free from the terror of having her only child kidnapped and wrenched away from her by a revengeful husband, suggested that Jay should be sent to a really excellent school in the South-West of England, where bad Mr. Inglefield would not be able to trace her. She deemed this a better idea than a harassed flight up to the Highlands, which was apparently all that poor distracted creature could think of, to keep her ewe lamb in safety.

"I'll be glad to pay the fees till she's old enough to leave. You can't hide her up in the Highlands for ever. But your husband would never think of looking in a school crocodile in Hampshire."

"Hurray!" shouted Molly, when told of Jay's destiny. "Hurray! Hurray! Hurray!" She turned cart-wheels; she exulted; she behaved like an unnatural little sister. "Jay is going away. Hurray! Hurray! Hurray!"

Lorna shrugged her shoulders, and Susan said: "Good thing somebody's pleased."

Jay was fourteen now. But Nature perversely backed up Lorna, for she looked no more than ten, so could still be used as a Visiting property, during the holidays. She prayed that no one at her new school would ever find out. At St. Catherine's, her home life receded like a nightmare; she abandoned herself utterly and with zest to the normal routine, and continued to excel in mathematics, and in games where a light build was no handicap. Though popular, she gave herself no airs; on the contrary: "She's trying not to let any of us see that she's a little unsure of herself," reflected the headmistress, an acute psychologist; "I wonder if that has anything to do with having her fees paid by Miss Butler and not by her own mother? It often has that effect."

She missed Molly, of course; but instead of Molly, she had Daphne and Clorinda. Daffy and Clo were a pair of amiable idiots, lovely to look at. "They have sweet dispositions," the headmistress told their mother, suppressing the further information: "and are practically half-wits."

Jay found that she could bask lazily in the admiring affection of Daffy and Clo as on a bed of roses without thorns. No sharp little questions, sharp curiosities, sharp comparisons. Being with Daffy and Clo day and night was the exact opposite of the house of jeopardy. Had anyone remarked to the phlegmatic pair: "Jasmine Blake never invites you to her own home in the holidays and never tells you anything about her people," they would have exclaimed in chorus: "Nor she does." But the idea was too brilliant and stimulating for them to reach it of their own accord.

After a year, Jay left suddenly and did not write to them: Visiting was over, and Mummy said: "My lamb, I'm sorry, but I'm afraid I can't afford St. Catherine's for you. It's a very expensive school, you know, and I won't have my children paid for out of other people's pockets."

Chapter Five

Benares Lodge, Huntingdon Terrace, had sheltered them ever since Jay was ten and Molly nine. Somehow their mother had contrived to keep their real address inviolate all through her second long Visiting period; her mechanics were inspired. Even Susan, unwilling ever to admire without adding a pinch of nutmeg, exclaimed over and over again: "Beats me how you do it!"

Now Lorna decided to move: "This house has too many associations," and her eyelids flickered sadly, implying that all her nearest and dearest had been buried from there.

No. 31 Netherby Park Road, Ealing, was not quite so nice, but it was in the same style. Lorna had to spend what she called "her savings," all that was left of their months of affluence, on papering and painting, alterations to the hot-water system and the kitchen stove. Moving was always a drain, she said. "We shall be hard up for quite a long while, my chicks. I don't want to take Molly away from Miss Rolandi's; she has started so nicely." Miss Rolandi's was a school of acting, mainly for children in their teens, where Molly had recently been sent on the advice of Miss Collins: "She's a born comedienne. I really don't see, Mrs. Blake, how you can do better for her future than have her properly trained." So, for the next six months, Lorna faithfully skimped her household and paid the fees. Jay attended the Polytechnic for a course of book-keeping and accounting. "One has to give them a practical education," said Lorna. "I'm not old yet, but one never knows, and when I'm not here to look after them—"

Life was monotonous; free from peril. But one Saturday afternoon Jay and Molly came home from the local cinema to find all the air disturbed. Something had agitated Lorna. Her equilibrium was back at a precarious tilt, yet not quite the same as in Visiting days, when she had been nearly all the time in high spirits, with the air of one who had it in her power to bestow favours. This time she was just a worried little woman hardly knowing where to turn; clucking and dithering, as though the virtue had gone out of her. Yet here was the shock; the old slogan: "Run along quickly and put on your things. You're coming out with Mummy. No, not you, Molly. You stay at home. Jay can come. Oh dear!"

Then a brief argument with Susan. "It, *would* happen on a Saturday when they're all closed, though I don't know anyhow if he would let me overdraw such a big sum."

"I can't see for the life of me why you're putting yourself out. You haven't bothered about him all these years. And it can't do him any good, poor fellow, only turning up for the end and the funeral. All this fuss about decency and respect."

But the obstinate traditions of The Nook, of Clifford's Bay, of Benares Lodge, spoke in Lorna's reproof:

"It's *right* that I should go up and take the children. One must let bygones be bygones. Though where and how I'm to get them into black as well, with all this rush —Susan, while I'm out, go and buy two broad black sashes. Oh, and hats; two black felt hats; the shape doesn't matter.

Oh dear, one has to think of everything at once. If only I had our fares— if only there were some relation or an old friend! Being poor cuts one off from everybody. I hate asking strangers."

Out of consideration for calamity, Susan controlled a far too brief reply.

"I don't know, I don't know …" Lorna picked up the current number of *Mayfair*, and, distracted, put her finger at random half-way down the page of "Society Chat." Then she opened her eyes and read:

> "The pretty wife of the Hon. Ambrose Bristow, M.P., has the novel idea of decorating her house in sea-shells and white stucco—"

Jay came lagging downstairs in the ordinary clothes she put on for the Polytechnic every day, but wearing the old green tammy on curls loosely pushed forward, as a concession to this semi-Visiting period. She was prepared, if necessary, to mutiny. Nothing would get her back into that horrible sailor-suit. To her surprise, Lorna did not seem to notice.

"Have you washed your hands, darling?" she asked absently.

Two hours later, Molly heard the gate click.

"Jay! Jay, I'm up here. Well?"

"It was beastly," said Jay. She threw off her cap and coat, and flung herself moodily on the bed.

"Worse than usual?"

They had to talk about it this time, for the event was not inevitably part of the rhythm, but once again a mystery.

"They didn't believe a word of it. They didn't give her anything. And it was Mummy's fault. I've never heard her do it like that, muddled and nervous and contradicting herself, and not seeing that she was going quite the wrong way about it; not stopping in time and oh-dearing and repeating her stuff—"

"Which stuff?"

"New. We've never heard it before; at least, I haven't, and I don't think you have. About a mental nursing-home up in Scotland."

Molly shook her head.

"Inglefield?"

"No, Blake. She showed marriage lines, of course, and some faded letters and old photographs, and said Father was alive really, but she had always let the children think he was dead because remembering was so terrible, and now he was dying and she had to go up and see him for the last time and it was only decent that his babies should be at the funeral. And Mrs. Bristow said: 'I've never heard such a thin story in all my life. You'd better be off.' And: 'I warn you, I may consider it my duty to enquire into all this, to protect other people.'"

Molly went white: "Oh, Jay—" But she stopped herself from saying: "Does that mean she'll go to the police?" Jay must not be frightened while there was still a chance of escaping prison.

A confused atmosphere of shame lay over the house. Their mother talked for a long time shut up with Susan; but she remembered to say: "Hush, the children!" and "Run away, my chicks," when they barged into the room, not allowing them to hear. And this was different, too, after Visiting.

The next morning, Sunday, she and Jay and Molly moved into cheap rooms in North Kensington, and stayed uneasily for a fortnight till Susan, impatient and snappish—"A lot of extra expense when you're hard up, and no reason"—persuaded Lorna to return to Netherby Park Road.

"Beats me what you're afraid of. You didn't leave no address, did you? Though you could have, this time, and no harm done. Running away to shiver in lodgings, when you're as right as a trivet. Upsetting the children and upsetting everyone. Why, you could have looked that honourable Missis straight in her silly face and said: 'Well, now go and do your worst, and what about it?'"

Lorna confessed: "Yes, I was stupid. I lost my head. It seemed so—so dreadfully indelicate, having to ask for money. Even for the children's sake."

←→

After the woman had gone, Grace Bristow went to the telephone and dialled a number. She intended to warn all her friends with well-known names living in London, that one of these crook women was going about with a trumped-up story of a husband dying in a lunatic asylum in Scotland and not having enough money for her fare. Visitors of this kind were nothing new, either before or after her marriage to an M.P., for Grace Bristow had been an amateur Interior Decorator, and always in the papers; "though why that should make them suppose I've oodles of money to give away—" She had been beguiled two or three times, and then crossly discovered her mistake. She was a conceited soul, and it gave her a pain not to be in the right. But this Blake woman could hardly hope to beguile anybody: it was preposterous; she had neither the nerve nor the audacity for a career of swindling. Still, you might as well put your friends up to it. They had done as much for her, several times.

Shirley Dennison was about the eleventh on her list. Some of Grace's indignation had spent its force by then:

"Hello, is that Miss Temple herself? How is our little sunny mop of curls?"

"I wish your parents had christened you Greta, instead of Grace," was the reply, cool and faintly exasperated.

"Listen, Shirley. I've just had one of those women here. You know, begging, with a cock-and-bull story which she did so badly that I wonder she bothered to do it at all. But I thought I might as well put you wise, in case she came to you. I've told Kathleen and Norah and Percy and Tommy and the Barclays."

"Busy you've been. How shall I recognize your pal?

"She's got a little girl with her. At least, not so little, about twelve or thirteen, I'd say. Rather pretty, long fair curls, wearing a most awful old green tam-o'-shanter; borrowed, I expect."

"What? The tam-o'-shanter?"

"No, Shirley. How maddening you are this evening. The child."

"'The Property Child' wouldn't be a bad title for a short story. Did you fork out anything?"

"God, no. Do you take me for a charity institution? Besides, I'm telling you, she wasn't genuine. Usually one wonders; but this creature was so nervous and muddled and frightened and kept on gasping and repeating herself and contradicting what she had said the minute before, I sent her flying at last, when I said I'd take her story to the police with a full description."

"And are you going to?"

"Not yet; I may presently. She said she had a husband in a lunatic asylum in Scotland; I remembered the address, and I'm writing up there first to find out if it exists, and if it does, if they've ever heard of a Mrs. Blake, and if her husband's an inmate, and had they sent for her urgently to see him before he died?"

"I don't think that's very kind of you," said the cool, mocking voice at the other end of the wire. "We've all got to live somehow. Well, good-bye, Grace. I'm off on a lecture tour."

"America again?"

"Lord, no, I've only just come back from there. They won't be able to bear the sight of me in America for another two years at least. No, this is the Northern Cities: Stockholm, Oslo, Gothenburg—rather fun."

"I'd much rather lecture than canvass for Ambrose. That ghastly by-election! Think of me in four days' time trying to flatter the voters in Welsh. Good-bye, my dear. Do you know if the Cranfields are in town? I think I'd better just get on to them and queer the pitch for dear Mrs. Blake. You're not nearly as grateful as you should have been, Shirley."

"No. It's a profession like any other. I wouldn't give her anything myself, but I'd let her have her chance with the mugs."

"Hullo? Shirley?"

"Oh, it's you, Grace. I thought you were in Wales, bothering the constituents."

"We start this afternoon. I just wanted to tell you, Shirley— because fair's fair—"

"So it is, Grace, so it is."

"I've heard from Scotland. The lunatic asylum. Would you believe it, that poor Blake woman was telling us the absolute truth the whole time. We were wrong from beginning to end."

"Us? We?"

"Every word was true. It's been corroborated. She *had* a husband up there; he *was* dying; they *had* written and asked her to come up and bring the children. And she wasn't able to. Shirley, can we ever forgive ourselves?"

"We must try," said Shirley, giving in to the plural. "What are you going to do now? Leave cards on her, or a hundred pounds?"

"That's the devastating part of it. She went off without leaving me any address. They're frightened when one talks of the police."

"Funny, if she was telling the truth."

"Yes. It *is* funny. I never thought of that."

"Ask her when you see her."

"Shirley, I told you, I don't know where to find the poor little soul. She's lost. It's been a lesson that we ought to feel ourselves far more responsible for each other's troubles; *melt* together more; we're each so hard and apart in our crusts—"

"The asylum secretary would supply the address, if you wrote again."

"So he would, yes."

"Then you can melt together like anything."

"I've got to rush off now and be a political wife. When I get back from Wales, I'll put it all straight."

"Bet you forget," murmured Shirley, after she had rung off.

The solitary excursion was never explained to Jay and Molly; it remained to jeer at their youthful reliance on precedent. After that, they lived in tolerable peace for nearly three years, making every sacrifice to thrift and prudence. Lorna worked her fingers to the bone, she said; but they kept within their income, and made some nice new friends. Every summer they went to Clifford's Bay. The sailor-suits were sold with a lot of other old clothes when Mummy had a big turn-out. The hag who bought them held them up to the light and murmured in disparaging tones that they were barely worth carting away.

Chapter Six

"My advice is *don't*," said Susan, with sinister emphasis on the "don't."

Lorna gave her a small sweet smile, and shook her head. The shake meant: "I know what I'm doing, *and* I'm going to do it."

"Start fresh, if you must start at all," Susan went on. "Though, mind, I think it's a sin upsetting the home now they've nearly grown-up and Jay ready for a job and Molly in pantomime. But if it's in you and it's got to come out, why, find a fresh place. There's a proverb about dogs goin' back to their vomit."

"You never sound natural when you preach." Lorna was still smiling. She walked restlessly round the room, plumping up cushions. Her eyes were bright and shallow and obstinate.

"Common sense isn't preaching, that I know of. You went begging to this Mrs. Bristow—how long ago is it? Two—three years ago?—and you muffed it. Well?"

"That's just it," said Lorna. "I wasn't feeling like it at the time, so I muffed it."

"Narks you where you keep your pride, don't it?" Susan grinned viciously. Nevertheless, Lorna always had amused her, always would. There she was, at it again. Though you might have thought, after that one mess-up, she ought to have been scared enough to stay settled down for good. Let the children work to keep her in her old age.

She put forward this attractive proposition.

"Oh, I can keep myself, thank you, Susan dear."

"One fine day that'll lead to you being kept at the nation's expense."

"Don't be a fool."

"Didn't you say the honourable Missis believed you was telling her a pack of lies, and she was going to make enquiries?"

"It happened that I was telling her a pack of truth."

"Yes, that's the funny part of it. You *was* telling the truth, that time. And yet it was one of the only times you didn't get away with it. Nasty suspicious people there are in the world, aren't there? God, I could die laughing!"

Lorna mused: "She wrote up to Scotland first, and had an answer from the asylum superintendent saying it was quite true that Mr. Leonard Blake was dying; quite true that they had communicated with the wife, poor soul, and asked her to rush up and bring the children if she still wanted to see him alive; quite true that Mrs. Blake wasn't able to come. The Hon, Mrs. Bristow would have been terribly ashamed of having doubted such a sad story."

"There you are! Being so sure, you could have afforded to sit tight in your home, and even left an address for her to come along later, with a fat handbag and I-beg-your-pardon-Mrs.-Blake. I said so at the time. And you all shaking and in a fright because you thought you'd done something not quite respectable."

"I feel different about it now. Besides, I had a letter from her. That's how I know she wrote to Scotland."

"Never told me, you didn't." Susan was offended; she could tolerate anything but reticence.

"I felt too awful about the whole thing, then. I didn't want even to read the letter. I put it away."

"How did she get the address? What did she say?"

"From the Superintendent. Only that she was sorry for her mistake and would I come and see her."

"Very kind, I'm sure."

"So I'm going."

"At last, and nearly three years after. You're a scream, you are. All right, go along. I hope you'll make a clean-up. Taking the children?"

"Jay can come. She likes it. Molly's grown too tall. Besides, six evenings a week and two matinées—I don't mean her to overtire her strength."

"Wonderful notices she's got."

"Yes, bless her. She's a born actress, and no amount of praise seems to turn that little head of hers." The warm maternal love in Lorna's voice overlapped for a moment the gambler's indifference to home ties.

But Jay, her eyes dark with panic, mutinied:

"I won't come."

She had known, of course, she and Molly had both known by every sign and signal, that it was due once again. The between-period of peace was over; longer than usual, except when their mother had forced herself into that one mystifying visit during her "un-Visiting" mood; and had lost confidence.

"I'm nearly eighteen," Jay swiftly added six months to her age. "And I've passed all my examinations. And I won't, I can't, I simply *can't* go Visiting any more. I suppose you'd like to put me and Molly back into sailor-suits and holey socks? And grow my hair into long curls again? I expect you'd like Molly to give up her career so that we can come with you and help you to tell lies and lies and lies—"

It was out now between them, declared in open rebellion, this thing which had always remained so carefully unspoken. It was out almost without a sound, as though glass were being shattered on a thick carpet; for Jay spoke in a half-whisper from a dry mouth; only her eyes were wild and miserable.

Her mother hardly dealt with the crisis at all, except by a shrug of the shoulders and a nonchalant: "Whatever I may have had to do, was for your sake and Molly's." The platitude came out mechanically, as though she could not be bothered to be convincing.

But the girl's passion was now all the more desperate, from an unwelcome memory that she herself had years ago been thrilled by the alliance; had welcomed the break in their ordinary humdrum life; had even been tempted to collaborate, half in fear, half in excitement. ...

"No mother has ever done what you've made us do. Molly hated it so, she nearly died of hating it. One moment you told us we must always speak the truth and never ask for anything, and the next—Oh, what's the good! But I can't bear any more."

Her mother went over to the looking-glass and began patting her hair into place with a familiar warning gesture:

"Molly has a more contented nature than you; I've had to manage on a very tiny income, but you never accepted being poor. It nearly broke my heart to keep on refusing you the luxuries you begged for: violin lessons—"

Jay had wondered which way all this was leading. Now she knew. Mummy had been padding towards the last two words. She had laid hands on a whip.

"I can't stay at home," sobbed Jay. No, they could not live together any more, she and her mother. Too much had been said. "I'm going away."

Lorna was still at the looking-glass, her back towards her daughter. But now her voice was indulgent and motherly: "Jay, my darling, I think you don't know what you want yourself, except to make a big scene over nothing. Stop being a little goose, and stop criticizing what you don't understand. When you're older you'll realize that it's not easy for a woman left without a husband, with two children to bring up and educate. I've done the best I can."

Molly came home from the matinée of *Dick Whittington,* and found Jay sitting on her trunk, already packed. It did not take long to tell what had happened.

"Yes, go. I'm glad."

"You were glad when I was sent to St. Catherine's. You're always glad, Am I awful to have in the house?"

Jay asked not touchily, but in humility. She was sure of Molly's love, but never sure of her own possible "awfulness."

"I'll never stop missing you one single minute," Molly gave her sister one of those slow, breathlessly attractive smiles which were her only resemblance to Lorna. "Except," conscientiously, "while I'm actually *being* Whiskers." Whiskers was the cat in the pantomime.

"Then what about when the show comes off? Join me?"

"I'm all right. I'm booked for *Naughts and Crosses.* A heavenly part.

They spoke to me about it today. Anyhow, I'm not at home much. Besides—"

"Never mind 'besides,'" Jay interrupted quickly. She may or may not have guessed that Molly's "besides" had meant: "I'm safer than you, when Visiting begins; I've hated it steadily, always. I'm in no jeopardy."

"Where do you mean to go?"

"You remember Daffy and Clo Carberry? I used to talk about them a lot, and they'll help find me a job, Their people are architects or something in Southampton."

"You haven't kept up with them, have you? Perhaps they've forgotten."

But Jay was sanguine. She could not help it, remembering how they had worshipped and admired her, followed her about, quoted everything she said, copied everything she did, begged for her notice, praised her to the other girls.

"Three years doesn't make a lot of difference. Daffy and Clo are the faithful kind."

"You'll have to stay here till tomorrow. My bank doesn't open before ten."

Ever since Molly had been earning—and Whiskers was her third part—her mother had prudently and wisely insisted not only that Molly was to open an account in her own name, but that she was to lay by at least two-thirds of her salary. Lorna reluctantly accepted a pound a week towards housekeeping expenses, which she declared was the greatest help in the world.

"Oh, Molly, I don't want to have to take your money."

"Ass. Of course you've got to."

"You're the youngest. I ought to be earning more than you."

"One always earns more on the stage to begin with. You had to pass your exams."

"Thank God I did. Now I'm qualified, it oughtn't to take long. You know," after a pause, "Mummy *has* been good over our educations. She's stuck to that being important, whatever—"

"Yes."

"Molly?"

– 118 –

"Yes—"

"You never say much, do you?"

"What's there to say?"

"It beats me how you can play the fool, as Whiskers, and make even me roll about in my seat and my stomach ache like a cave, and yet be so serious at home."

"Look at Dan Leno and Grimaldi and—and Charlie Chaplin. Not," Molly explained carefully, "that I'm boasting. But all clowns are melancholy in their homes."

"I'd have thought one acted as one feels."

"It doesn't work that way. Are we going to tell Susan you're going?"

"Why not? The old scoundrel doesn't care what we do."

"I bet she's committed a murder or two, on her nights out."

Jay laughed.

"All the same, I did want to get off before Mummy came home. We had a hell of a row."

"Is Mummy out now?"

"Yes, she's out."

Their eyes met. Visiting had begun again.

Suddenly Molly exclaimed in delight: "Of course, today's Friday. The ghost walks on Friday. I've got a week's screw on me now. Here you are: six pounds. Directly you let me have an address, I can send you a whole lot more. But this will do to pay your fare to Southampton."

A phrase well known to both of them, but it fell oddly from Molly's lips: "to pay your fare to Southampton."

PART IV

The Enemy Boy

Chapter One

Alexander Muir-Leslie, late of the 17th Lancers, sat up in bed on the twenty-seventh floor of an hotel in New York, and went through his Teuila fortune-telling cards. He did this as a sort of Mantra every morning between breakfast and reading the paper. There were no definite reasons for getting up early, and he was soothed by the combination of the cards and their coincident similarities or contradictions from yesterday morning. Today Calamity came out in the fourth line of "What You Don't Expect," next to A Surprise on the one side and A Caller on the other. Calamity was pictured as a dancing devil hurling javelins.

Alexander scowled at him; it was unlikely he would have a Caller; nobody called on him; so that disposes of your Calamity. And anyhow, here in the fifth row, not quite touching it, but at right angles, was the Sun, and that meant Good Fortune predominant. The Fair Woman whom he called Sylvia did not come out at all this morning; nor the Dark Woman, but a Woman Between Colours, next to the Sun, was in the line of Bound to Come True. Yesterday morning the Sun had come out in the third line, the Wish line, where it was luckiest. On the morning that it did not appear, Alexander always laid out the cards for the second time to give the vapid day a chance, but his soul knew that this was unworthy of his intelligence.

Satisfied, he gathered them up, laid them aside and picked up the newspaper. Reading it from end to end was also a formula; he was not particularly interested in the events of the world.

But today on the middle page a paragraph appeared in prominent type, announcing Sylvia's engagement.

She was engaged to a New York proprietor of a prominent group of periodicals: Parker B. Harland was on a visit to the Old Country, and there he had met the beautiful socialite, Sylvia Mainwaring, and fallen in love with her at first sight. It was a true Romance. They were to be married at St. Margaret's, Westminster, in five weeks.

And six years ago she had been engaged to him, Alexander Frederick Muir-Leslie.

During the five and a half years of his exile he had almost forgotten the woman responsible for dividing them. Now hate and the desire for revenge, the desire to kill, rushed back with the strength of a physical impact. He lay in bed and thought, not of Sylvia, but of Lorna Inglefield.

Lorna Inglefield.

And he thought he would kill himself, but not today, because he felt too ill. His head ached and his legs trembled. In a few days, when he was better and able to take definite action, then he would kill himself.

There was nothing else to be done. He had no hope, Sylvia was engaged, and presently she would be married to this Parker B. Harland. It was queer that, although he had had no word from her all these years, he had never thought of her getting engaged to another man. She had become static in his mind, not progressive, remaining at the point where she had just written him that terrible letter.

He stayed in bed, mechanically keeping to his old routine: breakfast; Teuila cards; morning newspaper. His routine was a rope along a steep staircase. He had to cling to it or he would fall.

He thought of Lorna Inglefield incessantly, and more than of his faithless love. Lorna—Lorna—made a two-note sound in his mind like the monotonous sawing of a cricket.

About a week later, his eye ran down a column on the literary page of the paper, of little interest to him until he came to mention of an author's birthplace.

"Shirley Dennison, the well-known English author, whose powerful proletarian novels ... return tour of America ... staying at the Algonquin ... concluding lecture before returning to England will be given tomorrow in the Brooklyn Town Hall Born in 1894 in Market St. Dunstan's, England, Miss Dennison led an uneventful life until the world war … drove an ambulance … colorful and vital first novel *Flanders Fires* … glad to welcome such a distinguished personality. …"

"Market St. Dunstan's." The words stared at Alexander starkly and significantly from among the wavering, meaningless print.

Market St. Dunstan's? it had some link with Sylvia.

"Neil Inglefield with Lorna Mason in the Church at Market St. Dunstan's."

Of course! Then this Shirley Dennison who had been born there might be able to tell him all he wanted to know. At last here was another clue towards the finding of Lorna; his first since he had let Neil Inglefield slip away from under his thumb.

I'm too ill to get up, thought Alexander. Yes, Lorna Inglefield had ruined his life, and now he was ill, very ill. With all the sweetly simple absorption, the freedom from embarrassment of a man with a fixed idea, he sent a telegram to Shirley Dennison at the Algonquin, with an urgent summons to his bedside.

Curious as to this unknown Alexander Muir-Leslie and his extraordinary message, she went. They knew her at his hotel, so she mentioned to Sidney, the Head Porter, that she was going up to Captain Muir-Leslie's apartment, and if she did not reappear in the next seven days they could break down the door and search for her body.

Sidney reassured her. They had known Captain Muir-Leslie for quite a long time. He was always going away and coming back. Apparently quite a nice gentleman. Harmless. English. Screwy.

She believed it when she found him sitting up in bed looking not unlike Don Quixote, and intently studying through his monocle four rows of highly coloured picture-cards laid out in front of him; the pack in his hand, ready to lay out the fifth.

She was astonished out of regard for polite preliminaries, even had the situation called for them.

"What in the name of Mike is all this about?"

Alexander looked up at her gravely, and bowed.

"Miss Shirley Dennison? I hoped I would just have time to finish this and be up and in my dressing-gown when they rang me from downstairs, But these elevators!" He shook his head. "You never know. Sometimes they stop on every floor, and sometimes they bring you up in a flash. It's so good of you to come."

"Not at all. I was delighted." If he could be formal, sitting up in bed and playing picture patience, then so could she. "Do finish what you were doing."

But it was fantastic, first his telegram and his urgency, and now the cards.

"I will, if you really don't mind. Won't you sit down? Over there by the window is the most comfortable chair, I think. The view up Fifth Avenue—"

"I'd rather stand here and watch, if *you* don't mind."

With a gesture he made her free of Teuila and all its oracles. Then he read the fifth row and gave a low gratified "Ah!"

"Yes," said Shirley. "What?"

"It's the Caller again. You. Nobody could call that a coincidence, could they? A Caller next to the Wish. That's the Wish there, the Ship. Usually if it comes out in any row except the third, which is the Wish row itself, it doesn't count. But next to the Caller, why, it's extraordinary. Yes, and I remember now, about a week ago, a Woman Between Colours. After Calamity and before the Sun. I remember quite clearly. Or was it before A Great Surprise? That's A Surprise, the Jack-in-the-box up there. But it doesn't mean much with Disappointment beside it." And he added quickly: "We can discount Disappointment. It might read as any trivial thing, like the coffee not being good; it wasn't this morning; I had to 'phone down to them." He studied the cards again, rapt, as an astronomer might study the heavens. "A Woman Between Colours?" He studied Shirley; then looked back to a picture of a lady with black hair and a red rose in it: "That's nearer you," unwilling to admit it. "The Dark Woman; under the Sword, for Danger. But I don't know—there's a lot of silver in your hair, making it much lighter. Which would you call yourself, honestly now? Dark or Between Colours? One can't cheat, or the whole thing means nothing; nothing at all."

Very gently, Shirley put a hand on his bony shoulder. She did not speak soothingly as though to humour a child or an invalid, because she guessed that this man had been mortally hurt, and at all costs his remnant of dignity must be respected. "I should say distinctly Between Colours, if I'm the Caller."

"Good." Alexander sighed with relief. Then picked up the cards neatly and put them back in their case. Shirley sat down in the chair by the window. She supposed she had been sent for because he had read something of hers which appealed to him and seemed to carry a personal message. To judge by her fan mail, her work was full of personal messages, but never yet had it led her into such fantastic contacts.

"Miss Dennison, you were born at Market St. Dunstan's? Did you live there long enough to—to know people? People in the neighbourhood?"

"I lived there on and off till I was twenty."

"Did you know Lorna Inglefield? She was born Lorna Mason. Did you know Neil Inglefield?" Not again was he going to bide his time; wiliness had lost him his one clue, nearly six years ago in California. But here was hope again, rich with promise. In a few minutes, perhaps, he would be able to get up and dress and return to England; go straight to Sylvia just in time to stop her marriage; prove that that woman was a cheat, that his persecution had been justified … ("Oh, Alec, Alec darling. Forgive me. I'm sorry. I was wrong.")

"Oh yes," Shirley replied. "I knew Lorna. She wrecked my love and ruined my life." She was so used to being flippant now about the whole episode that it did not seem worth while to mention it with decorum, especially to a strange man with bony ridges on his shoulders who sat in bed and told his own fortune by picture-cards.

"Not really!" he cried, discovering the ecstasy of a companion in misfortune. "By Jove, not really!"

"At least, which Lorna do you mean? My own dear little Lorna Mason's mother married Neil's father, and I believe that he was called Neil as well—"

"Then there was a Neil father and son, and a Lorna mother and daughter?" Alexander worked it out, his wits galvanized into rapid assimilation of all this entrancing fresh material. "And did they marry too, the daughter and son?"

"Lord, no! Young Neil hated her guts."

"Then she was using her mother's marriage certificate?"

Alexander lay back exhausted among his pillows. Sylvia was as good as won again.

"Captain Muir-Leslie, did you know our little Lorna?"

He brushed the question aside.

"You'll come back with me to London, won't you?" But the question was purely perfunctory. Of course Shirley Dennison would come back with him to England, immediately. "I shall need your assistance, you see, to show that she was impersonating her own mother. My God," it suddenly occurred to him, "and I could have heard this years and years ago from Neil Inglefield."

"How are you mixed up with Neil Inglefield? Captain Muir-Leslie, what's it all about? What's our little Lorna *doing* with a bogus marriage certificate?"

He smiled at her, a quizzical military smile. Ah, the ladies, always curious, always asking questions, always wanting to know; even the clever ones who wrote books. But he was prepared to humour her. So he told her the story of the woman who had visited Sylvia, and all its consequences.

Sylvia shone angelic in the foreground. And the woman, a detestable, lurid figure, crept in from the shadowy hall.

"But this is libel, if she goes about making everyone believe that Neil Inglefield married her and left her penniless with two children. Neil ought to know."

"I've been writing to him with that intention for six years," said Alexander, with a not unnatural tinge of bitterness.

"Telling him this?"

"No, one doesn't put it in a letter. Asking him to come and see me. If he hadn't rushed off in such a hurry, that time in California—"

Privately, Shirley had an idea of a not unreasonable motive for such an exit. Alexander's full tale, covering all preliminaries, justifications, descriptions of Sylvia, denunciations of Lorna, and what the fortune-tellers had to say about it, had occupied very nearly three hours.

"Where did you address your letters?"

"Care of the Neptune Hotel Company."

"Here in New York?"

"No. In London."

"They'll have headquarters in New York too, if so many of their hotels are scattered about America. Where's the telephone-book?"

Shirley found the number and rang up, asking if Mr. Inglefield were in America, and if not, where?

Alexander watched her movements gratefully, admiringly, yet faintly disturbed. It seemed to him that Shirley was not concentrating quite in the right place. She ought to have been booking their staterooms on the next boat back to England and Sylvia.

She rang off and turned round in a glow:

"We're lucky. He's at the Neptune hotel in Florida. I'll wire him. He might as well come along if he can get away."

"Do you know him well enough to send for him?" asked Alexander, a little dazed by the pace of modern life, now that he had a stake in it again. She smiled at him.

"Well, you didn't know *me* very well until this morning, did you? Actually, I haven't seen Neil since he was sixteen and I was twenty, but we always hit it off well. How will this do? 'Lorna Mason spreading libellous tale against you stop think important you should take action stop join me quickly as possible to hear details. Shirley Dennison, Hotel Algonquin, New York.'"

"But," Alexander protested, "you haven't mentioned me."

For all her compassion, Shirley treated him to one small nip of irony: "I'm saving you as a nice surprise."

Chapter Two

"But, Shirley, who *is* this man you're taking me to see? I'm shy with strangers."

"I told you; the man who brought the good news."

"About Lorna? Bitch! Wait till I lay hands on her." For Shirley had already given him an outline of Lorna's professional activities and how he was involved, only suppressing the fact that he had already met Captain Muir-Leslie and been on the brink of hearing it first-hand. She thought Neil deserved punishment for previous unkindness towards Alexander.

"This is his room. You mustn't upset him whatever you do; he's ill: nervous breakdown; the Man in the Iron Mask, or Six Years in a Coffin. I'm getting him right, but it's uphill work. Captain Muir-Leslie, I've brought Mr. Inglefield to see you."

"God!" said Neil.

But he realized that King Bore, as Alexander had always stood written in his mind, had been really ill, and still was in a rotten bad state; so, after one pregnant look at Shirley, promising to deal with her later, he made a quick recovery and introduced into his greeting something warmer and more courteous than his previous monosyllable: "This is a bit of a surprise, sir. Shirley doesn't seem to know we've met before; I was called away suddenly, and we never finished our talk."

"And you never received my letters either?"

Stumped, thought Shirley. But as it appeared about time that Neil was rescued, she interrupted with a skilful: "About Lorna—" and so blotted up all Alexander's attention.

"Lorna isn't safe," Neil declared. "I shall have her prosecuted directly we get back. The little darling. And always so damn plausible. I was the only one who saw through her from the start. 'The enemy boy,' she used to call me. And I'm not sure that she isn't carrying on the joke now and giving herself a lot of vicious pleasure, a few return jabs for what I did in putting Marcus wise to her."

"'Master Marcus'?" In spite of himself, Alexander's attention was caught. Master Neil and Master Marcus. The blanks in the story were fast filling up. "That was your brother?"

"Yes, my elder brother."

"The time has come," remarked Shirley, "for one of those fine old-fashioned scenes in the play when the family lawyer sits down heavily and says: 'Let us now cast our minds back to the circumstances as they happened in 1820.'"

Alexander's eyes, deep-set in their hollow caves, wistful as those of a monkey who has fallen out of a tall tree and suffered fatal damage to his strength, moved slowly from Neil to Shirley and back again. Their apparent lack of seriousness on such serious matters as hate and heart-break, confused him.

The younger generation—yes, he was prepared to make allowances for the younger generation, remembering how an older generation had had to be lenient with him. But these two were roughly his own age; Miss Dennison older, and she wore spectacles with scarlet rims which did not improve her keen, rather aquiline good looks. Yet their tempo was quicker, their outlook flippant, their idiom slapdash.

"I should like very much to hear—" he began courteously. After all, he would still be in time to stop Sylvia's marriage, as they were sailing tomorrow. "I would very much like to hear how this woman first came into your lives?"

"Go on, Neil."

"My father married again. He was always marrying; Hollywood was his spiritual home, only he was fifty years too early. But this time he picked a wrong 'un. Mrs. Mason, a widow with one inconspicuous daughter, Lorna; plain and demure and a bit quaint she was then; a Kate Greenaway."

"Strap shoes and a sash," murmured Shirley.

"Well, no, because she was my age already when she came into the family; nearly sixteen. It must have been just the mittened effect she produced; a fuzz of brown hair, and helpful ways about the house: tripping upstairs and fetching things. She had to be helpful to make any mark at all, otherwise she'd have been utterly overshadowed by her mother. My stepmother was a very beautiful lady, you see. Remember her, Shirley?"

Shirley nodded. "Yes. Sad like a legend. Everyone wanted to wait on her. I thought her wonderful."

"I didn't." As contemptuous as though they were boy and girl back at Market St. Dunstan's, he the quick-eyed one and Shirley the dupe. "But Dad, of course, thought nothing good enough for her. As for the wistful look in her eyes—well, she'd blued everything a few weeks before she met him, at the tables in Monte Carlo, and that makes you wistful."

"Neil, I didn't know that."

"Oh yes, Mrs. Mason was a fierce gambler; all she cared about was baccarat. But her hearing was beginning to go, so she came back to London and went to a throat-and-ear specialist who told her there was no hope. Then, luckily for her, she met my father, and suppressed this little item of information. She was getting worse, but very slowly, so she gobbled him first, and a few months later told him that she was afraid there might be 'something a *little* bit wrong' with her ears, just some slight trouble, but had she better go and see a specialist? Dad took her up to his own man and afterwards had a private interview with him, and then broke it to her very, very gently. They were both heart-broken and unselfish together. She kept on and on saying if only she had known beforehand, of course she would have refused to marry him: Oh dear, she had ruined his life, and what was he to do tied to a deaf woman!"

"How did you know she had already consulted a specialist before she married him?"

"I was a sceptic from the age of two, remember; and boys have a normal reaction against their stepmothers; look at Hamlet: if it had been his father who had loved and married again, how even more difficult he would have been. I never trusted the Masons from the start; they were much too sweet and self-effacing. It occurred to me to stroll round to a few other throat-and-ear specialists and ask them to verify the name; it was a shot in the dark, but I found out what I wanted. The man wouldn't tell me anything, of course, but it was the date which damned her. I didn't know if I wanted her damned or not. A young man always likes to prove himself in the right and cleverer than his elders, but it wasn't funny watching my father and knowing he must never know—"

"You didn't tell him? Oh, I'm glad!"

"Shirley, I'm a hard brute; legions of managers that I've sacked here and there from the Neptune Company will tell you that. But I'm *not* a monster. Dad was the kindest old man in the world, and he and Marcus, the servants, the village, everyone treated the poor lady like a saint. She suffered, certainly, but she lay soft while she suffered. That was the big idea when she married him."

"And Lorna? Our little Lorna? Did she know?"

"You bet she did. Probably it was her idea at the start: to shelve responsibility. She pretended to love and adore her pretty mother, but I believe she resented her down to the very soles of her feet. Her mother gave her no chance to expand; mopped up all the limelight; and our little Lorna liked power from the first. She planned to get it through Marcus. She did the Affectionate Little Sister act to Marcus who had never had a dear little sister of his own; used to slip her hand into his and gaze up at him wistfully, and cling, and do odd jobs for him on swift and silent feet. In a hundred ways she praised his sex and his stature. One day she meant to be Mrs. Marcus Inglefield and run everything her own way."

"I never guessed that, either," breathed Shirley, "though I saw her slip her little hand into his often enough. He seemed to like it."

"Oh, he liked it all right," grimly.

"Neil, what happened to Lorna after she had pushed me out of Market St. Dunstan's?"

"Dad took her mother to Monte Carlo to die. Then, a bit later, he died himself, and the home was broken up."

"So you lost sight of her?"

"Not altogether. I knew some people who knew the man who

married her. In fact, he had stayed at the Hall once or twice. Leonard Blake. A splendid-looking, broad-shouldered, Norse, dumb-animal sort of type."

"'Blake'?" repeated Shirley. "'Blake'?"

"Yes. A very usual name. Why are you turning it over and over with your umbrella and prodding at it?"

"I don't quite know. Something looked up out of the fog and then vanished again. Is it true that Marcus lives up in the North now, and controls the liquor traffic, sitting on a barrel and crowned with vine leaves?"

"I hate to break it to you, Shirley, but he looks like a barrel, he doesn't sit on one."

"My beautiful, slender, romantic Marcus?"

"Your beautiful, slender, romantic Marcus. He has a good-natured buxom wife and seven children. All their names begin with 'G'."

"With 'G'? Why?"

"I expect it gives him some obscure sexual satisfaction," Neil declared, with a side-glance towards Alexander, who let his monocle fall out and twiddled it.

"Girls or boys?"

"Six girls and a boy, and another coming along."

"Gertrude—" began Shirley, "and Galswinthia and Gladys—"

Alexander, interested in spite of his disapproval, contributed: "Guinevere."

"You've been reading the *Idylls of the King*," laughed Shirley.

At once he forgot Marcus's children and began to mope. Frequently he had read aloud Tennyson to Sylvia.

"And Gwendolen, of course. There are plenty to choose from for the boy: Gordon; Geoffrey; Gerald. But what are we to call Marcus's next infant if it should be a girl?"

"'G' is an infernally difficult letter." Alexander was getting cross as well as interested. "Why did he have to choose 'G'? Gloria!"

"*I* was going to say 'Gloria.'"

Neil, just to be tiresome, suggested it might be twin girls, "Grace," shouted Alexander triumphantly. "We forgot Grace."

Shirley suddenly sat up:

"*Grace!* Of course. That was it. Still, I could hardly have been expected to lay hold of it at once. It was three years ago, and I wasn't particularly interested." She turned to Neil with an air of one bringing a goldfish out of the top-hat: "I suppose that Lorna's husband, Mr. Leonard Blake, went out of his mind, so she put him away in a lunatic asylum in Scotland?"

Neil stared at her, amazed. "That can't be just a lucky guess? Yes, he went out of his mind, though I don't know where they put him. She's got that on her soul too, our little Lorna, though they called it a repetition of shell-shock. He was a war-hero and she captured him at the height of his D.S.O.; a flamboyant answer to me and Marcus and her mother and all her enemies. But Blake had no money, only his salary; and Lorna just the small income she inherited from her mother. I don't even remember what Blake's business was. There were children, I believe. I only heard of this, third- or fourth-hand. He'd been shell-shocked all right, but he had recovered. He was simply crazy about Lorna. A single-minded obsession, no one else counted—"

Shirley crossed between Neil and Alexander to get an unnecessary cigarette. She already had one between her lips.

"Steady on that," she murmured to Neil, so that he just caught the words, and obediently swerved off the subject of male obsessions by the unworthy feminine, to discourse with relish on Lorna's temperament:

"I fancy she hadn't much use for straightforward sex. Excitement, yes, but not excitement in the conventional way. It looks now as though she got it principally from going round wangling money out of the pockets of sentimental mugs."

Alexander muttered a protest, and Neil went on hastily: "You know— (damn, I keep on forgetting that man!)—I imagine that lots of born gamblers aren't much good in bed for the same reason, that they've found another outlet and a better one, they think. Anyhow, she refused him, poor chap, and he was much too humble about it all; he should have knocked her on the head and dragged her along the bedroom floor. Instead, he had a meek affair with his employer's wife. Neither was much good at hiding things. No brains. And when the boss found out, Blake got the sack and went right off his rocker again. Lorna to blame every time. I lost sight of her after that; or rather, I lost sight of the people who knew the people who had friends who knew Blake; and I'd forgotten her existence till that sinister wire from Shirley. It's not going to be easy to run her to earth now, though I swear I'll do it."

"I swore I'd do it too," from Alexander, "six years ago. But I achieved nothing. Nothing at all. Look at me now."

Shirley patted his shoulder. She had come to feel that this derelict Don Quixote was her own special responsibility, windmills and all:

"You handed it to me on a plate just now. You yourself and no other. G for Grace, you said. Grace is Mrs. Ambrose Bristow, a very conceited lady somewhere in the tenth row of my friends. She rang me up a few years ago to warn me against one of these visiting crooks who had tried to swindle a fare to Scotland with some bogus story of taking a child up to see a dying father in a lunatic asylum. A Mrs. Blake."

"Mrs. Blake?"

"Mrs. Blake. Now you see why I put Grace and Blake together, and made Lorna."

"Then she wasn't Mrs. Neil Inglefield every time?"

"Apparently not. The funny thing is that she performed so badly that Grace didn't believe a word of it, hustled her out of the house with threats of the police, and then checked up on her story, which turned out to be true from beginning to end. As Grace had rung up all her friends to warn them, she now rang up all of them to unwarn them again; she was almost repentant; as repentant as Grace could ever be. Isn't it a queer coincidence, though, that Lorna should have gone to Grace, who rang up me, who knew Lorna, though I didn't know it *was* Lorna till Alexander sent for me because I was born in Market St. Dunstan's and therefore I might know Neil Inglefield. Throw me a cigarette and 'phone down for the loving-cup. Highballs, they call them here.

Neil said: "I never have believed in coincidence and I never will. So I'll have to turn religious instead. This is the hand of God."

"You're both wrong," Alexander corrected him quietly. "It's merely extraordinary that a vile woman should have gone on her way for so many years, and that this should be the first, not the hundredth, coincidence to confound her. Especially if London was her beat. The hand of God, you say? No, but the devil's hand in holding off coincidence all these years."

Neil and Shirley looked at him, surprised. What he said was deeply true, and wiser than their flippancies. Yet up till now they had been regarding the situation as entirely theirs, to deal with in speculation and presently in action, and Alexander as an amiable idiot in the doldrums; a foolish victim; an absent-minded invalid; a pathetic child; a wooden-headed ex-soldier.

"Anyhow, she's got it coming to her now," declared Neil. "And I don't see what can save her." He flung out the challenge carelessly into space. "Our first visit when we get to London will be to your friend Grace for the address. And then we go straight on, all three of us, to pay a call on Lorna and thank her for what she has done for us."

He expected a revengeful assent from Alexander, but only got a dim smile and a shake of the head:

"I think perhaps if you will excuse me—" as though Neil had been suggesting a social call of no importance, "—I shall be busy. If I may leave it to you." For now he did not care any more about vengeance on the unknown woman, known at last. Let Inglefield attend to it or not, as he pleased. Six years ago, the one thought tearing him had been to make her pay for what she had cost him, but now the hounding instinct had exhausted itself; now all he cared for was to see Sylvia again, bringing her just enough proof that she had been wrong to jilt him, when she would at once break off her new engagement, saying: "Alec, forgive me. I love you." And grief and anger and his long desolation would slip away like a bad dream. "Alec, forgive me. I love you. ..."

Chapter Three

←—→

On a warm but moonless night, half-way across the Atlantic, Neil and Shirley were strolling round the boat-deck. Both felt that ease in each other's company which blends mental equality and liking with complete physical indifference. Presently Shirley said: "I'm worried about that man."

"Uncle Alexander? Why? He's in radiant condition; velvety, like a rose opening in noonday sun."

"Quite. That's what I'm afraid of. It's all done on confidence. He's been slowly declining to live for six years, his face turned to the wall. This change is too sudden."

"You've done wonders for him, surely?"

"I've done nothing. But I'm fond of the poor brute."

"So am I, in an odd sort of way. He's a bit like an adopted child, isn't he? Though why we should have chosen that one, when we could have had hundreds of rosy bouncing babies with blue eyes chosen from any orphanage—What's biting you, Shirley?"

"Fear's biting me. What do you think is going to happen when Alec marches like a conqueror into Sylvia Mainwaring's presence and says: 'Darling, here's your own Alec back again. I was right about that woman; you were wrong. It's been proved. Now chuck your present fiancé and we'll be married on Monday'?"

Neil scowled, flung away the end of his cigarette over the rail and lit another.

"Yes, I see what you mean. It *is* abnormal, his optimism. And I expect she's forgotten that such a woman as Lorna ever existed. Life goes on, after all."

"His didn't. His stopped."

"I'm surprised that this Sylvia creature hasn't married twenty times since they quarrelled."

"Just chance."

"There's just a chance, then, that she did care terribly for Alexander, and that when she sees him again she *will* throw away her present fiancé?"

"I'm afraid not, Neil. It's all too simple. With Alec, time has stood still since Lorna's entrance. With Sylvia, who is obviously a pretty fool, a bit stubborn, a bit spoilt, sentimental, resenting contradiction, shallow water anyhow, with Sylvia time will have flowed on. I'm frightened, Neil."

He reminded her: "'Men have died from time to time and worms have eaten them, but not for love.'"

"I'm not so sure."

"You've been in love yourself, Shirley, and here you are, quite tough and happy. Or aren't you?"

"Quite tough and happy. But I'm a woman."

"My handsome brother wasn't worth it, Shirley. I was—I am—fond of Marcus, as you know. But he and Alexander's Sylvia make a pair. You haven't really let his memory stand in your way, have you?"

A shrug: "It depends what you mean by in my way."

At the time it happened, she had felt like Alexander; she had wanted to die, not in a negative fashion, life gradually sliding from her grasp because she had no more tenacity to hold on, but a fierce positive desire to cut herself off from bitterness by a sharp stroke of death. For she had been humiliated as well as robbed.

In social class, she, the orphan niece of the District Nurse, living with her aunt in Market St. Dunstan's, was obviously so far below Marcus Inglefield, the eldest son of rich Mr. Inglefield of the Hall, that a happy wedding would be as improbable an ending to their romance as between the village maid and the squire in a Victorian penny novelette. And Shirley was too deeply in love to desire any picturesque handicaps. She tried to tell herself that it was silly to mind, and that class distinctions were beginning to mean nothing in 1913; yet still she felt tremulous and diffident whenever she thought about Marcus; still she was a trifle too impudent and outspoken when actually with him. She was twenty and he was twenty-two, and he was Shirley's whole world and her weather, her sunrise and her sunset. She believed, from a million signs less visible than the difference of one blade of grass from another, that he loved her too; but he was a shy boy, in spite of his good looks and his fine career at Oxford. When little Lorna Mason was added to the group of young people in and around the Hall, it struck Shirley once or twice that Lorna was acting as a sort of junior A.D.C. in the service of the young man whom she called her big brother, and wistfully adored. Shirley thought it rather sweet of Lorna. The kid was only sixteen, and Neil, stepbrother of her own age, had not made her welcome in her new home; had teased her or treated her with mock politeness; so no wonder she clung to Marcus.

"Neil's my enemy," she once told Shirley, her lip quivering, her eyes round and unhappy. "But I suppose he can't help it; because he never wanted a sister, so it must be horrid for him to have me living here. But Marcus doesn't mind, so it's all right. He doesn't even mind that I'm so ugly and he's so beautiful, and I tell him simply everything. You love Marcus too, don't you?" And Shirley at twenty had underestimated the precocity of sixteen, and thought the kid had meant like when she said love; Shirley had smiled, rumpled the fuzzy brown head, rather large for Lorna's thin little body, and told her not to be a goose, she wasn't ugly at all, not really. She had—here a search for Lorna Mason's good points—she had a long, graceful neck with a sweet little innocent dint at the nape, and—and quite pretty feet and ankles. And that little surprised lift in her eyebrows as though wondering at her own temerity in daring to live and be here at all; and though she was pale now, when she was a bit older she could use rouge and lipstick. "Even now, when you get excited and flushed, and wear that pretty white and silver scarf Marcus gave you for Christmas—"

So Lorna had cheered up, and tripped away to see if she could do anything for anybody; her mother or her stepfather or Corry the butler who was getting old and was always so kind to her and Mummy. Lorna responded to kindness, Shirley thought, a trifle too poetically, like a snowdrop in the sun: she did not actually lift her drooping head, but you could sense the warmth running all down that grateful little stalk:

"I wonder if Neil really hates her, or if he's just at an age when he must rag somebody."

Marcus and Neil had arranged a house-party that Easter. The Hall was full of pretty girls and young men, impetuous or languid. Shirley had not been invited to stay, because she lived in the village a few minutes away from the gates, but she came up every day to play tennis and other games, or to practise the new tango steps just coming into fashion from the Argentine. Dancing, and especially the tango, was the craze that year and with that generation. They competed incessantly, and each desired to excel. Some had the gift naturally and some acquired it, but one of their number, the most enthusiastic, never acquired it at all. That one was Marcus.

They were discussing Marcus and his eccentric clumsiness on that particular afternoon which Shirley was to remember now, as she had on and off for the past twenty-one years, always with that slightly sick, wrenched feeling below the heart.

Marcus himself had just been summoned away from them by his father on some business connected with the estate.

"It's a queer thing about old Marcus. He's got an ear for music, he's keen on dancing, and he *knows the steps*, but he can't dance. What is it?"

"It looks terribly funny when he puts his whole soul into it, as though he were shuffling along on snow-shoes; long steps and a sort of shoving movement."

"You know, he *would* do that exhibition tango last night. How he could, with all of us standing round and grinning and clapping and marking time, is beyond me."

"Shirley, you managed somehow to look as if you were enjoying the agony, clasped in his arms. What did it feel like?"

Shirley could truthfully have replied: "Like heaven." She knew as well as the rest that Marcus was no dancer, that he lacked some essential instinct of grace and poise, but she was not aware of it when actually in his arms. He might hold her contorted at the most excruciating angle, and it would still be Marcus whom she loved so passionately that it was sheer amusement, though it had to be secret amusement, to stand here with his friends casually discussing and criticizing his dancing as though he meant nothing to her. The secret had to be kept, of course; never, never must anyone guess until he had given her the open right to defend him, to declare he danced like a prince. So now she mingled her chatter with theirs, proud to let no difference appear between the way she spoke of Marcus and the way they spoke.

"How does he hold you? Show us!"

"Oh, spread-eagled against him, quite rigid, his right shoulder hunched up ..."

But Lorna, devoted little pseudo-sister, had heard it all. She slipped away from the careless group and waited till Marcus was free and alone, and then told him—what?

How had she achieved it? By telling him plainly that Shirley and the others had been making fun of his dancing, laughing and imitating him?

That Shirley should have betrayed him. He said that he never wanted to see her nor speak to her again. Her defence, clear in her own soul, was too weak even to be uttered. When you love a man terribly, misunderstanding is complicated into such a tangle that it can never be unwound. She faced him, and listened, and knew him deeply wounded, implacably resentful. Then returned home and told her aunt that she could not stay at Market St. Dunstan's. She went to London and into hospital, in training to be a nurse.

Six months later they were already using her in Flanders; she was lucky; she needed guns to silence the memory of that scene with Marcus.

It occurred to her now, on their way to England in 1935, to ask Neil, who had been present during the scene when they had imitated Marcus's dancing, whether he knew anything of the sequel, with little Lorna in the rôle of Cupid's messenger? His reply startled her:

"You don't suppose, do you, that she trotted up with the information that you had been imitating him doing an exhibition tango, bang out like that?"

"Didn't she?"

"Shirley dear, where's your sense of character? As though Lorna ever acted straight when she could act curly. 'Marcus darling, I've got something to tell 'oo which will make 'oo so happy. Otherwise, of course, I wouldn't tell 'oo because I love 'oo too much.'"

"Make him *happy*?"

"'They've all been making fun of 'oo, downstairs. I mean, making fun of your dancing, but of course that doesn't matter a bit because they're so silly. Nobody could mind what they said, and anyhow you dance beeyootiiully and I expect they're jealous. But what I *know* is going to make you so happy that the rest won't matter, is that the *only one* who didn't join in and say anything at all, was Eunice. And please, Marcus darling, I've guessed that you love Eunice. And she wouldn't say a word, while Marion and Shirley and Tom and all of them were laughing at you. Oh, Marcus darling, aren't you glad, *glad*?'"

"Oh, my God!"

"Yes. Clever, wasn't it?"

"She *couldn't* have believed he was in love with Eunice?"

"Eunice my foot. That was just the Lorna touch, practically painless. Painless for Lorna, I mean. If she had told Marcus straight out, it would certainly have done you just as much damage, but she would have damaged herself, too, as a tell-tale-tit and the bearer of bad news: the messenger whom they used to kill in Greek drama. And the amiable idea of pushing you out, was to wriggle herself in, one day, when she was old enough. So it was up to Little Sister to remain pure and wholesome in the sight of Marcus. But who could possibly blame an ingenuous child who had hoped to give him pleasure and only happened to make a mistake over which girl he loved?"

"Were you there when she—"

"No, of course not. Lorna knows better than that. Marcus let it out when he was on leave, about a year later. I cooked her goose then, and she's never forgiven me."

"That's why I suppose it still gives her a sort of delight in saying you were the father of her children and blackening your name."

"Bless her little heart, she doesn't know that the good ship Nemesis is ploughing the waves two days from England. Shirley dear, you're not crying, are you?"

"I'm laughing like anything."

"So was Pagliacci. I'm never comfortable with someone who laughs hollow and cracked because they've lost someone

"My child, where's your sense of proportion? Twenty-one years ago. Since then I've been through the War and had about a hundred love-affairs and my hide is thick and pickled, and I've been several times round the world and become a moderately famous author and had my appendix out and lectured to an audience of two thousand at a time and even read a few of my press-cuttings. And who cares about Marcus?"

"A hundred love-affairs, Shirley?"

"Say ninety-nine."

"Ninety-nine," said Neil obediently. "Is there any hope that if Uncle Alexander doesn't click with Sylvia he'll then turn and marry you?"

"As a solution, neat but not gaudy. I prefer them gaudy. Did Lorna act distressed when she saw that she had hurt Marcus instead of making him glad, *glad*?"

"She clasped her little hands about his neck and hung there, weeping, begging to be allowed to do something to make up for what she had done."

"You're guessing."

"I *know*. I know all about her. I know her unholy motives and reactions. I always did, and I do now. I can't go wrong over Lorna. I *am* the enemy."

"Considering that you can't be a day more than sixteen," Shirley crushed him, "I'm surprised that you should already have risen to a position of some discrimination and authority in the hotel world."

"Listen, Shirley. I cared for my father. And for Marcus. I'm even fond of our wreck of a spruce, well-set-up military man. And I've always been faithfully attached to my friend, Shirley Dennison. Does one need to have remained a boy, to be coldly, wrathfully on the side of the victims? And as for you, Shirley, in spite of the books of travel and the appendices and two thousand lovers and all the other wonderful things you've just described, I believe you've simply done time since that Easter of 1914."

Chapter Four

Grace Bristow said how amusing to see Shirley after such a long absence, and how well she looked but just a bit tired, near white, in fact, the fashionable colour, and how jolly to meet Mr. Inglefield who was almost a celebrity (she did not say "almost"), for to anyone who had stayed in a Neptune hotel it was obvious that somebody with initiative was behind them, and the one thing that she believed in, speaking as a politician's wife, was initiative; she always told Ambrose, he's the member for East Ledford, that the second she saw him getting into a rut she would leave him and then where would he be?

"Still in the rut," Shirley suggested briskly, putting an end to the patter. "Grace, do you remember speaking to me about a woman called Blake? A Mrs. Leonard Blake who came to you for her fare to Scotland?"

"To reach her husband before he died? Indeed I remember. I shall never forget how cruel and suspicious I was, simply because cynical people are always warning one against giving help to strangers. I feel now that I would far rather be swindled nine times than not come to the rescue the tenth time when it's a genuine case. It's taught me always to act on my own instinct, swiftly, like *that* and *that*." She made a complicated gesture of clapping her hands as though to crush a wasp high on her right and another on her left, symbolizing swiftness of action. "You know, Shirley, when I rang you up the first time, while I was still doubtful, you took the conventional line."

"Did I? Yes, I'm ridiculously conventional. The point is, at the moment, did you get her address? It's a forlorn hope that she won't have moved since then, but—"

"But she came to see me only a few weeks ago. Of course I can give you her address. That is, if you want it so as to be nice to her; she's had trouble enough, poor woman."

"Oh, come off it, Grace," began Shirley impatiently. But Neil, realizing from a certain complacence in the mental curves of Mrs. Grace Bristow that she had faith in her own judgment and no one else's, thought it wiser first to get the address, and only afterwards to enlighten her as to the spirit in which they sought it,

"Lorna Blake is a very old friend of mine," he interposed. And the deep ring of goodwill in his voice caused Shirley a gasp of admiration. "In fact, she's rather more than that: my father married her mother, so she's my stepsister, only I'm afraid I lost sight of her years ago."

"Oh, Mr. Inglefield, how interesting! And what a coincidence, I should say what a *lucky* coincidence for her, that I told Shirley about her, and that Shirley knows you. But for me, you might never have been brought together again."

"I couldn't be more grateful," Neil declared with one of his charming smiles. And Mrs. Bristow, in a benevolent glow towards herself (always), and towards Lorna Blake and her stepbrother Mr. Inglefield, only leaving out Shirley, who had not improved since her last American tour but no doubt they spoilt her over there, went to her desk, and after some rummaging, produced Mrs. Blake's address in Ealing and gave it to Neil, who controlled his hand from snatching it and his eyes from a triumphant glance at Shirley.

"You couldn't have come at a better time for poor Mrs. Blake, because, although she's not actually a blood relation, her pretty little daughter Jasmine would be your stepniece, wouldn't she? And perhaps, if there's no one else, you could give her away."

Neil made a mental note that pretty little Jasmine would be one of the two daughters kindly fathered on to him by Lorna during her Mrs. Neil Inglefield incarnations.

"I'm interested in anything you can tell me about Lorna. And then when I see her I needn't be tactless and ask too many questions myself. She used to be peculiarly sensitive as a child. And the world," added Neil, "is apt to be very brutal to sensitive women."

This produced from Grace Bristow the whole of Lorna's story in a glow of rosy light, going back to three years ago when she had had Lorna's pitiful story confirmed by the Superintendent of the asylum. She had then obtained Mrs. Blake's address from the same source and wrote a very kind letter asking the poor woman to come and see her again and condoling with her on the death of her husband, "though of course it was the best thing that could have happened to him poor fellow, and one couldn't wish him back for the little girl's sake—"

"You keep on talking of 'the little girl,' Grace. There are two children, both girls."

Grace shook her head. "No. Only one. A sweet little thing, Jasmine. She didn't look more than twelve when I saw her, but she must have been older because now she's of an age to many—That's why the mother came to see me again, after such a long interval. She never answered my letter, and I'm afraid, you know what by-elections are, I was so anxious for Ambrose to get in, the whole thing slipped from my mind until a few weeks ago when Mary brought in a note and said the bearer was waiting. Then I remembered at once and of course I said I'd see her. I didn't keep her waiting a moment. She was looking much younger, somehow, than the time before; no, not exactly younger—I can't quite describe the difference—it was too intangible. She even held herself better, as though her frame of mind had adjusted itself, and she had found the right way to tackle her difficulties. The first time she had hedged and repeated herself and been silly. But now she was quiet and clear and really quite dignified. She thanked me for my letter and said not many ladies would have owned they were in the wrong like that, and that it took a fine character to do it. She said she couldn't bear then to have accepted my invitation to come and see her because she was so ashamed of having seemed to beg from me and it had been only desperate need which had given her the courage and she had seen that I hadn't believed her and she didn't blame me at all, but if she had come to see me again I might have offered her money and she couldn't have endured that, for anyhow her poor husband was dead and beyond need of her."

"A very proper frame of mind," said Neil gravely. "So this time she didn't want money, just a cup of tea and mutual apologies?"

Mrs. Bristow looked a little worried. "I did ring for tea, yes. And we talked about her husband. She said his real life was over and we couldn't wish him with us again."

"Us? Why, he never was with you, was he?"

"Shirley, when you're in this mood—Besides, we were referring to shell-shock in general; we have a responsibility towards these men, every one of us. Were you in the War, Mr. Inglefield?"

"I got in for the last year of it."

"Ah! … Her little daughter Jasmine was growing more like him all the time, she said. The poor woman had evidently been devoted to him and was now devoted to the girl—"

"Grace, I'm sorry. I can't bear this Rhapsody in Blake. The poor woman, as you call her, has planted enough trouble to make the finest herbaceous border in the country. What tale did she pitch this time? And did you check up on it?"

"No," replied Grace coldly. "Naturally I didn't. I took the advice of people like you and 'checked up,' as you call it, on her story the first time she came to me, and every word of it proved true."

Shirley did not answer. She was aware that here was their weak point. Also Neil was taking a wicked delight in Grace, stroking down the glossy fur every time that Shirley rumpled it up.

"Did you say that my little stepniece is engaged to be married? I do hope poor Lorna will have an eligible son-in-law who can make things easier for her, now she's not so young any more."

"That's it, Mr. Inglefield. He's *too* eligible. That's why Mrs. Blake is so distressed about it all. I got her to confide in me. Her daughter is deeply in love with the young man, but she's proud. I expect it's their hard life and the father and all that. Eighteen is the most sensitive age. She couldn't bear to go to him with nothing; nothing at all; not even a few simple new clothes. You know they are not quite our class, the Blakes—" (she had forgotten that Mr. Inglefield's father had married Mrs. Blake's mother, and used the explanatory tone that Ambrose was wont to employ about the minor tradesmen in his constituency) "—those sort of people are always so conventional, it's comic how much importance they attach to things that we've learned not to bother about; weddings, for instance: the bride's parents supply the household linen and the trousseau, and the wedding should take place from their house. The silly girl actually wanted to break it off rather than go to him like a beggar, so her mother said she said."

"King Cophetua," suggested Neil, one eyebrow intelligently cocked to show sympathy and imagination with pretty, proud Jasmine Blake, plus a humorous understanding with the brilliant psychologist Mrs. Bristow, and no communion whatever with his friend Shirley, put in exile for the afternoon.

Grace laughed. "Yes, well, there you are. But Cophetua's maid was *really* a beggar, you see; bare feet make all the difference; this Blake girl was fussing about her shoes and stockings; But the mother could hardly bear to think that her child's whole life might be ruined for want of such a small sum."

"How much? Fifty pounds?"

Grace was thrown off her guard by Shirley's nonchalant acceptance of what had happened.

"Twenty."

"So she got it out of you?"

"Shirley, there was no question of *getting* it out of me. I'm not a dupe. I know human nature, don't I? I gave this sum voluntarily; an atonement, if you like, for what I refused before. I owed it to her."

"Have you been invited to the wedding?"

Grace shook her head. "Mrs. Blake wouldn't dream of telling the girl that she had been given a present. It would be easy to pretend that—well—let me see—"

"—that it had turned up suddenly in the mattress?"

The suggestion was ignored. "She happened to be a woman of natural delicacy. She said that she could never have accepted the money from a stranger. I could hardly with any delicacy at all have thrust myself into their poor little home—"

"I've never seen so much bloody delicacy all in a bunch: the girl's delicacy about not marrying her rich young man without half a dozen of everything, and the mother's delicacy and your delicacy—I shall be sick in a moment."

Neil could restrain them no more, after Shirley's last remark. He reminded himself that he had the coveted address, so he might as well let them rip. Grace and Shirley had one of the merriest rows he had ever had the pleasure to witness; merry and stimulating. He waited till the final insults had been hurled, and then dropped an unrepentant Shirley at her flat and took the taxi on to Lorna's address in Ealing.

Just before Neil parted from Shirley at the entrance to Curzon Mansions she asked: "Neil, you're still boiling over, aren't you?"

"Do you doubt it?"

"Just now, I wondered—"

"That's all right," Neil reassured her. "You weren't made for the Diplomatic Service, Shirley. If you and I had stood shoulder to shoulder, hot and indignant, you might have whistled for Lorna's address." He did not add that a man always feels a slight detachment when two women go into battle. Right down the generations of male ancestors, the message is handed: "Women, just women; keep out of it."

Shirley, subconsciously wise to this attitude, did not press the point. She only said: "I never knew I was so vindictive, but I should hate Lorna to escape now."

"She can't, or only by act of God."

"Don't think it's altogether because she divided me from Marcus; that's too long ago. Nor because she had the insolence to use your name and blacken it; nor even, though curiously enough, I mind this most, because of the mess she's made of Alexander. But those two children,

Neil: quite suddenly, from something Grace said, I wondered what sort of nightmare childhood can it have been, dragged round by their mother to strange houses, visiting strange people, having to hear her telling them strange lies, having to see her take their money—"

"You've too much imagination, Shirley." Neil took her hands and held them firmly for a moment. "Go in and sit down quietly and pour yourself out a stiff drink. And leave the rest to me. I promise you it's all right."

It was a long drive down to Ealing, and Neil had plenty of time to think about the picture Shirley had presented to him, of childhood deliberately exploited and helpless. By the time he reached Shepherd's Bush, his anger against Lorna was again as hot as hers. And the woman had dared to swindle under cover of *his* name: Mrs. Neil Inglefield. Perhaps one day of his own free will he would give that name to a love as yet unknown. That was his business entirely. But now the guarded name had been snatched and scribbled over: "my husband, Neil Inglefield—" The notion gave him acute discomfort, as though someone dirty had worn his favourite suit of clothes. Queer, he mused, that riles me more than her spreading it about that I had abandoned her and my children and left them penniless.

Neil Inglefield had had the disadvantage of being confirmed too early in scepticism. He was by far the most intelligent and the most independent personality in his family. His father and his mother had both been credulous, gentle and romantic. And his elder brother, Marcus, had resembled them. It was left for Neil, the youngest Inglefield, an ugly, attractive boy with a restless brain, to stand a little apart and watch them pass trustfully through the world which he himself lightly mistrusted. He was naturally affectionate, but he learned to place a guard upon this; and as he grew older, he grew prouder of his freedom from emotional delusion. The intrusion of the Masons, mother and daughter, into his actual family circle, capturing his father, threatening to capture Marcus too, made him desperately unhappy; though again he would not admit it, and pretended to enjoy stripping them naked of their pretences; though this was a matter for his own inner satisfaction alone; his father and his brother, he was aware, had better be left to reside in any fool's paradise that suited their temperament. Neil came of age, mentally, years before he was twenty-one.

He had confidence in his own strong management of life and in nothing else, except here and there a friend. He was only conceited about his own ability to measure himself up, without adding or subtracting from an honest total. He set an artificial value, far too high, on his own immunity, and so he knew very little of what was really going on anywhere, because of an imperious, perpetually inconvenient compulsion to preserve this immunity within a wary six-foot radius, and allow nothing human inside. Being critical adds quite a lot of fun to life, though, of course, not nearly so much as being uncritical. And when he forgot to be wise to the invariable motive, or to remove his feet, which were, after all, not more precious than King Canute's, from a zone where they might get wet, he could enjoy the company and affection of his fellow human beings with relish.

The result of all this was the man whom Shirley had summoned by telegram to New York about a fortnight before; a man of whom a casual observer might have said he was good-natured, easy-going, boyish, charming, mischievous; but who actually, as Shirley realized, had become intolerant and authoritative; knew too much and yet not quite enough of men and women; certainly not enough except from a ruthless angle. His job was bad for him; it had encouraged his tendency to exalt efficiency and condemn tenderness.

And yet Neil could have been tender: she discerned a strain of it in his treatment of Alexander; one might have expected him to be contemptuous of a conventional English soldier who had been fool enough to let slip his grasp of life because a stupid pretty girl had thrown him over for an even more stupid reason. But Neil had been very sweet to Alec; and very sweet, too, with Shirley, when he was not ragging her or guarding himself from betraying that he liked her. Shirley had hopes of Neil, but she had her doubts too. That was why on an impulse she had appealed to him in the name of sentiment: "What sort of a nightmare childhood was it?"

Chapter Five

←→

No. 31 Netherby Park Road, Ealing, was a pleasant little house with a pseudo-cottagy look about it, bright chintz curtains in the window, bright blue paint on the door, and a brass ship for knocker. It was difficult to associate it with anything sinister, but quite easy for Neil to associate it with the Lorna he had once known, with her quaint sedate ways, and clothes which carried an indefinable message that the dressmaker who cut them had been dreaming of Kate Greenaway before she took up the scissors.

In a black temper, Neil hoped that she herself and not a servant would answer his ring and knock; then he could allow himself to lose control without any further tiresome delays.

But the girl who opened the door had not the remotest look of Lorna to justify the loosing of a thunderbolt.

Neil remained so long silent that Molly had to speak first: "I'm the only one at home. Did you want to see anybody?"

"Mrs. Blake. Will she be long?"

"I don't know. Yes, she usually is when—"

"When?"

"When she's out," Molly finished lamely.

"I'll wait."

Not "Please may I wait?" "I'll wait" was the ultimatum of a conqueror, an enemy marching in to take possession. Molly wondered who was this man with the dark face and the grey eyes almost green, amazingly full of light where you expected to find them brown or black? Who was this man with the arrogant way of holding himself, and the sort of clothes she liked, worn in the way she liked?

Perhaps for a fleeting moment she allowed herself to believe the best had happened—perhaps he had fallen in love with Jay, although he was

– 153 –

so much older; and had come to Mummy about that. Then Jay would be safe for ever; you could see at once that he belonged on the right side of law and order.

"Will you tell me your name, if you're going to wait?"

"Neil Inglefield."

"Neil Inglefield!"

He was not prepared, though he might have been, for the shock her face betrayed; the conflict of joy and bewilderment; the struggle to maintain aloofness.

"Please come in." Before Neil had collected his reserves or felt about for his wits to have them handy, as a gangster might make sure of his gun, he found himself sitting comfortably in a round armchair with soft cushions in an utterly Lorna-esque sitting-room, a smother of chintz and battalions of brass and a curtsey towards modern but not very modern homecraft. A room, figuratively speaking, that wore bunchy skirts and a mob-cap. The girl drew up to his side a Benares table with ashtray and cigarette-box, and matches in an irritating box with a long tassel, and tried to make him name whether he preferred tea or whisky-and-soda. ("I hope Susan has her usual bottle in some place where I can find it")

"Nothing, thanks." He was puzzled. Why was she treating him half as a criminal, half as a person who had an undoubted right to be there; and—Oh God, tears were streaming down her face in a bright flood; yet until she owned by word or gesture that she was crying, he was impotent.

"You're Jasmine?"

"No, I'm Molly. What a good memory you must have," politely. (Though that's an idiot thing, she reflected, to say to one's own father. He named us himself, for all I know.) "We call Jasmine 'Jay.' She's living away now." Earnestly she plodded on, trying to entertain him with appropriate conversation: "I'm afraid I don't look awfully like you, but I think, no, I'm sure"—anxious to supply the right touch—"that Jay's got your mouth." Her chief desire was not to let him feel he was being reproached for his long desertion; to save him from the mortification, at his age, of having to accept censure from a chit of seventeen, and his own child. After all, a couple of howling babies, both girls; and who knows, face up to it bravely, what Mummy might have done to an honest man; he looked honest.

"Let's get this right," said Neil. "Jay's got my mouth?" Then suddenly light struck through the fog. Christ! thought Neil, I'd forgotten. Or rather, because Lorna had called herself "Mrs. Blake" to Grace Bristow and was obviously Mrs. Blake in her own home, he had taken it for granted that the children knew who was their real father.

And now what does a man do? Easy enough to break the news that you're the long-lost parent, when the girl is not aware of it; but the reverse situation, break the news that you are not her father when already she treats you in the filial spirit, that was a hundred times more disconcerting. He had never felt less paternal in his life. Yet she had better be told without any more delay. You could not insult a girl of that quality and endurance by continuing to masquerade in the spirit of cup-and-saucer comedy.

"I'm not demonstrative," Molly began, still protecting herself by an air of severity, for she feared that she might have already disappointed her father by not impulsively flinging her arms round his neck. "But perhaps you're not either, and so we both would rather know each other before—before—before we—"

"I knew your father," said Neil gently. "Leonard Blake got his D.S.O. in the War and thoroughly deserved it, but of course that was before you were born. Listen, dear, I don't know if they—your mother—if anyone has told you that he died two or three years ago, up in Scotland." He saw in her eyes a sudden recognition of some relevant incident, and went on quickly in the same voice that he carefully kept matter-of-fact and friendly: "He was never well enough, after the War, to be at home. A good many of us were in the same boat. I'm sorry." He heaved himself out of that absurd plump little armchair and walked over to the window, turning his back. She would need none of his help in assimilating this, but she might need time; at least he could be merciful and give her that.

Lorna must have been in the habit of alternating her real marriage certificate with the bogus one she had used for Sylvia Mainwaring and no doubt elsewhere, showing Lorna Mason married to Neil Inglefield, so both names would be familiar to Molly. For some reason the girl had linked her birth to the wrong one. Or had it given Lorna a bitter amusement to tell the Blake children that they were really the daughters of the enemy boy?

"If you're not my father, but you *are* Neil Inglefield—?"

He swung round at the note of sheer panic in her voice.

"—then perhaps the police have sent you," finished Molly, but too low for him to hear. She had been expecting the police on the doorstep for years, ever since she had first learned there were reasons why they had to take flight from their home, leaving no address.

Shirley had said, appealing to his imagination: "What sort of nightmare life has it been for those two children?" Yes, but could she not have foreseen that that very factor might stop him from prosecuting Lorna, not urge him on. Whatever else happened, this child's mind must be brought to rest, and at once. She was like a young captain desperately searching round for more reserves than she actually had, hastening them up from every side.

Neil smiled at Molly. "Sit down and relax," he said, "I'm not the police." And then, doing her the honour of frankness up to the limit where it was possible to be frank: "You're right this far, I *was* angry over—well, a wrong idea your mother had had of me, and I *did* come down here to make a scene, so it's lucky she's out, isn't it? otherwise by now I'd have been bellowing and throwing furniture." His tone, careless, undramatic, inviting her to be amused at the picture of a man's way of showing temper, had more of an effect on Molly than the random words he used. She could not wholly surrender yet to blissful relief; she still kept steady eyes on him as though at any moment the tiger might spring; but a little colour was beginning to come back to her lips; the worst panic was over, for she remembered: Jay isn't here any more; Jay's away and safe; so it's all right. And with Jay all right, the danger was no longer tense nor even serious. With Jay all right, serenity returned and a philosophic: "It had to come some time. Now let's tackle it."

"My mother has had a specially hard time, one way and another," said Molly, her heart thundering, but with the staid manner of a nurse explaining a confidential case to a not very intelligent doctor. She sat down, obedient, to his suggestion, and lit a cigarette. His being nice made it all, funnily, more difficult instead of easier. "She was terribly particular about educating us well, so that we could earn our own livings if she couldn't be there any more to—to—to do things for us. And so there were times when she got nervous. I suppose over-anxiety and no husband and trying to keep within her income. It was a very tiny regular income, I don't know how much. And though she was strictly economical, sometimes for years, she hated not to give us treats, and painting Christmas cards doesn't earn much extra. We'd have done without the treats, but Mummy—my mother—when she was nervous and worried—I think she got carried away sometimes, and if during those times she said things about you—" Molly flushed scarlet. She could guess now that she had had a little while to puzzle it out, why he had come down here to make a scene and throw furniture. If only one were allowed to break through loyalty, home loyalty, family loyalty, how lovely to rid her mind of the whole burden; just roll it off at the feet of this stranger whose name she knew so well; who was looking at her, while she plunged on with whatever extenuating bits of truth she could gather and use, with such an expression of deep understanding in his eyes that Molly realized for the first time how you could be thrilled by kindness as wildly as though it were a passionate declaration.

"Never mind what your mother said about me; I expect I irritated her when we were young and first knew each other." He was absorbed in his wish to help Lorna's young daughter keep her dignity inviolate. She must have been humiliated enough. It made him sick to think of what she had been through; and yet by a miracle she had preserved her integrity after years of Visiting with Lorna, used as one of Lorna's pathetic properties and a further incitement to generosity from strangers. He suppressed a natural longing to burst out with all that he would like to do to that devilish woman. But Molly could not be reassured by these primitive means, so he repeated: "I expect I was irritating too," actually joining her in the game of finding excuses for Lorna.

But this line produced a wholly unlooked-for effect. Molly had a childish lapse from sentinel duty, a lapse even from discretion. Until now, she had been neither old nor young, with the ageless wisdom born from a weary necessity to be perpetually vigilant, but her next suggestion was a disgrace even to seventeen. Assuming from his last remark that he and her mother had been long ago obviously in a position to irritate and hurt each other, she leapt eagerly not only at a false conclusion, but well beyond it:

"I needn't be a burden to you. I earn quite a big salary now. Of course, you wouldn't want me or Jay hanging round your neck. But we're self-supporting and I'd be quite willing to be on my own; it would be rather fun, in fact, after living at home for so long—"

Neil was hopelessly bewildered: "What's all this about? I'm glad that you're self-supporting, it's a damn good thing. But—" What in hell did she mean by "hanging round your neck"? She was enchanting now, without any fear or strain left in her face, just babbling like any other very young girl:

"You can talk quite openly with me. I'm on the stage, and you get tough very quickly with all you hear. If you and Mummy—when you were both quite young—and your coming back like this in a rage wanting to smash things shows that she's still in your blood; hate is very near love, isn't it?"

"Not always," said Neil grimly. "But please go on."

"Mummy runs a home awfully well; she knows all the handy things about whom to send for in emergencies and what takes out stains and the right quantities when you order vegetables—" Then an awful possibility struck her, to account for his lack of response; her cheeks dyed scarlet again. "Oh, do forgive me if you're married already," she whispered. "I never thought of that."

And Neil laughed outright. He could not keep it back. Considering all the circumstances, no more rich or comical notion could have been devised than that he should marry Lorna. Up to the decorous purpose revealed in Molly's last sentence, he had supposed she meant them merely to renew an affair which she suspected had prematurely ended in a quarrel during their headstrong youth. But the infant was fundamentally sober and domestic: first she had him planted as her father; now she was arranging him as a stepfather. And she imagined, bless her, that she was being worldly-minded and tough and doing the best for everybody concerned.

"No, I'm not married, Molly, but you see I'm your mother's stepbrother, so I doubt if it would answer if we got married, apart from any incompatibility of temperament."

"Stepbrother?" She knit her brows over the new facet.

"Your mother's mother married my father when she and I were about sixteen." But he was sorry he had mentioned this when he saw the girl growing older again before his eyes, as she fitted the marriage certificate into its place: not her mother's, but her grandmother's, only Mummy had used it as her own.

She had had enough for today, and more than she could bear, though she had borne it so well. Courage he might have expected, but from where did she get her breeding? And her amazing decency? God, she's a darling, thought Neil. He cursed himself for being undeserving of the privilege of helping a girl like this; it needed delicacy like the tip of a moth's antennae, and his was like shoe-leather. Delicacy—He remembered how Shirley told Grace Bristow that there was too much bloody delicacy all over the place. Never mind about Shirley now; he would have to deal with that presently. Now it was time he went. He could not do more for Molly than just cut the tension and leave her alone. Yet one day, and soon, he knew, perhaps she knew it too, everything would be candid and clear between them, and they could go straight on from there.

"Molly, what do you want me to do? I'll take my orders from you. Shall I go before your mother comes home?"

"You're the kindest man I've ever met," said Molly.

"And are you going to tell her that I've been here? You needn't, you know?"

"I'd rather not. It would worry her terribly." She accepted his generosity with a little sigh of relief.

Neil had never, had any special belief in telepathy, but some curious intuition made him say now, not in the form of a haphazard statement, but definitely, as though replying to a message, pleading for him to ease her mind on yet one more point before he left: "Your grandmother, the one who married my father, had a passion for gambling, you know. I hope," he added, adopting the tone of a middle-aged man chaffing impetuous youth, "I hope you haven't inherited it? One can't always help these things, when they are passed on from one generation to another."

"Thank you," she replied simply. And after a pause: "We were taken to see her grave once, Jay and I; it's in Monte Carlo. I suppose that was her favourite place, if she gambled."

The clock struck seven, and Molly glanced towards it and then away again. Her mother might be home any moment now.

"At what theatre are you acting, Molly? If I mustn't come back here—"

She told him. And he quickly said good-bye and left her.

"Shirley!" Neil strode into her study, prepared for any amount of rough handling as a blackleg. His blood was racing and he felt splendid. What an absurd fuss they had been making, he as well as Shirley and Alec, about a trivial matter. Everybody got what they could out of everybody else, and Lorna's methods were just a variant in technique. Or, granted that she was outrageous, it was simply not his business any more.

"Why are you sitting in the dark?" He could just see her, a listless outline in front of a small fire, not reading nor writing nor even in a pleasant reverie.

"Neil? No, don't put the light on, my eyes hurt. Did you see Lorna?"

He gave no direct answer.

"You remember, don't you, Shirley, that I said only an act of God could save her? Well, the act of God has happened."

"Two, perhaps," said Shirley. "Go on."

He told her about Molly. "—and that's final. I'm not going to prosecute, because I can't do a damn thing to hurt the child. Lorna's safe from me for ever. Shirley, Molly's absolutely honest and absolutely beautiful."

"And Lorna gets off on that?"

"I'm afraid she must. It can't be helped. Life's funny."

"It couldn't be funnier," Shirley agreed. "I'm the only one who has a legal case against her. You haven't, and Alec hasn't. I can't help what he may say—" Shirley roused herself with an effort:

"Alec won't say anything. He shot himself about an hour ago." A long silence. "They 'phoned me from his club. Instantaneous, or I'd have gone round." Then: "I'm sorry I had to announce it at such an effective moment."

"Had he just been to see Sylvia?"

"Yes, of course."

Neil said grimly: "Lorna again."

"Yes, Lorna again." He discerned, even through the dusk, that her look at him was a final question. He turned away. And Shirley understood that that was his final answer. Neither had to put it into words. Men and women were callous and single-minded when they were in love. Molly was now his story, just as Sylvia had been Alexander's. Alec's death had been a shock to Neil, but it made no real difference. One day he would marry Lorna's daughter. And Sylvia would marry Parker B. Harland next Wednesday week as arranged. Alexander was dead, and Marcus lived up in the north and had seven children whose name all began with "G."

"And that's that," said Shirley aloud. "Did she give you a drink, or will you have one now?"

PART V

Lady Bountiful

Chapter One

<->

It was a murky evening in January when Jay brought the bunch of balloons to Sally Greene's door. Sally was the charwoman's child. Mrs. Greene cleaned the offices of Walker, Dudley & Son, Architects, and then went on to clean other houses and offices in Southampton; she was rarely home before six o'clock.

And Sally had nothing to do; the streets were gloomy and unattractive, darkness falling limply from a damp sky. She had nothing to do and nothing nice to think about, which at seven years old was a hopeless state of affairs stretching on into melancholy eternity. In summer at least she could run down to the docks and see the huge three-funnelled liners moving out towards the horizon. In summer in the sunshine Southampton was a gay city. "Nothing to do. Nothing to do," chanted Sally fretfully. For she loved colour and movement. Even when Mum came home presently, that would not add to the liveliness of their two drab semi-basement rooms, nor to the drab weather outside. Mrs. Greene was a patient, not a cheerful charwoman. She was glumly kind to Sally, but Sally wanted life to be all bells and balloons.

She had had a balloon at Christmas, given to Mum free in the market: blue, with "A Merry Christmas" printed in sprightly red letters. But that there cat had got at it almost at once, in one vivid moment when Sally had not known whether to scream with excitement at the danger and the loud bang and the cat's astonished backward leap, or to sob with grief at seeing her treasure lost before she had had a chance to toss it flashing in the wind.

"Nothing to do," the child sighed again, bored by the stuffy room. She was in the same mood that had inspired Shelley to his "Lines Written in Dejection near Naples."

Suddenly there was a knock at the door; a happy sort of knock, thought Sally, not sharp like the rent-collector nor timid like Mrs. Reynolds from opposite when she wanted to borrow a lump of margarine because she had run out.

Sally opened the door, and stood gasping. She hardly even saw the young lady with the golden hair and shy appealing smile, dressed in a shabby coat. She only saw what the young lady was carrying: a whole bunch of glowing coloured balloons; not one alone, but twelve—fourteen—a hundred, a world of balloons.

Sally stared at them, enchanted. Mum had said: "You can't expect something for nothing till after you're dead"—but surely she was still alive when there had been a knock at the door and balloons had floated in? Presently, of course, they would float out again, but meanwhile they were so near she could stretch out a finger and touch them, taut shiny satin globes, frail and yet somehow strong.

"You're Sally, aren't you? I've seen you once or twice at the office, when you fetched your mother. She told us how disappointed you were over your Christmas balloon; the cat got it, didn't he? So I've brought you these. You mustn't let pussy—"

Jay stopped, dazzled by the glory in the child's eyes.

Miss Emerson kept a very plain table. On the terms she charged for room, breakfast and dinner, no profit could be made except on the food, and not much on that, for the guests at The South Riviera Private Hotel earned at the utmost stretch from thirty shillings to three pounds a week, or else earned nothing, but clung desperately to the remnants of an income or to the fringe of someone else's income. Even today, Easter Monday, she could not see her way, that was how she equivocally expressed it, she could not see her way to providing anything extra festive for dinner; anyhow, her best guests contrived to take themselves off on some sort of holiday outing, and only the dregs were left on either side of the long narrow dining-room table; the German refugees, Herr and Frau Hartmann with their young son; old Mr. Nichols whom arthritis had banished from the municipal orchestra, and Miss Matcham, a carefully preserved gentlewoman in the early fifties.

Miss Emerson dealt out the stew, which was mostly potatoes and turnip.

"And where's Madame Soboleff, I wonder? She's not out, I know, because the Brydens invited her to accompany them; very kindly, I thought, considering how doleful she always is at Easter, remembering old days in St. Petersburg and not calling it by its new name, poor thing."

Mr. Nichols said: "They used to make a great feast for Easter in Russia, I've always heard. Giving each other presents and so on."

And Miss Matcham said with a little giggle: "I expect she's known all this time where the Russian Crown jewels are and won't say."

"Now how *could* she?" began Miss Emerson, who had also begun life as a romantic, but had learned hard sense. It was difficult not to snub Miss Matcham when, far from shore, so to speak, she stopped swimming and began to float. And all this time the Germans were wishing hard that the talk had not fallen on refugees. It was a desperately uncomfortable subject for them, who only six months ago had been rich and respected citizens of Munich. Carl, their son, their darling, heard none of this, luckily. He was in a happy dream, as always, since that golden day six weeks ago when he had been given a violin to replace the one which the Nazis had smashed.

"Vill somevun open the door?" cried a deep gay voice from the further side. "My hands they are full."

"Why, it's Madame Soboleff. She sounds pleased about something!" Miss Emerson signed to Maggie to stop slapping plates on to the table and attend to the summons.

Enter then all the spirit of Imperial Russia before 1917: Madame Natasha Olga Tamara Soboleff, smiling, nodding, mysterious, hospitable, carrying in one hand a large jar of Astrakhan caviar, in the other a bottle of vodka; gifts from the Magi, and no skimping either.

Madame Soboleff sat down on the opposite end of the table from Miss Emerson, and dispensed royal helpings. The vodka made them all very lively and coy and affectionate. They drank Madame's health, and then Miss Emerson's, and then, with enthusiasm, the health of Jasmine Blake, who had stayed at the boarding-house during her first five weeks in the well-known firm of Walker, Dudley & Son, Architects, and who had remembered, the dear child, that Madame Soboleff adored caviar and got very little of it.

"But it's not only presents but the spirit you give them in," cried Miss Matcham. "Easter Monday, when you'd be feeling a little blue perhaps, Madame, and not forgetting the vodka to wash it down. And look at how she got hold of the date of Miss Emerson's birthday and filled the house with all her favourite flowers: Parma violets and mimosa. Why, the South Riviera looked like—" she stopped; it sounded so silly to say that the Riviera looked like the Riviera. She giggled instead, and went on archly: "My turn next, I hope, while the going's good."

Maggie, who had slipshod heels and permanently tired feet, exchanged a look with her secret friend Carl, over Miss Emerson's head. She was a slut, but a grateful slut; and though she had told no one else about those six pairs of expensive silk stockings that crunched sensuously in her hand when she picked them up and fondled them, she had felt impelled to tell the German boy, because her soul was full to overflowing, and he drew such lovely music from his violin that you couldn't keep things from him.

"It's clear enough, of course, that her people must be very wealthy indeed."

This romantic legend had started to drift round like thistledown from the first day of Jay's arrival among them; now, corroborated by so many delicious presents given swiftly and impulsively without thought of their cost, it was no longer impalpable on the breeze, but tough as truth itself.

"Social life and being presented and all that, it's all very well for a girl with nothing in her, but nowadays if they have any character, they'll break away and get their own experience. All sorts of new ideas get put in their heads, reading politics and economy—"

"Not much economy about caviar, is there?" Miss Matcham giggled. She was eating hers largely heaped up on to a fork, instead of spreading it on thin slices of bread as the others did. "Well, if she's the Modern

Girl some of the newspapers are so down on, all I can say is, she's a great improvement on the other kind, and may she go on. Why, she never spends one penny on giving herself a good time: orchids for the poor, but bread-and-scrape and a mattress stuffed with stones for herself."

This speech did not make a great hit with Miss Emerson. She was not "the poor," although Jay's wanton wealth of flowers had coloured a certain dinginess in her daily life; and while Jay had stayed at The South Riviera, she had certainly not slept on a mattress stuffed with stones, whatever other austerities she may have had to practise.

"She's proud," continued Miss Matcham, not at all abashed by Miss Emerson's haughty look down the table. "Proud and sensitive, which I for one understand very well. And reserved, too. If you ask her a personal question, not that I ever have, she'll say with that pretty, quick look of hers: 'Please don't ask me. Don't let anyone ask me.' Naturally she was ashamed of her mother having so much money and trying to marry her off to a horrid elderly man with boils and a title. And she refused point-blank to be presented."

"*Fabelhaft!*" cried Frau Hartmann in admiration.

Madame Soboleff began to babble about the Little Father and the Czarina and the Court of Russia. Because she was hostess, Miss Emerson let her have a run for her caviar; then, turning to Miss Matcham:

"Did Miss Blake actually tell you all this story?"

"What story, Miss Emerson?"

"About the old husband with the title, and refusing to be presented?"

Miss Matcham took up her glass and sipped the last few drops of the vodka: "They say one should throw back one's head and toss it down one's throat, don't they, Madame, without touching the mouth at all? I'm sure I've heard that's the proper way, but I'm not sure if I—Well, Miss Emerson, not actually in so many words, but the impression seeped through. It just—seeped through. Of course, I'm quick at filling in bits by sheer intuition. You can tell I'm like that by the way I handle jigsaws, which the psychologists say is most revealing."

"Ach? You have study in our language, then? Freud, Jung, Adler—"

"All of them. But I'm quite positive she did actually confide in me about not wanting to be presented."

Mr. Nichols murmured that it was, when you came to think of it, a barbaric ceremony. And Jay's prestige at The South Riviera was enhanced not only by the Russian feast she had provided, but by this engaging picture of her turning her back on barbaric ceremonies, choosing rather to live amongst the workers, simply and austerely sharing their stern conditions, sleeping on a mattress stuffed with stones.

Betty Forsyth was using the coffee interval at eleven o'clock to collect some outstanding subscriptions of five shillings each for a wedding-present. One of their number, Ruby Mitford, was shortly going to be married, and had already left Walker, Dudley & Son, thus making it easier for Betty to chivvy the girls in the accounts' room, and shame them by telling them loudly what had already been amassed. Helen Mitford was in the room, the plain elder sister of the bride, her head bent crossly over her knitting, but Betty did not think it necessary to lower her demands on Helen's account. "Three pounds fifteen shillings already," Betty announced, "and at least four more fives to come, that's another pound. Four pounds fifteen, call it five, pounds. Oh, and my own, of course," she added in sudden comical diminuendo which made her companions laugh: Good old Betty! "And my own, of course," they mimicked her.

"Jay? No, you've given yours. There's the 'phone, Rose."

"I'm filing," Rose stated placidly. She had been doing nothing at all for the last ten minutes, and hoped to do nothing for the next ten.

"Nelly Ann, another shilling owing from you."

"Duck of ducks, let it stand over till next week. Honestly, I haven't any change."

"You haven't had any for days. How d'you manage to get about? Good God, there's plenty of change at Walker Dudley's, isn't there, whatever else there isn't?"

"Smuggle in one more, Hopkins; my cup was only half full." The office boy went off obediently with the thermos, to the café opposite. "Shall we send in a cup to Orphan Annie?"

This question of whether to pamper dignified elderly Miss Anne Paynter, Mr. Dudley's private secretary, was solemnly debated anew every morning, but Miss Paynter still went without coffee.

"Now for suggestions. Helen, what has Ruby had to date?"

"Four cocktail sets, a bridge table, six bath towels, a dinner service, eleven cigarette-boxes, a case of coffee-spoons and a set of hand-painted table mats." Helen brought out these items as though each one had been a separate stinging hurt; as though she could not stop remembering that Ruby was a younger sister and should not have been married first. "The loveliest of all her presents was anonymous."

"My dear, how romantic! What was it? I suppose from some other fellow who'd been crazy about her, only she never guessed."

"I expect so. There were plenty. Only she guessed all right each time."

"Well, what was the thing? Jewellery?"

"No, a glass figure holding a lamp. Psyche, I think. Lalique. Ruby's thrilled. It's so light and graceful, it makes a quite ordinary room look absolutely—" Words failed.

"Lamps are right out, then, for our present."

"I suggest a case of cutlery."

"Bound volumes of something or other."

"A clock."

"A suit-case."

The telephone rang again: "Yes, Mr. Ernest?" Then: "Jay, Toby wants you."

"What, straight out, just like that? We all know he wants her, but in my young days," mocked Nelly Ann, "young men concealed their preference by a decent—"

"Oh, come off it," laughed Jay, and ran blushing downstairs to the younger partner's office, carrying her notebook.

She had started in the accounts room, and it was surprising she should not still be there, as her flair for figures far transcended her shorthand.

Mr. Macdonald, the chief accountant, had been delighted with her, though at first he had resented her entrance into a department already fully staffed. But the young son of the firm, Ernest Dudley, "Toby" to everybody in unofficial moments, discovered after a few months that it became wearisome to invent perpetual excuses for coming in search of Jay, so he wangled her into the more accessible stenographers' room. His father and his uncle had their private secretaries, but Toby, who was out on inspection a good deal, had no one permanently to work for him, and had been used to send for one girl or another to take down his letters and keep in order his desk, his accounts, his appointments, and all the minor troubles connected with his job. It was not many years ago that Mr. Ernest had still been Master Toby; he was really too young for a partnership, but his father was so proud of his only son and so anxious to fulfil the dignity of the firm's title: "Walker, Dudley & Son" (he had been "& son" himself, previously, to the founder of the firm), that he was saying, more or less: "Let the boy win his spurs," before Toby's university days were over.

"It's a funny thing"—Betty looked at the door through which Jay had just vanished with the effect of a leaf, a bubble, a drift of smoke; "the floating stenographer" they had named her, but good-naturedly—"It's a funny thing, but none of the Dudleys seem to object to this Jay and Toby business. We've all read diligently in our novelettes about the pretty typist tripping in from better days, and how there's always blue hell to pay when her employer's son falls for her. In fact, I never know how they manage to get it right by the last chapter. But the Dudleys are cooing over it like pigeons."

"What do you expect? They *are* pigeons. It's falling into a box of chocolate creams to get among that family; not an almond nor a bit of nougat in the whole box that you can get your teeth into."

"What about Walking Wilfred?"

"Yes. He's nougat. And he wasn't too keen on Jay. But he's only an uncle. All the same, luck for her that his liver broke down after she'd been here a month. When's he coming back? Does anyone know?"

"Month after next, I've heard. Just in time to forbid the banns."

"I don't see why he should. Jay is probably a good match even for Toby, if we Knew All."

Helen Mitford said suddenly:

"It was Jay who sent Ruby the Lalique lamp."

"Did she? Did she, Helen? Are you sure? How can you know, if it was anonymous?"

"I don't believe she did," remarked Betty, "because she forked out her five shillings for our united present, and she wouldn't have, if she was giving separately."

"Betty, my sweet, you must cultivate large ideas. If the girl's able to afford six or seven pounds for a Lalique glass figure, that wouldn't prevent her from chucking away an extra five shillings to keep herself from being suspected."

"But why shouldn't she say, if she'd sent it? She's given most of us heavenly presents. Look at Nelly Ann's blue enamel. But they were always quite frankly 'With love from Jay.'"

"She didn't want to embarrass the rest of us by giving so much more than we could afford."

"That makes her a bit too good to be true, doesn't it? I shall burst into tears in a moment."

"She *is* too good to be true." Helen abruptly put aside her knitting and got up from the low window-ledge. "I must fetch the Merlin Park Estate estimates." As she passed the others, a faint trail of very subtle, very expensive perfume brushed through the air. Betty sniffed it with knowing appreciation: "That's Guerlain's 'L'Heure Bleue,' or I'm a Dutchman. It's not like our Helen to be so fragrantly intoxicating. Do you think she's been consoling herself by getting at Ruby's trousseau scent?"

"Helen? Lord, no; rugged honesty is our watchword."

Rose Dixon, who was the most recent arrival in the accounts department, asked: "What are Nelly Ann's blue enamels? I never see her wearing them?"

The other girls shouted at the vision of Nelly Ann with a necklace of hairbrushes. And Jay's room-mate explained:

"I saw them in the window of The Gift Shop. My old toilet set was awful. You know what it is when you see something you want to scrunch, it's so attractive, and it gets on your mind and you can't talk of anything else. And then one day I came home and found them all laid out on the dressing-table. I was so stunned, I could hardly say thank you. But she stopped me, anyhow. She said my face was enough: the little fiend had actually got hold of my Kodak and was lying in wait with it; she caught me with my mouth wide open and my eyes rolling like saucers. She's a darling," finished Nelly Ann warmly.

"Are her own things luscious?"

"Lord, no. Tuppence plain, like all ours. And she kicks up a hell of a rumpus if we're in debt on the household bills. Says we've got to keep within our income."

"Overdoing it."

"Yes, these rich girls who come and live with the poor are always the most drastic. She must have been reading a lot," Betty continued, not aware that she was echoing Miss Matcham, for whom she would have felt supreme contempt; "political and sociological sort of stuff: The Economic Conditions of the Black-Coated Workers …"

"If you think, Betty my dear, that you've been a black-coated worker for the last hour and a half, you've done nothing but put a tick against three names and pick our pockets for Ruby's wedding-present. Whom I never liked either, alive, dead, or married."

Madame Roxane Guilbert was celebrating her sixtieth birthday. She was celebrating it by a hearty orgy of tears. She had been governess with the Carberrys for many years, so they were used to her Gallic temperament. A big rollicking woman like a symbolic figure of La Gloire in a pageant of France; a warm heart and lewd eyes; a lewdness which matched nothing in her soul nor indeed in her past, which had been a perfectly proper affair of *jeune fille bien élevée* a small *dot*, a *manage de convenance* and a *bon petit mari* killed in the War. That air of flamboyant lewdness, then, was an accident, but it materialized all that an Englishman had once hoped to encounter in Paris during that jovial period when it was still called Gay Paree. The Carberrys all adored Madame Guilbert. There is no French for the idiom: "being put upon," but Roxane did not need it; Roxane ran the house and Mrs. Carberry and Daffy and Clo and the servants and Nanny and any of the Dudley clan who happened to stray within her range, particularly Monsieur Norman himself, head of the firm and the family, but good-temperedly despised by her for his weakness, sweetness and lack of initiative with the ladies: *"un an de manage,* one son, Tobee, and one wife who die on her child's bed—*Parbleu,* is that enough for a tranquillity of twenty, thirty years to follow?" She was cheery, efficient, warm-hearted. She never preached to the young, but though she found no sermons in stones, she certainly and triumphantly found sex in everything; and much innocent enjoyment in believing the worst without a moment's hesitation, and broadcasting it under the conviction that the worst was the best. She was afraid of domestic animals and screamed when they came near her, which created some natural difficulties in a country house in the New Forest, full of children. The children ragged her and she ragged them back again, answering what were usually termed "embarrassing questions" so frankly and fluently that embarrassment died of neglect. Clo was her favourite in the family; and next, Clo's first cousin "M'sieu Tobee." She was a distant relation of the Duke—was it of Orleans or Bourbon?—who ought to be King of France. It was understood that she was privileged to weep on her birthday.

But this year, the 8th of June brought genuine disappointment. All her presents had been *pratique,* stout, excellent presents, durable presents; Madame Guilbert had thrown herself into one apparent ecstasy after another on receiving them, but it so happened that though she could use them all, she desired none.

Et quoi, alors? Was she an old woman that she should be given felicity in the guise of hot-water bottles and bedroom slippers? Was she a professor hankering for the Oxford Dictionary and a new spectacle-case? *"Ne suis-je pas femme?"*

Daffy and Clo knocked and rushed in simultaneously, followed by the younger tribe. They delivered two large boxes, one heavy, the other light, into Madame's hands: "By post. They've just come." And stood waiting while she opened them.

The first, in elaborate swathes and packings of sawdust and tissue paper, contained a pale green glass bowl; the second, masses and masses of lilies of the valley, fragrant and glamorous.

"*Ah, mon Dieu, les fleurs de lys de mon beau pays!*" exclaimed Madame, clasping her hands, their hands, any hands, with short intoxicated bursts of tears. It must be remembered again that she was a relation of the King of France: to send her lilies of the valley was like sending her Versailles and the Tuileries, embroidered banners and the pearls of Marie Antoinette.

The younger Carberrys eyed her with horror. It was not in their schedule that grown-ups should cry. Besides, there were always plenty of flowers in the garden and in the meadows beyond the garden; more than anyone in their senses could want. This was therefore a damfool birthday present.

Daffy bundled her sisters out of the room. Meanwhile, Clo was searching through the two boxes for a message,

"Here we are: *'Bonne fête et beaucoup d'amour, de Jasmine.'*"

"Oh, the dear little one," cried Madame, splashing the water from her ewer into the bowl, and caressing the delicate sprays as she untied them. "*'Beaucoup d'amour'*—we do not say that in our language, as you say 'much love,' whether it is love you feel or merely *amité*. You will remember that, Duffee, and you, Clo? And I will remember always the tender heart that could think of the birthday of a tiresome old French governess."

"You're not tiresome," swiftly from Daffy.

And: "You're not old," from Clo.

And that being arranged, they sat down upon the floor and babbled of their school-friend, Jay: how sweet she was and how generous to everyone; how surprised they had been when she arrived last autumn in quest of a job, any job they could find her; she did not seek favours, but hard work, for she had run away from home: ("Don't ask me why, please don't. I'd much rather not say. But somehow I must earn my own living and keep out of debt.")

Madame interrupted: "Yet it is not possible, no, that out of her salary she buy me these rare lilies of May, and the bowl that is like rippling water in the shade of the green willow at the end of your garden, and still that she can afford to clothe herself and eat herself and bed herself, yes?"

"She lives like a Spartan boy. She'd let the fox gnaw her side."

"And though Daffy and I have tried to give her things to make her more comfortable, she won't accept. She says: 'No—please don't, I'm quite all right, and I'd much rather not,' and then tells us something funny about the office to change the subject."

"She must have her own money still. Only she's so scrupulous, she won't live differently from the other girls in Uncle's firm. She's just like the princess who felt the pea under the eighteen mattresses, isn't she, Roxy?"

"*Mais non*, she is not so at all. That famous princess, she was a girl without breeding, or there would not have been all that fuss and so many mattresses and the groaning and the display. A true aristocrat would have said nothing of it, *mais rien du tout. Mais la petite Jasmine, c'est du vrai sang.* I feel for her a great affection, *une vraie tendresse.* If I had a child, a little one"—Madame Guilbert looked as voluptuously maternal as though she had borne at least a baker's dozen—"she would have resembled our Jasmine. When she marries, if it is from this house, it is I who will pin her veil *et les fleurs d'oranger.*"

It was delightedly taken for granted at Admiral's House by Fripp's Hard, that their first cousin Toby would presently propose to Jay and she would accept him, giving Daffy and Clo the opportunity to walk together as bridesmaids in pale yellow. They had discussed it, in fact, with everyone except the principals, and even Jay and Toby might not have escaped, had not Mrs. Carberry forbidden it. She would not admit that Daffy and Clo had any serious faults, but she allowed that their puppy clumsiness and their puppy gambols of affection, their exuberant leapings and their liability to overturn the work-basket and get their large paws caught in the wool, had occasionally to be restrained by adult discretion. Their Uncle Wilfred had once remarked with sardonic affection that they should have been boiled for four and a half minutes instead of for slightly under three.

So they beamed on the prospect of the marriage, without an atom of jealousy; and prepared to dress Jay for the Prince's Ball, like an exceptionally pretty pair of Ugly Sisters in a revised version of the legend of Cinderella.

"Mother heard from Uncle Wilfred this morning. He says that all the oaks in South Carolina are draped with something called Spanish Moss, and if he had anything to do with it he'd get in an army of unemployed to cut all the stuff away. Mummy said: 'Yes, but what's that got to do with us? I do wish your uncle didn't write such *scolding* letters.'"

"He'll be back next month," put in Clo. "I think Toby had better hurry up and marry Jay before then. He can manage Uncle Norman; we all can; a guinea-pig could manage Uncle Norman, he's so perfectly sweet. Besides, he'd love Jay for a daughter-in-law. But Uncle Wilfred's hard as nails. Daffy, isn't he hard?"

Daphne nodded. "Worldly," she agreed. "He tried to pretend at the beginning that Jay had been wangled into her job through favouritism, but he had to admit that her arithmetic was a credit to the old school, and quite up to form, even for his precious Walker, Dudley & Son."

"But he said to Mummy: 'She's after the boy.' I heard him. 'She's after the boy,' in that maddening 'you can't fool me' voice that elderly men like to use."

With the one exception of Wilfred Walker, the Dudley family were salt of the earth without any salt in their composition at all. Their mutual admiration was unbounded, except again in the case of Uncle Wilfred, who stood a little aloof and wished that Norman and his sisters, Lucy and Mary, and the girls and young Toby, and all their adherents, dependants and employees would stop growing roses over every lattice-work, and learn to see plain facts plain. He had no unreasonable objection, for instance, to the little girl whom Daphne and Clorinda had lugged in from their old school; and she was not, as he grimly suspected at first, a useless intruder. Nevertheless, he saw no purpose in squealing with joy when his cousin's only son fell for her like a ton of bricks. Time enough for Toby to settle down and marry in another ten years. Besides, she looked fragile enough to break if you dropped her. In his opinion, since little Blake came into Hampshire, the whole group, business and family, surrounding the Dudleys had become more juvenile and sillier. As some people are germ-carriers of certain diseases, so Jay seemed to carry and diffuse an infection of bird-song and dewfall which Wilfred Walker found maddening and unbusinesslike. But he had nothing against the girl except that instead of tramping about as though her feet gripped the solid earth, she moved as though gravity did not trouble her: "A handful of petals on the wind," Mary Carberry agreed sentimentally; "a swing without visible cords—"

"Don't be so absurd, Mary; how can a swing be without cords? It would be a board suspended in mid-air. And what's that got to do with our new junior accountant? 'Pon my word, I don't know what's got at you all. Norman was always fatuous over a curl of golden hair, but really you and your girls might show a bit of common, decent, sensible jealousy in the matter. I tell you, she's after Toby. If you won't see it, you won't. Well, good-bye." And off he went for his health on a six months' holiday to the Western world. He had no capacity for sunning himself sweetly without thought of the morrow, so he varied the boredom by picking up oddments in the way of the latest air-conditioning equipment, insulation, shop fronts and reinforced concrete designs; and hoped, without much justification, that on his return the house of Dudley would have ceased to wobble in every breeze.

The lilies of the valley, were all arranged in water now, a shallow pool of delicate white bells with scalloped edges; Madame Guilbert proudly ran backwards to regard them from every angle. Then she addressed Daffy and Clo, still squatting on their heels on the rug. "I tell you it would be better that they marry at once, those two, and not only because the good uncle he returns, but presently is the month of July, of August, *la grande chaleur, lune de miel*, honeymoon—"

Daffy chanted: "'Honeymoon, harvest moon—'"

"But when the young blood is restless and there is no honeymoon, what of the harvest *après la chaleur*. ..."

Madame Guilbert was enjoying a vicarious orgy, with Daffy and Clo listening, so innocent, so attentive, so very, very foolish, so puzzled at this symbolism of moons and harvests, "You 'ave both read with me de Musset? *Tu le rappelle, Duffee?—'Poète, prends ton luth, le vin de la jeunesse fermente cette nuit dans les veines de Dieu. Mon sein est inquiet, la volupté l'oppresse—' Reponds, alors, vite;* from where is that took?"

"George Eliot," replied Daffy, flustered. "No, I mean George Sands. Roxy, do you think Clo and I ought to speak to Toby? Clo has always had a lot of influence with him, though she's four years younger. Tactfully, of course, and not mentioning anything about honeymoons, nor bringing you into it; just an encouraging hint that he's to hurry up and go at it. Or would you like to tackle him, as you're French?"

"*Mes enfants*, it would not be *convenable*; I am not her mother—"

"But she hasn't a mother who's any good to her any more. Her mother persecuted her."

"Yes, she hated the whole idea of Jay getting experience among the proletariat so as to really understand The Problem. She's the type of woman who would have said, why don't they eat cake? I think it was noble of Jay to break away; she's got much more character than I've ever had."

"Or than I've ever had."

"No, you've got miles more character than me, hasn't she, Roxy?"

Daffy and Clo wrangled amiably for some little while, bestowing large chunks of character on each other. Madame Guilbert interrupted: "Did you ever see *la mère de* Jasmine, at the school where she was with you together?"

Daffy knit her brows with an effort to remember: "I think so, at one prize-giving. A large brazen-looking woman with swaying hips; platinum hair and dripping with furs, a sort of Boadicea, quite different from Jay. Unless that was someone else. But we were never asked home to her house, though we were her best friends."

Sergeant Dale, door-keeper at Walker, Dudley & Sons, was surprised when he reached his home one evening to feel the air quivering with music. He had a wife and a sister-in-law and a mother on the premises, and four children, the eldest twelve, but not one of them played any musical instrument, so that together they could not have formed the orchestra now sending waves of melody through the kitchen door and through the front door and out into the semi-rural street, its trees dripping and flaming from the wash of an April shower. Sergeant Dale was dripping and flaming as well: for he disapproved of all surprises; he liked duty and plans and organization and a sober, decent pace to life. But April, as he frequently said, was a ticklish month and interfered with pace and plans and organization; with everything, in fact, save duty.

And now what was this freakish spontaneous burst of music to greet his homecoming, instead of a savoury burst of steak and onions? Had someone lent them a gramophone? He didn't hold with borrowing. One day when he could afford it, he meant to give them a gramophone, second-hand, perhaps. Ben, his eldest, was crazy on music, you couldn't get him away from the band when there was a band. Still, no money in that.

He flung open the door. The setting sun blazed in through the small tightly shut window, past the curtains and the geraniums and the ornaments; blazed on to the group of children standing entranced round the portable wireless set in the middle of the kitchen table. The three women in black and faded brown and dingy purple formed an outer ring; they still had their occupations checked in their hands, the one a pudding bowl, another her knitting, forgetting to put them down when the music had burst so gloriously from the walnut box and streamed through the room.

Standing a little aside as though she had nothing to do with the conjuring trick, her mouth quivering into a soft smile of pure joy as she watched Ben, was a young lady with fair hair and a shabby coat, whom he recognized as Miss Blake who had been employed with his firm for only a few months and who had never given him any trouble as some of them did, goodness knows.

London Regional tactfully chose to bring its hour of B.B.C. orchestra to a close just as the sergeant was beginning to wonder if anybody was going to take notice of him ever again, a man in his own house!

Benny moved a little nearer to the wonderful box. His eyes were starry, his hair clung damply to his forehead, he could hardly breathe, he was in heaven. And it was not going to be taken away, this kingdom of harmony; he could release it whenever he chose; it had been given to him, Benny Dale, for his own.

"Oh, George," explained Mrs. Dale, a little worried in advance, for her husband was a fine man and had won many medals which decorated his chest, but he did discover so many things that were not right for the children, and so very few that were. And when there's four in the family besides Mother and poor Florrie, and you have to manage and not owe a penny … "Oh, George, Miss Blake has brought our Benny a wireless same as we've always wanted and you promised to get him some day. Isn't it kind of her? We was all listening," she added rather superfluously.

Sergeant Dale was a little slow on the uptake, but he always liked to have things accurate. "It was a gramophone I meant," he corrected his wife laboriously. "I never thought of a wireless set. I never was one for mechanics. And it wasn't a promise: perhaps, I said, *perhaps*, if you're a good boy—"

Ben, too dazed to be aware of menace trembling in the air, put out one finger and ran the dial around until it found music again from another station. He could do this all day and all night now, if he chose. It was his to control. He crooned a Te Deum of joy with the invisible crooner inside the music-box.

Jay said anxiously: "I hope you don't mind, sergeant? I didn't know who Benny was, when—"

"He didn't ask for it, I hope, Miss? None of my kids—we never have been beggars, me and the missus, and I hope we never will. If he asked—"

"Oh, no. No, of course he didn't. It was all me, all my fault." She might have been pleading forgiveness for a crime. "I saw him leaning against the railings, listening, outside a house in St. Michael's Square. The window was open and the wireless was playing, and then suddenly they switched it off before he had finished listening." How could she make this burly stolid lump of six-foot-two understand the awfulness of that blank helpless look on the child's face, standing outside the window and beyond the railings while rich people, privileged people, turned music on and turned music off according to their whim. "So I just said: 'What's your name?'—and came here tonight," she finished, careful not to add: "And I do wish you'd stayed away." It had been so lovely and exciting, to enter Benny's home swinging Benny's miracle in one hand.

But Sergeant Dale was not a cruel father. He just wanted to make sure that everything was in order, that the new acquisition had not been solicited, and that gratitude had been duly and coherently placed on record.

"It's more than kind of you, Miss, to think of my little chap, when a trumpet would have done—" He was a bit confused as to his own meaning, which was that Miss Blake, for her position as one of the junior typists to the firm, must have spent far too much and out of all proportion in giving this present to the door-keeper's son.

"Ben, don't stand there staring as though it was conjuring tricks. I hope you thanked the young lady proper?"

Ben's enormous brown eyes moved slowly from the radio to his father, from his father to Jay.

"Oh, please, yes, he did," cried Jay, dismayed. She did not want to hear actual words of thanks, ever. It was intoxication enough to see with her own eyes the glamour she could bring.

But one of the sergeant's four children was spiteful, the one next in age to Benny; Gert did not deem it fair that the music-box had not been parcelled out into four exact shares, one for each of them, so she cried out: "Benny hasn't said thank you, dad, not once. I waited for 'im to say it same as you taught us we should, but 'e didn't: 'e just took it as though 'e had a right."

"Benny my boy, I'm surprised—" began the sergeant in a ponderous crescendo.

But Jay was already in flight. She ran to save, not herself, but Benny. Once there had been a rich little girl and a poor little girl; a benefactress on the one side, and on the other the humiliation of having to receive, always to receive, and say thank you in front of everyone.

Chapter Two

Toby Dudley had battled through a week in the rain without Jay, and it had been unendurable. This was how he put it. Actually, he had been impatiently inspecting the restoration of a large dilapidated early Georgian house, some forty miles away. The owners had not been satisfied with the progress made and were venting it on the foreman. Norman Dudley thought it wise that Toby should remain on the spot for a while. The boy took nothing seriously and must learn that business meant to plod instead of to play; he had a good sense of period, though inclined to be impatient with the mechanical drudgery of estimates and specifications.

Jay was not officially Toby's private secretary, although more and more boldly he used her in that capacity instead of sending discriminately for Nelly Ann Ryman or Helen Mitford. But he could not go so far as to take her along with him wherever he went. And it had been bad weather all the time; not that he minded; sunny weather was wasted unless he and Jay were together. But now he was home again, it was Saturday afternoon, and the heavy July rain was being blown towards the west.

He was somewhat mollified when his Aunt Lucy, who kept house for him and his father, was able to inform him without even waiting for him to ask, that Jay was spending the weekend over at Fripp's Hard with the Carberrys, as she often did. Aunt Lucy, like her brother Norman, her sister Mary, her nieces Daphne and Clorinda, Madame Guilbert, the children, the dogs and all the rest of the unworldly clan, smiled benignly on the romance and put up no impediment. There were even moments when Toby revolted against so much tender encouragement; could have wished the air less balmy. His manhood was like an army in weak piping times of peace, longing to test its strength. Part him from Jay? Just let them try. But nobody tried. Daffy and Clo were even a trifle irritating, the way they continually patted themselves on the head for having brought him and Jay together. Jay was exquisite. Jay was incredible. But what a pity that he, Toby, could not be the only one to know it and defend his knowledge against prejudice and intolerant attack: "I don't care if she *is* only a typist in my father's firm—" and so forth.

They were not yet actually engaged. Again Toby was conscious of a slight disinclination to face the pelted confetti and goodwill that would be immediately showered on them. Besides, Jay was only nineteen, and measured even younger by her frail childish build, though she always declared, laughing, that it was deceptive, and that she was strong as an athlete.

Still for once he did not object to Aunt Lucy making courtship easier with her obliging information. No sense in wasting a July afternoon in search of Jay, when she was anchored at his cousins' home.

Toby walked up bare-headed through the rain. His red hair was brilliant against the dripping background as he came across the lawn and softly through the French windows, for he had a glimpse of an equally brilliant orange sweater sitting over in the bow window, back turned towards him, absorbed in a jigsaw puzzle. He knew that sweater well; had even seen portions of it left on his office desk with two pink knitting-needles stuffed through a huge ball of wool, when Jay had been suddenly summoned away by Mr. Macdonald. "You're colour-blind," he had teased her on her return, "or you couldn't use magenta needles on orange wool."

"Why not? They're Russian ballet colours. Once I saw them mixed up and falling down a wall."

"The whole Ballet?"

"Flowering creepers. The two colours looked heavenly, twined together. It was near Monte Carlo."

"Dear me, Miss Blake, have you travelled?"

"Oh yes, Mr. Ernest, I'm quite a traveller. Monte Carlo before I was fourteen."

"It broadens the mind, doesn't it? And don't call me 'Mr. Ernest.'"

"Mr. Ernest suits you."

So she had finished the sweater while he was away? What cheek. He felt tenderly that he had a personal stake in it, and should have been beside her to draw out the magenta needles and burn them in the flames between the carved sides of the Adam mantelpiece; then to inspect the finished work and say with an imitation of Mr. Macdonald's slightly carping Scotch accents: "It's nae sae bad, but there's a muckle o' drapped stitches in it."

He stole up behind her, absorbed in fitting together the pieces of the half-finished jigsaw. ("Speaking dispassionately," said Toby to himself, and no young man had ever been less dispassionate, "I should say she's the prettiest sight of this century, and a new wonder of the world.") Aloud, he remarked over her shoulder: "That entire section lifts much higher and becomes part of the coach on the other side. At least, it would if you hadn't got it upside down. Here—like this."

"Oh, *Toby!* Toby, you pig, now the whole thrill has gone." But how lucky he had given her cause to rail at him, so that she need not say "So you're back," casually, fighting to keep the startled gladness out of her voice. "I've been at it ever since lunch doing the donkey-work, and you break in and take the profits."

"Donkey-work's right." Toby's heart was thumping so hard that it got in the way of his throat and voice. "Anyone but a donkey would know the difference between a horse's harness and a leaded window. Look," he reversed two pieces.

"Oh—yes. Yes, perhaps. May I help, Toby dear, or is it your jigsaw now?" For he had seated himself in her vacated chair and taken control of the whole thing. "You've done this one before; you must have; nobody could—Oh, Toby, *not* that bit; I'd been saving that one specially to put in last of all."

He took no notice of her cries and revilings, but went sternly on. He was a handsome youngster in an ugly freckled sort of way; well-built, flaming red hair, brows bumping forward over light blue eyes, a wide attractive smile, good bones, hands that seemed to have a nervous sense of whatever they were at without fumbling. He could hear Jay's soft breathing as she leant against him, grabbing wildly for bits of the jigsaw, trying to force them into crevices where they did not belong, crying out with rage when a lordly Toby took them from her and laid them down in their proper place in the pattern. Presently he dumped a parcel on top of the puzzle without any more apparent emotion than if it were a piece of cheddar cheese. (Will she like it? Will she hate it? Will she call me "Toby darling"? Will she wear it always? Was I a fool not to have chosen the little peacock instead?) "Here—take it."

"For me?" whispered Jay. She broke the sealing-wax, unfolded the paper, and opened the small cardboard box; resting on cotton-wool was a pretty diamond clip in the shape of a sailing-vessel.

"Oh, Toby, it's so sweet. It's so pretty. You're so sweet. But Toby—"

"Like it?" stolidly. "I don't know why you amateur jig-sawers can't do the frame first and then fill in the livestock. It's the only possible way. Now when I—"

"Toby."

He swung round at the note of distress in her voice.

"Toby, I can't keep this, honestly I can't."

Disappointment made you heavy as lead, thought Toby, till it was a wonder you didn't sink right through the ground into the cellar.

"Sorry. It was stupid of me. Never could choose the right thing. There was a peacock—But perhaps you don't care for any sort of clip. I looked at cigarette-cases, but this was something you could wear—"

"I wish I could. It isn't that I don't love it. It isn't that I prefer peacocks or cigarette-cases or anything else. Only—please don't, Toby; *please* don't give me presents."

"Why not?"

"I don't like taking them."

"You're ridiculous sometimes."

Her eyes were full of tears, they felt hot as flame.

"I'm not ridiculous."

"Yes, you are. Living in a cell with a hair shirt, that's what you'd like to do. It's—it's ungenerous not to accept."

"I'm not ungenerous."

"You keep on saying you're not everything. I'd like to buy you whole arcades full of diamonds."

"I know. That's just it. This *is* diamonds. It's valuable."

"It isn't really valuable; only a bit of trumpery I picked up with my eyes shut."

But Jay knew. Her instinct could tell what was trumpery and what wasn't.

"You don't understand."

"I always swore that the first time a girl said 'You don't understand,' I'd leave her."

"Leave her, then. Turn on your heel with an oath. Do what you swore."

"Jay—dear. What about your birthday? Will you take it then? When is it?"

She shook her head. "I'm a girl in your father's employ, and—"

"My God, Jay, you *can't* be as prim and old-fashioned as that; you simply can't; you're behaving like a heroine in a play, A silly play," he amended.

A moment of silent tension.

No. She thrust the little ship back into the box, closed it, slipped it into Toby's pocket. Then she flung her arms round his neck and kissed him full on the mouth. She had never done that before.

"Oh, Jay!" he gasped.

"Look at the sky. Blue. It cleared up behind our backs while we were quarrelling. Come on, Toby, let's go out. Let's go down to the estuary."

She rushed on to the verandah, leapt the steps and across the lawn, calling to the two sealyhams, Hengist and Horsa, who followed her at full pelt, yelping and somersaulting with ecstasy that the dullness of the day was over. In a moment Toby had caught her up:

"You devil. My sweet."

Madame Guilbert saw them, as she stood on the schoolroom balcony shading her eyes from the fierce rays, and sped them with a lusty shout which the wind shredded to tatters before it reached them; but Toby looked back and saw the old governess gesticulate like the goddess of procreation in a French mythological farce, and laughed and shouted: "*Bon soir*, Roxy!" A dip in the water-meadow hid them from sight. But Madame Guilbert had had a glimpse of Jay which caused her to sigh gustily, reflecting that at no moment of her own circumspect maidenhood could she ever have looked so impudent in happiness as the girl running free in her grey trousers and orange sweater, the sealyhams twirling and tumbling at her heels. Jay did not mind how nor where her hair was blown, nor the sun beating into her eyes; she did not carry a wrap in careful provision lest she should be cold later on; she had no need to bother about high heels that might turn her ankle unless she tripped warily: all these rueful handicaps which were the self-imposed burden of middle-aged and elderly ladies like Madame Guilbert. And even when she had been, like Jay, at the mating age, forty years ago, her courtship had been *comme il faut* according to her period and her parents' convictions; her proper little fiancé instead of pursuing her madly through the long grass to the water's edge, had stayed in the salon and asked permission to woo her chastely, by the sundial. Had it been good, had it been bad, *la surveillance?* Roxane could not tell. Pastorals in Dresden china. She sighed again, and returned to the empty schoolroom, hoping that this crazy shepherd and nymph of the twentieth century would remember at least that the grass was wet when they flung themselves impulsively headlong, seeking the earth, as she knew they must sooner or later. If not today, tomorrow, when it would rain again, *bien sûr*. Her bosom felt warm with protection, laced with envy; restlessly she wandered downstairs in search of company, and passing the butler, Norton, threw him a smile of such blended roguery, such mysterious significance, that it startled both his manhood and his disapproval. He was used to Madame Guilbert, and he had fought in Flanders and could read foreigners like a book, but you could never be sure what they were up to. Better be careful.

"Roxy," said Mrs. Carberry in the drawing-room, "I've just had to speak to Norton severely about the silver, and I'm still trembling. Did he seem upset when you passed him just now?"

"I did not see him," Madame declared with perfect truthfulness.

Jay and Toby, reunited, were in high spirits which had to be worked off somehow. They saw Daffy and Clo sailing on the estuary with the Bishop's two sons, in Toby's boat, the *Good Fortune*, and shouted insults at them when they jibed standing and nearly overturned.

Then they found someone's motor-boat, *Ohi*, tied up in the bright ginger-coloured rushes, in the process of repainting, and abandoned for a week-end; its spawn was beside it: "Tender to Ohi." Jay and Toby seized the paint-pot and brushed in the word "Be" in front of "Tender to Ohi." It looked unutterably wistful in the sunset, and they went off rocking with laughter,

"I'd like to have a boat named after me!" cried Jay. "I can't imagine anything more exciting or complimentary. Only one would have to die early, so that people would cry every time they looked at the *Jasmine*. But it oughtn't to be *Jasmine*," she babbled, while Toby privately resolved to buy a yacht as soon as finances would allow and even sooner, merely to please her with the christening. "It ought to be 'The Susan Jane' or 'The Saucy Kate' or—"

"Those are fishing-boats. You couldn't call a yacht Saucy anything. Look here, I'll tell you what we'll do; we'll re-christen the *Good Fortune*; people often wash out one name on their boats and give them another.

The *Jasmine. Jasmine the Second*," he repeated softly, trying it over to get the flavour on his lips.

She cried with some dismay: "But I'm not the second, I'm the first. Or have you been friends with another Jasmine?"

"Of course not." Nevertheless he preferred "Jasmine the Second": it was more sophisticated; "We'll have a special ceremony."

A flash of blue rose from the reeds and streaked across the water. "A kingfisher! Look, Jay!" Then he laughed. "I apologize."

"Why?"

"An hour ago I nearly said you reminded me of a kingfisher. But I'd forgotten; they've got awful figures and short legs and big heads. You're like—"

"Never mind what I'm like," said Jay. "Like a girl in an orange sweater, I suppose. I do adore not living in London. I do love it here. I do love Saturday afternoons when it's been raining and then the sun comes out. I do love water gurgling and chuckling and slapping the posts. I do love to see a great liner moving round the curve and through the lawn at the end of your father's garden; it's so absurd: you happen to look up from tennis, and there's the *Berengaria*, huge and stately. I do love living at the sea-end of Trumpet Street. I love the paddle steamer clunking along early in the morning, and a whole bunch of cranes leaning together against the sky just before it gets dark; and the colour of the old warehouses, red-brown and purple-brown with faded green shutters. And I love dancing at the Pier Pavilion and sitting in the little Museum Garden and feeling like Ann Boleyn."

"What a collection. Didn't you ever come to the New Forest for holidays when you were a kid?"

"No. Molly and I used to go to Clifford's Bay."

"Is Molly your sister?"

Jay nodded. "She's on the stage."

"Is she? I believe I've heard of her. Molly Blake. What's she in now?"

"She's on tour in *Naughts and Crosses*, up north somewhere. It ran for nearly a year in the West End."

"Are you fond of her? You tell me such funny things about yourself,

Jay. No information. I'm left with nothing except that you once went to Monte Carlo, are good at figures, and get excited when you see a Cunarder in the garden."

"Isn't that enough? I think I could put those together and make a girl."

"Yes, but what sort of a girl?"

"An ass of a girl, Toby."

Chapter Three

One might suppose that 2 a.m. would be an hour of remorse and terror, lying awake and remembering that next week the auditors were due on their yearly visit. She was almost bound to be exposed. Yet she was neither apprehensive nor penitent. She did not turn and twist on a feverish pillow, but slipped her left hand under her cheek and lay there smiling a little into the darkness, in a debonair reverie which bore no relation whatever to reality.

It had been so lovely, giving from her abundance, giving everyone just whatever they wanted, not caring for the price, but only to know that save for her this special fragment of happiness could never have existed; more glorious than any glory she had ever imagined, though she had always longed to play Lady Bountiful.

And it had all happened so naturally, as though it could not be otherwise: hearing about poor little Sally's bunt balloon, and the delicious thought darting through her mind: "I'll bring her a whole bunch, one of every colour there is." Balloons did not cost much, and that day was Friday when, as Molly would say, "The ghost walked." Sally's face, Sally's eyes—Oh, not a doubt about it, if you had the gift of divining so exactly what was wanted, it would be unfair, ungenerous, not to use it. Nelly Ann's blue-enamel toilet set, Madame Soboleff's caviar and vodka on Easter Day, Benny Dale's radio set, and flowers, flowers everywhere all the rime, flung lavishly, heaps of flowers, a glorious perfumed profusion in all directions, wherever they could bring solace or intoxicate. For Jay herself was intoxicated by the ardour of giving. She could not stop, and she did not see why she should. Balloons were cheap, they could be given out of her three pounds fifteen a week salary; but for violins and Lalique glass and flagons of L'Heure Bleue, funds had to be provided. She saw herself as a modern Robin Hood: take from the rich to give to the poor. Everyone had admired Robin Hood. He was a sort of gallant saint.

If, reflected Jay, she had bought one thing for herself, kept one penny of the stolen pounds, some question of dishonesty might justifiably arise. But she had been scrupulous and exact to spend only within her income, as she had been taught from childhood. Even Toby's little diamond ship she had refused. It was such a pretty sparkling little ship, she would have liked it to pin on to her best thin summer frock, the one that clung and floated, the light soft green of baby ferns. She could have clipped it just where, the folds crossed, not far from her heart: the little ship that to her was Toby written in diamonds. But it wouldn't do; it had cost too much; it would have been wrong to accept it; at least one knew what was right and wrong, so it was no good pretending one didn't

What a summer it had been, what a light, shimmering summer of bells and balloons and flying gold. Until this summer, she had not even begun to live. Like a happy little colt, immune from jealousy as St. Bernard was immune from rain under an invisible umbrella, Jay ran through fantastic meadows as though they were safe as the home paddock.

Yet during the past seven months Jay had been robbing the firm of amounts that varied between five shillings and twenty pounds at a time.

Take from the rich and give to the poor. Was she deceiving herself? If it had been only that, would she have felt so flat and listless on the

one occasion when she tried sending a gift anonymously? She never repeated that experiment; no kick to be had from it. You hated actual thanks, but even kings used to toss purses of gold to the populace who never bothered where the money originated.

And now it was July, and the auditors were arriving next week to go through the books at Walker, Dudley & Son. Yet Jay did not quake, nor see the prison walls looming; nor did it occur to her to escape while there was still time, before she might be stopped. On the contrary, a gambler, she was thrilled by the magnitude of her stakes.

Toby would stand by her through thick and thin. It did not matter in the least if it were found out that the accounts had been twitched crooked here and there: "I didn't keep a penny. I made the poor happy." Her back to the wall, her words simple and eloquent: "Yes, I did it for them, and of course I'm not sorry. You can do what you like to me."

And he: "I'll stand by you, darling."

Reverie was hot and gay. She was Robin Hood, the friend of the oppressed. She was the King of France distributing largesse. She was a profligate, recklessly gambling for others to scoop up her winnings. "There's no need to drag you into this, Toby. I can face it alone." ... "Darling, you re the bravest girl I've ever known and the most generous. How can you imagine that I'd give you up just because there's danger? If you're not afraid of danger, nor am I." ... "I'm not afraid."

Bells and balloons in the air. Smiling, Jay fell peacefully asleep. Silly to stay awake, just because the auditors were coming next week.

Chapter Four

←→

Madame Guilbert sat between Daffy and Clo at the back of the court under the gallery. It was strange to find herself at the Assizes of an English cathedral town, not only a spectator but deeply concerned, personally interested, terribly, afraid for one of the accused. There were six cases, and Jay's was the one before the last: "No. 5. Blake, Jasmine." She read it in the Calendar of Prisoners which the Under-Sheriff had handed her. He was a friend of the household and had often dined with Mrs. Carberry at Admiral's House, so he had found them good seats downstairs among the witnesses and the potential jurymen instead of upstairs in the gallery with the mere spectators. Mrs. Carberry had refused to come. She had said: "I can't, Roxane. It would be too painful; that poor silly girl. I was fond of her, we all were. We would have welcomed her as Toby's wife, and all the while she was doing this to him: making out false expense sheets in his name; getting his signature in all the wrong places; it's incredible."

Mais oui, it was incredible. To be sitting here watching for *la petite* Jasmine to come up those stairs from the cells: *la petite* Jasmine who had sent her that great bowl of *fleurs de lys* for her birthday, a gift so subtle, so sympathetic. But how could they know then that the money which had been spent on the *fleurs de lys* and all the other beautiful presents which the generous young girl had scattered about, had been robbed from her lover? *"Bonne fête et beaucoup d'amour, de Jasmine."* The bad French had acquired a special pathos. Jasmine whom they had loved so tenderly, who had always been so sweet, so gay, so much a child of the family:

"No. 5. Blake, Jasmine … Offence … on a day between the 15th day of April 1935 and the 31st day of June 1935 at Southampton did fraudulently convert to her own use or benefit certain property, that is to say ten pounds nine shillings and fourpence in money entrusted to her by Ernest Dudley in order that she the said Jasmine Blake might pay or deliver the same to John Edward Jones, stationer. ..."

Madame Guilbert did not wish to go on reading that terrible list of charges, but she could not help herself:

"On a day in May 1935 at Southampton, forging a document purporting to be a Bankers' cheque and Order for the payment of thirteen pounds eleven shillings and fivepence, drawn by Ernest Dudley ..."

Ernest Dudley; that was Monsieur Tobee. Toby had fallen in love with *la petite* Jasmine. They had been such a happy boy and girl, running hand-in-hand across the wet lawn. Madame Guilbert, remembering how she had stood on her balcony and watched them and had wept with pleasure at their happiness, now wept again more bitterly at the betrayal of Toby.

"Don't, Roxy. You mustn't, here," whispered Clo fiercely.

Roxane dabbed her eyes with her handkerchief and sniffed loudly; and Daffy on her other side, less fierce than Clo, also whispered "Roxy, *please* try not to. Listen; there are the trumpets—That means the Judge is arriving."

The fanfare of trumpets for an instant demolished the sense of chilly grey reality which was pressing down upon Madame Guilbert's heart. They sounded nearer now; just outside. They sounded inspiriting; trumpets meant glory and romance and pageantry. Perhaps, after all, the law which provided trumpets would not be too hard on *la petite* Jasmine. The Clerk of the Assize and a group of counsel in the well stood up, their faces turned expectantly towards the door by which the Judge's procession was to enter. The rest of the Court also stood up. Madame Guilbert wondered in a flurried way if she should curtsy; she had forgotten to ask; now it was too late; already the Under-Sheriff had appeared carrying a long staff with ivory carved top. The Judge was a splendid figure with his mediaeval scarlet robes, his flat three-cornered hat, a full periwig with formal white curls from the period of Marlborough framing that broad handsome judicial face. The High Sheriff clanked behind him in uniform with scarlet and silver frogs. He carried a sword. His face, too, was familiar to Madame Guilbert, both from the Carberrys' dinner-table and from various hunting-prints and portraits of colonels and brigadier-generals which the Carberrys and Dudleys hung on their walls and never looked at. The Mayor in his robes; the Judge's Marshal; now they were all seated. Madame Guilbert, had she known the idiom, would have said that British justice was easy on the eye. She was deeply impressed by all the subsequent ceremonial of the first day of the sitting, when the Clerk of the Assize chanted a long highly flavoured piece about God and King George and the Lord Chancellor, and the counsel bowed low to the Judge, and the Judge, the Hon. Sir Piers Layton, Knight, gravely returned the gesture with a flourish of his three-cornered hat. Then he swept out again with the High Sheriff, the Chaplain, the Under-Sheriff, the Marshal, and the Judge's clerk.

"What does he want to go out for now, before he's done anything?" plaintively asked a woman sitting near Madame Guilbert; and the man beside her replied in a tone of tolerant amusement: "Gone to change into something a bit more simple for everyday."

Madame Guilbert noticed that the pattern of the wigs formed by the counsel's heads as they bent together and conversed in eager professional undertones was a patchwork of clean white and dark dirty-grey. Feeling a little more vivacious since she had seen the Judge's face, which, stern though it was, was lacking in all cruelty or self-satisfaction, she remarked to Daffy: "*Regardez donc,* that one there, *là bas,* laughing at a joke. It is time he should buy himself a new wig. Feelthy hair."

But Daphne Carberry at least knew better than this. She explained to their obstreperous French governess that the older and more experienced counsel were very proud of their seasoned wigs and clung to them madly until they actually fell to pieces on their heads: "The clean wigs are still babies on the job; they're longing for them to get 'feelthy.'"

"*Tiens,*" Madame Guilbert turned from Daffy to Clo. "*C'est rigolo.* You 'ear, Clo? *C'est rigolo, ça.*"

But Clo affected not to hear. She refused to be involved in any conversation with her sister. The fact that Madame Guilbert sat between them was significant of the havoc which Jay had worked in the Dudley and Carberry households. All their lives the sisters had been inseparable; it was as much a treat for them to sit next to each other and have their intimate whisperings and jokes about whatever was going on as if they had not met for years. But when the shock of Jay's arrest burst on them and they realized that the pretty friend whom they had adored and helped, and desired no credit nor thanks for helping, was simply a thief who had defrauded their uncles' firm, they had clung together and been horrified and utterly miserable in perfect accord. But then the question had arisen of their cousin Toby's reaction to what had happened; and here, for the first time in their lives Daffy and Clo could not find it possible to agree. It was the end of their unity, for Daffy remained loyal to romantic friendship; she burst out with sentiments of such incredible foolishness that even Madame Guilbert could not remain a partisan. She was furious with Toby for "ratting"; she declared he should have stuck to Jay through thick and thin; that his love was pretty weak and rotten if it couldn't stand up to whatever she had done, poor darling. "In fact, it's not what I'd call love at all. It was just passion."

But Clo, somewhat to her own amazement, discovered in herself a fundamental integrity too strong for her to accept this attitude towards the whole dreadful affair. Just because she and Daffy had been responsible for getting Jay a place in the family firm, just because they had seen Jay as flawless and a darling, and their whole-hearted delight had encouraged the prospect of Jay married to their idolized cousin Toby, so she was now all the more outraged at Jay's betrayal of so much loving trust. She refused to be pitiful: "Toby's quite right. It wasn't what she did, it was the way she did it."

"You're hard. You don't know about temptation."

"Yes, I do. And I'm not hard. I can't understand you, Daffy."

"And I can't understand Toby."

"I can. He's hurt to death. Why, she exploited him, that was what was so awful. She exploited his being in love with her. If she had only broken the till and taken the money, that's different. But because he trusted her to fill in cheques and make out expense sheets and things … He was her cats-paw. Do you think that's pleasant for someone as decent as Toby to have to remember for the rest of his life? A fat lot of good, Uncle Norman sending him away. It'll follow him all round the world. He'll never be the same again. He'll be bitter. He'll be a sceptic. Perhaps he'll hate girls always, because they'll all remind him of Jay. Do you remember his face," Clo's voice shook, "do you remember his face when he came round to us that day, just after he'd heard?"

But Daffy remained stubborn:

"It's all very well. But if he'd *really* loved her, he wouldn't let Uncle Norman send him round the world. He'd stay till she came out again."

Nothing could budge either from her conviction. Madame Guilbert agreed a little with both, sometimes with neither. Always she tried to keep the peace. It was desperately hard work. She would be glad when this trial was over; it was tension gathered to its most unbearable moment. Toby, under stress, had revealed himself more the cousin of Clo than of Daphne. The auditors' revelations had been a ghastly shock to the boy; he had been bewildered, frantic, out of his mind; but there had been no question, once he had been assured of Jay's guilt, of doing the romantic act and "standing by her through thick and thin," as radiantly visualized by Jay herself, and later by Daffy. His girl was a wrong 'un and that was all there was to it. He had been duped into robbing his own firm; his father's and his uncle's and his own. That they had been so gentle about it, even his Uncle Wilfred, made him feel worse, not better. They had made him a partner in spite of his raw youth, and because of him they had lost over seventy pounds, not that that mattered as a sum of money, but it was through him.

He would have to cut her out altogether.

Jay had pleaded guilty before the magistrate, following the discovery of her theft, so now there was no need for Toby to be in court. He was only a conditional witness and had not been called. Directly the trial was over, he was due to leave the country for the good old-fashioned cure of a trip round the world to make him forget.

His father, who had from the first been fond of Jay and prophesied she would be a ray of sunshine in the house, and other sentiments equally characteristic of kindly, charming old muddlers, was profoundly grieved at the catastrophe, refused for some time to believe it, and even then would never have consented to prosecute but for the businesslike insistence of his brother-in-law and partner, Wilfred Walker, who had just returned from America when the auditors made their discovery. Walker was not in the least vindictive in the matter, but, on the other hand, as a good citizen and practical man, now that his original opinion of Jay had been justified, he sturdily refused to allow any lachrymose nonsense to stand in the way of what the firm would normally have done to any girl in their employ found stealing from them.

Jay had refused bail and declared that she wanted no counsel to defend her. Since her arrest, she had been alternately wildly excited and no less wildly silent, in that her silence only seemed to conceal a sort of animated reverie which went on and on creating heroic solutions to her predicament. Apparently, though she pleaded guilty, she had no idea that in terms of austere reality she had done anything wrong. She kept on asking for Toby. Then at last, on hearing that Toby not only would not see her but was about to leave England for an absence of months or even years, she dropped like a lead plummet from her exalted state, turned sullen and unresponsive, and put up a dead resistance to any attempts by her friends to comfort or help her.

"We must send for the mother, of course," said Mrs. Carberry and Mrs. Dudley and Aunt Lucy and Madame Guilbert, all deeply distressed and anxious. The mother came down, was met by Mrs. Carberry, taken to see Jay, but met with no more success than the others in rousing her from her mood of stupefaction which was the effect of too rapid a transition from the gay stained-glass-window fantasy of bells and balloons, love and popularity, Lady Bountiful and little princess, meadows of flowers and white sails on the river, to a grim metamorphosis of harsh iron and cold stone.

"She is *farouche*," remarked Madame Guilbert to Mrs. Carberry, summing up in a word for which no translation existed in English. "Not even the mother can melt her, you say? *Ah, la pauvre femme*! Her 'eart must break. She was to you sympathetic?"

"She seemed a nice little woman, yes. It's hard to tell when you meet someone under such abnormal conditions. Of course she was terribly distressed. Rather dowdily dressed and anxious not to be a nuisance. Not much personality, I thought. She will arrive again for the trial, of course."

"She 'as already return to London?"

"What was the good of her staying? She said she had to get back to her work, and she could do nothing for Jay. She works very hard. Apparently they're badly off; well, we know that now. It's a pity we didn't know it before, or we might have suspected something from those floods of expensive presents and checked them before it was too late."

Nevertheless, in spite of and against Jay's reluctance, Norman Dudley in his private capacity as the girl's friend had asked his sister to instruct solicitors to brief a counsel for the defence, and he would be responsible for the fees; as his own firm was prosecuting, he could hardly let his name appear in the matter.

The procession swept back through the Judge's entrance. Sir Piers Layton was still wearing his robes, but he had changed into a much simpler wig. He seated himself on his big chair and gave a signal that the actual work of the day could begin.

Madame Guilbert watched with fascinated curiosity as the first prisoner came up the steps into the dock between two warders, standing until the indictment was read by the Clerk of Assize. It was like being at the theatre, she thought, trying to fight down a suffocating panic at the thought that these were real men and women, real boys and girls, and that the theatre had nothing to do with it. As a stage production, it would have been faulty; the pace was too slow; there were long halts; the dialogue jerked and rambled. Like most of her nation, she was an ardent and critical playgoer, and she would have had many caustic things to say of the proceedings had they been behind the footlights. But this was daylight, and it was a court of law. There were no graces of setting or decoration to soften the fact that each person who came up those steps and stood behind that rail was in unbearable danger of losing his freedom.

The first was a case of manslaughter: Madame Guilbert only saw the man's expression for a moment before he turned to face the Judge: dark nervousness kept under tight control. He was very thin, and his cheek-bones stood out more than they should. He had been driving his car, and pulled out from a queue when he had no right to do so, run into a girl on a bicycle and killed her. He pleaded guilty to dangerous driving, not to manslaughter. A map of the road was passed up to the Judge, who bent over it intently. The Counsel for the Prosecution had only to point out the facts. The Judge was lenient; imposed a fine and disqualified the man from holding a driving licence for two years: "the consciousness all your life of what you have done, should be almost sufficient punishment." But at least, reflected Madame Guilbert with a sigh of pent-up emotion, at least he will be free. He is free now. She would never have dreamt that she could have felt such relief on behalf of an utter stranger.

Then ensued a certain amount of comic stuff about paying the fine before he left the court.

"But if 'e 'as it not in 'is pocket," exclaimed Roxane audibly to Daffy, "*enfin*, one cannot be a conjurer. Why do they not let 'im owe?"

The next case took some time: a solicitor who had speculated with funds and shares entrusted to him by his clients. There were eleven charges, and he pleaded guilty to each one as it was read out. His Counsel respectfully submitted that he wished it to be known that his wife, the headmistress of a girls' school, had had no share or benefit from his transactions, knew nothing whatever about them, but might nevertheless have to give up the school in consequence of the vicarious slur on her reputation. Apparently he was better as a husband than as a trustee, for his wife was said to be devoted to him and he only anxious to clear her of any possible scandal in the matter. The Judge laid stress on this in his passing sentence, more or less indicating a strong hope that the pupils' parents should pull themselves together and not be tiresome about this. He spoke quietly, but with so much tolerance and imagination that Madame Guilbert had a vivid mental picture of a cloud of mothers and fathers, particularly mothers, rushing up the road and through the gates of the school, flapping censure and agitation, tearing their tender offspring from the classrooms, shooting them back to their unblemished homes.

The solicitor was given a sentence of three years' penal servitude. Roxane sighed again. A large-hearted woman, she could not help wishing that no one need be condemned, but could every one of them leave this court of law singing glad songs of liberty. Yet she had to remember that solicitors who loved their wives had yet behaved with the very reverse of loving kindness to certain aged victims with very little money.

"*C'est difficile,*" murmured Roxane. And her heart began to beat fast at a renewed stir round the dock, thinking, "*maintenant c'est la petite Jasmine.*"

But there was one more case before Jay; also a young offender, a boy of about twenty who had broken the padlock of the gas-meter in his home and robbed it persistently of whatever was put in.

"But his mother and his father, could they not see it was broke?" Madame demanded, first of Daffy and then of Clo. And an instant later the Judge asked the very same thing, which gratified her enormously. The Chief Constable gave evidence confidently and professionally that the boy's father was dead and his mother bedridden: "From where she lay, m'Lud, she could not see the gas-meter."

"*Ah, mon Dieu!*" exclaimed Roxane under her breath; for it seemed to her a pitiful feature of the case, that from where the mother lay bedridden she could not see the gas-meter with the broken padlock. From where she, Roxane, sat, neither could she see much of the young barber's assistant. His clothes were bunched up about him in an odd shapeless way as though they were only held round his person by the belt of his old raincoat. She never saw his face at all. The Judge warned him severely that if he kept on his present courses and his present attitude of mind against authority, he would undoubtedly spend the rest of his life in and out of prison. Then he gave him three years in Borstal.

"*Mais qu'est-ce que c'est que ce Borstal?*" demanded Madame Guilbert.

This was Jay at last whom they were bringing up.

Madame Guilbert, leaning forward with protruding eyes and breath heaving in and out in short gasps, got one glimpse of the girl's face as the stairs twisted up into the dock. After that she only saw her back as she stood or sat between two female warders; but the lines of her shoulders and her back, like her face, were expressive in their utter lack of expression, frozen and hopeless. She wore a shabby navy-blue coat and navy beret and a dark green woollen scarf. She had lost that look which Madame Guilbert had always so admired, of flying sea-foam with the sun on it. Her skin was pasty and dead, her mouth sulked, and her voice, too. And the governess, who had hoped that at least *la petite* Jasmine's ethereal personality would make its own wistful appeal to the Judge and spectators, leant back again in her seat with a sharp pang of disappointment.

A man sitting just in front of Madame Guilbert muttered to the woman beside him: "Young, isn't she? Didn't ought to have been living away from home yet. I'm sorry for her parents."

"I am her mother," said the woman he was addressing. She spoke in a low voice, but Roxane heard and sent a great wave of sympathy flowing forwards to envelop this tragic Mrs. Blake who had to sit there, hard-working, respectable, a widow, and see her little daughter in the dock.

"But perhaps," Roxane reflected, though finding it hard to glow and expand with her usual hopefulness, "perhaps they will not punish 'er this time. He 'as a good face, the Judge. It would be lucky if he had a daughter himself of the same age. Then he could not fail to be gentle." It was hardly a logical basis for optimism, British justice being an impersonal and well-balanced thing, but—

"Guilty," replied Jay four times in answer to the four charges in the indictment. "Guilty." But she said it defiantly as though each time she meant "Not Guilty." For what did they understand of it, these men who had caught her and dragged her here and translated into clingy grey all that lovely glowing happiness she had scattered around her in the spring and summer? Largesse? But the largesse had dwindled and gone stringy in the joyless legal conception, till now it was nothing more than charges read by the Clerk of Assize:

"Jasmine Blake, is that your name?"

"Yes."

"Jasmine Blake, you stand indicted for Felony, namely forgery contrary to Section 2 (2)a of the Forgery Act 1913, and the Particulars of the charge against you state that you on a day in May of the year 1935 at Southampton in this County with intent to defraud did forge a valuable security to wit a Banker's cheque or order purporting to be drawn by Ernest Dudley upon Lloyd's Bank Limited for the payment of thirteen pounds eleven shillings and five pence. Do you plead Guilty or Not Guilty to that charge?"

"Guilty."

"And a further count in this indictment charges you with uttering that cheque knowing it to be forged and with intent to defraud ..."

And hearing the name of Ernest Dudley repeated over and over again in connection with the further charges brought, Madame Guilbert, hitherto a little more inclined to sympathize with Daffy than with Clo, suddenly realized what a terrible blow this must have been to the integrity not only of the firm but of the whole family, and especially to Ernest Dudley himself. As though echoing her thoughts, she heard Clo mutter: "It's damnable"—and turning dismayed from one sister to the other, saw that Daphne was flushed and Clo white, and that both were struggling indignantly not to cry. She patted the hand of first one and then the other, but she knew that Clo and not Daffy had been right: Jay had done an appalling thing to the two faithful chumps who had won her a job in the firm of Walker, Dudley & Son.

By the time she was able to pay attention again to what was actually happening in court, the Counsel for the Prosecution had ended his succinct arraignment; and the Counsel for the Defence, briefed by Mrs. Carberry's solicitor, was doing something legally known as "shedding tears." His line was obvious: this young girl had been put in a position of responsibility for which she was still far too childish and inexperienced.

("It's not fair. He's throwing the blame on Uncle!"

"*Tais-toi, ma petite.*"

"But it's not fair. Why, it's Uncle who got him to defend Jay."

"'E 'as to do what he can. Your uncle, *il est bon comme du pain*. He will understand.")

Toby's susceptibility was alluded to with tolerance; and then Mr. D. L. Randall, the experienced Junior Counsel, hushed his eloquence to a crooning note as though he were rocking a baby in a cradle, while he reminded His Lordship that this young girl, though she had indeed by devious means laid hands upon money which was not her own, had lived scrupulously and in spartan fashion within her means: that her clothes, the food she ate, the lodgings she occupied, the pleasures she afforded herself, were perforce of the simple severe nature which could be adequately covered by the sum of three pounds fifteen shillings a week. She had no debts. She had stolen, but unselfishly. It was less a criminal than a mistaken attitude towards life and morality. A psychologist might say that she had a "Lady Bountiful" complex, but what it amounted to in ordinary phraseology was that she had lived in a sort of dream-world, but unselfishly, with imagination to realize when other people were unhappy, and how unhappiness and the drabness of their lives could perhaps be softened by the arrival of an expensive and beautiful present at the opportune moment. He went on to enumerate some of the different ways in which Jay had squandered the stolen pounds: children, old people, lonely foreigners—

It made a touching list, and Madame Guilbert prayed fervently that he would not mention the *fleurs de lys*. Luckily, however, he became so enamoured of the violin which she had given to Carl Hartmann that he stayed there and went no further.

Finally: "M'Lud, I need call only one witness, the mother of the accused."

"Is that necessary?" asked the Judge, for it was getting late, and he had apparently, one way or another, made up his mind about Jay.

The Counsel for the Defence promised not to detain him long. And Mrs. Blake went into the witness-box and took the oath, swearing in the usual hurried slurred gabble to speak the truth the whole truth and nothing but the truth.

Jay did not look once towards her mother. A keenly observant spectator might even have noticed that she turned her head a little in the other direction from the box, as though she had no concern with the insignificant figure with tragic eyes and a convulsive swallow in her throat: the typical weak but respectable widowed mother of an erring child.

Mrs. Blake created a good impression, not by the way in which she gave her evidence, for she murmured and stumbled and repeated herself and failed to understand what the Counsel said, but because she was so obviously the mother who had tried to do her best by a foolish headstrong daughter, and had not succeeded very well; Demeter blamed herself for Persephone's plight in hell. "Perhaps I spoilt her. When she begged for pretty things, I couldn't bear to say no. Perhaps I should have impressed it on her that we were poor and I couldn't afford luxuries. … Yes, I worked very hard. … Yes, I had a small income of my own, but it wasn't easy even then to fit in everything. … No, she's not an only child, and they both had to be educated, only Jay went to St. Catherine's. … Naturally I couldn't afford to pay for it myself. A kind friend of ours who took an interest in Jay … Yes, it may have given her extravagant ideas. I know she's not bad at heart. I *know* she isn't. Young girls run wild sometimes and then they don't seem to mind what they do. I hope so, I do indeed"—in reply to the Counsel's suggestion that her daughter had always had a good home. "I tried to make it so, but you know what it is." Her evidence faltered when it became a question as to whether she had approved of her daughter's occupation at the firm of Dudley, Walker & Son, and how much she had seen of the girl since she came to Southampton.

"I didn't want her to leave home," murmured Mrs. Blake. "I thought she was too young and would be better living with me, for her first job, anyhow. And as girls do when they are a little hot-headed and won't be interfered with, she flared up, so we were out of touch ever since she came here, nearly a year ago now. But I kept on thinking I'd hear from her. I suppose I ought to have come down, but it was difficult to get away, what with one thing and another. I blame myself, I do indeed. More than anyone."

Sympathetic eyes followed her as she went back to her seat. A bad daughter of a good mother was the general verdict. One of the spectators up in the gallery whispered to another lady beside her: "Yes, I knew them when this one and her sister were little girls. They played with my own little girl, Kathy, down at Clifford's Bay on their summer holidays. Jay was an extraordinarily pretty child, but I always preferred the other one, Molly. She was more honest, and it showed, even then. Poor Mrs. Blake, she was so nice and kind, but a little ineffective, I always thought. When I read about this case coming on, in the *Western Sentinel,* I said to myself: "I'll drive over and see if it's the same one. It's only two miles. Terribly sad. Luckily my Kath's away and hasn't heard about it. I must try and see Mrs. Blake afterwards; if I miss her, one of the officials will give me her address, I expect."

The Police Inspector was giving his evidence, as he had already done in two or three other cases. Madame Guilbert was deeply impressed by his firm and resolute manner when compared with that of less experienced witnesses. Every word could be clearly heard, and he knew whom he should be addressing and which way to turn his head. As for taking the oath, she could imagine him doing it on his head.

He related all that he had on his records about Jay's past: the date of her arrival in Southampton, the boarding-house where she had first lived, the rooms she had shared with another girl. The Judge asked whether it were true that the Dudley family had treated her like a daughter? and the Inspector replied that they *had* treated her like a daughter: she had been always at the house of one or the other of them, Mrs. Carberry or Mr. Dudley. No previous convictions.

"What," asked the Judge, "has her behaviour been like since her arrest?"

"Quite satisfactory, m'Lud. At first she had a lot to say. Seemed indignant at the charges brought, wanting to explain why she didn't deserve them. Latterly, however, I understand she has"—pause—"relapsed into almost total silence."

That was all, then. The Judge leant across from his seat to talk to the Clerk of Assize just below him in the well. The Clerk of Assize then asked Jay if she had anything to say before sentence was passed upon her?

"Yes," Jay raised her eyes to the Judge and spoke with soft confidence, as though they were alone together. Everyone in court leant forward in breathless surprise. It was unusual, especially for a young prisoner, to become articulate from the dock. Generally they passed up a letter to the Judge, containing what they wished him to know, not trusting themselves to find words at a moment like this.

"I did no harm. I made them happy. I didn't take money from anyone who would miss it. I didn't spend a penny on myself. He told you that, but I'm not sure if you noticed. It's not wrong, is it, unless you're doing it for yourself? There must be a difference, if there's any difference in anything. I kept strictly within my income, for me. But everything round them was hard and narrow and grey, and I changed it all. I'm glad I did. Their eyes when they thanked me. … It makes you feel like heaven, to be thanked like that. I thought people would understand. I didn't mind them finding out. But all they care about now is who the money belonged to, not what I did with it—"

She stopped and buried her face in her hands.

There was a tense silence. Madame Guilbert prayed that the Judge's heart would have been touched by this outburst; that he would be lenient. *Elle était si mignonne, la petite Jasmine.* … She ought to have been outside among the flowers and the running water, not in here waiting to be sentenced.

One of the wardresses touched Jay's arm and whispered something to her. She could not be sentenced with her face buried in her hands.

The Judge in passing sentence admonished her gravely. "You appear to think that what you choose to do with money is a fair excuse for the way you obtain it. You have obviously got twisted ideas about life. That is an utterly dangerous point of view. You've had a good home and a good education. Perhaps, however, you were a little spoilt and not taught clearly enough the hard fundamental difference between right and wrong. You can still learn that, if you are prepared to accept the lesson and not push yourself angrily against it as you are doing now. You will be sent for three years to Borstal. That does not necessarily mean that you will stay there for three years. The length of your stay will depend entirely upon yourself."

Chapter Five

Outside the court in the gathering dusk, Madame Guilbert with Daffy and Clo ran into Lorna and impulsively laid a hand on her arm.

"I am sorry. I regret, with all my heart I regret, but perhaps it will still come right. Forgive me that I ask: you have seen her, the little one? I notice that you left the court after her case."

Lorna was touched by the real, warming sympathy.

"She wouldn't speak to me. It was no good. To turn away from her own mother, as though I—One of the wardresses was very nice. She said they often did that to their nearest and dearest. It's no good my staying. I must get back to London."

But Madame Guilbert could not have that. It sounded so desolate.

"You will come back with us at least for a little while? After so much strain you will be tired, hungry. It shows itself. Already you know Mrs. Carberry. These are her daughters. All of us we loved *la petite Jasmine, n'est-ce pas, Duffee? N'est-ce pas, Clo?* Permit that I introduce myself: Roxane Guilbert, for many years I have been in the family a loving friend as well as governess—"

Lorna jerked back as though in some strange, almost violent repulsion from the other woman.

"Are you sure," in a choked abrupt voice, "that you've always been a loving friend to Jay? Are you sure that you weren't her enemy? That it wasn't you, perhaps, who—"

She swung round and walked quickly away.

"*Mais, mon dieu!*" gasped Madame Guilbert.

What was wrong? What had she said, speaking straight from a compassionate heart?

"How frightfully rude!" from Daffy.

"But that, it was more than rudeness. It was a woman suddenly possessed who answered me thus. So timid in court, so grateful at first when I spoke to her of the catastrophe. And how could she have thought it that I—I of all others could be enemy to her poor little daughter? No, it must be the shock which has given her a frenzy. Let us go home, *mes enfants*. Three years. It has not been a happy day."

It must have been an instinctive desire for the deepest quiet that could be found, after the glare and publicity of the courts, which took Lorna, after her brief interlude with the Carberrys' French governess, out of the street and into the sanctuary of the cathedral close. Here the sense of peace was almost physical, something you could touch like velvet. In the fading light the houses hardly showed the mellow claret of their bricks, the sturdy simplicity of design with which the Queen Anne and early Georgian period still rewards us, their harmony of portico and fanlight; but back from the front gardens the lights were just being lit, one after another, making an irregular pattern of amber squares. For the one or two people who, like Lorna, were strolling along the diagonal path across the lawns to the cathedral, past the ancient yew and the group of tall feathery elms, the feeling of looking back at these windows might have transcended mere aesthetic pleasure; they might easily have felt: If

I belong to this, or at least if there is no reason why I should not belong to it, then here is security from all harm.

Lorna's steps halted. She heard the sound of trumpets approaching from the town, accompanied by the mediaeval clatter of horses' hoofs: the Red Judge was being driven in state to his lodgings at the far end of the close. The procession swept into sight, and now the peal of trumpets was clear and triumphant: Three trumpeters on horseback in front of the car and three behind. The frieze of lighted windows could be seen slipping in and out behind the procession as it passed and slowly disappeared again.

For a few moments the church and the law had been in alliance to bring panic to a woman standing in jeopardy beyond their sanctuary.

PART VI

Chameleon

Chapter One

Lorna let herself in at No. 31 Netherby Park Road, Ealing, called to Susan, and then went into the sitting-room and sank down with a tired sigh into one of the round bunchy armchairs. Mrs. Anderson had made a mistake and put her into a slow train, and she had been too upset to care. The comfortless journey had taken nearly three hours.

Susan came in, a good deal more subdued than usual.

"Tea?" she asked briefly, and already up in arms against whatever invisible person might be suggesting that she should show any sobbing demonstrations of sympathy over what had happened.

"Yes, please."

"Expected you earlier."

"Mrs. Anderson came in while I was packing my case last night and made me go home with her."

"Who's she?"

"It doesn't matter. Aren't there *any* letters for me, Susan?"

"Lots. Most of 'em registered. That's why I put 'em in the drawer. Some came here, and some I fetched from Thompson's. There you are, you can read 'em while I see if the kettle's boiling. Take your mind off your troubles."

Lorna looked up with a wan smile, pushed back her hair, and then caught at Susan's hand in passing: "'Our troubles,' isn't it, this time?"

"Poor little soul," muttered Susan; "thinking it was as simple as all that to diddle 'em. But Jay was always the fool of the two." She pulled her hand away and hurried off into the kitchen. Brooding witchlike over the kettle, she thought: "Odd, though, the luck *she's* had, so far. Time and again I expected we were for it, sailing so near the wind. But she's right, it's instinct what picks out them as won't be likely to prosecute. Ah, boiling, are you? Right, now we shan't be long! There's a good many women, after going through this with a daughter, would have asked for a good stiff pick-me-up. But she'll never take to drink, not that one: 'A nice cup of tea and then I'll feel better,' same as it might be the vicar's wife. Lord, she's a queer fish and no mistake. Times I'm not sure if she don't believe half them tales herself, the way she looks at me soft and reproachful when I pull her leg a bit: 'What I do, Susan, I do for my children's sake, to give them an education.' Yes, and a pretty place one of 'ems landed herself, education or no education. She's not been acquitted, or the old girl'd 'ave brought her along. Poor kid. And poor other kid too; it'll break Molly all to bits when she hears. They're neither as tough as their mother, and if *she* isn't the best entertainment to live with!—Not far off twenty years now, and still I don't get sick of it. Well I suppose wondering if every knock's going to be the police does ginger up life a bit. Though, mind," she apostrophized the tea-caddy, as she scooped up three spoonfuls of Indian tea and stared absently at the picture of "The Stag at Bay" on the lid, "mind, I'm glad she's taken to this letter game instead of going round herself. Safer on the whole. And with Thompson's a twopenny bus-ride away, they're not so likely, unless they watch outside, to find out where we live. And pays just as well, too, if not better. But I don't think she enjoys opening letters as much as pushing past the butler and pitching the tale herself. Ah well, it's a profession like any other, and all according to your lights—Out of the way, puss; and you don't get *your* lights till tomorrow, so it's no good pushing up against my legs when I'm carrying a tray." But Susan's tone was melancholy, even while she rated the cat. She was no cuddler by nature, but she regarded Lorna's family as her own, and now what could she do for Jay? Not that she knew the verdict yet, nor the sentence, though she had hunted through the evening papers and the cheaper London dailies, but none of them had any space to spare for a minor embezzlement case in the south-west of England. Now if Jay had been murdered—

Susan watched Lorna drink her tea. At the end of the second cup:

"Went against her, I suppose?"

Lorna nodded. "Three years in Borstal."

"Thought that was only for boys?"

"They have one for girls too. Only one."

"Three years? Damn and blast 'em, that's hard. A good deal worse than prison if you ask me," added Susan cheerfully. And the ghoulish side of her was compelled to give Lorna a few unpleasant details, from the rich fund of her imagination, of what Borstal did to its inmates.

"Susan, I don't want to hear!"

"Oh, all right," not in the least offended. "In fact, I can understand that," Susan allowed handsomely. "Did they call you as witness? Did Jay"—she sank her voice—"did she give you away?"

"What was there to give away?"

Susan chivalrously determined that this was no moment to ejaculate: "Come off it!"

"You saw her afterwards, I suppose? Carried on a bit, I shouldn't be surprised? She was never as quiet as Molly when things went wrong. Up and down like a fever-chart, that was Jay. Mackurial, they call it. Did she make a speech from the dock?"

Lorna nodded.

"Ah, that ought to have done her some good. She's pretty enough. Or would you say she'd lost any of her looks? How much was it she'd lifted? Over seventy pounds?" Susan gave a shrill whistle of admiration. "Well! Chip of the old block, ain't she?"

Lorna made no reply. Her fingers played with a letter in her lap. It was from a very kind lady who quite sympathized over Mrs. Blake's two little girls so desperately wishing they had pretty frocks like other children for their school breaking-up party; yes, it *was* hard if they were the only ones to look shabby and darned and threadbare: "So, instead of the money, I'm sending you an evening-dress of my own that I have had to put away for some time for sentimental reasons, but I would like to think it was bringing happiness elsewhere. It is a little baggy and voluminous and old-fashioned, so, as you say you are clever with your needle and meant to make two new frocks for them yourself if you could afford to buy the material, I am sure you will have no difficulty in converting this one into two. Give Joyce and Margery my love and tell them I hope they will look very nice indeed and have a very good time at the party."

And now "Joyce" was in prison, and "Margery"—

"Susan, you remember I said you weren't to mention Jay if you wrote to Molly?"

"What? Still?" Susan's voice was glum with disappointment. She had been looking forward, in a sort of way, to writing that letter, sparing Lorna but pouring out her scorn for the whole firm of Dudley and the entire paraphernalia of justice, law and order, adding what she would have said to them if she had but had a chance … "The whole lot of you stuck up there, so pleased with yourselves, against one poor little white-faced kid that wanted a bit of fun and didn't quite know her way about how to get it. Lord, I'd be ashamed!"

"She's got to know some time," argued Susan, apropos of writing to Molly.

"I know. But we'll let her be happy as long as possible. She'll be home in three weeks and then I'll tell her myself."

"What'll she do, d'you think? Rush off and see Jay?"

"She'll want to, of course, but it won't be any good; they won't let her have visitors; or if they did, Jay won't speak."

"What do you mean, 'won't speak'? Didn't she speak to you?"

"No. That's what hurt me so. My own child. And I wasn't going to blame her, Susan, not for one moment, as most mothers would have done. I only wanted to hug and comfort her a little and tell her we'd do everything possible, and if it was no good, that she'd find her home just the same afterwards, because I'm sure she'd have been punished enough by just knowing how unhappy she'd made me. But she wouldn't melt at all. She wouldn't let me get near her. She pretended not to care what they did to her nor what was said in court or anything. It was terrible, Susan. My little Jasmine. Of course she'd had a shock. And then that boy—"

"Let her down, did he? They're all the same. What did she expect?"

"Quite a lot," whispered Lorna through her tears. "She was a romantic child, you know. And when she found out what real life was like—"

– 218 –

"Life's a bastard, and so's that there young man, from all you tell me. Was it 'im found out and called in the police in the first place?"

"No. Someone got suspicious, the French governess, I should think, and spoke to one of the partners in the firm, the boy's uncle; and he got in the auditors. That's how it happened, I believe, though I can't be sure, I got so confused with all those charges, and my head was going round and round."

Susan threw her a sidelong look, affectionate, doubting, humorous. Common sense told her that architects did not have French governesses spying about in their firm, the first to scent anything crooked. And, moreover, she had heard that motif before. Lord, it dated from one day a long way back, when Jay and Molly were kids and Jay ill and Lorna came home having been, so to speak, Visiting with Molly.

"No chance, I suppose, they'd let me make a chocolate layer cake and send it to her there?"

"No, you dear old thing. But it's a nice thought, and you shall make her a chocolate layer cake every day when we get her back."

"Ah, she'll need fattening up. She'll be skinny. Jay, too, that was always so dainty in her food, picking and choosing; and in her clothes too; she won't 'arf like having to put on coarse stuff next to her skin that other women have worn first, and scrubbing with yellow soap and—"

"Susan, stop!"

Susan stopped, aware that this was a period when a little consideration might be shown, though she told herself rebelliously: "What's the good of blinking facts?"

"Is there a parcel for me? A large parcel?"

"Yes; come to think of it, there is; with the paper half torn off an old broken cardboard box. Why, what's inside?"

Lorna smiled teasingly, making an obvious effort to shake off her dejection. "I can't be sure, but there's probably an evening-dress inside, 'a little baggy and voluminous and old-fashioned.'"

"Cripes!" exclaimed Susan. "What's the good of that?"

"If the material's decent, I may get six or seven shillings for it. Unless, Susan dear, it suits you. In that case I'll present it to you for a dance-frock."

Susan giggled, hauled in the parcel, opened it and shook out the kind lady's response to Lorna's wistful letter about her two little girls and the school party: an ornate evening-dress of 1910 vintage, pink net over a purple satin foundation. The net was embroidered in a pattern of pink and gold beads, edged with a heavy fringe of pink and purple, and across one shoulder drooped a battered trail of purple velvet orchids.

"Cripes!" ejaculated Susan again, holding it out. "I'd look a treat in this. Shall I try it on?"

Lorna agreed, amused at the idea, glad to be back again with her volatile domestic.

Susan did not bother to leave the sitting-room, but pulled off her apron and her old print dress and arrayed herself in the purple and pink.

"Don't I look a treat?" she demanded, posturing for Lorna's benefit, "You wait, I'll 'ave all the boys after me. Old Sammy Thompson, him of the newspaper shop, he's a bit larky already, but when he sees me in this, 'e'll 'ave me on my back in no time."

She picked up the skirts that flowed around her skinny legs and stout shoes, and began to dance with extravagant gestures and high kicks, singing:

"Maisie, she's a daisy,
Maisie, she's a dear,
For she likes the boys to chaff her
And the men to photograph her
And they all cry Whoops when they see her on the pier—"

A knock and ring at the front door.

Susan stood still. "That 'ud be the post, at this time. More letters to sign for. But I can't go to the door looking barmy like this." Susan winked. "It won't do to let 'em think we're a disorderly 'ouse, will it?"

"I'll go," said her mistress.

So Lorna opened the door to Neil Inglefield on his second visit.

Chapter Two

<->

"Good evening, Lorna," said Neil cheerfully and firmly. "Here's your profligate husband home again. Glad to see him?"

He had forgotten for a moment that this was Molly's mother, and, in fact, his future mother-in-law. This was little Lorna again, as at Market St. Dunstan's, when he had been the enemy boy taking a wicked delight he had never bothered to conceal in putting his finger through all her transparencies and twisting all her demure little plots.

Yet if the sight of him had been a shock, if she felt any fear at his form of greeting, he thought that she concealed it well. Though perhaps she somewhat over-emphasized her welcome:

"Neil! dear Neil! Now, do you know, if an angel had come to me and whispered: 'Choose of all the world whom you would most like to see here on your doorstep for a good chat about old times,' I should have said: 'Neil Inglefield.'"

"You would, would you? I'm afraid some of this chat is going to be about new times, Lorna, and there's no angel about anywhere for the moment. What the bloody hell do you mean by going round saying I'm your husband who ran away from you? Not," he added politely, "but that it wouldn't have been an honour and a pleasure—"

"To run away from me?" Lorna gave a little laugh. Her eyes were round and bright and wary. "How you tease, Neil. You were always a tease. Sometimes, you know, I used to think that you went a little too far; I mean, that you didn't consider enough that very young girls have sensitive feelings. But I don't mind that, now we're both middle-aged people."

"Now we're both middle-aged people," he repeated. "Won't you ask me in, Lorna?" And knowing his way to the sitting-room, he strode past her and had thrown open the door and entered before she could stop him.

Susan was standing on a low chair in front of the chimney-piece mirror, so as to get a good sight of herself in her fine ball-gown. At the sight of Neil, she nearly toppled off.

"Good Lord!" he exclaimed, taking an unexpected encounter not nearly as cleverly as Lorna just now. "Susan Orris. My sainted aunt!"

The young men at Market St. Dunstan's and the neighbourhood had never had any complaints of Susan as their sainted aunt or in her semi-professional capacity, but it was a little disconcerting to come face to face with her like this, without any preparation, in Lorna's sitting-room, more than twenty years afterwards. Her extraordinary get-up prevented him from realizing that she was living more or less respectably as cook-general-parlourmaid-housemaid-nurse-ladies'-maid. Molly had mentioned Susan, of course, in her rare moods of childish reminiscence: rare because they had to be so pathetically pruned and edited; but there were many Susans, and he had not given a thought to this particular specimen since she had disappeared from her native pastures.

"Mr. Neil!" Susan scrambled down from her altitude with a spontaneous grin of pleasure at the sight of a face she had always liked pretty well, even in the dark. Then she saw her mistress standing just behind Neil and suddenly recollected certain illicit uses of a certain marriage certificate: Lorna Mason to Neil Inglefield; recollected that a few years ago she had become aware, on her annual Armistice Day visit to the village, that Neil was on Lorna's track, or had put emissaries on her track, a dapper military-looking bloke. But the hue and cry had died down without results. Now here he was in person, and, Susan thought in a fair-minded way, with good reason not to be pleased. After all, a man's name was his own, wasn't it? And Lorna had bandied it about a bit, dragged it in the dust and then rubbed it further in with her heel. Had he brought the police with him, she wondered, her loyalty bristling in defence of Lorna right or wrong. As though the poor dear hadn't had enough recently, without this on top of it.

"Mr. Neil! Well, troubles never do come singly. Nice of you to look us up. I'd thought of you as a beeyutiful picture in a beautiful golden frame, and now 'ere you are, large as life and handsomer than you was even in your clothes. What'll you drink? Aow, it's all right," at a gesture from Lorna deprecating such careless hospitality, "I've got a bottle of whisky in, if you haven't."

Neil glanced quizzically from Susan to Lorna: "I don't want to appear too curious, but are you two ladies sharing this house?"

Lorna's reply was outrageous in its demure suburban respectability, but at least it settled the situation:

"Susan has been my faithful maid and companion for a great many years," she explained, definitely that nice Mrs. Blake of No. 31 Netherby Park Road. "She was just trying on a new dress when you came, Neil. Otherwise, of course, she would have opened the door to you. If you have any different memories of her when you were a foolish boy, she's sorry for it now, and there's no need to bring it up. Let the dead past bury its dead. Susan, please make some fresh tea as quickly as possible."

Susan, quelled, and with only a half-hearted grimace in Neil's direction, departed to the kitchen, kicking her train out of her way as she went. Neil was for a second equally taken aback by Lorna's staid little air of virtue and reproof, which gave her an opportunity to say: "I'd rather you didn't unsettle Susan, please, Neil. I had a lot of difficulty with her at first, but now I believe and hope she's given up her old ways. The children were a great help."

This was a mistake. She was confronted again by a determined man of thirty-seven, and, where she was concerned, a man formidable in temper. A man, moreover, to whom she had done an injury.

"Yes, the children. That, Lorna, is what I came to see you about. Jay and Molly."

"You know Jay and Molly? But you can't. Just their names, perhaps," she babbled. "You must meet Molly one day."

"I have met Molly. I'm going to marry Molly—one day," he echoed sardonically, destroying her poor attempt to continue on a bogus social footing with him. And he told her of his first visit to Netherby Park Road.

"... So you see, Lorna," he finished, using again that bantering tone which he knew she detested because it served as a sort of tin shield against which all her shot rattled ineffectively, "you're quite safe from me now and for ever. You don't deserve it, but you are. No one could regret that fact more sincerely than I. What danger of prosecution you may be in, of course, from other victims of your racket as a professional beggar, I don't know. You seem to have had extraordinary luck in escaping the law so far—"

He stopped suddenly, for Lorna had given a little gasp and then begun to cry. Real, not crocodile tears. She cried like a child, her mouth open and making whimpering noises from the throat. He had supposed her tougher than this, and not likely to succumb so easily; it was grotesque, but, unwilling as he was to recognize it, rather moving.

"Look here, Lorna," roughly as though they were again boy and girl of sixteen at some unimportant phase of their constant battle. "Look here—shut up! What's the good of crying? You must have known I should find out and come down on you some time. Besides, I've just told you you're safe; I won't ever prosecute. I couldn't, caring so much for Molly—"

"Molly!" It came out now, between gulps of pure sorrow and desolation; there was real cause for her crying, and it was not her own peril, past or present.

"Molly—she's—she's never kept anything from her mother before. If she cares for you—if she cares, I've lost my baby—"

"I hope so." His voice was stern again. The moment of compassion had passed. "What have you done to your baby, and to your other baby, if it comes to that? My God, Lorna, there isn't a brute in the whole criminal calendar who could have dragged his children through a worse hell than you did, year after year, when they were helpless. If you'd had a grain of imagination you might have realized what they went through; what Molly went through, anyhow. Still, the fact of her not telling you about me needn't send you off into floods of tears. She kept it dark out of pure decency, so that you should go on sleeping at nights. The news that Neil Inglefield had come to call, might, you know, have suggested a charge of libel and false pretences, rather than teacups and a nice gossip."

At that appropriate moment, Susan, dressed now in her usual

slatternly uniform, entered with the tea-tray, dumped it down with a loud rattle at the low table between Lorna and Neil, and sulked out again.

Lorna had recovered her control now. The feeling of the teapot in her hand prompted her to ask the visitor in her most refined manner how he liked his tea: "Milk? sugar?"

"Neither, thanks."

"And how is everybody? How is Marcus?"

Their eyes met. Hers were dancing with malice and an odd sort of enjoyment of the situation. Still, he thought ironically, she hasn't heard one-half of it yet.

"Marcus is very well, thank you. He's married to a most charming, beautiful and accomplished lady, and is thought highly of in his profession. They have seven children. No, eight. And they live at Carlisle."

"Carlisle? That's right up in the north, isn't it? Carlisle. I'm glad he's happy."

"I'll swear you are." He smiled at her as she passed him the cup. "Dear little Lorna," he murmured. "You've got a lot to answer for, haven't you? Alec's death, amongst other things."

"Alec's death?"

"Alexander Muir-Leslie. He shot himself. And the cause can be traced, my sweet stepsister, directly back to you."

"But I've never heard of him."

Neil went off into a shout of laughter. "My God, I don't suppose you have. Isn't this an amazing world? You've never heard of him, and but for your dainty activities he'd be alive now, married to Sylvia and happy as a king."

"How can I be responsible?"

"You can be, even for someone you've never seen, if he kills himself because of something you've done."

"I do wish," said Lorna, turning peevish, for the interview was a strain on top of her week of strain, "I do wish you'd stop laughing in that—that harrowing way, Neil, and either share the joke with your hostess or go away."

"Your dismissal is a bit out of character as a hostess, surely? You haven't offered me 'just one more cup' yet, and I haven't drunk this one. I don't break bread with you, my pretty. But I can't go away until I've told you why I've come." He pulled from his pocket a folded newspaper, a London daily paper, the *Westminster Tribune*, which pursued an intelligent, faintly highbrow policy. He handed it to Lorna and indicated the place where she was to read; rather less than half a column relating a somewhat unusual aspect of a case on the Western Circuit: A girl named Blake, who had misappropriated some seventy pounds of the funds of the firm of architects where she had been employed; her counsel declared: "A psychologist might say that she had a Lady Bountiful complex …"

"That's your girl, isn't it? Molly told me she was working for an architect."

"Yes," said Lorna, wearily pushing the paper away. "It's Jay. But I'd hoped it wouldn't be in any of the London papers."

"This is the only one. I happened to see it during lunch. The point is this: Does Molly know yet?"

"No. I've kept it from her. I wasn't going to have her worried until I could break it to her myself."

"Yes, well, that would have been all right if it *had* been confined to the local papers. She's in the north and this was the south-west, but some kind soul is sure to see this or hear of it and identify it with Molly Blake's sister and tell her. Anyhow, we can't risk it. I'll go straight along to Edinburgh, only I had to find out first; for all I knew, you might have sent for her—"

"Drag Molly into a sordid thing like this? My Molly? Neil, you don't understand!"

No, thought Neil, I don't. A lot that went on inside Lorna's head remained, even more since this interview, an intriguing but sinister mystery. All that he had fathomed and could set apart as truth was her passionate, her genuine attachment to both children. Yet even her love did not save them from being callously used as pathetic assets, on and off, during those ghastly ten years when they were small enough to be of value.

"Yes, go up and break it to her, Neil, as tenderly as possible." Suddenly he found she was treating him as her ally, a kind and considerate son-in-law from whom she had no secrets. "Molly is devoted to poor Jay, you know, and this is going to hurt her terribly. One of the things that comforted me during my worst times was seeing how there was never any jealousy or quarrelling between my two babies; though Jay was so pretty and Molly so talented." She flickered into a smile of raillery which made him feel slightly sick. "I expect *you* would call Molly the beautiful one."

He got up and pushed back his chair, so that it fell with a thud. He simply could not endure being on these terms with Lorna. Though for Molly's sake he would do nothing to damage her, in his feelings he was still the enemy boy.

"Lorna, you'd better hear this frankly: I'm not in the least softened towards you; I resent strongly that things have worked out so that I can't put the police on to you, I have no tolerance in me and I don't wish you to think I have."

"Oh, Neil, but we *should* be tolerant. After all, we're fellow-humans; we should try to realize, as I did for Susan years ago, with our imagination if not with anything else, how trouble might drive us and drive us—"

"Did trouble drive you and drive you to tell strangers that you were married to a man called Neil Inglefield who gave you two children and then sloped off and left you penniless?"

"I only did it once or twice. In fact, I think only once. It was for the children's sake. Whatever happened, they had to be educated, and my poor Len—"

"I know about your poor Len. And you're right to pity him. He was an extremely pitiable case." Neil heard himself being censorious and upright to an extent which he would have hated in another man under other circumstances; but he felt as though this stuffy pseudo-Tudor sitting-room with its teacups and plump cushions, its flowery chintzes and brass ornaments, were crowded with Lorna's victims: his father, Marcus, Shirley, Blake, Alexander, Jay, crying aloud what she had done to them. Why couldn't she at least have played her beastly games alone?

See where it had led Jay; what it might have done to Molly but for some invisible touchstone of integrity that she had mercifully been given where there had been no other mercy.

He strode to the door. Lorna followed him.

"That's enough, Lorna; go back to your tea."

"Neil, you'll give Molly my love?"

"For what it's worth."

"Does she love you?"

"Yes, thank God."

"She's very young to marry. Afterwards—you'll let me see her, won't you, sometimes?"

"As little as I can help, my dear."

"It's a wonderful match for my little girl. I wouldn't stand in her way." That was Lorna in her imitation of gratified motherhood. "Leatherette," thought Neil.

Then, surprisingly, she was genuine again. As when flying above cloud you look down and suddenly see a small homely green field, before the billowing silver closes together once more.

"Yes, you're right. As little as you can help. Oh, Molly—But you're quite right. There was Jay."

Susan's dignity prompted her to remain in the kitchen and continue resenting Lorna's reproof: "As though I'd been anyone," she murmured indignantly; meaning, as though she had been a cook-general in service with a perfectly conventional mistress who was kind to her but did not allow liberties, instead of larky, impudent Susan Orris of Market St. Dunstan's, freakishly attached to that strange creature, Lorna Mason, Lorna Blake; and perhaps the only being on earth who knew most of the time what she was up to, and could grin and say "Good luck to her!" or "I could die!" meaning the exact opposite, that she could live, rejoicing, with Lorna.

But still, to tick her off in front of Mr. Neil from up at the Big

House—"When many's a time—Oh well, what's over's over. But whose fault was it, I should like to know, that he found me dressed like gran'ma going to the ball?" Still, poor soul, she had had enough to try her this last week: "For all her ways, she's fond of them kids, and for all that she kept on saying so, she's done a lot for 'em, and they've not often had a cross word, and plenty of treats too, on and off, where another woman would have gone and spent it all on herself. Who'd have thought that Jay would have been and gone and got herself jugged like this, her with her delicate looks and modest manners that sort of coaxed you before you knew where you was. *Jay!* Why, she'd have let a mouse out of the trap and then made you think it was all right she should have done, after all your trouble to catch it. It's cruel to think of her nipped by the law, whatever she's been silly goose enough to go and do in her sleep.

"Must have been a bit of a shock, no doubt of it, to go to the door expecting the post, and find Mr. Neil, what she'll never give over thinking of as the enemy boy. Wonder what he wanted? Maybe if I went in now and cleared away the tea she'd not be so arsie-tarsie. If he's going to set the police after her for using his name without a right to, I may as well know, and the sooner the better. The Stars say this will not be a good week for family Blake and Co.—'Abandon for the present all thoughts of asking your employer for a rise.' In I go, prepared for the worst."

But she went in cautiously, all the same.

Lorna did not hear her. She was sitting with her back towards the door, absorbed in her letters. Those she had read were scattered round, on the table beside her, on the floor, on her lap, cheques and postal orders among them, loose and pinned on. She was smiling a little.

Susan watched her absorption: "Is that what means most to her, after all? An out-and-out menigma, that's what she is."

Chapter Three

Sir Halmar Barnard was not often in his London flat. Before he retired, two years ago, he had been a big man in Tarmouth; and since his retirement he had proved in some ways even more of a local asset, interesting himself in a hundred charities, sitting on committees, with an interest in the two important newspapers of that part of the country, a churchwarden, president of the golf club, a continual prize-winner with his marrows. His leisured usefulness had spread and spread; he used his influence (he called it his poor influence) for the promotion of peace, better trade fellowship, sport, and general harmony everywhere between everybody.

So it happened that he was now in town for a few days as a delegate to the World Conference on the Promotion of National Understanding; and had recently been interviewed on what he personally thought were the prospects for National Understanding, including How he Occupied his Leisure; Is Fifty a Man's Most Active Age?; Are We Justified in turning our eyes from Home Stiles to help the Lame Dogs Abroad?; and Can we Find Utopia in This Material World? Naturally, with a man of such wide interests, his mail was always on the bulky side. He was now reading a letter for the second time. It was a letter of appeal, and he did not know the writer, but it interested him peculiarly because it seemed to call from him that very gift of imagination which he insisted was the stained-glass window through which fell the rich lights into an otherwise chilly chapel. That was the very phrase he had used in his interview.

"DEAR SIR HALMAR,

If you feel directly you begin to read this that I should not have written to you and that it is an impertinence as I am a total stranger and where can my pride be, please please tear it up and don't read any more. But you with your rare imagination, for indeed, believe me, it *is* rare, will understand how when one is in deep trouble, as I am now, the kind of trouble that, as a German poet said, keeps one awake and crying sitting on the end of one's bed all night long wondering if the gods can hear you, that the very last people to whom one can possibly appeal are one's own friends and relatives, especially if they have warned you not to be rash and enterprising. No, one turns to a stranger, and if one chooses well he will say 'Let me help you,' instead of 'I told you so a hundred times.' Or, at the very worst, he will say and do nothing. And that is better, too, if one still has a rag of dignity left.

I'll be as brief as I can: I am a woman earning her own living for a great many years now, and entirely dependent on it. On the whole, by not taking many holidays, I have managed nicely and grown to love my work which is very delicate embroidery, quilting and trousseau orders, with a special line for petit point reproductions. A few months ago when I was looking up some needlework designs in the South Kensington Museum I got into conversation with a very clever woman, or so she seemed, and nice too, who was in the same business as mine but in Carlisle, so she said. One is lonely and one talks, you will understand that too. She talked of partnership but I had no capital, so it fell through. Then she suggested that I in London should do work for her firm in Carlisle. After she had got back she sent orders for several small things. I dispatched them and got paid, not immediately but generally a few days afterwards, which gave me confidence and I had nothing to complain of as to their terms. Then I had a valuable order on which I had to make a large personal outlay. It was copying a petit point set of chair covers for some big country-house drawing-room. I won't bore you with details, dear Sir Halmar, you will know that the outlay for specially designed canvases of this nature is comparatively enormous. I worked night and day on this order, hoping to satisfy them so that I could stick to this line, which is more profitable than lingerie. At last I dispatched the order registered and received a bare acknowledgement. This did not alarm me and I waited, as usual, for them to pay me, but nothing came except silence. I wrote to the woman who was my original friend in the firm, but my letters were returned 'not known' and my heart sank. Meanwhile the wholesale houses are pressing me for payment. There is only one thing for me to do and that is to go up to Carlisle and see for myself if there is any firm or any woman; I mean, of course, the woman whom I'd met in the museum and who played such a wicked trick on me. I can hardly believe that I was ingenuous enough to trust to her, but she was so plausible and so nice it never occurred to me that her story might not be true and that she was what they call in America 'working a racket.' If only I had someone with experience and wisdom to advise me on these things. It is hard to be forgiving because I believe now, looking back, that the woman actually enjoyed deceiving me. When I get to Carlisle I must, of course, employ a solicitor to help me at least to redeem my petit point. I believe, don't you, that that would be more sensible than to put it in the hands of a solicitor in London? After all, when they are on the spot, they *know*. But I haven't even my fare up, let alone the expenses of employing a solicitor. And I dare not leave my address here until I have paid at any rate a large part of the twenty pounds for my outlay on the work, as they are threatening proceedings.

I cannot bring myself to say 'Will you help me?' After all, why should you? Though if you could—I am half crazy with worry. If I get back my work, I shall be able to sell it and repay you anyhow part of a loan, but you will know yourself that it wouldn't be honest for me to promise this.

I am broken and at the end of my tether. If I cannot get some help by Friday next, you will read in the papers of just another commonplace tragedy, but you will know how it was forced on a lonely and desperate woman.

God bless you,
(Mrs.) Lorna Blake."

Sir Halmar read this letter through twice, very attentively. It impressed him, but not to the extent of immediately sitting down and answering this piteous Mrs. Blake with a cheque for twenty-five pounds. He was sentimental by nature, but neither generous nor impulsive; a big, fair, ruddy man of Danish extraction, his very fairness and burliness gave an instant impression that here was no mere bought knighthood, but an incarnation of protective chivalry: "Sir Halmar: Help me, Sir Halmar!" And help he very often did, with advice, with letters of introduction, with personal escort and free passes, with the most strenuous efforts to interest other people on behalf of a good cause or an unfortunate victim; help with sympathy, with solemn eyes and sentences broken by sincere feeling, a deep kind voice, reassuring pats on hand and shoulder; with addresses noted down and "You can mention my name; you'll find Sir Andrew extremely easy to talk to when he hears that I've sent you." Yes, he was always ready to put himself out, but it took quite a clever man or woman to induce him to take out his fountain-pen and write a cheque with it.

He married when he was very young, and was left a widower not many years afterwards; an obstinate widower, people said, obstinate in that as in everything else. His character, like his appearance, had a sort of firm ruddiness which defied interference, so he did not marry again. His two daughters, when they grew up, looked after him until they married and went off with Empire-building husbands. He managed just as well without them, though he could be very touching on the subject of his own forlorn condition. Burly men can always contrive to seem even more forlorn than their smaller, quicker, slimmer fellows; they cannot dart about here and there and find sanctuary in crevices; their only chance not to appear helpless and derelict is when wearing a policeman's helmet.

But fancy trusting a woman whom you pick up in front of a glass case in a museum, and after five minutes' chatter sending her a whole package of valuable goods! Really! Really!

Sir Halmar called: "Alfred!" Then, as the click of the typewriter from an inner room did not cease, he strode across and flung open the door. "Alfred!"

What emerged, prompt and cheerful, was known to Sir Halmar's friends as "the pink lizard." In colouring he might have been Sir Halmar's own son, but not in build, for he was tiny; an array of pink gums above his teeth expressed perpetual prompt cheerfulness. He had been Sir Halmar's secretary for six years, and the two got along very well together.

"Alfred, tell me what you think of this?" he handed him Mrs. Blake's letter. "I find it very distressing, very distressing indeed. I must do something, undoubtedly, to help the poor silly woman."

Alfred, seeing that compassion with a touch of contempt for the female sex was what was required of him, composed his face to lines denoting these reactions, put on his rimless glasses, which he had taken off when his employer called him, and read through the seven and a half pages of small slanted handwriting.

When he had finished, he read them all over again. Sir Halmar always read everything twice, and Alfred had modelled himself so faithfully in imitation that now he could not have stayed contented with one perusal even had he so desired.

"Now tell me, Alfred, and answer quickly on your instincts before you have time to think the matter over. Is—this—a—sincere—appeal—or—is—it—not?"

"Not," said Alfred, answering wrong. Then, seeing a frown flicker across Sir Halmar's eyes, he amended; "not insincere, definitely. Not bogus. This, in fact, may be the one case out of every dozen which we're always looking for." He was the more emphatic because he had so nearly failed to divine the answer which would tally with Sir Halmar's own conviction.

"Good; that's what I thought. A woman of taste and breeding, too; a woman of our own class; you noticed?—stained-glass windows, and Goethe. Shall we say slightly redundant? Well, perhaps. But, poor soul, she wanted to reach my feelings, she had to reach them, and she had to feel her way in the dark. As it happens, complete simplicity, a stark simplicity, would have pleased me more, but how was she to know that, Alfred?"

Alfred did not know how she was to know that. Also he was having rather a busy morning with a good deal of correspondence on hand, and thought he had better bring Sir Halmar to the point.

"For how much would you like me to make out the cheque?"

Sir Halmar winced slightly at the word "cheque."

"I was thinking of five pounds."

"Five pounds," repeated Alfred, knowing perfectly well from long experience that in the end it would not be five pounds.

"You see what she says: she proposes to go up to Carlisle and interview a solicitor there. Supposing she is altogether destitute—and it's a hard life for a woman struggling alone in the world, especially a woman like this—supposing her to be altogether destitute, five pounds would easily cover her fare and give her, say, two or three nights in Carlisle while the solicitor made inquiries."

"Oh, easily," Alfred agreed; "in fact, Sir Halmar, I see no reason for her to spend two or three nights in Carlisle. An hour should prove to her whether the firm exists or not, or whether it has ever existed; but probably a solicitor might take several weeks to investigate the swindle."

"Then there would really be no sense in her stopping in Carlisle at all; two or three days would be worse than useless."

"Much worse," said Alfred. "But on the other hand, I doubt, Sir Halmar, if she could go up and down on the same day; that is, without excessive fatigue."

Sir Halmar's eyes twinkled: "I shouldn't like her to be excessively fatigued." He often lightly mocked his secretary's penchant for a formal vocabulary. Yet, if he could save himself the expense of a night in Carlisle for Mrs. Blake—"

"How long does the journey take?"

Alfred went into the inner room and returned with an ABC.

"The faster trains appear to take five hours. And five hours back. But the solicitor might not be able to give her an appointment immediately, and she would need a good square meal." It became apparent that humanity was to win over thrift.

"Three pounds, do you think?" with a doubtful look. "Or three pounds ten shillings?"

"The solicitor's fee—"

"Oh, I'd pay that separately," hastily from Sir Halmar.

"You are showing great generosity, if I may say so, Sir Halmar."

In the simple natural way which civilized behaviour forbids, Sir Halmar wanted to reply: "Yes, I know." As it is, he had to deprecate: "I'm afraid not, Alfred, I'm afraid not. If I had obeyed my first impulse, and we all like ourselves in the rôle of fairy godmother, I would have offered to make good her loss over the covers. But all is not lost yet, and should we recover them, and we can help her to make every effort, it would be a great deal better for her self-respect. This letter shows how painfully she shrinks from the idea of accepting money."

"Oh, I'm sure she never would have asked for it," put in Alfred, still playing about with the pages of the ABC. In his busy life, he very rarely had the chance to look at it; but all these hotels at the beginning were most fascinating, so that perhaps he was not quite so alert to Sir Halmar's psychology as usual, otherwise he would never have added: "If they weren't threatening her with proceedings—"

This was an annoying reminder. "They always threaten some time before they actually pounce," said Sir Halmar briefly. "A tradesman has only got to put the word 'solicitor' in a typewritten letter, and the women run round screeching like barn-fowls. They'll wait. When she returns from Carlisle, she'll be able to assure them that something has been done. Something practical that they can understand. Two pounds ten you said, didn't you, Alfred?"

"I'm afraid that won't quite answer, Sir Halmar. The monthly return to Carlisle, third class from Euston, two hundred and ninety-two miles, pop. fifty-seven thousand three hundred and four—"

"Leave out the pop.," Sir Halmar advised him. "I haven't even begun dictating my morning letters yet. What's the fare, monthly return? There would be no day returns in places as far as that."

"Monthly return, seventy-eight and nine; no, that's first-class."

"First-class would embarrass her," decreed Sir Halmar. "Terribly, terribly. We mustn't make blunders of that sort, must we?"

The gums flashed: "No, indeed. Third-class, fifty-two and six return. Two pounds twelve and six. So I'm afraid two pounds ten shillings—and one night and lunch and dinner and breakfast and lunch—"

"My dear fellow, she'd have had to have lunch and dinner and breakfast and lunch if she stayed at home."

"That's very true," said Alfred, but not altogether convinced, nevertheless, that it would not come under the heading of Sir Halmar's expenses. Directly you travelled, you had to have a sum to cover the trip. Otherwise you were out of pocket. This poor woman whose confidence had been so grossly betrayed and who had got herself into such a sad mess, did not at this moment of crisis seem to have a pocket to be out of. He stared at Sir Halmar and Sir Halmar stared back at him. The expenses were rushing up again. Soon they would have returned to their original five pounds.

"Look here," exclaimed bluff Sir Halmar suddenly. "Damn it, why need she go up to Carlisle at all? It's a frightfully long tiring journey; and she's sure to be run down, lying awake at nights and tossing about." Somehow or other the vision of the woman who wrote this letter lying awake at nights filled Sir Halmar with soft fruitiness. Nowhere in the letter was there any indication that she was beautiful, but helplessness and appeal so often take the shape in a man's mind of wet blue eyes uplifted, small fluttering hands with shell-pink nails, delicate features, golden hair. "Why need she go up to Carlisle at all?" he repeated stubbornly. "There must be some better way of getting hold of the name of the best solicitor there. You can find that out for me, Alfred. She can write to him giving him full details, names, dates, etc., and he can do the rest. And send her a letter that she can show those infernal badgering tradesmen. What do you think, Alfred?" Alfred thought it much more sensible.

"Then in that case it would hardly be necessary to send her any money."

"Not at all necessary. Not ready money, that is."

"Yes, that's what I mean, ready money. Of course I'd stand the solicitor's costs, but that's not ready money." One could far more equably bear the thought of an unspecified amount to be paid at some unspecified date in the future, than of an actual five-pound note, a fair and glistening vision in the air and then wholly gone.

But just when everything was so satisfactorily settled, Alfred made a most annoying suggestion:

"'If I cannot get some help by Friday next,'" he quoted, "'you will read in the papers of just another commonplace tragedy'—You know, I wish we could arrange speedier relief from her troubles. Solicitors—I don't particularly know if this applies to Carlisle, I would hesitate to say—" again the gums flashed rosily, and the eyes behind their glasses looked waggish, "but solicitors on the whole are a slow race, you know, they are not express engines. And there's no doubt about it, this gang with whom Mrs. Blake has got involved are likely to vanish rapidly with their unscrupulous profits."

"She couldn't stop them, even if she went up herself. So what—?"

"I was thinking of a private detective," said Alfred in triumph. "I happen to know a very good firm, most discreet, in Cornhill; and if I told them, making sure that it would go no further—'Sir Halmar likes to hide his charities under a bushel,' I'd say—but if I mentioned that you would make yourself responsible for the expenses, they could send up one of their best men immediately. I believe it's the usual thing to make a deposit of, say, five pounds—"

Sir Halmar nearly wept. Here they were again, back at that five pounds. And the matter had gone too far for him to say: 'Wipe it out and do nothing.' Besides, his sentiments were already involved. One could not be so brutal as that towards Lorna Blake, Lorna all forlorn, fair Lorna with the tears in her gentle—no, her gentian-blue eyes, trusting him, believing in him, her little fingers all pricked and scarred from the harsh needle. "Stitch, stitch, stitch, in poverty, hunger and dirt—" No, he was sure that she could not be dirty: "And you shall wash your body and keep your linen white"—That was Lorna. Sir Halmar was very fond of poetry. But five pounds deposit for a private detective, and who knows how much more it might cost? He stared resentfully at Alfred, whose expression gradually lost its Jack Horner complacence as he realized that he had failed to pull out a plum. Yet for a moment he did not see how to recall the suggestion and be Sir Halmar's good boy again. And Sir Halmar did not see how he could save his five pounds and still be Lorna

Blake's gallant benefactor. It was as much a deadlock as Sheridan had devised for his duel in *The Critic.*

Sir Halmar had an inspiration. "Colonel Henshaw!" he exclaimed. "Of course, the very thing. Much better than either a private detective, or than letting the poor woman go herself. My old friend Bob Henshaw, Chief Constable or whatever they call 'em, at Belcastle. I haven't seen him since he went, and that must be, let me see, four years, but I'm quite convinced that I've only to write and ask him, and he would attend to this matter for me. And he's the proper person to attend to it. These racketeers are always afraid when something official comes along in big boots to round them up."

"Belcastle." Alfred carefully spread out the map from the beginning of the ABC.

"You've got Scotland," said Sir Halmar over his shoulder, and Alfred blushed and quickly reversed the map.

"Now here's Carlisle, and here's Belcastle. No, they're not very close to each other. A good forty or fifty miles, I'm afraid, if not more. Fifty-five, taking the scale to be—"

Sir Halmar interrupted. "Now look here, Alfred, you must train your mind to make larger gestures; not to get cramped. It's an inessential detail, surely, whether the Colonel has to spend an hour or an hour and a half in his car, when probably he's touring round the country all day. I'll write to him personally. He'll be delighted to oblige a friend. And I'll write to Mrs. Blake, too, with my own hand, and reassure her. It gives great satisfaction to a woman of this type to feel that a high official of the police force is actually interesting himself in person in her affairs. That'll help her to sleep tonight, better than aspirin. Though if she could see the Colonel—"

Halmar flung back his fine Norse head and laughed at the memory of his friend's pippin strength. It was a fine thing to be a Viking.

Chapter Four

For the moment he had saved that glistening precious five-pound note. But directly he received her frenzied telegram, heard her voice, urgent, desperate on the phone, he knew sadly that it was as good as lost again, as bad as lost. He would be lucky if it were no more than five pounds. That was what came of sentiment and sympathy, two traitors to carefulness. The telegram must have been sent off, he reckoned, the instant she had his letter. It read: "Some dreadful mistake for heavens sake do nothing till I see you Lorna Blake." And the telephone call was even more frantic: a husky, stammering and yet curiously attractive voice besought him to give her an interview immediately. It kept on repeating, as in the telegram: "There's been a terrible mistake." But Sir Halmar was offended. This was all too dramatic, too intimate. His benevolent instincts, his desire to help a poor creature in trouble, had risen to the five-pound standard, fallen, risen again, and finally adjusted itself: he had been prepared to write to Colonel Henshaw, didn't mind the trouble in the least, was willing to ask an old friend to take considerable time and pains to set right an injustice to a stranger. Well then, why should she not show her gratitude by behaving sensibly, letting him have the details he required and then settling down to wait?

"Really, my dear Mrs. Blake, I'm a very busy man and London is not my home. I have a good deal to attend to here before I return to Tarmouth." Her excitement alarmed him. All that burly ruddiness covered a soul that was somewhat less than brave. "Really, Mrs. Blake, I so seldom give a personal interview. I should be besieged if I did. You can have no idea. If you could calm yourself and tell me what you wish me to write to Colonel Henshaw, or to withhold when I write? It would be a great pity for you to lose this opportunity. Colonel Henshaw—"

She rang off.

He was exasperated, and yet in an odd way sorry, as though some rich pleasure had been snatched away from him. Alfred found him extremely difficult to deal with during the next hour or two. Tact, Alfred kept on saying to himself; show tact; tact. He was not admonishing Sir Halmar, but himself. Alfred was a nice person. His ambition was to be a statesman. He saw himself in the Cabinet at a crisis: tact, that's the main thing, Tact Before Action, not Action Before Tact. A good slogan for the world to remember—

And then the woman burst in on them. She had left Webster no time to announce her while she waited in the hall. Afterwards he told Alfred that she had cried out almost before he opened the door: "I have an appointment. You *must* let me in. It's life or death." And had rushed through him as though he were air. Webster was very unlike air. So Alfred realized the onset must have been imperious and dynamic as the Winged Victory rushing to avert cataclysm.

But all this was afterwards. For the moment, here she was in Sir Halmar's presence, and here was he, Alfred, out of it. For her first words had been: "I must see you alone. I must." And Sir Halmar had yielded without demur.

He had found her entrance startling, but that was nothing compared with the shock of her first revelation. She had been silent for a moment after Alfred's exit, as though rallying her strength now that she was actually in here at last, with butler and secretary both disposed of; so he began with some careful remark, chosen and modulated to calm her, about how pleased he had been to have found it in his power to suggest some practical solution for the grave problem she had set forth in her letter; when she hurled herself upon his last words.

"It's not true. It wasn't my letter. I never wrote it. Sir Halmar, you must believe me, I can't be responsible for the consequences if you don't let me tell you about this dreadful, dreadful mistake. I never wrote that letter—"

"My dear child, of course. Of course not. Certainly you shall tell me. Now would you like a glass of sherry first? a little light sherry;

– 241 –

Manzanilla? All the ladies, I believe, feel the better for a glass of Manzanilla."

She shook her head, but thanked him with a sudden very sweet smile. Sir Halmar was bewitched by her smile; it was so merry, so childish, such pretty curves, anyone but a brute must have smiled back at her. She was, he thought, beautiful in a subtle way; a way that most men might not have noticed in the first three minutes, but he was never taken in by mere surface value. Something a little foreign about her: those brilliant eyes, the grace of her long neck. She ought to wear earrings, opal drops, fire in a milky cloud. Unless, of course, she was superstitious. A Russian mother or grandmother might have accounted for her enchanting husky voice, the expressive movements of her hands, too fluid for a purely English type, too free from self-consciousness. And the way she had wound her chiffon scarf round her throat and shoulders and upper arms so that it delicately stressed the unnatural heat of this day at the end of October, that was foreign too. And he admired pale slender women.

"Sir Halmar, I never wrote that letter. I shouldn't dream of it. It's dreadful even to think … a begging letter … a letter as good as asking for *money*, God knows what my little girl would say if she heard. But it's happened before, and I'm afraid it'll happen again unless I—Oh, I wish life weren't so difficult!" This last was said in an undertone, as though angry with her own weakness. "One oughtn't to be soft," she continued on the same gently chiding note, "ought one?" she flashed up at Sir Halmar. "Come, own up. You think that all women, especially alone as I am, are too soft, too foolish, too confiding? And that's why they get themselves into muddles and have to appeal to a man like you to help them out?"

"My dear lady—"

"But it's true. It's true, only not in the way you think. I haven't even the faintest idea what she wrote to you, except that it's always the same in the end. It's always to ask for money."

"*She?*"

"Yes. Our governess. Miss Gardiner."

She was calmer now it was out. But Sir Halmar remained stupefied. He did not know what to think or say.

"Please, Sir Halmar, might I see the letter? I dread reading it, but it will be easier for me to explain once I know just what she has written in my name."

He unlocked his desk and produced the letter.

"Yes, she's even imitated my writing again," murmured Lorna Blake.

He had to admire the courage with which she read the letter through from end to end; then with sudden passion tore it across into small pieces.

"And now," she said, looking up at him as he bent over her solicitously with the glass of sherry which against her will he had sent for, and poured out while she was reading, "now that it's destroyed, I can explain better. Thank you very very much. What a lovely colour. Like amber with the sun shining through. It's very good of you to spoil someone whom you must still think of as trying to swindle you."

Sir Halmar declared with absolute conviction that from the very moment he had set eyes on Mrs. Blake he had known that was impossible. "But your *governess*! Surely, my dear Mrs. Blake, not that it's my business, but ought you to keep her if she forges your writing and uses your name? It's criminal, you know, using someone else's name to obtain money under false pretences."

"I know, oh, I know. But so far I've managed to protect poor Miss Gardiner; Gardie we always call her. And as long as it's only my name … You see, she doesn't use it to get anything for herself. She never has, and that's what would make it criminal, wouldn't it? Poor soul, she's simply devoted to me and to my little girl. She's been with us for years, and she can't bear it when things get really tight and I have to economize and can't give the child simply everything. My husband, while he was alive, used to say: 'Get rid of her.' Just like that. It only happened once before he died, but he was furious. He couldn't see really that she was, is, terribly pitiful. Do you think, too, that I ought to get rid of her?"

"I certainly do," he replied gravely. "She may be devoted as you say, but all the more reason—Am I to understand that nothing she said in that letter was true? There was no swindling woman at the museum? No bogus firm in Carlisle?"

"Nor anywhere. She picks up anything that's around, when she's working up for this, and just weaves it in: someone may have mentioned Carlisle to her, casually—There's not a word of truth, except, frankly, that we are rather hard up; but nothing desperate; not the way she describes it, as though we had to beg. I was brought up in a very old-fashioned way; lots of people nowadays, I believe, think nothing of borrowing, but my mother would have been appalled. She was such a sweet dumpy old thing, and as honest as the day."

She looked at the fragments of letter which she had hurled against the electric fire, forgetting in her wave of anger that it could not burn them to ashes.

"How untidy of me, in your beautiful room. Do forgive me. I feel a little as though I had come here and soiled it." She bent to pick up the fragments, but he forestalled her. "Leave them alone, my dear; Webster will see to it presently. But I confess I'm alarmed, very seriously alarmed, at the notion that you are letting your tender heart, your too vivid sympathy, leave you at the mercy of—You say she has done it before?"

"Three or four times at least. I've always found out in time and had to rush round to explain. It's so painful. Once I actually had to take the money back, and it was ages before the man could be persuaded that I was in no need of it and hadn't cadged it from him. He was an M.P., too. No, I won't tell you his name, it wouldn't be fair to poor old Gardie. And each time I had to be so stern with her, it was terrible, she cried and cried and swore to me she wouldn't ever do it again. I've always managed to keep it all from my little girl, Gardie's devoted to her, simply devoted; she's her slave; she has no life, outside us. Sir Halmar, doesn't it make a difference that she would have spent not one penny on herself? That it was all, every bit of it, given unselfishly for others? Doesn't it?"

She looked up at him with the trusting limpid gaze of a child who expects that the wise man will speedily make clear the confused criss-cross of print on the page set before her to read. It happened that this was just the sort of talk for Sir Halmar to revel in. Oh, the luscious rewarding feeling of someone who comes to you to say that, after all, she does not want money, instead of after all she does. It was like having hard cash poured into his palms; like having it actually handed to him tightly wadded into a stocking. It was amazing to suppose money had gone flying out, and then see it flying back, as it were, trebled in value from this fancied sojourn in a limbo of sheer loss. And it was not that she was weak; far from it: strong as the beat of swans' wings flying down the river. And yet all that strength, that strange foreign enchantment, was being used to persuade him to do nothing for her, nothing at all, except advise her. Every moment was a positive enchantment. All that strength, and yet she deferred to him, asked him to dictate to her what she should do. He was heady with the compliment. It so happened that no woman could have found a surer way to bewitch him than first to let him think she desired his money, and then amazingly lighten him of this fear.

And now they were going to have a long, fascinating, ethical discussion. He could see it coming towards him as a small boy sees a parcel being brought containing the desired clockwork train. A discussion, partly on an abstract problem, and partly on one which called for practical masculine administration. He drew the opposite armchair up to the fire, and subsided into it, smiling. Then remembered, stopped smiling, and looked experienced.

"Mrs. Blake, I feel very anxious about you. Yes, indeed I do, although I have known you such a short time. But I want you to make me a promise. I want you to promise me that you will send this governess of yours, this—Miss Garnett, did you say?"

"Gardiner," she corrected him. "And I'll promise you whatever I can, Sir Halmar. I owe you that, because you've already helped me so beautifully over a painful situation for both of us."

"It's been a very happy situation for me," said Sir Halmar, and wondered if she had understood him.

There was a pause, and then:

"And the promise?"

"Ah yes, the promise. I want you to promise to send Miss Gardiner right away out of your life. The greater the distance, the better."

"I couldn't. Sir Halmar, I simply couldn't. Apart from any question of feelings, the fare alone would make it not possible; I—"

He interrupted: "Mrs. Blake, you must bear with me if I'm crude, will you allow me to pay for her fare?"

She looked straight at him, and he could not tell if he had offended her by the suggestion. Her dark eyes were shadowed, her lips quivered. There was a vibrancy in the air behind them as though she were willing him to guess her thoughts.

"No," he spoke suddenly. "No, you mustn't. That's just what you must *not* think."

"What mustn't I think?"

"That there's still the slightest doubt left in my mind. That I—that I—" he was blundering about like a bee against a window, "—that I wouldn't have dared make you such an offer if your letter—Ah, but it was *her* letter, and I do realize how you must hate every word of it, with your name signed in what looks like your writing. It's just because of that, that I'm so urgent you should get rid of her; and it's because you're soft-hearted that I want the whole responsibility to be mine, down to the last farthing. You see, Mrs, Blake, it will make it easier for you to let me do it all, choose the place, South Africa, South America, whatever it is; choose the boat, pay her fare, everything."

Alfred, in the inner room, wondered what his employer could be pleading so loudly and earnestly, with so much vigorous youth in his voice.

"Has one a right? There's a poem of Browning's—'It's a dangerous matter to play with souls.' Isn't it a terrific responsibility for you, playing with my poor Miss Gardiner's soul? Torn away from us, and really for no reason, for she's not to blame if she doesn't think it wrong, is she? To ask on behalf of others, is that a disgrace? Can it be? A sort of Lady Bountiful complex? So many do it and are blessed for it; nuns, for instance, when they come round collecting. Have I shaken you?"

"No," replied Sir Halmar sturdily. "You're eloquent, but you argue like a woman. There's too much heart in it. You haven't shaken me in the least."

"Then how should I feel if I heard that poor Gardie had thrown herself overboard, just before they reached Table Bay?"

"You would feel nothing, I hope. You've done nothing. It's out of our hands since you've come to me. If I choose, I could prosecute this woman, this governess of yours, for having tried to get money out of me on false pretences."

"I know, I know. That's why, when you wrote about the Chief Constable—the police—prosecution—it all seemed so near. I was terrified for Gardie. And now, instead, you're offering to pay her fare to South Africa. In the spirit of pure clemency. It's a miracle."

"In the spirit of practical consideration for you, my dear. You've had too much to bear from her."

Her liquid gaze was still fixed on him, with some question threshing about in her mind which had not yet been settled by his solid argument.

"We are, aren't we, or we might be, responsible for someone we have never seen, and who because of something we've done, kills himself?"

"Herself," corrected Sir Halmar. "Well, I take all the responsibility; fair and square, I take it. Now what do you think of me?"

She was one of the few women he had ever met who could rise from an armchair without any apparent effort, as though flowing upwards. She smiled at him again:

"I would rather not tell … fair and square … what I think of you."

He turned away his head, and an even brighter rosiness spread over his wonted flush of good health.

"Fair and square," repeated Lorna, and her inflection showed who was in her mind to be decorated with those adjectives. "But what will *you* think of *me*, Sir Halmar, if I accept? Miss Gardiner's fare will, after all, cost more than the chair-covers. Asking for things—it's against decency—"

"No."

"Deportment, then," and she saw him twinkle tenderly at the prim word. "Yes, deportment. No one ever gets a present which they haven't asked for."

"You certainly have not asked me for this."

"You can't convince me. I'm a gold-digger, after all. But I'll accept her fare gratefully," and he had an impression of a tiny joke which leapt from her mind, like a fish that twisted brightly out of the water and back again. The simple joke had pleased her, then? that she had, after all, proved a gold-digger.

"But there's one stipulation. You mustn't see her before she goes. Poor old Gardie, I'm afraid you're right in everything you say, but I can at least protect her from that much shame."

Sir Halmar agreed to the stipulation. He did not particularly want to see Miss Gardiner. Such a meeting could not profit either of them, and, from a social point of view, had no chance of proving a sparkling success.

Chapter Five

←→

They had only been engaged two days, and, at Lorna's urgent request, the engagement was still a secret, when she said to him one evening at dinner in a quiet and perfect little restaurant in Albemarle Street: "Halmar, I have a confession to make."

He gazed at her fondly over his glass of deep-coloured Richebourg. His beloved did not drink wine. She had told him, laughing at herself, that it was too much of a strain to pretend she liked it, and she had better be candid from the very beginning and drink the tea or lemonade she preferred; and sometimes, when she felt exotic, a glass of sweet cider.

"I worship you in rose-colour," was all the infatuated man found to say in answer to her last remark.

"I'm afraid you *see* me in rose-colour." Lorna shook her head in mock deprecation; the earrings he had given her, fire-opals, for she had declared she was not in the least superstitious, dangled and quivered with light at every movement. He reminded her, when he had bought them: "Opals are only semi-precious stones, you know, and not at all expensive. You would have done much better for yourself to pretend you were superstitious. It doesn't pay to be honest."

But her answer had been: "One can't help one's nature. Besides, after we're married, I'd be sure to forget and give myself away."

"Say that again, Lorna my darling."

"I'd be sure to forget—"

"No. 'After we're married.'"

"'After we're married,'" she repeated, and he beamed at her like the sun at high noon from a shadeless sky. For he lacked eyebrows.

"Well, how about this dreadful confession. Tell me where you've hidden the body and we'll see what can be done."

"It's my little girl. Something about her that I haven't told you yet. You may not forgive me—"

Sir Halmar took another sip of his Burgundy. He had realized already, even during the short period of his felicity, that there might be something dubious for him to learn about Lorna's little girl; for she had not been produced yet for his inspection, and since Lorna had accepted him they had talked entirely of themselves and of the future. Lorna had been so delighted to hear that he had a big country house several miles away from the town of Tarmouth. She said it had always been her greatest wish to live in the country and never see London again; and when he had spoken of his present *pied-à-terre* in Berkeley Mansions as being too small for two of them and therefore he would have to exchange it for a larger flat, she had cried: "Don't do that, please, please, Halmar. I shall never want to come with you to London when you have to go. I'd never dare move about among famous or brilliant people in London. And I'm quite sure all your friends must be famous and brilliant. I should have nothing to say to them. So leave me down there with my gardening gloves and my store-cupboard, and I shall be perfectly contented. You know, I'm really a housewife at heart, though I've had to be domestic on such a tiny scale. I'm the sort of woman who gets a thrill out of going through the linen-cupboard or counting jars of home-made jam. And as you like wine, I'll stretch a point and learn how to make dandelion wine and cowslip wine and—oh, elderberry—" She broke off and laughed gleefully at the sight of his disgusted face: "Now what's wrong?" she teased him.

"You can call those, *wine*?"

"So do several thousand other people. In the time of Good Queen Bess the women gave it to their heroes to drink when they came back from doughty deeds on the Spanish Main"

"Heroes didn't know better, in those simple days. They'd have something to say about it now."

"My dear Sir Halmar," she sparkled back.

He stopped her lips with a kiss.

"Now remember, that's the penalty. 'Sir Halmar' indeed."

But she repeated directly her lips were free, sedately lending pomp to his title: "Sir Halmar—"

"Lady Fair?" He was delighted at having found a retort. Presently, after another little interlude of badinage, he found yet a better substitute for "Lady Fair": "Lady Wimple." Now, when she called him "Sir Halmar," with its association of Vikings and the North and men with winged helmets, he could always fling back "Lady Wimple," asking her to bring forth her possets and her cordials and her firkins of elderberry wine. Never before had he met anyone with such a flow of intoxicating conversation, that just matched his own and stimulated him to further wordy frolics. She was perfect.

Yet in all this, he noticed, there was no further word of her little girl.

"Come, my dear, don't be afraid. Tell me. I'm quite prepared, you know, for all the small burdens of step-fatherhood. I have had two of my own, though now, thank goodness, they're grown-up and married and away. Not that I don't miss them," he added hastily. But his children had been a great expense and not always considerate. One of them had even told him lies, and one had called him "an old has-been" no more than seven years ago.

An old has-been! He, Sir Halmar Barnard, only two or three years over sixty, prop of Tarmouth, consulted by all, his free advice listened to with deepest deference: "You ought to have been a lawyer, Sir Halmar." Blessed by the poor, knighted by the King. "Has been," indeed. He already felt a warming of his heart towards Lorna's little girl, whom he felt sure, with such a mother, must prove modest and respectful and affectionate, and enchant him with her pretty ways; in spite of the mysterious bogey just attached to her, of; "something you won't like."

"She's on the stage." Lorna rushed it out in one breath. And then looked up fearfully at her betrothed to see how he had borne the shock.

He threw himself back in his chair and roared with such bluff laughter that other diners glanced towards their dim alcove in surprise.

"You're the sweetest, most old-fashioned Lady Wimple that ever lived in a shoe," he cried. "Did you really think that today, in 1936, a reasonable man could possibly mind the idea of the stage as a profession?"

"Perhaps I am a little old-fashioned," Lorna admitted. "I've never been quite happy about it, but Molly showed such talent from the time she was quite a little girl, that I had to give way. I remember when she was going to play Bottom in *The Midsummer Night's Dream*—" She related, laughing a little at herself, how she had determined to save money by providing a home-made ass's head, and what a fumbled failure it had been, so that at the last moment the school had had to send up to Clarkson's.

"Bottom? But that's a strange part for a little girl. And naturally, I was thinking of her as still a little girl."

"That's very sweet of you, Sir Halmar."

"Not at all, Lady Wimple." He raised his glass to her with a courtly gesture.

"Molly's seventeen. She's a comic genius. She went to Miss Rolandi's Children's School of Acting and they gave her her first part in the West End, Dick Whittington's Cat, before she was sixteen. She was never any good in what they call straight parts. I should have preferred seeing her as Titania or Alice Fitzwarren or Tessa in *The Constant Nymph*. But Molly, bless her, prefers playing the fool, I've seen her audiences rock with laughing when she clowns. Perhaps she's going to be like Gracie Fields. I don't know."

"Is she amusing at home?"

Lorna shook her head and the opals danced again.

"Not often. It's rather a pensive child, but very sensible. One of her mistresses said Molly reminded her of Alice Through the Looking Glass, just because of that; Alice always kept her head, didn't she, even when she went on getting smaller or larger, which I'm sure would have worried me terribly—" Now that she had broken the ice, Lorna babbled on and on about Molly, and no one hearing her could have doubted her passionate love for her ewe lamb. "It's silly and sentimental to call her that, I suppose, but what I should have done without Molly during these long lonely years—"

"All over now," he assured her.

And: "All over now," she whispered back, with a little tremulous smile.

Halmar thought that even in the two days they had been engaged she had somehow changed her personality. At that first interview, and surely no couple had ever met more strangely than they, she had struck him as faintly exotic, exciting, her origin laced with some hot gipsy streak, perhaps; an enchantress in spite of herself. But now the foreign element had died, or had he invented it? She was cosier, more of the domestic type that would light a fire but never start a conflagration; she suggested dimples and mob-caps, honeysuckle in the porch and a kettle on the hob; church, too, on Sunday morning; an English church. Now that she was to be Lady Barnard, he was glad of this change in her personality. Her voice was less husky, more confiding; as for the impression she had first brought into the room, of a flying sunset tangled behind swaying trees—Rubbish! Imagination! Why, some of her ideas were positively cherubic. He was not even quite sure any more that opal earrings did suit her style. His mind hunted for other semi-precious stones to replace them later on: amethysts, now what about amethysts? No nonsense about amethysts.

"Tell me more about my stepdaughter. Is she pretty? What am I to say to her?"

"She wasn't as a child, though it was a dear little face. But everybody seems to think her quite beautiful now. And you'll see her almost at once; she's been on tour and comes back tomorrow; that's why I had to tell you."

"Oho!" cried her fiancé "so the confession was wrung out of you, was it?"

"I'm afraid it was."

Yes, he was absolutely right: She had dimples, very subtle dimples, not the kind that hit men in the eye. What a prize she was. How he looked forward to showing her off to all his friends and relations in Tarmouth and the neighbourhood.

"Does she know about you and me?"

By now his brandy had been poured out and his cigar lit. He moved his chair round and took her hand.

"Halmar! The waiter's looking."

"Treat for him."

"No, she doesn't know yet. I shall have to tell her, shan't I? It's absurd of me, Halmar, but it does make me feel a little shy."

"It's admirable of you. Was she very attached to her father?"

"Oh no, she hardly remembered him."

"Well then, I don't think we shall have much trouble. You say she's a sensible girl. I'm very fond of young people, Naturally, at first the idea of a stepfather goes against the grain; Hamlet isn't always a boy, you know. But I'll make a bit of a fuss of her, and she's bound to be pleased at the thought that you're going to be looked after at last."

"Oh, Halmar, one other thing: I've always managed to keep it from Molly about poor Miss Gardiner, you know, and the tricks she played. She was quite fond of her governess, though nothing exaggerated. Modern children, I think, are subconsciously a little scornful of foolish sentimental people. She probably used to wish that poor Gardie wouldn't pet her quite so much or weep over her and give her silly little presents, the wrong things at the wrong time."

"What will you tell her, then? Just that she's gone to South Africa for her health?"

"Oh, something of the sort," vaguely. "She had been coughing a lot (that was quite true, you know), and dreaded the winter, and an uncle

- 253 -

turned up who was willing to pay her fare to South Africa, so I packed her off without any argument."

"Funny how near the truth one can get," remarked Halmar profoundly. "An uncle did turn up, didn't he? if I may call myself poor Gardie's uncle—"

Lorna cried: "Oh, I'm so glad to hear you call her that; it shows you've softened; that you've forgiven her. You were a little hard at first whenever you spoke of her."

"No wonder. For years she had put you in the most ambiguous and humiliating position. Now she's gone for ever, I can afford to soften. Poor Miss Gardiner."

"Poor Miss Gardiner," echoed Lorna. "Then there's no need even to mention her in front of Molly. I'm a bad actress, and I should find it difficult to—what's the word?—dissemble."

"You don't have to dissemble. Gardie's of no importance except that she brought us together. I'll forgive her everything for that. How shall we tell your little girl we met?"

Lorna absently ran the soft folds of her scarf up and down between her fingers, as she considered. "Do you know, I believe she won't ask. Molly's not inquisitive. She takes things for granted, in that pensive way of hers. If it should come up, the simplest way is always the best! I'll say I was in some little legal difficulty and had to go to you about it, and you were very kind and helped me out."

"Bring her to dinner tomorrow," commanded Halmar, "I'm anxious to make friends with this pensive maiden. That's just one of your own delicious nineteenth-century words; I shall always call my stepdaughter 'the pensive maiden.' Are her affections engaged?"

"Yes."

"What is it, my darling? You shivered."

"Somebody walking over my grave. What were we talking about?"

"We were talking about Molly's young man. Do you like him? Shall we ask him to dinner as well, or doesn't he live in London?"

"He lives in America. Don't speak of him, I—I don't like him. I hope it will come to nothing. No, no, I don't. That was wicked of me, I know

– 254 –

he'd look after Molly. I want her to be happy. It's just my private feeling, or perhaps it's vanity. He doesn't like me."

"My darling, I refuse to believe in such an unnatural young man. Wait till he gets to know you as I do. He can't have met you often, if he lives in America."

"Only once. Halmar, what's that lovely green drink in the little glass they're carrying to the table over there?"

"That? That's crême de menthe, the ladies' delight. Shall I order some for you?"

She said no. She said yes. She said might she leave it, if it was dreadfully bitter? She faltered. She tasted. She exclaimed, surprised, that it wasn't bitter at all, it was sweet, only it burnt her throat. She begged Halmar to finish the rest, so that it shouldn't be wasted. She pretended to be hurt by his refusal. She playfully commanded him. She took another sip and said perhaps it was not so bad. Halmar promised to get in a supply for her especial benefit, down at Beechcroft Manor. She chided him for masterfulness, and said she was not going to allow it—

And that lasted until he said good-night to her, on the doorstep of No. 31 Netherby Park Road.

Chapter Six

Shirley sat alone in her study trying to write, but succeeded only in producing some very complicated designs over the margins of the foolscap paper, designs that floated off into beautiful rounded arabesques curling and uncurling within each other, untrammelled by life with its abrupt and angular circumstances. Her meditations, looping, overlapping, brought in Alec and Grace and Molly, Marcus, Neil, Jay,

Lorna and herself, with a host of subsidiary irrelevances. Alec's death had shocked her into realizing that her behaviour after a disappointment in love had hardly been better than his, except that she had talked less of it. Certainly, spread over a period of more than twenty years since she had lost Marcus, it looked as though she had had a tolerably active and successful career, but ransacking her mind and soul she could not find much in either to justify herself. Alexander at least had had the justification of continuing to think Sylvia perfect and that he had therefore been robbed of perfection, which was, indeed, a thing to worry about. "Men have died from time to time"—the lines always drifted up whenever she thought of Alec—"Men have died from time to time and worms have eaten them, but not for love." Still, Rosalind didn't know everything. "To think I squandered my whole will-to-live on a man who calls all his children names beginning with G. And the world in the state it is now."

After that, she got to work, offering herself for whatever job was urgent and topical; trying, if it were too late to alter the mood of lazy bitterness which had become so natural as to be part of herself, at least not to let it dictate what was worth while to do and what wasn't. She had professed herself sceptical on the subject of committees, experts, and "the proper channels," but now she found that these people who formed shapes in order to deal with confusion, really did achieve more than could be dismissed by a shrug of the shoulders. Shirley had always been a tolerant free-lance, too laconic or else too impulsive; all her views and principles weakened by a sense of irony, and by her far too final opinion of herself as an individual of no solid value, but only amusing views and rambling affection. She had quarrelled once with Alexander on this very subject. He had been shocked to the bone when Shirley declared that she had had affairs out of indolent kindness, or, characteristically underrating impulse, just to be obliging; a might-as-well mood; marriage, she maintained, demanded live passion: the very fire which most men and women deem essential only for their interludes. But Alexander, in his obsession, upbraided Shirley for her slack ideas, yet once availed himself of her kindness ... and then added his infidelity as a postscript to his remorse-on-account-of-Sylvia saga, cursing himself for the lapse. As though it mattered, Shirley had reflected, listening ironically while, regardless of her presence and certainly of her feelings, he did both sides of a dialogue containing Sylvia's supposed reproaches and his own arguments, all very comforting. It was one of the most amazing things in wonderful nature, Shirley reflected, the extent to which men could be oblivious of her feelings. She did not go so far as to believe that all women were exposed to this amazement; but rather that some damnable provocation in herself, some challenge of which she was not aware and would gladly dispense with, invited it.

But now Alexander had died for love. And Neil, who should have avenged him, had achieved final justification of Shirley's sense of irony by falling deeply in love with the child of the very woman who had been responsible.

He had brought Molly and Shirley together shortly after his first visit to Netherby Park Road. "I'm not asking you to do your best to like her, Shirley, or any nonsense of that sort. You won't have to do your best. Molly is anyone's peer, age or no age."

"Calm down," Shirley advised him. "This isn't the Zoo in a thunderstorm. And I'm not proposing to patronize Molly, if that's what you mean, simply because I've had nearly a quarter of a century longer in which to make a fool of myself."

"No. But because Lorna's her mother—"

"Is that why you glared? Oh, if God can make a rainbow, He can give Lorna an honest daughter. Though it's funny that He should want to."

"Other young girls," said Neil, "well, you can see them trying to be honest, but her honesty is without effort, like a waterfall."

Shirley's friendship with Molly was of the satisfying nature which sometimes occurs when there is such disparity of age as between a girl of eighteen and a woman of forty-one. Shirley could not but be delicately flattered that Molly should so instantly have preferred her company to that of any youthful contemporary; more flattered than if Molly had been quite a child, for she remembered that children so often have not the power to roam afield and must take what is nearest, and do so indiscriminately. And again, they have often, though the grown-up rarely admits it, material advantages to gain. But Molly became simply Shirley's friend; spoke freely of her own thoughts and affairs and never asked for Shirley's, not because she was an egoist, but because the diffidence of her youth caused her to be certain that Shirley would not be likely to honour her so highly; and anyhow, at forty-one, if you were Shirley, you were so wise and experienced and strong and scornful that you could manage your life without needing to make confidences.

Shirley and Neil, after taking counsel, had decided, as far as Molly was concerned, to handle the whole situation of Lorna and her Visiting as a perpetual joke. It seemed as though this were their best technique to save a strain on Molly's loyalties. Compassion she would not stand, and they were aware of it; she knew it was there, and could be called out if necessary. And for the trio never to speak of Lorna at all would have been an unending discomfort; sudden silences; things half spoken and snatched back again. No, the joke was best, and Molly caught at the solution and assisted it so swiftly and gratefully that it was evident they had chosen what she would have chosen herself. Shirley believed that with Neil for her love, and herself as a friend, Molly was as happy now as was possible since the catastrophe which had befallen her sister. Jay's trial and sentence was not more than three weeks ago. Neil had gone up himself to Edinburgh with the bad news, and Shirley had had a heart-broken letter from Molly, unconsciously revealing how severe her vigil had been all through her childhood, for it was a letter showing no surprise, Neil, too, had said Molly was not surprised. She had hoped passionately when Jay first went to Southampton that sanctuary might fold around her for a time, and this hope had been betrayed, but it had been slight compared with the recurring cycle of her fears.

Molly was arriving that day in London after a three months' tour. Shirley had expected her to dinner, but she had had a hasty telephone call: "Darling, I can't come. It's maddening. I've got to go and dine with some pompous old friend of Mummy's. But I'll try and break away, and rush round later."

Suddenly she saw Molly herself come round the corner. She was walking, almost running, her olive velvet cloak blown back from a thin dinner-dress of snowdrops formalized on a soft green ground. Under her arm she carried an enormous melon, half out of its wrapping. The melon seemed to have a desire to escape, but Molly tugged it along ruthlessly. Now she was directly under Shirley's balcony.

"Molly!"

She looked up quickly. Her cheeks were flushed, her eyes stormy; her usual serenity had been whipped to a tempest.

"Coming!" she called up superfluously. "Oh, Shirley *darling*!—" She dropped her encumbrance, picked it up with an impatient gesture, and as though she lugged the yellow world and would be glad to put it down, disappeared under the jut of the balcony to the entrance of the building.

Shirley smiled. "Bless her—" But she was anxious all the same. What had happened to get the child into such a state? It could not be Jay's fate any more; that would be a continual sadness, but Molly had known about it already for three weeks; and just now, as she fought her way up the road, sudden rage and sudden betrayal were her companions. A ring at the door and then Molly burst in.

My God, reflected Shirley, it's bad, whatever it is.

"Here, darling, this is for you. Do take it. I've left home for ever this time. There's been hell to pay. Can I stay here with you for a bit? Mummy's going to be married again, but it isn't that."

She flopped down upon the rug, but was up again in a moment, tried another chair, tried the arm of Shirley's chair; marched up and down the room as though she were Napoleon on board the *Bellerophon*, Shirley said, or an infuriated colonel with an Eastern liver.

"Oh, if you don't want me—" Molly began, with complete confidence that Shirley did.

"If I don't want you, you'll remove yourself and your luggage, is that it? and find another home for lost bairns before I can say water-melon. Is that the only luggage you've brought, by the way?"

"It's not luggage, it's a present. I don't know why I brought it, either, except that I saw it yesterday on a barrow, before it began to look large and silly, and I thought: 'I'll take this down to Shirley,' knowing you like them. I meant to stop the taxi on my way home from Euston, you see, and just lay it in your hall-porter's hands and smile and say: 'Please give this to Miss Dennison. It's Scotch.' Only Mummy upset it all by being at the station with a car the size of a baronial hall, upholstered in pale grey suede. *His* car. I dined with them tonight. He—he calls her 'Lady Wimple.'" Molly collapsed into half-sobbing laughter.

"Steady," put in Shirley. "We can't bear too much at once. 'Lady Wimple' did you say? Is he Sir Somebody Wimple?"

"He's Sir Halmar Barnard. 'Lady Wimple' is playful, like 'La, Sir Halmar'; 'Lud, Lady Wimple.'"

"Sir Halmar Barnard. It sounds incredibly respectable. Lady Barnard." There was awe in Shirley's tone which anyone not aware of the peculiar situation might easily have put down to a speculative envy on the part of the woman with no husband, for her contemporary who had just achieved the promise of a second. "God, Molly, how does Lorna do it? Suppose you stop pouring out drinks and leaving them in every part of the room, and take one glassful and empty it. You look all in. Surely my baby girl doesn't mind being given a stepfather?"

"*Of course* I don't mind. What sort of an ass do you take me for? It's been the object of my life to get Mummy happily settled. But, Shirley—" The girl sprang up again, flame in her eyes. "—It's Jay. She's denied Jay. Three times for all I know. Just because Jay's in prison." The damning words were pronounced as steadily as though she were saying "because Jay's in the country." "She told the man she had only one daughter: 'My little girl, my Molly.' Shirley, wouldn't it make you feel sick and horrible? Could anyone be more cowardly? Any mother, I mean?"

"It's pretty bad," said Shirley, facing it with Molly and not attempting a palliative.

Lorna's younger daughter raved on:

"She pretended to me it was for Jay's sake: to save Jay's pride; she said: 'Jay would prefer it.'" Molly tore that up as though it were the flimsiest chiffon. "Even if it were true, and it isn't, Jay's pride doesn't come into it; it would only be a top layer which might make her want to hide herself and her name from a stranger coming into the family. But, underneath, Jay would *want* Mummy to stand up and say 'Before we go any further, I've got two daughters, and one, the eldest and prettiest and loveliest and sweetest, has got herself into a mess. I expect most of it's my fault, but anyhow, if you want me, she's part of me, mess and all.'" Molly paused. Then rushed on quickly; "Mummy had to tell me on our way home in the car. She was taking me to dinner with him directly I'd changed, and I'd have burst out with anything unless I'd been warned. She didn't seem to realize that there was one thing I wouldn't stand for: denying Jay." Molly's mouth and chin were stern as a Roman sentinel's casually invited to leave his post. "I said I'd do the dinner, and that's damn well all. Now I'm through. That"—with a lapse into practical affairs—"is why I took the melon along to his house so that I could come straight on to you when it was over. I won't sleep in Mother's house again."

Shirley realized how very deeply Molly's loyalty had been betrayed, by her abandon to the use of wild phrases and dramatic decisions. Molly's serenity and poise were usually so established that she and Neil agreed they were immature and barnstormer beside her; and that she made them feel ashamed of their uncontrolled tempers and over-coloured statements.

"Molly, I'm going to love having you here, that's one good result of an ill wind. Have you brought your things?"

"No, Susan can send them round in the morning, every rag.

But Molly's first passion was subsiding, though her disdain of Lorna's treachery remained steadfast, and her purpose as inexorable. Shirley knew that if Lorna had told Sir Halmar she had only one daughter, she now as surely had none, and wondered if the woman herself knew it? Probably not; had she known, she might have risked telling her fiancé; she might have gambled protection, wealth, an establishment, tide, and the love of a good man, all the things by which she had contrived miraculously to encircle herself, rather than forfeit Molly. Her first mistake on a big scale. Lorna's instinct, which had guided her walking between precipices all these years, must have been weakened beyond redemption. She would have known she had lost Molly, could she have heard how the girl said just now: "She denied Jay. I wasn't going to stand for that."

Would even a rich and uxorious husband be worth the loss of Molly and Jay?

"What's he like?"

"Sir Halmar?" Molly's voice was serious, but mischief gleamed in her eyes. "Well, he's over sixty and ever so much handsomer than Neil, for instance. He'd look nicer still with wings sprouting on either side of his helmet. A beautiful golden Norseman, the kind that rushed out into the water waist-deep and hauled their ships up on to the glittering sands, shouting 'Skaal!' He did actually say 'Skaal' to me, when he invited me to drink his health and Mummy's, I think he enjoys being a Norseman, though his family have been settled in England for ages. He took a lot of interest in my profession, and told me jolly anecdotes about Scandinavian actresses and French actors who used to give seasons at Her Majesty's—'though I expect you hardly recognize the pronoun, ha! ha!' And every now and then he looked at Mummy, sharing with her that sort of you-understand-me-without-words thing which married people get."

"I've seen it," remarked Shirley grimly. "You needn't describe it. Fun for us, isn't it?"

Molly laughed. "Oh, I don't mind." And her laugh was clear and free from irony, so that Shirley remembered, as she had to every now and then, that she had stood for over twenty years on the wrong side of experience, and young Molly was still, happily for her, across the water and far away. "I didn't mind, but I couldn't live with them anyhow, I thought it would be waste of time to pal up, so I remained rather cool and frosty, and toyed with the succulent food he had provided for me, making great play with my knife and fork, as we have to when we do old-fashioned drawing-room comedy."

"What did you have for dinner? Don't spare me any of the grisly details."

"Chocolate pudding and ginger-pop,

"Liar!"

"Oh well, lobster and grouse and a wonderful ice-cream bombe—same thing from Sir Halmar's point of view! 'We'll give the child a slap-up dinner'—Oh, and we had the most heavenly wine I've ever tasted," added Molly, unaware that here she had, after all, fallen into the trap laid by her future stepfather, and that the sweet golden full-bodied wine he had provided for her to drink during the welcoming banquet was one which a grown-up palate would not have touched until the dessert. "All through dinner he joked about the stage and my 'future' and this and that. Mummy didn't join in much; she was badly upset, though she hid it pretty well, because, of course, I'd had it all out with her before we got to his doorstep."

"I thought you said just now that she caught his eye and was amused?"

"No, he caught hers, but that's different; he was imagining that her side was all right. I did eat an awful lot of the bombe, though I'd told myself that food was going to choke me. It's funny the way it doesn't when it's as lovely as that. And by then, Sir Halmar was beginning to arrange how I'd spend all my holidays with them: 'I'm afraid there won't be any holidays,' said I, all dignified, and he wagged his magnificent blond head—you can't see them turning white when they're so fair—and said: 'Ah, but even Bernhardt and Ellen Terry had to rest sometimes, you know!' And he said that when I came down to Beechcroft Manor there'd be a pony for me to ride—"

"No, Molly, you're trying me too far. Behave yourself."

"I was a beast," Molly owned unhappily. "It couldn't be helped, but he *was* trying his best to be decent, and I couldn't let it go on. I said: 'I'm sorry, sir,'—I don't know why the hell I called him 'sir' like that, all grubby little schoolboy—'I'm sorry, sir,' I said, 'but when you and Mummy are married I'm going to cut myself off. I'm financially independent.' It wasn't a thing I could say with manners, so I just didn't try, and it came out even rougher and gruffer than I'd meant, and all the beautiful party lay broken in bits. 'You needn't wait, Webster,' and the butler shimmered away like Jeeves; I'd never understood how butlers shimmered until I saw Webster do it. And then he said to Mummy, ever so tenderly—you know, Shirley, he's going to be good to her and I'm terribly glad because he's all right in every way that matters—'My dear, you mustn't take our Pensive Maid too literally. Leave us alone and I'm sure we can arrive at an understanding.' Shirley, isn't that a rum expression, arrive at an understanding? Arrive in a carriage and pair with footman, at a rather stately trotting pace. If you don't understand to begin with, how can you ever arrive at it? The Pensive Maid felt a beast, but a quite implacable beast, because apart from decency," Molly argued hotly, "Mummy was a *fool* not to stand by Jay. I swear he'd have taken it. He'd have been shocked to the core, of course, but that's what cores are for. And it would have given Jay a chance, when she was free again. Still, I couldn't butt in on her arrangements, however guarded and shameful they were. I do think self-preservation is shameful, don't you, honestly, Shirley?"

"Honestly, Molly, yes."

They were both silent for several minutes. Molly's mind was racing back through the years. She had been so glad when Jay had cut herself off from their mother and their mother's house, so profoundly glad, thinking: "Now Jay's out of it; now she'll be safe, even if the police do come"; and the police had come, the inevitable police whose fancied tread Molly had heard so often ever since she was eight years old, but they had followed Jay, and left Mummy to marry Sir Halmar, to be taken leaning on his arm into the drawing-room, to sit there and wait in case her champion and protector might have to say something which could possibly pain her a little. And Jay, Jay was in prison. Molly's indignant heart swelled and swelled till she felt she could not bear it. She began to talk very fast again, burlesquing the end of her narrative:

"He came back to me all modern and hearty and before I expected him, so that he found me nibbling biscuits madly. I was dreadfully nervous, which I wouldn't have been, of course, if I could have told the truth. It was so silly, having to sit there sulky and obstinate while he did frank contemporary stuff about his own girls being grown-up and married and not needing him any longer, and so his sweet young wife's daughter, his wife's *only* daughter, blast him, blast her, I mean—Oh, blast everybody! He was really rather a pet. I'd have stayed with them for months and liked it, if Mummy hadn't been a coward about Jay. And just imagine, Shirley, he had the cheek to inform me that I was being old-fashioned, and that the Viennese school fully explained the step-parent complex. I thought: 'You'd look blue and funny if you saw all that's going on in my head at this moment.' You needn't tell me, Shirley, that that's not the noblest way of getting through a bad half-hour, comforting oneself on those 'Ah, you don't know what I'm thinking' lines. I felt cheap enough, and I wasn't amused, really. It isn't even as though I'd been sacrificing myself for anybody about anything."

"We never get a chance of straightforward Eric-or-Little-by-Little sacrifice nowadays. It's all mixed up and a mess."

And Molly echoed: "All mixed up and a mess. He lost his temper with me in the end, and I'm not surprised. I should have, too, in his place. Said I was ungrateful and ungracious and not even trying to be co-operative, which made me feel like a chain of stores. And, of course, that I didn't deserve such a gentle mother. Shirley, I'm not at all sure whether I ought to marry Neil, now? I can't for years, anyhow, because I've obviously got to be ready for Jay when she comes out," added Molly in a tone which she carefully kept casual and slangy. "She'll need a bit of seeing to, I expect; Jay's never been much good at looking after herself; she goes flying around, and then lands in a frightful tumble. I wonder if I ought ever to have said I'd marry Neil."

Shirley had been afraid of this. However, now it was out, she could tackle it. Fighting Molly was like swimming through waves that were clear and cold as crystal; she was young, of course, and ruthless; the spray stung you sharply; but at least you could see where you were swimming.

"Why shouldn't you marry Neil? It's a perfectly simple proposition. Of course you'll have to look after Jay, silly young chump that she is. Nobody's going to deny that it's your job, but luckily Neil won't put up any irritating competition; he doesn't need looking after; he's not that boyish sort of man who runs up with a pair of grazed knees to show his mother, or his wife if he hasn't got a mother, Neil's packed with faults, but he's adult. You can take on Jay, and he can take on you."

"I know he can." Molly was gazing dreamily through the open window and beyond the balcony to the moon, a golden bowl loosely pendant between the earth and a black velvet sky. "I know he can. And he isn't packed with faults, Shirley. He's got one or two at the most."

"You could find three if you were hard put to it," drily.

"But as far as you're concerned, Molly, and I'm talking sense now not ecstasy, he has one big asset: he knows it all from A to Z. You don't have to explain or cover up." ("Not that you ever would," Shirley added in silent parenthesis.)

"About Mummy, you mean, or Jay?"

"Both. So what's the point in not marrying him, say in a couple of years, directly after Jay gets home? I'll take on Jay for you during the honeymoon. She ought to keep me busy. And afterwards—Well, Neil won't sentimentalize, but he'll be decent; you can trust him for that. And helpful, which is more than you can say for most men."

"Of course he will," hotly. "And of course I can trust him. But look here, Shirley, ought I to have children? I couldn't bear to marry Neil and not have them."

"I knew Neil when he was a horrid little boy; if your children and his will be anything like that, you have my deepest sympathies. But all the same—"

"It's not that, Shirley, you know it isn't. You're wilfully misunderstanding, as Sir Halmar kept on saying to me tonight. It's that if Jay takes after Mummy, and we know now that she does in that one thing—"

"Then your children would take after you. Or, if the worst comes to the worst, after Neil. It's a perfectly cheerful prospect. Don't fuss."

"Was I?" cried Molly in genuine horror. "I hate people who fuss. But, Shirley, I remember—"

"Yes? Yes, darling?"

"Mummy said—it was at the beginning of one of her comfortable stay-at-home times—she said how lovely it would be when one of us married and had children of our own, for her to love and play with. Shirley, suppose one day she borrowed one of my babies!"

"Borrowed? Molly," sharply, "that's nonsense."

"We were inside a bus once, Mummy and Jay and me—no, just Mummy and me, and the bus had stopped and the conductor had gone outside, and a woman came along lugging a baby in a dirty shawl, a real beggar woman; she got on to the step and then right in, whining that it was for the poor biby's sake and for the love of 'eaven kind lidy. … The conductor came down and turned her out and she spat and swore at him, and the people in the bus started saying it was a disgrace, and that nine times out of ten these babies were hired so as to make it easier to wring money out of soft-hearted people. And I couldn't really see any difference, except that I was a bit older, and Mummy was clean."

Shirley fought down a strong desire to cry. One day Molly would be grateful to her, and Neil too, heaven knows, if she could succeed in dealing drastically with all these delicious little legacies which Lorna had left with her younger daughter.

"Suppose you use a bit of sense. You had some before you over-ate at your stepfather's tonight, and tossed down too much of that heavenly wine. First of all, if Lorna is marrying Sir Halmar Barnard, she won't be in any further need of earning her living by that rather peculiar profession of hers; and secondly, if, in spite of that, she should ever come to you and say: 'Lend me your baby for the afternoon to lug round the streets in the pouring rain and a shawl,' I gather that you or Neil or both, or your nurse, or even at a pinch myself if you all happened to be out, would be quite capable of saying: 'Sorry, no. Go somewhere else.'"

Molly couldn't help laughing. "Thank you, Shirley darling. Really thank you, not sarcastic. You make me feel that I've been fatuous."

"You have. But it's the first time."

"Neil's baby …"

"Croon away. Are you sure you can wait for it two years and then nearly another year?"

"Just, but only by the skin of my teeth. It's queer to think that my

– 267 –

babies can't help being called Inglefield, when I used to think for years it was our real name which we weren't allowed to use."

"Did you never ask?"

"Ask who? Mummy? Oh no." Molly frowned: "Does that seem odd? We just took it for granted that we called ourselves Blake but that the Inglefield story was true, the one she told Visiting whenever she pulled out that marriage certificate. It sounded so much truer than the others. But we simply couldn't ask her; we didn't even discuss it together, Jay and I, except once or twice. I suppose it's funny that we shouldn't have, but while one didn't speak of it, it wasn't quite so much there."

Shirley understood. It would have been like breaking through into horror itself and touching it. She said, musing back to an incident that she had not thought of for some thirty years: "When I was a child, I was sent to stay with some rich relations; rich, that is, compared with the way we lived at home in Market St. Dunstan's, Aunt Lucy and I. Aunt Lucy was the District Nurse. But these people I stayed with kept two maids. The one who was supposed to look after me, Angèle, was a Frenchwoman. When I was in bed one night, and all the grown-ups were out, I was woken by Angèle rushing into my room screaming, the cook after her, calling out names, Angèle locked the door behind her and flung herself on her knees next to my bed. She took me in her arms and said that Cook wanted to kill her: *elle était méchante! C'était une putain.* Cook was beating on the door; she was a thin little crooked woman; and kept on crying out in a thin little crooked voice that Angèle had had a man in her room: *a man! a man!* It was dreadful, the things they screamed at each other through the locked door; Angèle was terrified and hysterical. She told me Cook was mad, and she had only me to protect her. Almost the worst thing about it was seeing her in a nightgown and dressing-gown, with her hair down and her face staring white, all pulled and drawn, when up till then she had just been a respectable maid in a black dress and cap. That sort of metamorphosis does something to a child. Somehow, I forget how, it all calmed down, and next day one would have thought nothing had ever happened. Except that every night while I stayed there, I lay awake for hours in bed in the dark, waiting for the whole ghastly thing to happen again: the screams and the flying footsteps, and then Angèle to hurl herself shaking across bed."

"You didn't tell anyone." But Molly made it sound like a statement, not a question.

"No, I never told anyone. I couldn't. And a few years ago noticed the same sort of psychology in a novel I was reading: A group of children in some foreign country; they were standing at an open window, and there was a crowd below and no one was looking after them, and suddenly their brother fell out of the high window into the crowd and was killed. And they just closed up and never spoke of it again. It's fantastic, of course, but there you are; I believe it might have been true."

Molly asked: "Have you ever put what you just told me into a book? About Angèle and you and the thin little crooked cook hammering at the door?"

Shirley smiled and shook her head "Haven't you been told, Molly darling, that authors never put themselves into books?"

"Don't they? Don't you? Shan't I find you in them anywhere? I thought I had, once or twice."

"Always a very attractive woman?" said Shirley gravely.

"Yes. Always. Why shouldn't she be?"

"Another woman writer once told me that as you get older you stop making yourself the heroine, and slip into more and more subsidiary characters, until it isn't even yourself any more but just one character who somewhere or other in every book reflects your own views. She needn't be you at all; age can be different, looks, sex even. But all the same, directly that character reflects your standpoint, you *have* to make her attractive. It's a sort of vanity compulsion."

The girl listened with that air of wide-eyed respect which always tickled Shirley's humour, as of one infinitely honoured at hearing "writer talk" first hand, and determined to be worthy of such honour, however dull and boring. Suddenly, however, her expression altered into radiant life: it was a quiet street, and she had heard footsteps she knew beyond the open window below the balcony.

Shirley, subsided. She knew that in a few moments she would be feeling solitary as death. She knew that it was unreasonable to mind. She waited. Presently the front-door bell rang and Neil strolled into the room with a casual air of a man who expects to find only a nice elderly woman friend. Then he saw Molly. She went straight across the room to him and he moved forward and took her hands. Still they did not speak. They had advanced towards each other as though between the walls of an invisible corridor, so that neither would nor could swerve an inch to the right or to the left from that splendid inevitable encounter.

Shirley thought: "This is what writers mean by 'a great love.' And I'm damned if I can think of a better phrase for it," she added. "And I'm damned if—*Why* did I have to be in on this?" For she was fond of arrogant Neil Inglefield, and fonder of Molly, but Neil had a strong look of Marcus grown older, and Molly was Lorna's young daughter.

PART VII

Done by Mirrors

Chapter One

Mrs. Dingle sat in her usual inconspicuous place a little more than half-way down the long committee table, and watched their chairman with adoration, thinking: "How beautifully she does it." Even the Hon. Mrs. Parker had been heard to say that Lady Barnard was quite an asset, and that meant something, thought Mary Dingle, from the Hon. Mrs. Parker, who owned the beautiful old house in which they were holding the meeting. Look at Lady Barnard now, using her authority so gently; not bullying those ladies who either would not or could not keep to the point; looping them back every time from those fascinating little excursions into local talk, reminding them that, after all, they were here this afternoon to make the final arrangements for the Elizabethan Fair in aid of the German Refugees, and that the question of whether Mrs. Warnford had been supplied with a new novel at the lending library which Mrs. Norton had asked for and been refused two minutes before, was neither relevant nor helpful.

"Quite right, Lady Barnard, quite right," cried Mrs. Dingle in her soul, though she rarely spoke her thoughts aloud in that company, which was the élite of Tarmouth and its neighbourhood. Mrs. Dingle wished that she had the personality to handle people with such deftness and tact as Lady Barnard used; she handled, she did not bludgeon them, that was the difference between her and Mrs. Parker. Mrs. Dingle was proud to sit on the same committee; it was a privilege; and one day perhaps Lady Barnard might single her out for a special smile and a few words of commendation: "I have noticed, Mrs. Dingle—or perhaps Mary, now we know each other so well; may I? and you must call me Lorna—"

"Oh, I should love to. Lorna suits you."

"Does it?" smiling. "It's just a name, you know. Tell me why it suits me?"

Mrs. Dingle, one part of her mind still moderately attentive to the discussion going on all round her, the other, happier, cosier part weaving this dialogue with the object of her hero-worship, would then reply; "Well, you mustn't think me impertinent, but though you dress so beautifully and your hair always looks as if it had just been waved and you can come into a room as though you didn't know that everyone was looking at you and saying, 'There's Lady Barnard!'—all the same, there's something romantic about you, and I think it's that which inspires people and makes them want to do as you say: over those stalls at the Fair, you know; and which of them to have the hand-made lingerie, which is, I suppose, the most attractive and I think you ought to have it yourself. And I can imagine you doing even grander and braver things—Not that I don't think you're brave, because I do, to have tackled Mrs. Parker like that; none of us dared before you came. I'm not a bit surprised that Sir Halmar won't do a thing without you. He told the Archdeacon only yesterday …"

Oh dear, now one of those absurd arguments had sprung up which was so nearly a quarrel that but for Lady Barnard and her subtle authority, must have ended as they always used to, in somebody raging and somebody bursting into tears and somebody saying they were insulted and somebody haughtily leaving and having to be fetched back and placated. Mrs. Dingle, recalled from reverie and reproaching herself for inattention, had to pick up what odds and ends she could of this particular discussion, and discovered that it was based on some wearisome question of red tape; a burning problem had arisen and must be settled instantly, as to whether *only* the artist refugees who were to be given their chance to sing and play and get engagements should perform in the little concert hall which was to be one attraction of the Fair, or whether the committee might bring in local talent, which, after all, was terribly important if local patronage was to be mingled with the lordlier patrons on the programme. The question was urgent because the order to the printers had to go that day; but the vice-president had just objected to the discussion on the grounds that it had not been included on the agenda and must therefore wait till next time.

"Do, please, Lady Barnard, let us try not to conduct our meetings in this hoydenish fashion."

Mrs. Dingle held her breath, waiting to see how her idol would handle this. ("Those dark furs make her look a little pale, but I think she's right not to wear rouge; Mrs. Parker looks quite blowsy next to her. I wish I hadn't given up writing notes for the *Tarmouth Tribune* fashion page, then I could say how distinguished she looks in that wine-coloured cloth and the diamond earrings. Mrs. Fogarty looks dreadful in earrings by day and not much better by night. Oh dear, that *is* a little unkind of me, but then I liked Mrs. Fogarty so much better before Lady Barnard came. Ah, I'm glad she's settled that.") For the chairman had not cut the red tape, but very carefully, smiling a little, disentangled the knot; and now a more amicable discussion was in full swing again and she was able to lean back and relax.

Mrs. Dingle wondered what was in Lady Barnard's thoughts at this moment: her eyes were half-closed, her gloved hand absently scribbling on the sheet of clean pink blotting-paper in front of her; the line of her neck reminded Mrs. Dingle poetically of a weary swan; she surmised that Lady Barnard was thinking of the dreadful plight of those poor refugees and the heart-breaking stories they told. The pity of it all! She had been truly wonderful, not only at organizing the whole thing but in dealing with individual cases. Mrs. Dingle had heard her giving them all her compassion, and yet not thinking smugly that compassion would be enough, but exerting herself in every practical way. At that moment, Lady Barnard laid down her pencil, lifted her hand, and patted her hair with an abstracted gesture as though she were standing in front of a looking-glass but not seeing what she did. "She has forgotten to drink her tea again" (the ladies of the committee always had cups of tea beside them to stimulate debate). "There's such a thing as caring *too* much. I wonder if I dare ask her to come in and have some proper tea with me? It's on her way home. They can't be much longer now. I will, I really will this time. There can't be many more meetings, and I may not be on the next committee where she's chairman." (For Mrs. Dingle took it for granted that, where there were committees there would be Lady Barnard ruling in soft dignity from a chair at the head of the table.)

The meeting was over at last, and as Mrs. Dingle pushed out into the hall with the others, she was uneasily conscious that she had not greatly contributed to the furtherance of the relief schemes. On the other hand, she had not been a positive hindrance like Dodo Perry who was always at least two questions behind the others, and would argue passionately and persistently several moments before she realized that her point had been abandoned or settled several minutes ago. Silly Dodo with her perpetual: "I should have gone into Parliament!" What would she have done in Parliament? except put a very severe strain on their courtesy. One of the reasons you so respected Lady Barnard was her almost unfailing courtesy. Of course she could afford to be, with so much poise.

And at that moment Mary Dingle became aware of that very voice, charming and a little husky, saying to her: "Can I give you a lift, Mrs. Dingle? I pass near Grove House and I don't see your car anywhere; I always know that nice boy with the broken nose who drives the car; he was so helpful once when we had trouble with the petrol gauge."

Mrs. Dingle was thrown into so many states of gratification that it was difficult to pick out one for reply. That Lady Barnard should offer her a lift! That Lady Barnard knew where her house was! Quite a nice house, but nothing compared with Lady Barnard's beautiful place a few miles outside Tarmouth. That Lady Barnard should actually know Tom by sight, and his broken nose! Her amazement was not in the least snobbish; Mary Dingle was no snob; the tumult of joyful surprise was wholly on account of the other woman's riches of character. She quickly suppressed the fact that her husband was using the car and that she had meant to go to his office close at hand and wait there to drive home with him; and controlling her ardour, sedately accepted Lady Barnard's offer.

When they had been two minutes side by side under the rug in Sir Halmar Barnard's luxurious Bentley, she asked: "Won't you come in with me and let me give you some tea? It'll be half an hour at least before you're home, and I noticed that you left your cup quite untouched, just now. You know," boldly, "you give too much of yourself at these meetings."

Lady Barnard smiled. "How observant you are. I didn't even notice myself that I'd left it. We broke up a little late and I ought to get home, because—I shouldn't really come in, but you tempt me. Thank you so much."

Mrs. Dingle remembered that the Barnards were giving a dinner-party that night, and she wished that there were some way of reassuring her companion that she was not in the least wounded that they had not been invited, she and Arnold. You can't invite everyone. And Arnold was not Sir Halmar's solicitor—

"Listen," she hailed the distraction of silvery trumpets and the sound of hoofs trotting nearer. "Doesn't it sound like the Middle Ages? That's the Judge going to his lodgings, I suppose. The Assizes opened today in Tarmouth. Yes, here they come."

"How picturesque!" Lady Barnard leant forward, interested, to watch the little procession go by. "I should have been sorry to miss this. Who is the Judge?"

"Sir Reginald—I forget his name; how silly of me. Sir Reginald something. Last year and the year before, it was Sir Piers Layton. It's a very sought-after job, my husband says. Here we are," she tried to smooth out the elated note from her voice. "It's so nice of you."

And presently, as though in bright-coloured fulfilment of a charm, they were seated like two old friends in front of the fire in the rose and beige drawing-room, and Edith had brought in the tea without hitch or delay, and the great coloured bowl of different shades of Michaelmas daisies behind Lady Barnard's shoulder had just the right effect in toning down the glory of the occasion and making it all seem natural and pleasant as a cottage garden. Arnold had called them cottage-garden flowers and asked her why she did not have dahlias in the room? But now she knew: dahlias were too flamboyant.

They talked lightly at first of the Fair and of the committee and how difficult it was to get anything planned on a big scale without hurting people's feelings.

"But you handle them so beautifully. I've watched you and tried to learn your method, if it is a method, but perhaps it's something which has just been born in you."

And Lady Barnard replied thoughtfully: "I think it is. At least, I'm certain that I have nothing so cut-and-dried as a method: a creed, perhaps, but that's not the same."

The subdued lamplight gave Mrs. Dingle confidence. She spoke in a low voice: "We find heaven in a creed," and gasped at Lady Barnard's quiet reply:

"We find each other, and those are the pilgrim routes to heaven."

"I am a little afraid of those routes; I wish I weren't." The confession was accompanied by a shy little smile, and Lady Barnard put out her hand with what might have been an impulsive gesture of friendship or else in eloquent appeal: "But you mustn't be afraid, not for one moment, Mrs. Dingle. I haven't had an easy experience of life. I've had to struggle. I've had two children to support—" Lady Barnard stopped. Mrs. Dingle wondered why her eyes were suddenly misted with tears. She picked up again with a rueful "—And one of the children was myself. I don't think I ever learned to be properly grown-up. I have had to ask for help sometimes, when pride would have been my enemy. As it is, faith was my friend. Oh, you wouldn't believe the kindness, the readiness to help, the compassion dormant in everyone if we could only be childish enough to appeal to it. I've sometimes longed to start a Great Movement and persuade everyone in Tarmouth to join, and then everyone all over England, and then all over the world. Then we should have no more of these wars, and no more refugees, or committee meetings to help them in their last hour of distress instead of their first moment. Have you ever had to be woken by an alarm-clock? It's such a dreadful name for anything so kindly and helpful as a clock. I always think they have such charming freakish little faces, like a flower, a pansy."

Mary Dingle was breathless. Never before had anyone sat in her armchair, a teacup precariously held, and spoken such bold exciting doctrines.

"Alarm-clock," she murmured. "No, it's true; I never thought of it before, but we ought, we certainly ought to be woken every morning by something less—less alarming," she finished with a little laugh. "Please, Lady Barnard, do tell me what you would do to break down people's fear of each other? After all, in a way it's natural, isn't it? After all, it begins with the animal in us twisting round in the grass to make sure it's safe to lie down; or taking refuge in caves." She was quite proud of herself for bringing out these points of natural history, though hoping that her very wonderful new friend would be able to demolish them. Which she did without the slightest difficulty:

"But we're not animals. If we were, I shouldn't have offered you a lift home, and you wouldn't so very hospitably have invited me in to tea, and we shouldn't be talking like this now. Imagine," said Lady Barnard, "imagine a squirrel and a kangaroo discussing ethics after a jungle committee meeting. Not that that was so unlike a jungle this afternoon," she added, a twinkle of mischief glinting from her large brown eyes.

Mrs. Dingle, on being told that she was discussing ethics, felt some of the elation of Mr. Jourdain when he became aware that he was talking prose; and that sly dig at the Charity Fair committee was delicious. She had a touch of whimsical humour herself, and so could appreciate Lady Barnard's.

"More like a farmyard than a jungle, perhaps. But do you really think that if we trusted our fellow human beings more, we wouldn't be terribly snubbed and let down?"

"Quite sure. Imagine, for instance, if we could break up this artificial taboo of silence, disregarding it. Suppose everybody spoke to everybody in shops and trains, as though it were the natural thing to do: 'Can you help me? I'm looking for a cheap nursing-home, my husband's so ill.' It wouldn't take long to get over the first surprise. People are grateful, not cross, when you appeal for their help. You broach a barrel of ale, but do you broach a barrel of kindness? of untapped generosity? What a cruel waste! We should be conscious of all the thrilling implications of every personal contact."

All this was so true, yet so bewildering. Mrs. Dingle's brain was a whirl of barrels and taps and alarm-clocks. She had been brought up to believe that pride was one of the finer qualities, and that it was ignoble and cowardly to ask for help. Yet now Lady Barnard, who must be right because she was always right, wanted to start a movement to reverse all these notions.

"Peace on earth," murmured Mary Dingle. "Isn't it odd," she chattered anxiously, refilling the teapot with hot water and holding out her hand for her visitor's cup, "isn't it odd how often the people who talk most about wanting peace do less than anyone else to bring it about?"

"Perhaps they don't really want it, in their heart of hearts." She glanced at her diamond wrist-watch, and gave a little cry of dismay. "As late as that! And here I sit talking, blowing lovely aerial soap-bubbles, while at home they'll be waiting. We began late today. Oh dear, I wish they wouldn't insist on reading the minutes quite so conscientiously; it mops up so much of our precious time. No, thank you, no indeed, no more tea, though I enjoyed it more than I can tell you. We must often meet and talk like this, mustn't we, when we can get away from the farmyard, you and I? Good-bye, Mrs. Dingle … May I? May I indeed? I should like to; Mary is such a pretty name. Mary Dingle, like an old-fashioned nursery rhyme. And my name's Lorna, if you can bear to use it. You're quite sure you won't mind taking the wood-carving stall? It's so splendid of you not to fuss and wonder whether it's important enough. I do so respect people who never lose their sense of proportion. Good-bye again."

She departed in an atmosphere of such charm and intimacy that for several minutes after she had gone Mrs. Dingle felt as though all the warm amber had been drained from the room. For several minutes she could do nothing but sit quite still, her hands pressed together, staring at the armchair on the opposite side of the fire, and repeating at intervals: "Lorna. Lady Barnard. Lorna Barnard. Mary Dingle like a pretty nursery rhyme. Mary and Lorna." Then she gave a little sigh, pulled herself together, and rang for Edith to remove the tea.

"That was Lady Barnard, Edith."

"Oh, I knew, madam," the parlourmaid's voice was hushed in awe. Her sentiments were feudal.

"And that reminds me, Edith," though she never explained what reminded her. "Is there any beer left in the cask for the master's dinner? I thought it seemed to be running short yesterday."

"There's some bottles, madam, if it has, just for tonight."

"You know he never likes his beer out of a bottle. Oh well, it's too late now for anything else. But I wish you or Cook would notice—"

She stopped half-way in a reproof. A rich husky voice was saying: "You broach a barrel of ale, but do you broach a barrel of kindness?"

Chapter Two

←→

Lorna flung off her furs and hat, and explained to Susan in a rush what she was to put out for her to wear for that night's dinner-party.

"I ought to have come straight home, but I was so stiff with boredom I couldn't endure half an hour's drive without a fire and some tea to thaw me on the way. Susan, I don't think I can endure another committee meeting. Sitting round a table gabbling or staring at a sheet of clean pink blotting-paper, so clean and prim and efficient, the very sight of it makes me want to scream."

"Better not," Susan advised, opening and shutting wardrobe doors. "You don't know where you'll leave off, once you begin to scream. I've run your bath. Why ever don't you put your foot down and say you'll not do any of them charity things no more? You've done 'em ever since he got you down here."

"Nobody got me. I got myself. And that doesn't make it any better, either." Lorna was sitting at the dressing-table with its triple mirrors and load of gold-topped bottles and monogrammed brushes, and was busy with her manicure-set; a faint scent of pear-drops rose in the air, then, using the brush with the precision of a genuine artist reduced to tinting Christmas cards, she painted on the rosy lacquer.

"Where's my polisher?" She held out her hand towards Susan, without looking up.

"Here."

Even that had its monogram heavily stamped: "L. B." Susan read it aloud as she passed it. "'Change the name and not the letter, change for the worse and not for the better.' Shouldn't wonder, too, if you hadn't. Always sighing and yawning and wishing yourself at the bottom of the sea. Why don't you drop some of this faith-hope-and-charity stuff, and do something to enjoy yourself?"

"Do something? Do what?"

"Coo, I don't know. Mr. Webster's got a roulette-board down in our hall. Fourteen bob I lost last night. Win it all back tonight, you'll see. Why don't you play bridge? Not got the brains for it?" Susan jeered.

Lorna was ruffled. Their attitude one to the other had not altered by a fraction.

"I play a very good game. I played every evening at Gleneagles, but it didn't amuse me."

"Came out even, that was your trouble. Never won and never lost."

"Well, there's no kick in that, is there?"

Susan grinned, "You're a fine one to sit on Peace Committees, you are, always talking about a kick. I'd say, if you asked me, the last thing in the world you wanted was peace. You're miserable when you get it, whatever my Lady Barnard says in her speeches."

Lorna laughed. "I expect you're right, Susan. I'm going to change my bath essence. I'm sick of *l'Heure Paresseuse*. We'll try—"

There was a knock at the door and Miss Soutar glided in, her hands full of plans and papers.

"Lady Barnard, I must disturb you just for a moment. I know you'd never forgive me if I didn't show you these beforehand, but they were finished rather late because the Judge of the Assizes, Sir Reginald Seymour, had to be asked at the last moment; and of course that meant altering the whole table, as he has to sit on your right."

"Of course," Lady Barnard assented, studying the table plan.

"You've plenty of time, Lady Barnard. Dinner's not till half-past eight, you know."

"I'd forgotten. I thought it was eight."

"And here's the menu, but of course you ordered that yourself, only Mrs. Rumford is driving everyone mad about it. And here's the list of who takes in whom. I wish we could find two ladies who didn't matter to go on either side of Sir Oscar Lawley. He's so trying and deaf and shouts so. And of course Mrs. Edgar Eaves is quite unimportant, but she won't like to be put down next to him. She always says she likes brilliant people. Isn't it strange, Lady Barnard, how the boring ones never seem to like to sit together? It's as though they could recognize bores quite easily, unless it's themselves."

Lorna said something whimsical but not anarchical. And Miss Soutar tried to look prim and indulgent both at the same time.

"And here are three telephone messages. Mr. Meade has a very bad cold and wants to know if you mind. He says he doesn't, but do you?"

Lorna stared at this problem and could find no solution. "What does Sir Halmar say?"

"He told me to ask you."

"And what do you think?"

"Well, people do mind, you know. But a man missing at the last moment—and Mr. Meade is one of our good conversationalists. We relied on him."

"Is he? Did we?"

"There's quick cold cures," put in Susan. "Cure you in two hours. At least, that's what they promise."

"We haven't got two hours any more. You must be dreadfully tired, Lady Barnard. They should let you off earlier, though it's difficult when you're chairman."

"Ask Sir Halmar again. I must have my bath now." And after Miss Soutar had glided out, harassed and burdened, Lorna flicked a quick little grimace across at Susan: "What a life! How many dinner-parties have we given since we got back from Gleneagles? And every one exactly the same. Sir Halmar told me last time I hadn't been in my usual spirits. Oh God, Susan—"

"Oh God's right!" retorted her confidante gleefully. Here was a marriage working itself out after Susan's own heart. "Look here, have you thought—"

Lorna paused on the threshold of her bathroom.

"Have I thought what? I can't think any more. My brain's as stale as last week's bun."

"Jay'll be corning out on the tenth."

She eyed Lorna speculatively. ("You never get to the end of that one. Don't suppose she ever gets to the end of herself.")

"I hadn't forgotten," said Lorna slowly.

"Then what are you going to do about it? Bring her here?'

"How can I? If I only could. How *can* I?"

"You know, you acted silly about that at the time. Why did you ever go and say you had only one little daughter, and her on the stage. Much easier to say two, and one in America or somewhere far enough. He'd have swallowed it all right and you wouldn't be in this fix you're in now."

"But why should I have?" Lorna cried, in real despair. "I had no idea when I first went to Sir Halmar that he was going to be my husband. Jay wasn't a permanent problem then. I had to explain away something temporary, something—difficult. Would it have helped me to have mentioned that I had another little girl in prison for embezzlement? Would it have helped him to trust me? to believe in me? You're so sweeping with your 'You should have done this, you should have done that.' How could I know that by the time Jay would be free again, I'd be Lady Barnard? Afterwards, when I realized he was actually going to propose, it was too late."

"What had happened that first time?" Susan asked in unabashed curiosity. "What tale did you pitch him? Must have been a fine one, with none of the tin-tacks loose, for him to worship you the way he has when he married you and ever since. Come on," she coaxed, "relax; tell us; give us a laugh. They're all so solemn here, Rumford and the whole bunch. That's the worst of what they call a staff. Makes 'em feel pompous. Give me a place as cook-general and a nice char to gossip with a couple of hours every morning, that's all I ask."

"You're not likely to get it here," said Lorna with a faint smile.

But if she were congratulating herself that Susan had been plucked off the agonizing subject of Jay, she congratulated herself too soon; already Susan had returned to it:

"She'll have to go somewhere when she comes out. Lucky for her she's got a sister. Molly'll take her in and look after her, and she's earning plenty now. But that won't go on for ever, girls being what they are. She'll be wanting to marry that there Young Neil though he's more than twice her age, and then where'll Jay be? You don't get a job in a hurry with two years in Borstal behind you? Like a bit of advice before you get into your bath?" And Susan hurried on in case Lorna said no: "Tell him all about it now. Cry a bit and throw yourself on your knees. Well, I don't mean go as far as that, but make him think you're going to. Men like it when we can give 'em something big to forgive. They grow fat on it, the smug little angels. Go on, give him a chance. Think what it would mean to her now, to come and live in a house like this, with you to take her up, and him too, what with his name and the respect of the neighbourhood. She'll need all that. I know Jay; she'll be raw, body and soul, but she'll heal again, with time and the right oils and creams and cotton-wool. *You* can do it for her: a mother's a mother, and Jay was crazy on you, for all the bitter things she might have said when you last saw her. Come on, tell him and give her a chance, poor bloody little fool. And in six months she'll be making pretty pictures about herself again: 'Miss Jasmine Barnard was seen at the Hunt Ball looking like an Alexandra rose.'"

Lorna still stood leaning against the bathroom door, her eyes sombre, tortured, fixed on a point just beyond Susan's head. Susan wondered what reply she would get to what she privately deemed a speech of much eloquence and psychological insight, but which actually was informed by more sense than either of the more showy qualities: "She might kiss me or she might cry or she might throw me out. Still, I had to have my say some time, so what's the good of bottling it up?"

… Suddenly Lorna yawned. She stretched her arms in a circle above her head and strained all her body into this gesture expressive of some terrific inner nostalgia that had been clogging all her hours and minutes.

"God, what a day it's been!" She relaxed, dropped her arms. "I must have my bath," and nodding at Susan with perfect amity, disappeared behind the closed door.

Susan stared: "Can you beat it!"

When Lorna presently reappeared, Miss Soutar was once more there.

"Oh, Lady Barnard, I'm so sorry to disturb you again, but there's a man in the hall. He's been before, twice, but you've always been out. He wants to see you personally and it's terribly urgent, he says—Oh, we know what that means, but I don't think he's one of the usual ones. He looks to me as though he might be genuine, so I hesitated before turning him away. Would you like me to give him five shillings and say you're too busy to see anyone?"

Lady Barnard and her maid, Susan, gazed at each other pensively through the medium of the triple mirror. Then Lady Barnard spoke in her most gentle, most compassionate tone.

"No, don't do that. Poor fellow, it's a little too drastic, I think, don't you, Miss Soutar? As though we were cutting ourselves completely aloof from the troubles of a fellow human being. It isn't as though he were asking for money, or is he?"

"Oh no. But then they very rarely do, do they, until they get hold of the person they want? Alfred tells me that Sir Halmar sometimes gets as many as four or five a week when he's in London, and of course this isn't the first we've had, but usually I don't let them bother you."

"You guard me beautifully, Miss Soutar," was Lorna's grateful acknowledgment.

"But somehow, as I said, I wasn't quite happy about it this time. I have always felt, though it may be sentimental of me, that I'd rather let myself be hoaxed nine times out of ten than risk sending away one person with a real story of distress."

"Yes, I agree. So would I. I think I'll see this man. Yes, I'll see him."

"Oh, but Lady Barnard, have you time? I could tell him tomorrow—"

"And he'll tell you tomorrow's too late."

A soft choking sound came from Susan's direction, where by now she had her head half in and half out of one of the big wardrobes.

"I mean," Lorna explained with a touch of dignity while she slipped into a flowing velvet tea-gown, "that his need may be really imperative. It's only twenty to eight and I can get rid of him in a few minutes."

A lot of his head was bald, though his birth certificate, immediately extracted from a packet of other worn-out documents and photographs from his little papier-mâché attaché-case, and handed to Lorna with a respectful bow, showed that he was only twenty-five. His name was Edmund Vincent Burgess. His clothes were clerkish, and his bright impudent blue eyes were somehow incongruous with the pencil neatly clipped on to the outside of his breast pocket. Hung over his arm was a carefully folded umbrella with one rib stark and unclothed. He said he was an Australian—

"And you want to go back to Australia?"

"I've got to go back." And, surprisingly: "I've got my passage. Here it is."

She held out her hand for the dirty envelope, but did not immediately examine what was inside.

"I worked for this," he went on, his head proudly jerked back. "Lord, how I worked. Not that I'm complaining. I like work. Keeps you from thinking how you've been had for a mug. I was a waiter for the last three months and we didn't shut till 2 a.m. and what went on—but there, you wouldn't want to hear about that. Or would you?" He flung her one of his rakish looks. "Sheltered ladies, I've noticed, like to hear a bit about the underworld fresh from the horse's mouth."

"I'd rather hear about you," murmured Lorna. And she sat down as an epicure to a well-flavoured meal.

Delighted by her interest, he told her a story which was a queer mixture of naivete, impertinence and an affected decorum. His old mother was very ill with rheumatoid arthritis. She had slaved like—like an old mother, to give him a chance in the art classes. He was dead nuts on art, fair dinkum he was. Then Exhibit Three from the attaché-case: a large certificate adorned with a design of prancing muses, easels, palettes, paint-brushes, masks, a winged horse thrown in for luck, and a declaration to the effect that Edmund Vincent Burgess, of North Street, Melbourne, had passed with honours as a first-year student of the Central School of Art and Sculpture.

Lorna glanced at it with a sympathetic smile. Anyone could see by his air of childlike pride that Exhibit Three at least was genuine.

"Humiliation is a better schoolmistress than prosperity. I used to think of that sometimes, when they blew me up if the mustard in the cruet had dried up again. Look here, I'd do you a picture, still life, Sir-Realist school—and I will, too—of a table in the dive I worked in and what it looked like after a few hours. Yes, and you can hang it up in your grand dining-room for a contrast, and say when your visitors tell you it puts 'em off their food, which they couldn't pay me a better compliment: 'Yes, I knew the artist. I helped him once. He sent me that out of gratitude.'"

"That is very kind of you. I shall look forward to having it. But now, as you already have your passage home—?"

Her pause indicated that this was the moment for him to make known the reason for his visit.

Twenty minutes later, as she swiftly finished her toilet for the evening, Lorna was amusing Susan by her graphic account of Mr. Edmund Vincent Burgess's performance. She was in excellent spirits, gayer than Susan had seen her for many months past; her eyes glowed, her mimicry was vivid. It was as though she had suddenly acquired a new relish for life, a gusto for its chance encounters which was lacking before.

"You know, it was terribly bad luck for him that he should just have walked in on me and not a much more probable Lady Barnard. He wasn't at all bad at it. The probable Lady Barnard might easily have been gulled. I was sorry for him about that," added Lorna thoughtfully, and Susan giggled.

"The folks you're sorry for!"

"Oh, Susan, you'll never understand what a relief it was not to have a true story to deal with, just for once. Not to have to be heart-broken. All those genuine cases we've had pouring in, poor devils who have lost everything, simply convulsed with grief or stony with bewilderment, and one had to listen and one could do nothing in proportion, however hard one tried—It tore me to bits. And suddenly on top of it this comic little lying devil. How I wish he could have broken in today on that collection of snobbish ladies muddling round a table with blotting-paper in front of them."

"Would he have put it over on them?"

"Oh yes, I think so. He really was quite convincing. It happened, of course, that I examined his passage rather too closely and saw the date on it was three years old, but he could have relied on forty-nine out of fifty not to notice that. It was just bad luck again."

"Then what did he want, if he pretended he had his passage?"

"Six weeks' arrears of rent for his room and a harsh landlord who wouldn't let him get away with his box. He asked for five pounds; that was another mistake; I could have put him wise to that. It's never a good idea to ask for a round sum. Four pounds eighteen shillings he should have suggested, or five pounds three and six. Still, he'll learn. He's young, although he was going bald. But it was a dear little chubby youthful face underneath."

"You seem to have taken quite a fancy to him."

"Good heavens, I want to be amused, amused, amused."

Susan was silent for a while after that outburst, but her thoughts were busy.

("Talks a lot more open to me now than she used to do, in Huntingdon Terrace and Netherby Park Road. Then it used to be patting me down into my place all the time: 'I don't know what you mean, Susan.' And 'Susan, the children!' And 'Susan, please remember I don't care to hear you talk like that.' Now it seems I'm a chip of the old block and the best friend she has. Funny. And she's using a lot more words than in the old days. Shouldn't be surprised if she wasn't working herself up again. All she needs is something to set her going, and whoops, we're off!")

Then a question occurred to her, so intriguing that she found it difficult to understand why she had not asked it at once:

"See here, did you give him the money?"

Lady Barnard was by now attired ready to receive her guests. Seated in front of the glass, her chin propped on the small flat stool of her interlaced fingers, she smiled happily at the three handsome women, two in profile, with diamond stars in their hair. Her eyes had a roguish glint.

"Did he get it?" repeated Susan, impatient for an answer. She had often wondered what would be the fate of any professional crook who might now come to Lorna with a hard-luck story. "Did you give it to him, or did you show him up?"

"I was going to give it to him. It's so humiliating to be exposed by a rich woman leading a conventional sheltered life and having no idea of the audacity, the boldness, the flair, the sense of character needed to live by your wits and to depend on no one; no one except yourself. That's the fun of it, of course: to judge swiftly and have the courage to act on what you feel is going to happen the very next moment, instead of waiting for it to have happened a moment ago; that's fatal; any fool can do that and not get any further with the job—"

She met Susan's eyes, mocking black slits fixed full upon her; stopped; and then continued with calm languor:

"No, I wasn't going to expose him. Or even snub him and turn him away, poor fellow. Always remember, Susan, that people who never climb on to a pedestal can never fall off it."

"You do beat the band," murmured Susan in admiration. "So he walked off with a perfectly good fiver, did he? All for showing a passage to Australia three years out of date."

"Oh no," casually, rising and gathering up her brocade handbag and a floating chiffon handkerchief. "For one thing, I hadn't got five pounds to spare, nor one pound, nor five shillings."

Susan nodded. She could not help knowing, as all the rest of the servants knew, and Miss Soutar and Alfred, that Sir Halmar gave his cherished wife everything in the world she desired except ready money.

"What do you want money for?" he would say to her. "You have the car, haven't you? There's everything you want in the house, and what there isn't, you can ring up and order and have it put down to the account or ask Miss Soutar to do it for you. However hard I try, my darling, I cannot imagine any possible way that you could spend sixpence in hard cash. All the flowers you could possibly want in the garden, all the clothes you can possibly want hanging in your wardrobe. And I must say you do me credit. And as for charity, well, we neither of us approve of promiscuous charity, do we? And you've only to come to me and ask me to write a cheque for this or that, and when I've looked into it—"

Lorna said to Susan:

"I promised him I would tell his story to Sir Halmar, and if my husband agrees with me that it was a very hard case, I'll send him the money. He left me his address and he quite saw that I made it a rule never to give impulsively without consulting my husband."

Then she floated through the door and down the corridor to the great staircase, leaving Susan speechless.

Chapter Three

Sir Halmar was delighted and proud when guest after guest came up to him to make their adieux, telling him that they had never enjoyed a party more, not even at Beechcroft Manor where they had been so often and so hospitably entertained. For this was not mere politeness, and he knew it; it had indeed been an unusually successful dinner-party, and the tributes were spontaneous and not cranked out by the machinery of politeness.

"Your wife," they said. And "Lady Barnard …" "Your wife is amazing

"… I have never seen Lady Barnard in such good spirits …" And not only to him, but from one to another. He felt rather than heard their murmurs of genuine admiration:

"She has such personality. Not domineering, you know, but subtle. It's genuine sweetness … She doesn't think of herself … And one knows that she really enjoys having us here; that she isn't just entertaining us as a social duty … Yes, that's exactly what I mean." And then, again to Sir Halmar: "You wouldn't believe, Sir Halmar, what good work your wife has done. She never spares herself. If everyone had the same spirit of national service … And never in the least aggressive. You know what people are … But we've had far less quarrelling and unkindness since Lady Barnard came among us … I always say she's a sort of peace-making influence … Look at your wife now, Sir Halmar. How well that colour suits her, and those flowing lines. You must be very proud of her."

"Yes, of course I am. Indeed she is. Indeed she does. She'll be delighted when I tell her that. Yes, I entirely agree with you. Thank you, Sir Reginald, thank you," to the Judge of Assize; "you can't have enjoyed tonight more than I, more than we both did … Thank you, yes, she *is* looking young. No, I don't know that we've had any special good news to account for it … Sort of *joie de vivre,* you know. Or what you scientists would call natural magnetism … Good-bye. Good-bye, Sir George; delighted to have heard your good news." But for a moment Sir Halmar looked a little less delighted. "May I tell my wife? Josie is a great favourite of hers, you know. To be made public tomorrow? Splendid."

The last visitor had been driven smoothly away down the avenue; the last congratulation on a most excellent evening still hung in the air. Sir Halmar beamed on his wife and repeated a few of the compliments which had been showered upon her. It amused him that she still hung back shyly, a little wide-eyed, from a compliment, hardly believing it could really have been meant for her.

"And upon my word, darling, they haven't said a word too much. I've never seen you in such good form. The way you led the conversation, and that battle of wits you had with Professor Middlemas! Why, it reminded me of the dialogue in a play! One of those brilliant comedies, you know, flying to and fro and everyone else holding up to listen. And you're looking well—an American husband would say 'like a million dollars,' but I hope I can find a prettier likeness than that."

"Find it, then," laughed Lorna. "Did you suppose I'd let you off?"

He found it: a dark red tulip, glossy and shapely. He asked if that deserved a kiss. She replied that it did.

"I'm so glad everyone enjoyed themselves; that it went off well. It's important to you in lots of ways, isn't it?"

"It's important to me that people should admire my wife and realize what a lucky fellow I am. Parker asked me if you'd had some specially good news."

She laid one hand on his coat-sleeve as though to assure herself of his solid presence. "Yes. Yes, I have had some good news. Do you know what it was, Halmar? I realized all over again that I was happy and safe and married to you. That was the specially good news I had had."

Sir Halmar had a slight beatitude. Then he asked: "But what brought it home to you so vividly?"

She was a little reluctant then to go on. He had to coax her, for it was evident that something had occurred which she was not quite prepared to tell him in detail.

"Do you remember our first meeting? We don't often speak of it, do we?"

"It was a little unconventional, shall we say, but nothing in it that need make you blush. That letter—After all, you weren't responsible for what's-her-name? that governess woman, Miss Gardiner."

"Poor old Gardie. I wonder how she's managing in a strange country?"

"You haven't heard from her since she went?"

"One letter. I tore it up."

"Ah!" He did not press her to say what had been in the letter. Thank heavens, he had got the woman removed to the other end of the world where she couldn't drag on Lorna any more.

"I was such a fool," she burst out. "I wasn't fit to live alone. Some women aren't. That awful moment when I had to come and see you at your flat and explain that I wasn't just a professional beggar. I was trembling all over. And then once past the threshold, your understanding! it was almost divine. Your chivalry. And not only words, but solid help. Strength, strength. They say a woman adores strength, but it has to be combined with kindness and then—Oh, then I could pray before it. Halmar, I can truthfully say that while I was on my own, working, fighting, trying to plan my life, trying not to be afraid, I was never happy for one single moment. I'm not that type. I was never rugged nor stalwart nor broad-shouldered, was I? am I?"

"I shouldn't have fallen in love with you if you had been, my dear."

"You might have been so different. You might have said dreadful things. Poor Gardie was always writing those terrible letters and signing them with my name. Always that nightmare uncertainty. And now … Oh, the difference! And it's all owing to you. I'm safe, I'm protected. If anyone appeals to my weak point, and you know how idiotically sentimental I am, all I have to say is: 'I'll ask my husband. My husband wouldn't wish it. I'll talk it over with my husband and let you know what he says—' Oh, Halmar, can you wonder that I'm passionately grateful simply at having the chance to do a little thing like making your parties a success. That man today—"

"Ah, I knew there was a secret. What man today, eh? Well, I'm not going to be jealous before I hear a bit more about him."

"Jealous? You needn't be." She was half laughing through her tears. "It was simply that he reminded me of the way you and I were first brought together. He was a poor little fellow in trouble, that's all."

"What was Miss Soutar about to let you be badgered? I thought she kept all that sort of thing away from you. I have tribes of 'em all the time."

"Oh, Miss Soutar's splendid. She always interviews them and sends them away and only tells me afterwards, looking as bland as milk. But this little Australian—she had an instinct. She felt his story was true. And directly I saw him, I was sure, without the slightest doubt. One *knows*, like a water-diviner holding a twig above the ground. When the twig begins to tremble … Besides, it was such a strange story: the fatal woman luring him over to England, and that grim, fine old father alone on the ranch, letting him go, not saying a word till he broke. And in contrast, the queer crowding jabber of waiters, Italian, Spanish, Polish, South American; and he quite bewildered among them, flying to and fro with a napkin over his arm … But you're tired, Hal. And, anyhow, none of this can possibly interest you. Let's go up. Darling Halmar."

"Darling Lorna, But that's all very well, first making me curious and then putting me off with a short instalment like a serial story in a newspaper. Waiters and fatal woman?—Join me in a nightcap and tell me all about it. I'm not a bit sleepy, and you look more wide-awake than I have ever seen you after a party."

She refused the whisky-and-soda, but she related simply and well the story of the eager Australian art student, the only son of a father who slaved to give him his heart's delight, a chance to express himself on canvas. And then the woman, indolent, insolent, well off, caring nothing for him, a woman who enslaved him so that he threw up his training at the best art school in the city, and stealing his next term's fees which his father had just sent him, used them for a passage to England on the same boat as hers. And when they landed in England, she just said good-bye over her shoulder, languidly like that, and went off with a man who had come down to meet her in a huge car. And he awoke—"

"'And found himself on the cold hillside.'" Sir Halmar had a taste for apt quotation, and "La Belle Dame Sans Merci" seemed to him particularly fitting for that wild tragic story.

"So he wanted his passage back, I suppose? And where do all the waiters come in, rushing about with napkins on their arms?"

"He didn't go back then. He was too ashamed. He couldn't bear to face his father. He got a job in a restaurant in Soho and lived somehow, fierce and miserable, and cold, icy cold with disillusion. But I think he had courage, don't you, Halmar? Months and months of all that. And then he saw in an Australian paper that his father had had an accident—no, wait, I'm wrong, it wasn't an accident, it was a hold-up. He was alone on the ranch, you see. It was in a lonely spot, and two or three brutes—" She shivered in the warm brightly lit drawing-room. "Halmar, they left him lying there all night alone, bleeding, while his only son, thousands of miles away in England, was spinning about with plates of spaghetti and stew and garlicky salad. I'd like to kill that woman, the one who got him away. Kill her."

"Now, now, Lorna, you're getting too worked-up over this. I grant you it's a sad story, but you ought to be inured to them now with all your refugee work. Mrs. Fogarty told me today that you had done a fine job; they didn't know how they'd have managed without you."

"This was different."

"I expect it was," her husband chuckled. "I expect the refugees' stories are all true; that's the main difference."

"I deserved that," said Lorna in a low voice, her eyes fixed on the ground; and Sir Halmar was stricken with remorse. Was this taunt all the reward he had for her, when the élite of Tarmouth had been congratulating him that night on his felicity?

"I didn't mean it, Lorna, I expect the poor devil *was* speaking the truth. What did he want from you? His passage back to Australia, I suppose? That's opening his mouth a bit wide, isn't it? What did you give him?"

He never seemed aware that he gave his wife no money and that she had little of her own. In his mind he had written himself down as an indulgent husband, and that phrase conveyed reassurance. Obviously an indulgent husband meant a petted wife who was given everything she could desire. And every sight of Lorna and every sound of her sweet-tempered gratitude re-established that amicable picture.

"But, Halmar, of course I wouldn't give money to any of these people, however much I believed their stories, and I don't usually, as you know. Of course I wouldn't, when it's against your principles. That's why I said just now I was so happy and so safe, because I *had* someone to tell me what to do when I'm so uncertain and credulous and foolish."

He told her that she was much too modest, and repeated to her again a few of the phrases he had heard of her that night. Embarrassed, she swept them into a corner and out of the way as though with quick strokes of an invisible broom.

"Anyhow, he didn't want his fare back to Australia or anything like that. He had saved up enough; tips, I suppose; he always knew he'd need to go back to his father one day, and so he rigidly scraped together every penny until he lost his job a few weeks ago. The slump. And perhaps he wasn't quite as good as the others. Inattentive. He confessed to me that all the time he had been longing and longing to hold a brush again and smell the paints on his palette—"

"Beastly smell," was Sir Halmar's comment. "So he had his passage? Well, then?"

"But he owed his landlady several weeks' rent. He could have gone off and left it, but she needed the money and she had been kind to him and he couldn't bear to. Hal dear, I want you to scold me. I've been weak and sentimental, and you haven't much use for sentimentalists, have you? I ought to have said No, straight out, but I said instead; 'I'll ask my husband. Leave me your address.'"

"Lorna, Lorna, you're incorrigible. Stick to your committees and let Miss Soutar deal with this sort of visitor."

"I will. I must. Oh, I wonder if I shall ever grow up and learn to handle life as you do, firmly from the very beginning. I'm so disgusted with myself. And this poor little artist, this poor little waiter, he's the victim because I gave him that much hope. He'll be disappointed every time the post arrives and doesn't bring anything. Please, Hal, scold me. I'm haunted; I've a sort of desolate feeling all round my heart."

"I can't have you with desolate feelings round your heart, blaming yourself and not sleeping. How much does he want?"

Lorna whispered: "Seven pounds fourteen shillings."

"And elevenpence?"

"Elevenpence? No. What made you think of elevenpence?" He patted her shoulder, and then, relishing the feel of the warm satiny skin, stopped patting and began to stroke.

"Lost, a sense of humour. Anyone finding same and returning it to the owner at Beechcroft Manor will be suitably rewarded. No, I merely suggested it because he was so plausible over the exact sum he needed. Seven pounds fourteen shillings, you say? Not a round sum, as it might be five or ten pounds?"

"You still don't believe his story or you wouldn't use the word 'plausible.' Don't let's talk of it any more, Halmar. What was it that I heard Sir George saying to you, which was to be made public tomorrow? Candidly, I don't like Sir George very much, mayor or no mayor. He's so satisfied with himself. 'You must know, dear lady,'" she mimicked the deprecating organ tones, "'that I have dabbled in the arts myself.'"

"Dabbled, has he? Well, now he'll have to dabble in a big way, for his daughter Josie's engaged. That was the news."

"I'm so glad. Who's the man? Josie deserves somebody nice. She's always been sat upon at home. Neither her father nor her mother realize how lucky they've been to have an old-fashioned daughter who doesn't rush away to be independent."

Her husband knew she was thinking of that defiant young daughter who had rushed off at the first hint of a stepfather. "My poor Lorna," he thought. And began to grumble aloud at the heavy expense of a wedding-present for Josephine. "It's a barbarian habit. The head of the tribe sells his girl, and we all have to roll in with handsome offerings according to how many head of cattle we have on our ranch—"

But the word "ranch" was dangerous tonight, and he wished he had not used it. "Better be something silver, I suppose. A rose-bowl, a tea-service, a set of finger-bowls?"

Lorna, seeing him really bothered, came to the rescue with an inspiration.

"A portrait of Josie! What could be more original? You know we're going to have a small exhibition for refugee artists at our Fair, so that they can get commissions. One of them, Karl Leismann, is a really first-class portrait-painter. I mean, in his own country and in good times he could charge—oh, well I don't know, whatever top prices are: a hundred pounds, two hundred? But he'll do Josie for practically nothing, I know, and thank God for the commission into the bargain. And *what* an advertisement for him to have it exhibited among all the wedding-presents. The Brantons are bound to make a splash with the reception. It looks like providence," Lorna finished breathlessly.

Her husband was delighted: "Jove, you're quick-witted, Lorna. Old

George has so often strutted as a patron of the arts that he's bound to welcome the notion of Josie sitting for Leismann, even if he would rather have had solid silver. There's nothing George likes more than the sight of other people spending good money. But your idea, why, it'll make every other present look vulgar and commonplace: A portrait of the bride by the famous Karl Leismann! Lorna," Sir Halmar finished in some excitement, "you've as good as put twenty pounds into my pocket."

He had said it, and though Lorna remained silent, her head a little bent, a faint musing smile playing about her lips as though she were merely echoing her husband's hearty pleasure, the word "pocket" as he pronounced it struck him as though it were a small electric current running from his wife's mind to his. "Pocket." "You've as good as put twenty pounds into my pocket." And he knew at once that what he had to do was to take out a fistful of this twenty pounds, say seven pounds fourteen shillings, and hand it to her for this beggar man whose story, true or false, had so powerfully stimulated her imagination. And he was bound to say, even without her testimony, and women always fancied themselves on instinct and so forth, that it sounded true enough as she repeated it. The circumstances were odd and arresting, unlike the usual run of these tales: the grim old father on the sheep ranch, indulgent to an only son who longed to be an artist. And then the woman, one of these cold, indifferent devils. And the restaurant where he darted to and fro with dishes, the air sizzling and steaming and rocking all around him. Yes, it might be true. And anyhow Lorna, tender-hearted soul, was fretting because she had been weak and given the man hope where she must have known there was very little hope to give. But women were all sentimentalists, you couldn't blame them for that. The number he had had to hoist out of the muddles into which they had landed themselves, all through sentimentality and making promises they couldn't keep. Playing the Lady Bountiful too, that was a temptation. Not but that Lorna had done really fine honest work for months past, for lost causes. They had all said so, tonight. He was in high good-humour. Lorna. She sat at the head of his table and did him credit. Every man envied him his possession. She wore her clothes with an air of breeding and dignity. She did not pester him for money. She made him feel that he was a wise man and a strong man. If she had a fault besides this tendency to a credulous disposition, which showed her, after all, to be essentially feminine, she was perhaps a little cold physically; he had no complaint of her tenderness; she adored him, she admired him, she had a sweetness and suppleness of disposition which made her every surrender to his wish an act of wifely grace which thrilled him. No, it was only that some man or other, probably her first husband, whom she spoke of hardly ever, must have been a brute to her, given her a shock, disgusted her with the whole business. He did not doubt but that in time he would win her to a more spontaneous abandon. Already tonight—Why, look at her, her very skin seemed to glow and tingle and her eyes were brighter than he had seen them since—Yes, now he came to think of it, she reminded him tonight of their very first encounter when she had burst in on him, a strange woman with a husky voice and an air of wildness, to explain about the letter she had never written him. Tonight she was alive with the same sensuous provocation. How had he roused her? Yet never mind how. The thrilling reward was for him, no one else.

"Time for bed, my dear. Look, it's past one o'clock. I'm not going to have you lying awake any more worrying about your Australian protégé. You can send him the money in the morning and be damned to it. Here you are, eight pounds. Get a pound changed and give me the six shillings change tomorrow."

"Yes, thank you, I think that's all." And Miss Soutar gathered up a mass of letters and papers and prepared to leave Lorna's sitting-room. But Lorna, sitting at the desk, called her back. "No, wait a minute. I want you to take this and register it."

She placed five notes for one pound each in an envelope, took an address from her book and copied it: "Edmund Vincent Burgess," she murmured as she wrote, "Post Office, Bath," and handed it to Miss

Soutar. "Can you send it off at once, if you're not too busy? I don't want it to wait for the rest of the batch. It's rather urgent."

"Of course, Lady Barnard. Did the party go well?"

"More than well. I think it's the best we've ever had."

"Yes, Alfred told me Sir Halmar was triumphant this morning."

"Men worry a lot about parties, don't they? More than we do. Oh, and by the way, get in touch with Karl Leismann, Mrs. Parker will know his address, and ask him to come and see Sir Halmar this evening. We have quite an important commission for him. Fix a time when I'm not booked up. I want to be there; it's always nice to see someone getting good news, isn't it?"

After Miss Soutar had left the room, Lorna sat thoughtfully fingering a little pile of money in front of her: two pound notes, a ten-shilling note and some silver. Then she rang and told Webster to send Susan.

"Susan, have you ever heard a recitation called 'The Gambler's Burial'?"

"Not my favourite joke," said Susan glumly. "I've had a bad run lately, I told you."

"When's the next orgy of roulette?"

"If you go telling Sir Halmar what I tell you, there won't be no next. Webster did say something about tonight. You're out, aren't you? and we need a bit of a pick-me-up after the way you kept it up last night."

"Well, here's a little present for you to gamble with. I expect it'll bring you luck, but don't say you got it from me."

She gave Susan the two pound notes, the ten-shilling note and two florins, leaving a couple of half-crowns and a shilling on the desk.

"Cri!" exclaimed Susan; "two pounds fourteen! You could knock me down with a feather. Been robbing the bank?"

"No. I spoke to Sir Halmar about that poor man who paid me a visit yesterday, and he gave me a little more than was needed to meet the case. I've just sent him the five pounds he asked for."

Susan regarded her with the grin of uneasy reverence with which an urchin at a party might regard a particularly clever conjurer. "My sainted aunt!"

"Not at all," said Lorna, modestly disclaiming the tribute.

"But look here," Susan slowly recovered. "That bloke that called yesterday. You told me he was a fake. He tried to bluff you with a passage to Australia dated three years old."

"He did, poor lad. But it wouldn't have been manners to have told him so."

"And yet you went and sent him a fiver? Why, in God's name, didn't you keep it?"

Her employer spoke in tones of cold punctiliousness:

"Because, my dear Susan, it wouldn't have been honest."

Chapter Four

Their mother's telegram ran: "Coming to see my darlings today five o'clock longing welcome Jay home love Mummy." It had been sent off from Paddington Station.

"I don't want to see her." Jay was shivering like a sick animal with damp staring pelt. "Need I see her, Molly?"

"I think it would be simpler in the end if you could face up to it, Jay. You needn't be alone. I'll be here."

Molly saw no reason to add to Jay's outcast bitterness by telling her that Lorna had told Sir Halmar, when she married him, that she had only one little daughter; so she found it difficult to answer Jay's passionate outburst:

"Why does she say 'welcome Jay home'? She didn't welcome me. She wasn't there. I came out two days ago. And my home, as she calls it, ought to be Beechcroft Manor. A proper mother would have met me and taken me there at once. Why didn't she? You can't drop in and see your daughters all grand and condescending on your way back from the dentist's, and call it welcoming me home, can you, Molly?"

'You can when it's our mother," said Molly. But she was pleased that Jay should be in a fury. It was at least more promising than that broken-stalk hopelessness. Jay apparently still reacted violently one way or another to Lorna's voice, even from a distance. Molly felt nothing at all about her mother any more. All her love was divided between her sister and Neil. All her friendship went to Shirley. She could never forget that betrayal of Jay working out her sentence. The cord was cut in that moment for Molly. She could even be amused when Lorna swept in, fulfilling in her poise, the drip of furs from her shoulders, the confident dangle of her earrings, Jay's cross childish prophecy of "grand" and "condescending."

"Jay. Oh Jay, my sweet baby. Darling Jay."

Molly was a little puzzled. Although Lorna's entrance and broken cries were over-dramatized, the girl's stage training and instinct assured her that her mother meant every word of it. And she was faintly moved, as by some far-off echo.

But Jay remained curled up in her chair with face frozen and averted; one shoulder hunched as though she were not being embraced, as though she were clad in cardboard. Lorna, distressed, turned in appeal to her other daughter: "Mollykins."

"Hullo, Mummy. You're looking splendid. I like those foxes."

Lorna tried to find a seat in the room where she could draw down her two little daughters one on each side of her. But the act required collaboration, and she had to abandon the gesture and do it verbally instead.

"I can't believe it," she murmured in that husky tender voice which always went richer and huskier when she was deeply moved, as undoubtedly she was now. "I can't believe that we're back, all three of us, just as we used to be in our happiest times. Do you remember Benares Lodge and what fun we had? Do you remember that dreadful donkey's head that I made for you, Molly? And now," smiling at her with tremulous lips and genuine tears dimming her eyes, "now you're the least donkey of the three of us."

"Oh, I don't know," replied Molly politely. "You've not done so badly;

I heard through Susan that you were the big noise on all sorts of charity works and refugees and committees and all that."

"Does Susan write to you?"

"Now and then. Not often. But she came in to see me a month or two ago with a Mr. Webster."

Molly's demure voice betrayed no hint of the mischief she felt at the sight of her mother suddenly becoming Lady Barnard displeased with the butler.

"That must have been while I was at Gleneagles. Really, Susan had no right to go dashing up to London with Webster and then telling me nothing about it. I shall have to speak to her."

"Poor Susan. Don't be too harsh, Mummy, she's such a sensitive down-trodden creature."

"Still fond of teasing, my squirrel? Jay darling, don't sit staring out of the window like that, as though I weren't here. Come and have a good cuddle down and don't bother about anything, while Molly and I talk about what nice things we're going to arrange for you."

A quiver shook the girl's body, but she still stared out of the window as though she had not heard, as though nothing concerned her, nothing to do with life or nice things to be arranged.

"Is she like this all the time?" Lorna sunk her voice. "Molly, what can we do? She's turned against me. She's turned against her own mother. It's terrible. How could I help what's happened? What did they do to her in that place? She's like a wounded bird dashing herself against the bars. I can't bear it. Molly."

This was just what Molly had dreaded. Coldly, a little disdainfully, she quenched Lorna's rising emotion.

"Please, Mother, don't get romantic. There's no need for it at all. If you have any plans for Jay, there's no reason why you shouldn't tell us about them, but you have your own life now, and really I can manage."

"I didn't know you could hurt me so much."

"I didn't mean to hurt you. I don't intend to let you hurt Jay, that's all."

"As though I would! You talk as though I were a monster. Isn't Jay my own little girl?"

"Did you say so to Sir Halmar when you married him?" sternly.

Lorna flung out her hands in a gesture of appeal which Molly remembered terribly well.

"But, Molly, how *could* I tell him then? It wasn't the time. It would have ruined everything. Are you still too babyish to understand that this is a world of facts we live in, hard material facts? I was thinking of you and Jay as well as myself. Jay's future more than her present. Then, there was nothing I could do for her. But later on—And I was getting too old to work. I was losing courage. You don't know what it is to go on and on, and then suddenly feel your feet beginning to slip and slip down into the abyss. Tired. I was tired out. All those years—and your father dying like that. And Jay would have to be provided for, perhaps for the rest of her life. Responsibility was crushing me. And then this chance came along. I took it, lying if you like, anyhow equivocating, for Jay's sake later on. Now—"

Jay turned round. Her eyes were not so blank as before. Her name repeated over and over again had penetrated, and she had listened perplexed to the rest of Lorna's defence.

"Lying about what?" she asked slowly. "What would have ruined everything? What were you doing for my sake later on?"

"Damn!" Molly muttered. Jay should have been guarded from this, in the madly sensitive state of her soul.

But Lorna said with a recovered dignity that reduced Molly to the status of a well-meaning but blundering schoolgirl: "Molly dear, you must leave us alone. This is between Jay and her mother, and I can't allow anyone else, even you, to misrepresent me to my own child. There are some things that you can't possibly understand yet, even using your imagination, which you haven't tried to do. You can come back in half an hour."

A sudden scream from Jay flashed between them, sharp as a sword.

"*No*. No. I won't be left alone with her. Molly, don't. You mustn't. Don't leave me. Molly, don't, don't!" She collapsed into stormy hysterical sobbing.

The door opened and Shirley walked in.

Neil and Shirley had warmly allied themselves with Molly in her passionate crusade to bring Jay back to life. They both felt it was too big a job to let the child tackle alone. If unswerving love and steadfast undaunted purpose had been enough, Molly had all this and to spare. But though she was no fool, she was too young and enthusiastic to realize at first that catastrophe had smashed Jay far beyond a younger sister s unaided mending.

Jay had dwelt in an aerial rainbow-coloured kingdom of her own fantasy. Two years of stone reality had left her still bewildered, defiant of kindness, mistrustful as a savage little animal; listlessly turning away from delicate pleasure in however seductive shape it was offered her; saying: "These have nothing to do with me." She saw herself as an outcast, but this time without any picturesque swagger to the part: all that had disappeared during those dragging iron-coloured months in Borstal. As for love, what link had she with love now? Molly had a lover, Neil Inglefield, and Jay accepted the name without wonder, as she accepted everything; though the fact that it was a name she had seen when a child carved on a tombstone in Monte Carlo should have swept her with at least a passing glimpse of a world full of freakish twists and diversion. Her mother also had a husband to shelter and protect her; her mother was Lady Barnard, respected and unassailable. Only for her, Jay, there was nobody; could never be anybody again.

Now and then she brooded over Toby; but worse things had struck her down than losing Toby as her champion and playmate. She had almost forgotten him; a grey mound of sullen days stood as a rampart between her and that unreal lilting flowery summer of bells and balloons.

"No," said Neil to Shirley, after the first meeting between himself and his future sister-in-law, "I shall never like her. She's meant too much grief for Molly. But I'm deadly sorry for her. She's been knocked right out, and it wasn't her fault originally."

"As though anything were anyone's fault, originally," said Shirley.

"Our little Lorna. What happened when you two met?"

"I said: 'Hullo, Lorna,' and she said: 'Shirley Dennison! Now if an angel had come to me and whispered, "Choose of all the world whom you would most like to see here on your doorstep for a good chat about old times," I should have said Shirley Dennison.' And then we attended to Jay, who was in hysterics—at least, Molly and I did; she wouldn't let her mother come near her. And before Lorna left she said: 'You must come and stay with me, Shirley.' And I said: 'That will be lovely.' That's all. She's grown almost handsome; I know now what they mean by a presence."

"When it's Lorna, I prefer an absence."

"Cheap. Of course, one was handicapped by Molly and Jay, or one might have spoken a few well-chosen words. We must all work together on Jay, Neil. The girl's terrified. One can't get near her. She pushes even Molly away. We've got to make her feel natural again, join her up with the living world even by the most frivolous things. Molly's taking her to Alphonse tomorrow to have her hair set in the new way."

"Is there a new way? Your head still looks like a black billiard ball with a white wing on either side. Quite effective but a little forbidding."

'That's to conceal my slack and unforbidding nature. You'd better arrange a theatre party, Neil. Get in two other men who won't put their foot in it too heavily, a man for her and a man for me—"

"And tea for two and two for tea," interrupted Neil flippantly. "What sort of men?"

"Nice men. Susceptible men. Men of easy conversation. Gentlemen who prefer blondes. And Molly can join us for supper afterwards. And a whole fleet of cars from the Neptune. Tails and white ties, the gleam of satin and the flutter of chiffon—"

"God!" from Neil. "What's all this novelette stuff."

"What Jay needs. Have you sent her flowers?"

"Every blessed day," said Neil. "Molly saw to that. Their rooms look like a film star's just landed from Hollywood."

"Did she say anything about them?"

"Rather. She said: 'Thank you, Mr. Inglefield,' in a flat little monotone. She must have had a sweet voice once. So then I said: 'You might call me Neil, I think.' And she said: 'Thank you, Neil,' in the same voice, completely limp. But she did watch me out of the corner of her eyes to make sure I didn't hit her, so I suppose that could be construed as showing some interest in a fellow human being."

"But, Neil, you're not telling me that they—"

"It's not part of the system, no. But, Shirley, my dear, try and imagine if you can what sort of companions she had. Some of them, anyhow. You can bet your life they weren't exquisite little creatures with lily-white minds. She's been badly hurt, that girl, and I doubt if you'll get her right by a shower of new frocks and silk stockings and transparent lingerie."

Shirley smiled ruefully. "We took her to Chez Simone, and all of us, Molly and I and the *vendeuse*, worked on her to try and make her declare what colours she thought would suit her best. It was like trying to pump life into the drowned."

"Drowned. Yes, it's a frail kid, no strain of sturdiness like Molly's. And as I said before, she's feeling naked and exposed to every cutting wind. Well, go ahead, and good luck to you. I'll do my share; the sooner we can get her sane and whole again, the sooner Molly will come to me. I can't stand waiting, and I've got to wait."

"Patient Neil," she mocked him.

Molly had made up her mind that she was not going to let herself be overcome by despair; but the days went by, and Jay still gazed at pleasure with eyes that were dull or frightened; still shrank from her sister's poured-out affection. And the efforts of Molly and Shirley and Neil seemed to be perpetually tipped up and rendered naught by a mischief-making Poltergeist, who saw to it that one of the two really charming young men whom Neil provided for the theatre party should immediately, with hardly any preface, have related an incident of the Juvenile Courts, and that the other should ask Jay if she knew Southampton and the New Forest. If they went to a film, you could almost hear the Poltergeist chuckle as they threw a trailer on the screen: "Coming next week, the breath-taking epic 'Reform School,'" which neither Molly nor Shirley in their careful choice could possibly have foreseen. The very beggar in the street, trying to make a sale with his shoe-laces and studs and buttons, whined out a tale of having been in prison and it was so cruel 'ard for a man to reform as everyone tried to push him down again and there was no chance to let him forget ...

Shirley, with the idea that desperately foolish measures might succeed where wise ones had failed, told Molly to take Jay to a fortune-teller on pretence of wishing to consult Madame Grania herself. And the exuberant Celtic lady, who was reported never to fail in a pageant of future events brightly coloured as a muster of peacocks, on this occasion and on first sight of Jay's cards gave a shrill Celtic wail and saw a large grey building with barred windows: "And would it be in the past now, or would it be in the future? Ah, what's the difference? Sure there's no such things as time, the past and the future are as one. ... And I see you crossing the water and goin' a long long way from the land of your birth. ... Here's a woman neither dark nor fair, between colour, with the dark furs slippin' off her shoulder. ... Yes, dearie, she's visitin' you tonight ... tomorrow ... yesterday ..."

Finally, not wanting to leave Jay alone one night when Shirley was not available, Molly took her along to spend an evening in her dressing-room, where, in the easy come-and-go behind the scenes, Jay for once shed her listless demeanour and became excited and defiant, and chatted about her past to a group of girls gone suddenly rigid with embarrassment. And then the young actress who shared the dressing-room with Molly was fetched by her best boy, and introduced him, and prompted by the Poltergeist: "Call the lad Toby," said Elinor carelessly to Jay; "his other name is too much of a mouthful."

"They call me Toby because I'm a faithful dog, added the young man. "You can't imagine a Toby who isn't faithful, can you?"

Chapter Five

←→

Alfred was of the opinion that this had better be stopped at once. And firmly. "This" was a letter addressed to Sir Halmar Barnard, Bart. (which he was not), in an uneducated writing on cheap paper, postmark Tarmouth, signature none.

"To Sir Halmar Barnard, Bart.
Dear Sir,
Look you ought to know this. Your wife that you think so grand has got a daughter just come out of prison. Embezling they called it but thief is what decent people call it. Careful not to tell you, wasn't she? Told you she had only one daughter, her on the stage. Well she's got two and one been in jail. Lord I could laugh thinking what a fool you've been. Had for a mug from the start and going about beaming as if someone had given you the crown jewels to take care of. Just a mug. One would think at your age you'd have learned not to trust any woman who chooses to pitch you a tale. I'm all for above-board and plain speaking. This letter isn't meant to do any harm. It's to put you wise. See?"

"Disgusting," thought Alfred, "really quite disgusting." His face boiled with chivalrous indignation, for he liked and respected Lady Barnard; they were on excellent terms; sometimes they even had little jokes together, about the sort of things that Sir Halmar forgot or wilfully neglected and pretended were not there, hoping that Alfred too would forget and let him alone. But sometimes, when they were not joking, Alfred was dismayed to see her eyes recede into some abstract distance. As though she had some secret sorrow in her past, reflected Alfred. For certainly Lady Barnard's sorrow could have no connection with her prosperous present and her happy marriage.

But recalling now this look in her eyes, Alfred felt his first spasm of uncertainty with regard to that pestilential letter. A secret sorrow in the past? Might that not have been a daughter in prison? And if it were, would he be best serving both Sir Halmar and Lady Barnard by showing this letter or suppressing it? He had full authority to tear it up if he wished. Sir Halmar's correspondence, except where it was obviously personal, was entirely Alfred's affair and could be dealt with as his judgment and experience dictated.

Anonymous letters. Horrible tainted things. And this one, like most of them, had that snarling note under its affectation of an honest desire on the part of the writer that everyone concerned should be as honest and upright in all matters as himself. Or herself, Alfred amended, perplexed and miserable. He re-read the scrawl. Then his common sense came to the rescue. After all, Lady Barnard was a *grande dame* to the finger-tips. Was it likely that she should have a daughter serving a sentence for embezzlement?

"And even supposing that such an incongruous tragedy had ever happened to her, would she, I ask you," said Alfred into the air, "would she have married Sir Halmar and placidly said nothing about it? and even have told him she had one daughter only, and brought that one daughter home to dinner? A most attractive girl, but foolishly resentful of her stepfather. Jealous, perhaps; now I come to think of it, she never appeared again."

Well, then, all that being safely established, what was there to worry about? Nothing. Nothing whatever. Absolutely nothing. Therefore Sir Halmar had better be shown the letter, discover the anonymous sender and deal very severely with him or her. No doubt some political enemy. Or no, that was unlikely, for though there was only one spelling fault, the whole balance and phrasing of the letter betokened that it sprang from what Alfred called "the lower classes." A servant who had a grudge against Lady Barnard.

He toyed with the idea of showing it to Lady Barnard's personal maid. She might supply a clue. Better, however, to take it straight to Sir Halmar. Susan Orris had a careless tongue. She was not Alfred's idea at all of a lady's-maid, who should be discreet and noiseless and highly superior. If he had a fault to find with Lady Barnard, *if,* mind you, it was that she allowed this Susan too much intimacy, too much liberty of speech. A lady's-maid should not be brisk and saucy, with an outrageous twinkle in her eye. He asked Webster once how Lady Barnard's maid was getting on at Beechcroft Manor. "Living in the country must be strange for her." But Webster, rather to Alfred's surprise and annoyance, instead of delivering himself of a few carefully considered adverse opinions, became almost enthusiastic over Susan, and came very near to saying that she was the life and soul of the servants' hall.

At that rather irritated stage of Alfred's musings, Sir Halmar came into the study to start on his morning's work.

"Anything special, Alfred?"

Without giving himself time to lose confidence in the decision he had reached, Alfred replied cheerfully: "Only this, Sir Halmar. I thought you'd better see this, just in case you'd wish me to take steps to discover and punish the sender. Poison pens. It's a scandal. All over the country, growing and growing." He went on talking nervously about poison pens, while Sir Halmar read what could not, thought Alfred, be a very pleasant communication, however baseless the purport.

Sir Halmar burst into exclamations of fury and contempt. He said several times: "I will *not* have it." He said he would not rest until he had rooted out the author of this scandalous message and brought him or her to justice. He and Alfred wondered together if it could be anything political. Then decided that personal malice was at the bottom of it, a desire to wound, to influence, to destroy happiness, to set fire to the home.

At first Sir Halmar seemed to have no doubt that it was directly shafted towards him. But when Alfred, very tenderly, for he was feeling towards Sir Halmar like a mother at the moment, brought up his own theory that it might have been written by an enemy of Lorna's, a servant perhaps whom she had dismissed and who was seeking revenge in the dirtiest possible way, Sir Halmar admitted that there might be something in that. But why invent such a ridiculous story which could be contradicted in two minutes?

"Perhaps the reptile hoped that it would plant a suspicion in your mind, Sir Halmar, that not all Lady Barnard's denials would altogether eradicate."

"Then the reptile was a bloody fool. Suspicion against Lorna, indeed." Sir Halmar strode to the fireplace, pressed the bell and told Webster to ask Lady Barnard if she would mind coming to the study immediately. "And say there's nothing to alarm her," he called after Webster, as the butler disappeared. Lorna must not be suffered to think for one fleeting shadow of a second that he could believe a vulgar anonymous letter directed against her.

He smiled fatuously in recollection of their first meeting when harassed by life, fleeing from panic, she had placed herself under shelter of his wisdom and experience. And it had never failed her, never. It was not going to fail her now. He spoke a few words to Alfred on the subject of perfect love translated into perfect trust.

Lorna entered. Sir Halmar met her and took her hand. Then he signed to Alfred to go, but to leave the letter behind. It struck him that Lorna was looking pale and queenly as though she had a presentiment that she was about to be arraigned; perhaps his expression had frightened her. He hastened to reassure her, even before he enlightened her as to the cause, that the sternness, the wrath, was not for her: She was now and for ever the dear object of his love, his respect and his protection.

After which, very carefully lest it should explode in her hand, he gave her the letter to read.

Lorna's eye sought the signature before she read. "Anonymous. Oh, Halmar, how—how degrading!"

He hardly allowed her time to read it before he broke in with: "Now, my darling, what you must understand at once, for my sake much more than for yours, is that I'm not asking for a single moment, as a more stupid husband might do or a husband with a stupider wife, whether there's even a grain of truth in it. The question doesn't arise. What I *am* afraid of hearing you say is that, loving and trusting you so proudly and freely, why should I ever have distressed you by showing you this letter? Why didn't I throw it into the fire, as I would any other foul unclean thing that I found lying about my study? Yes, it's on your lips. Don't say it, not till you've heard my argument. You and I, my darling, are citizens. As private people we could burn this, and forget that it had ever brought a trail of slime into our home; but as citizens it is our duty not to forget it until we have followed it up and punished the poison pen. Other people's possibly more precarious happiness is at stake as well as our own. The poison pen never stops at a solitary letter. There. I had to say this first so that you should not reproach me. Now, have you any notion what enemy could have invented this? Pure goodness often makes enemies, you know. Somewhere in the past, in the background, could there be somebody whom you've forgotten all this time who might want to do you an ill turn?"

He had stopped at last. Lorna never tried to speak until she was quite sure he would not be going on again. Now she gravely shook her head; her earrings swayed.

"I have no idea who might have written it. What's the postmark? Tarmouth? I don't see how anyone in Tarmouth could have known about Jay—"

"Jay?"

She faced him. Her eyes were steady; her voice under complete control.

"It's true, Halmar. I have two daughters, not one. And Jay was serving a sentence for embezzlement when we first met. I was afraid to tell you. I thought it might upset everything. I thought I should lose you. Now somebody who hates me has written you the truth and I won't lie about it. I didn't like lying about poor little Jay—"

She stopped on a choke of tears in her throat. But her husband could only stare at her stupidly, and in a stunned fashion repeat one or two of the words she had just spoken:

"Two daughters? You lied? Serving a sentence for embezzlement when I first met you?"

Lorna bowed her long shapely neck, but remained mute, waiting for him to realize; waiting for the thunderbolt, the earthquake, the forked lightnings and tidal wave, all those metaphors by which man likes to express his rage as Jove-like, lordly and catastrophic, instead of a fretful sense of injury fumbling for expression on a grand scale. She had a wine-coloured chiffon scarf twisted round her throat and falling in long graceful ends. Wine-colour suited her now, with that new rich dignity she had acquired, better than the flimsier flowered patterns by which she used to encourage a tendency to mere daintiness of style.

"Lorna!" thundered Sir Halmar, beginning to find his deeper chest-notes, "are you standing there telling me that this infernal libel is true?"

"Yes, Halmar, quite true. I'm sorry."

"You have another daughter? You have two daughters, not one, as I thought? as you told me?"

"Yes, Halmar."

"And this—this filth is true as well, that she's been serving a term for embezzlement?"

"It was my fault. She was so young, only eighteen, when she left home; not yet eighteen. And perhaps I'd spoilt her; perhaps I had brought her up to expect too much out of life. She was so gay, so sweet. It was hard not to spoil Jay. I should have told her more about reality. She believed that everybody would love her, everything would fall into her hands. You had only to hear her laugh, she—"

"Never mind about her," the chest notes had reached a bellow. Sir Halmar was stricken and yet he towered. "This is between you and me, between husband and wife." Then he broke, not altogether, but slightly: "Oh, Lorna, if you'd come to me at the time and told me the truth. Couldn't you have trusted me to say: 'Bring the little girl here when her punishment is over. I'll do my best for her and give her a second chance'? Or even now, two years later, now after you've lied, even now at the eleventh hour if I'd heard it not this way but from you direct—"

"Yes," Lorna agreed softly, "I know."

"But to hear it *this way*." He crumpled the sheet of paper in his hand and hurled it into the grate. It fell harmlessly just short of it, and Sir Halmar felt baffled. He needed a detonation to accord with his mood.

"Letting me hear it like this. Making me a laughing-stock even by the sort of mind that could compose that. God, I can't forgive you."

Lorna sat down and took a cigarette. Then she suggested that her husband should sit down too. She remarked she had something to say to him, something important. But her manner was so comfortable that it could almost be said to be chatty. And Sir Halmar, rightly believing that it was he who had had something important to say to her and this reversal of attitude was slightly impertinent, refused to accommodate himself either to an armchair or to the situation. The gibe in the anonymous letter, now that it was justified, was smarting pretty badly: "Had for a mug." It was quite true; he *had* been had for a mug. And by Lorna of all people, his dear, his perfect wife. And here she was, asking him to sit down. Looking enormously burly, and, as he hoped, impressive, he declined. He stood on the rug with his back to a blazing log fire, and scowled into the leisurely spaces of the drawing-room. Look at all he had given her. Look at it. And what had she done for him? Provided food for anonymous letters. Certainly she would have to move unforgiven about his house until long after Christmas. In April, perhaps, if she were properly contrite, and when with the spring the young beech-leaves—

"I must go away, Halmar."

"Oh?" shortly. "Well, perhaps it might be better for three or four weeks, until—"

"For ever."

Shocked out of his assumption of injured righteousness, he could only repeat in blank dismay: "For ever?" This was not at all what he had meant.

"I'm sorry, Halmar. You've been very good to me. You've given me such a great deal. But your knowing about Jay helped me to make up my mind. I must be with my poor little girl, now and for always. She needs me. You're strong and you can manage without your wife. But she is desperately in need of her mother."

But Sir Halmar had never seen *Candida*, and if he had, the reasoning would not have appealed to him.

"You haven't bothered much about her all this time, have you?" he exploded. "Good God, if this is how you felt, why did you only own up to one daughter when you married me?"

"Because I was tempted. You were so generous, Hal, so protective, so wise. Quite suddenly out of the blue you offered me a throne in the blue heaven. What I'd wanted all my life and never had: a man to look up to. A man who was stronger, a great deal stronger than myself. I dared not take the risk and lose you then. Now, now I must atone. Jay is delicate and unhappy and defiant. She's hating the world, I longed to be looked after, but you see I wasn't meant to be. It is I who must look after Jay."

Sir Halmar went through a variety of emotions while listening to this speech; the principal one, however, and the thought which dominated the others, was: It's all right. She won't stick to it. Here is her life, luxurious, sheltered; here at the head of my table, everyone looking up to her. Talk about the little girl being weak, why, she's pretty tender herself. She's a real woman. This is just sentimental mother stuff. Let her work it out of her system. It won't last six months.

"She's got her sister to look after her, hasn't she?" he said aloud. And Lorna slanted him a swift look as though to divine what had suddenly brought him into this state of satisfied calm. Then, turning her head again to gaze through the window opposite the fireplace, she gave a little swift secret smile: great ruddy chestnuts tossing in the wind and rain out there in the park; proud and splendid chestnuts even with their last leaves about to be stripped. She may have been thinking they were very like proud and splendid men; tall and ruddy men.

"Molly? Yes. Jay's with Molly now, but that can't last. Molly's the younger of the two, and, as you saw for yourself, not very stable. She's passionately fond of Jay, but she can do nothing for her. I can do everything. Besides, Molly is going to be married almost at once, and what will become of Jay then?"

Oho, mused Sir Halmar, so that's what she's up to? Though it was curious how Lorna, his beloved treasure, had within the last hour become an enemy with strategical plans of advance and retreat. *That's what it's all about: She hadn't meant to tell me about the girl till I got* this letter, and now she's working on me to invite her to live with us down here. She thinks that rather than lose her—

No, madam, no. I happen to have had a lot of experience of women and their little ways. I thought you were different from the others, but they simply can't help being tricky. It's in their natures. I was a fool—

But his thoughts checked on that and would go no further, for it was too like the phrases in the letter which had stunned him. Instead, he allowed his thoughts to reach back to the joyous moment when Lorna, whom he still loved and admired devotedly, would return to him purged of all this high-flown nonsense about the weaker and the stronger, responsibility and atonement, and which of them needed her most. As though it were some sort of silly competition (he had never seen *Candida*). Yes, he might well have allowed her to have her erring daughter to live with them had she been honest from the beginning, had she spared him the mortification of hearing about it in this unpleasant way. Women were no psychologists. He was not the type of man to be exposed to insult and then persuaded and wheedled by pretty feminine ways and wistful female tears into issuing invitations which he might earlier have done on his own initiative had he been given a chance. No, madam, no.

He stared down at Lorna, still gazing with pensive eyes through the window at the trees and the park. Of what was she thinking? That she would miss that park? miss it sadly and all that went with it? Never mind. Next year would be the happier for both of them; next spring. As for the girl, she could go and live with her married sister. Do 'em all good.

Susan gasped when, summoned to her mistress's bedroom by a much more than usually urgent and prolonged peal of the bell, she was confronted by a Lorna with laughing excited eyes and cheeks in a glow, already flinging her dresses from the wardrobe on to the bed as though she were tossing bouquets in a carnival. "Have all my trunks and suit-cases brought in. We must pack at once. We're going away."

"Going away?" repeated Susan, aghast.

In a spate of merry words, Lorna told her. Susan could not remember ever before seeing her mood so undisguised.

"Cri! if I didn't know how she hated the stuff, I'd say she was oiled. Still, she's one that can get oiled on her own plans!" Susan was feeling an amused detachment, and appreciation of a good show: "Lord, you never know with her, but this is the biggest she's ever pulled on me. Fancy chucking up all this, once she'd got it. Still, what's the good? If you're bored to death, no amount of carpets and tables and champagne for dinner can do you any good. Besides, there's Jay."

Susan reflected on Jay. "Good thing she should have her mother; she's like her mother. Good thing for Molly too; now she'll be able to marry."

Thinking furiously, she obeyed orders and began to pack, while Lorna rattled on: They were free for adventure and new encounters; they need never be bored again; they were going to America—

"Here. Wait a bit. When you say 'we,' how many does that count up to?"

For a moment, Lorna's pace was checked. She gave a puzzled stare at Susan's back bent over the trunk; then laughter returned. "Not quite the old firm, no. We must leave Molly behind, this time. Molly isn't ours any more; she belongs to the enemy boy. Still, bless her, we must all be happy on our own sort of road."

"I wasn't thinking of Molly. I was thinking of me. Sorry."

"Sorry?"

"I'm not going."

She knew, without having to turn round, that Lorna's main reaction was not dismay or the fear of loneliness, but the startled vexation of one who had been relying as a matter of course on good old Susan in the Sancho Panza rôle of lumbering faithfulness; sighing a little; even pitying herself; a bit of a burden: three to support instead of two, in a new and strenuous existence in a new and strenuous country.

That Susan's guess had been right was proved by the chilly note in her employer's voice as she asked:

"Then you propose to stay on here without me and with Sir Halmar?"

"Yes and no," replied Susan briskly. "You see, I'm getting fixed up with

Webster, and we're not sure yet whether we'll go or stay. Stay, I hope. Your husband's always treated me generous, and I like the climate and the house and the other servants. It's all pretty comfortable and not too haughty and ruling-classes."

"I'm very glad," said Lorna, smiling. "It's fortunate that Beechcroft Manor suits you so well. That's nice."

"No good getting riled. You know the old proverb about making your bed and lying on it. People always seem to think it means a bad bed and a bad night on it, but sometimes it's the opposite. This time, for instance; for me, anyhow."

Lady Barnard, on the verge of quitting the sybaritic surroundings where Susan had settled herself so finally with a wriggle of sheer pleasure, allowed a slight crossness to escape into her congratulations:

"I shouldn't have thought that Webster would have been your affinity. He always struck me as a little severe and melancholy. But perhaps—"

"Severe nix and melancholy my foot. You've been mistress here, you're Lady Barnard, you've only seen the butler side of him. He's a grand boy. We suit each other a treat. It was that there roulette-board of his," sighed Susan, a dreamy look creeping into her eye, "that first drew us together. It's been creeping on him for a long time, he says now. Ah well, I'm getting along in life, and it's now or never for a good husband."

She could not quite refrain from this much plaguing of Lorna. Lorna was so obviously disconcerted that out of her own enterprise in marrying Sir Halmar, her maid and companion of so many years should have made such excellent material arrangements.

Then she returned to good temper; laughed and admitted to Susan that she *had* expected an act of deathless fidelity, and been a fool to expect it. She kissed Susan warmly and sincerely, and wished her good luck.

"What beats me," said Susan, blinking rather hard and in her crossest voice, "what beats me is what you're making whoopee about? Is he going to give you a packet to pay for your get-away?"

"I'm not accepting a penny. Not one penny. I lived on my tiny income once and I can live on it again. I'm proud, Susan, proud."

"First I've heard of it. Then how do you reckon to get to this America of yours?"

"Oh well, I happen to have a small lump sum; a hundred pounds; it ought to be just enough for two second-class passages to America." And she added demurely, enjoying a joke that even Susan could not and should not share: "Poor Miss Gardiner, she didn't need it, after all."

"What's that?"

"Nothing. Oh Susan, Susan, think of having my Jay with me all the time. All the time, now. No one and nothing to keep us apart. It's too good to be true. She won't turn away from me, now that my whole life is hers. My poor sweet baby whom they shut up and tormented. I'll make her happy in spite of them. She's got a mother now."

"Had one for eighteen years that I know of, and didn't do her much good."

"Jay never got into trouble till she left her home. I shouldn't have allowed it."

"—Lord, how I'll miss you!" gasped Susan, without any apparent relevance.

Chapter Six

Directly Molly entered the bedroom and saw Jay, she knew that change had broken in during her absence. Usually when the younger sister returned after the show, Jay lay huddled together with the bedclothes tightly drawn up round her, pretending to be asleep; pretending too hard, for there was always an appearance of strain in the performance; she could not relax even to deceive Molly. But tonight Jay was sitting up in bed hugging her knees, her eyes had a smoky sparkle and her mouth curved in a smile half demure, half subtle.

"Jay!" cried Molly happily at the sight of her.

"Mother's been here," said Jay.

"Oh!" Molly casually began to throw off her clothes.

She reminded herself that Lorna was now right away out of Jay's life, in a world of her own; she could do nothing from such a distance; that last time she had appeared, she had been remote as Selene stooping to kiss Endymion, and far from having to fight her influence over Jay, Jay had resented her bitterly. Nevertheless, the rapt air with which her sister had said: "Mother's been here," started a faint premonitory thrill of horror. Why was Jay's mood so changed?

"What did she say? Did she bring him with her?" For it struck Molly that possibly their mother had at last taken the risk of acknowledging Jay to her husband, which might perhaps account for the illuminated letters in which Jay had spoken the words: "Mother's been here."

"Oh, Molly, I'm so happy. So safe and happy at last. I can't tell you how it feels, knowing she's going to be there always now to look after me."

"So it's that," thought Molly. "Oh well." Her heart lightened again. Jay as the debutante daughter of Lady Barnard, home from a finishing-school abroad, perhaps; Jay shyly but gracefully handing round teacups in the Barnard drawing-room; Jay in the hunting-field; Sir Halmar giving a ball for Jay; Lorna fussing about Jay's suitors. ... Funny, when you came to think of it, but quite a sound notion. "And Neil and I could get married almost at once," thought Molly with a leap of the heart.

It was odd that Jay had so readily consented to the prodigal rôle, and not remained proud and sullen.

"She has given it all up," Jay was still hugging her knees and laughing into a rosy future: "her rich husband and Beechcroft Manor and her position as Lady Barnard. She said none of it was any good to her without me. She has renounced it all. Sir Halmar knows about me now, but she doesn't mind. I think she's rather glad. It's me she cares for most. We're going away together, she and I, alone. We don't want anyone ever again except each other."

Molly was now drenched in fear. Fear searched deeply into her very bones. For though she sternly prepared for battle, her knowledge of her mother, and still more her knowledge of Jay, told her that she was fighting for a cause hopelessly lost. Already she realized that Jay was no more than a twisted paper spool that had been wound round and round with fine embroidery silk, and had acquiesced contentedly to the winding.

She sat down on the edge of the bed; "Listen, Jay darling, all this sounds a bit melodramatic, doesn't it? Are you sure she meant it and wasn't just putting on one of her acts? After all," Molly brutally reminded her sister, using any weapon that came handy, "we both have reason to know she can pull the tale quite effectively when she wants something, and the truth needn't have anything to do with it."

But Jay's new reverie could not be so easily dispersed. "When she wants something? Yes, I know, but all that was long ago. What could she want this time?"

"You, She couldn't bear to feel that you had slipped away; that you were rather despising her even though she was Lady Barnard; that her patronage and soft fox furs and oh-my-darling-child-let-a-mother's-heart-yearn-over-you didn't work."

"It didn't. Of course it didn't. So she's given it all up. That's *real*, to care for me as much as that. It couldn't have been easy, when you had got used to luxury and importance. And she wasn't just staging a scene, Molly. She was the first time she came, and I know the difference. She wasn't a bit dramatic this time. She didn't cry or anything. She only kissed me once. She was just comfortable, as she used to be in Huntingdon Terrace when we loved her best. That's why I felt so safe. I haven't felt safe like that for years. She was funny, too; we laughed together a lot, especially when she told me about Susan. Just think, Molly, Susan isn't coming with us. She's staying on at Beechcroft Manor and marrying the butler!"

"Not coming with you *where*?" asked Molly grimly. Her brain was tearing about, trying to find a loophole for rescue before this incredible thing actually happened; before Jay was finally encompassed.

"We're going to America. Nearly at once. In three days I think there's a boat. Not one of the big expensive ones. Mummy won't take a thing from Sir Halmar, not money or anything, except her own usual tiny income. Isn't it lovely?"

"And how are you going to manage?"

Jay answered in genuine innocence: "We can work."

Molly was afraid she was going to be sick. She clenched her hands hard and crushed down that deadly feeling of nausea. Did Jay herself acknowledge for one moment what this work was likely to be? No, she was still too starry, too intoxicated by the size and scale of the sacrifice made on her behalf; it gave her substance, where before she had felt thin and shadowy as the stale chilly air of a cell.

"Come on," whispered Molly to herself. "It's now or never. Come on." Desperately she flung herself against the situation; desperately recalled the past and what Lorna had done to them, trying to stimulate Jay's old defiant attitude against their mother.

But Jay was drowsy with a narcotic from which she did not wish ever to be awakened. She had had too much to bear and no resources to bear it with. Molly divined that ever since her release she had felt exposed and frightened and longing to be back again in the womb where nothing could hurt her; to be dominated body and soul by her mother and accept all that Lorna did as right and perfect.

Molly shed all scruples of decency; used every lever to try and raise Jay out of the perilous pit. She knew it was terrible to be fighting their mother as an unscrupulous enemy, but less terrible than the alternative which even now and even to herself she scarcely dared clothe in words! Surely it was fantastic beyond all fantasy to believe that Lady Barnard—

But Lorna's elder daughter would not let herself be drawn either into battle or assent. She listened to all that Molly said, but still with that amiable far-away smile on her lips as though nothing of this concerned her in the least.

"Yes, I know," she murmured several times. And: "Yes, of course I remember." And: "Yes, wasn't it beastly." And suddenly she flung her arms round her sister, pulled her down on the bed, and buried her face in a warm shower of kisses: "Molly *darling*, you've been such an angel to me over everything, always."

"But Jay, Jay, it's not being an angel. I love having you here. I've missed you more than I can possibly say. Can't we go on like this always? It's quite safe and snug."

Jay's sidelong look was affectionately mocking.

"For how many hundreds of years are you going to put off getting married, and go on being safe and snug with a beloved elder sister out of jail?"

"Even if I married Neil, you could live with us."

"I can't bear to have to be eternally grateful; I can't bear it. And as long as I'm here you won't marry Neil because you know Neil doesn't like me. Own up."

"You come first," said Molly steadily.

"No, I don't, Molly. I come second. Neil comes first with you, and that's natural. I'm glad. I'm not jealous. I couldn't be," quickly, "because I come first with Mummy. I wouldn't have believed it if she had just talked, but she's proved it now, hasn't she?"

At Jay's triumphant tone, like a challenge by trumpet, Molly knew it was over; knew, weary to death, that she was finally beaten

Chapter Seven

←→

Neil was idly twiddling the dial of Shirley's wireless while they waited for Molly to come in from her matinée. Suddenly he exclaimed: "Damn!" with a great deal of energy and disgust, switched off, and walked over to the fireplace where Shirley lay back in an armchair doing a crossword.

"Pinched your finger?" she asked without looking up.

"I've suddenly remembered. I clean forgot to get Father's marriage certificate back from our little Lorna that last time I went to see her. Was there ever such a fool? I suppose Mrs. Neil Inglefield will now be wandering from coast to coast across America, explaining with the hurt wide-eyed stare of a crucified child about the bad man who married her and deserted her and left her with two children to provide for—no, one, as she's only using Jay."

Shirley soothed "She's much more likely to use her Lady Barnard marriage certificate. It's grander."

"I don't know." Neil gloomily threw himself into the opposite chair. "Blake, Inglefield, Barnard; she likes to change the rings."

"She'll know you're going to marry Molly quite soon. Molly will be Mrs. Neil Inglefield. She wouldn't use that name. Whatever we may think about her, you know, Neil, she did love her children."

"'Can a mother's tender care—'" he mocked, "'Cease towards the child she bear?' Yes, it can. Every time."

"I wonder why she preferred to exploit herself as Mrs. Inglefield instead of Mrs. Blake? Molly said she hardly ever used her legitimate marriage lines."

"I can answer that one." As usual, whenever they talked about Lorna, Neil and Shirley became fascinated to the exclusion of all other topics. "She hated me more than anyone else in the world, and it gave her a sort of vicarious satisfaction to vilify me and pose as a martyr to my wickedness. Like sticking pins into a wax image of her enemy. She gave herself the same vicious pleasure by blackguarding a governess, an innocent Miss Gardiner, who once quite rightly did her out of her fare to somewhere."

"How d'you know?"

"Molly told me; she heard her do it once, but I expect it happened fairly often. A lot went on inside Lorna's head that we can only guess at."

"Neil, *what* goes on inside her head? Did she ever know herself what she was like? Does she really think she's good and persecuted and that we're all against her and that she was an excellent mother and that it was all done for the children's sake?"

"I expect so. Call it rationalizing on an awe-inspiring scale. It's maddening not to be sure of her mental processes, but we can only guess from what we see; from her effect on other people: on Susan, Jay, Molly, Alec, Marcus, Gracie, you and me and the lamp-post."

"Who's the lamp-post?"

"Sir Halmar Barnard, I suppose," laughed Neil.

"I can't imagine how she could bring herself to give him up after she had made such a catch: riches, power, respectability, an impeccable position, a devoted husband; it's unbelievable. All solid. All hers. After all, the life she had led up till then, the life she'll be leading again now, was touch and go all the time."

"Lorna always preferred touch and go, to bed and breakfast. And I expect there was a good deal of bed and breakfast with Sir Halmar."

"Even then—"

"She didn't need passion, you know. She didn't want men to be in love with her. She wanted power and a dangerous gamble and the fun of winning and putting herself over as a sweet saviour, till at last she came to believe it herself—perhaps. Perhaps not. And she liked planning sudden bold unexpected strokes of strategy when she was in a tight place, and annexing minor states and justifying that by a protective manner."

"Who's the minor state? Jay?"

"Poor little idiot, yes. God forgive me, I never liked her from the start."

"At least you and Molly are free to marry; her responsibility for Jay is over. What's going to happen, Neil, about your two jobs?"

His teeth flashed white and triumphant at being able to provide a solution, instead of having to ask Shirley's advice on the old problem of whether a husband should allow his wife to work, or whether a wife on the stage did not mean a husband in mischief? "We've settled that. We discovered that we should never meet at all if I went on travelling about for the Neptune Company and she remained a juvenile favourite of the footlights. It's never much fun for one to make a sacrifice and the other to have to stand about and hold it with a slight wobble. So we're *both* chucking our jobs. We're going to start a hotel together; somewhere in the Cotswolds, I think. Do it on a big scale, but have our own house just out of sight round the bend of the hill. Probably a home farm. Imagine Molly with calves and lambs and foals and fawns and puppies and all the rest of it."

"And all the rest of it," Shirley repeated.

"What do you think, Shirley? Will it do?"

"Anything you did with Molly would do." Shirley smothered a sigh, again finding it hard not to be envious. "You're such a pair of ecstatic loonies. Never mind. Molly deserves it. She's had a long wait."

"Haven't *I* waited?" somewhat injured. "It's much harder to wait for Molly than to wait for me. So I've had the worst of it."

Shirley filled in a couple of difficult clues in her crossword. Then she mused aloud, more as though working it out for herself than to enlighten Neil: "Most things that go wrong are due to impatience. This speeding-up of life, it's a mistake. If we could wait without even willing things to move forward any faster; wait for happiness, to learn a creed, to get thinner, fatter, for miracles, for misunderstandings to clear themselves, for lunch, for daybreak, for fine weather, for tomorrow, for pace in our shorthand, for the next bus, for rain, for rescue, for argument to finish, for sleep to visit us, for the soup to get cold, for the paint to dry, for the postman, for love to cease from vexing us—"

"Too difficult," retorted Neil briefly. "Lorna couldn't wait. She had to stir things up. That's why she sent Barnard that anonymous letter"

Shirley sat up; the paper slid from her knee: "Neil, do you mean that letter which blew up everything? the one telling about Jay? She sent that herself? *Lorna* did?"

"One can never know for certain," said Neil. "Yes, I rather think she did."

Chapter Eight

They paused at the end of the second rubber, for highballs, while Mrs. van Straten went on with what she had been saying after the first rubber:

"I do wish you'd seen her for yourself, Edith. You'd have been crazy about her. Tom was, weren't you, Tom? That's one of the things about having Tom at home all the time, he doesn't have to miss what happens during the day, as he used to. No, you needn't wink and laugh, Frank; Tom enjoys having retired and living up here and being able to walk out to the lakes just whenever he feels inclined, and—"

Edith Linden said hastily: "Go on telling us about your English visitor today."

"Oh, it was a terribly sad case. Terribly sad. I wish I could have done more for her. She was a very handsome woman, such breeding and delicacy. You could tell at once she had never had to *ask* for anything before in her life. I mean, things had just been laid before her, hadn't they, Tom? Tom felt the same. And the young girl, her daughter, she was very sweet and pretty too, but she didn't say anything, she just kept her eyes fixed on her mother all the time with such a look of devotion it would have nearly broken your heart to see. She was to have been presented in May if all this hadn't happened. I do think it's hard."

Frank Linden, who was one of the more hard-headed citizens of

Minneapolis and not as fundamentally amiable as the van Stratens, broke in with a hearty: "Well, what was this sad case? They've come a long way to tell it. You haven't even let us know her name yet."

"Oh, but that's part of her trouble. Her name is really Lady Barnard, and she was very much respected and looked up to, and did a lot of good in the town where she lived. Then Lord Barnard received a mean anonymous letter saying her first husband, a man called Inglefield, wasn't dead at all. He had just kept out of the way to be spiteful."

"Well, for crying out loud," from Edith Linden.

"And Lord Barnard actually lost his temper and blamed *her*. She's a very proud woman, and she thought it would be easier for her little daughter, she only has that one child, if she herself just slipped away over here and disappeared altogether and worked for her living. It was a sacrifice, but Lord Barnard was very attached to his stepdaughter and might have got over his anger quicker that way and had her presented all the same. But the girl followed her mother, gave up everything, her social prospects and simply everything, and here they are. And poor Lady Barnard doesn't even know if she ought to be calling herself Barnard or Inglefield. Tom and I both advised her to take her daughter out to the Coast and get some work there; with the winter coming on, they'll never stand it in the Middle West; the girl looks terribly delicate, like a white flower. And she said yes, she had thought of it; she had heard of the lovely sun and the warmth, but it was so far away and she hadn't enough for their railroad fares."

Afterword

About a quarter of the way into Jack Lee's 1947 film adaptation of *The Woman in the Hall*, Molly (played by Jill Raymond) tells her mother (Ursula Jeans): "I know the law well enough to know that, if they knew what you were doing with Jay, they'd take her away from you and never let you see her again."

The film is a largely faithful, if selective, adaptation of G. B. Stern's 1939 novel – the main difference being a happier ending, for those who might be considered worthy of one. But while much of the dialogue and scenes are taken directly from the book, this direct allusion to the law is an original addition. Throughout the novel, Lorna and her daughters are rightly wary of the police knocking at the door for crimes of fraud, forgery or even extortion, but there is no overt acknowledgement that her most constant crime is a form of child abuse. Instead, it is a constant hum in the background.

Midway through the book, Stern summarises the experience of 'Visiting' that Jay and Molly have endured through many years:

> You could not foretell what would happen, nor how it would
> happen. You wondered vividly what sort of a house it would be.
> Mummy never told you beforehand, she just let you wonder till
> you got out of the bus or the Underground and walked along—and
> suddenly she stopped and said: "This must be it." And then came
> the terribly hazardous game of getting past the servants. Sometimes

it was a haughty butler and sometimes a cross parlourmaid, except once by accident when it had been a darling Swedish woman with eyes like a kind cow, who wasn't a servant and gave them money as well as a dreadful heavy old typewriter. But servants or secretaries were grim and incredulous, and always put up obstacles; you turned icy and held your breath and your legs trembled like water.

In the twenty-first century, the imploring email, phone call or text has largely replaced the phenomenon of going door-to-door – or, in Lorna's case, to specifically predetermined doors – and asking for money with spurious reasons explaining why it is desperately needed at that exact moment. In post-War Britain, however, it was a common occurrence – more often for ex-soldiers and other men than for women, though Lorna and her daughters certainly wouldn't have been a total anomaly for the well-to-do households which fielded many similar requests. Some, of course, were genuine: before the creation of the welfare state or the National Health Service, the charity of individuals might be somebody's only recourse for help. As Marian Sinclair says in the novel, echoed by many other characters in similar phrasing: "All the same, I'd rather be swizzled by eleven crooks than send away one honest person."

Throughout the novel, we see much more from Jay's and Molly's perspectives than their mother's – particularly around the rationale for these 'Visits'. We may initially believe the lie of the contented family and share some of the girls' confusion about what is and isn't true in the stories that Lorna tells to her would-be benefactors. Our understanding leaps ahead of Jay's and Molly's, of course, and one of the affecting elements of *The Woman in the Hall* is seeing hope and uncertainty interweave in their slow recognition of what their mother is doing.

The moment that the realisation truly dawns is particularly striking. Jay has been 'Visiting with Mummy' and they do not talk

about it all evening. Instead, they perform the normal functions of families: eating tea, playing games and getting ready for bed. And then …

> A silence so long that either might have dropped off to sleep. Then across the room through the dark came Jay's voice, on a queer, thrilled note: "Molly, are we beggars?"

Stern leaves the question unanswered, ending the scene there. What makes the moment such a jolt is that it is the first time the word 'beggar' is used in the novel. They only discuss 'Visiting' – usually given that capital letter, making it seem like an official but mysterious activity. The idea that it could be considered 'begging' comes as a shock, and pierces to the heart of their sense of familial identity. Jay doesn't ask 'are we begging?' (that is, a question about what they are *doing*) but 'are we beggars?' (a question about what they *are*).

'Beggar' or 'beggars' appear eight further times in *The Woman in the Hall*, mostly referring to other people. One of the few other occasions on which it is used to describe Lorna and her daughters is when Neil explains he won't go to the police, but that she isn't safe from others doing so:

> "What danger of prosecution you may be in, of course, from other victims of your racket as a professional beggar, I don't know. You seem to have had extraordinary luck in escaping the law so far—" He stopped suddenly, for Lorna had given a little gasp and then begun to cry.

Lorna's uncharacteristic tears could have various explanations: the vision of a future in prison, of course, or (as she goes on to say) because Molly hasn't been open about her relationship with Neil. But Stern is judicious about when she uses 'beggar', and it's also likely that hearing the word is a further cause of Lorna's breakdown. She is forced to consider herself as a 'beggar', rather than the self-portrait she has painted for herself. To her respectable family, 'begging' is in a totally different category, even if it would be hard for any of the characters to pinpoint the distinction between what they are doing and what would constitute begging.

Perhaps it is the picture that Molly shares, remembering a bus journey with her mother. She recalls: "a woman came along lugging a baby in a dirty shawl, a real beggar woman; she got on to the step and then right in, whining that it was for the poor biby's sake and for the love of 'eaven kind lidy." The main distinction is clearly class, demonstrated in the phonetics of Molly's attempt to replicate the woman's accent. But the law did not – officially, at least – distinguish these activities on the basis of class.

When Molly refers to 'the law' in the film adaptation of *The Woman in the Hall*, what law might she mean? While the novel opens in the 1920s and spans a decade or more, the most relevant law was enacted in England and Wales in the middle of the narrative's timeline: the Children and Young Persons Act 1933. As well as setting a new minimum working age of 14 years old, it included penalties for anything 'causing or allowing persons under sixteen to be used for begging'. Section 4 under 'Prevention of cruelty and exposure to moral and physical danger' states:

(1) If any person causes or procures any child or young person under the age of sixteen years or, having the custody, charge, or care of such a child or young person, allows him to be in any street, premises, or place for the purpose of begging or receiving alms, or of inducing the giving of alms (whether or not there is any pretence of singing, playing, performing, offering anything for sale, or otherwise) he shall, on summary conviction, be liable to a fine not exceeding twenty-five pounds, or alternatively, or in default of

payment of such a fine, or in addition thereto, to imprisonment for any term not exceeding three months.

Lorna would be horrified if her children did their form of begging 'in any street', but 'place' certainly widens it to include the halls and parlours of the men and women Lorna targets. Later in the Act, in a section on the definition of 'in need of care or protection', it states that the fact of any child being found begging shall 'be evidence that he is exposed to moral danger'.

'Moral danger' may now sound like quite an old-fashioned term, and some of the phrasing of this section does indicate an unspoken expectation that the children in question are more likely to be found among working-class communities than the middle-class world Lorna inhabits – but it is equally clear that Lorna is breaking this law. These stipulations sit between a section on prostitution and brothels and one on giving 'intoxicating liquor' to children under 5. Lorna's discussions of violin lessons and exclusive schooling don't fit easily alongside these worlds, but Neil – and, later, Molly – are able to see that she is not, in reality, an exception to the rule. 'Visiting' is a form of child abuse. As Neil thinks, 'even her love did not save them from being callously used as pathetic assets, on and off, during those ghastly ten years when they were small enough to be of value.'

There is an irony that Lorna's unexpected elevation to the upper-classes doesn't bring money with it. While, as Lady Barnard, she is considered wealthy – and has the home, clothing, jewellery and connections of a wealthy person – she does not have access to cash. When on the other side of a 'Visit', she cannot give the man the five pounds he is after, or any amount at all, for 'Sir Halmar gave his cherished wife everything in the world she desired except ready money.'

Stern doesn't include much over commentary on the role of women in the early twentieth century, but this brief mention does help us

realise that agency and independence aren't accessible to many women in the period – even when they have reached the highest echelon of society, they may well be expected to go to their husband with each request for money. Nobody would have used the term 'begging' for this, but there were doubtless many cases where the dynamics weren't truly all that different. Lady Barnard must present her case, tell her story, and hope for her benefactor's generosity and benevolence – just as Lorna did under any of her various surnames.

Simon Thomas

Series consultant **Simon Thomas** created the middlebrow blog Stuck in a Book in 2007. He is also the co-host of the popular podcast Tea or Books? Simon has a PhD from Oxford University in Interwar Literature.

Well, then, since that has got you nowhere, stop being yourself.
Beat your way out. Escape.

Originally published in 1945, what begins as a domestic novel quickly evolves into a dramatic thriller. Penelope Shadow, like her name suggests, has made very little mark on the world, until she purchases a typewriter and becomes a sensation as a romance novelist. She can now afford to buy her own house, and employs a capable and attentive young man as house-keeper. But what are his motives? Is she in danger? As events twist and turn, she must summon up the strength and ingenuity of her characters as the novel moves to a tense denouement.

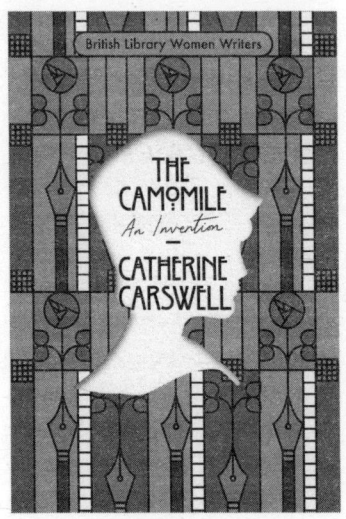

I have a Room! A room all to myself and away from home!

Set in twentieth-century Glasgow, this effervescent novel is widely considered a fictional counterpart to Virginia Woolf's feminist essay 'A Room of One's Own'. Desperate to escape her intrusive aunt and explore her creative talents, the vibrant Ellen Carstairs rents a room ten minutes' walk from home in which to find the peace and solitude to focus on her music and writing. Written as a 'journal letter' to her good friend Ruby, Ellen reveals her fluctuating ambitions and dreams as she endeavours to negotiate her place in the world.

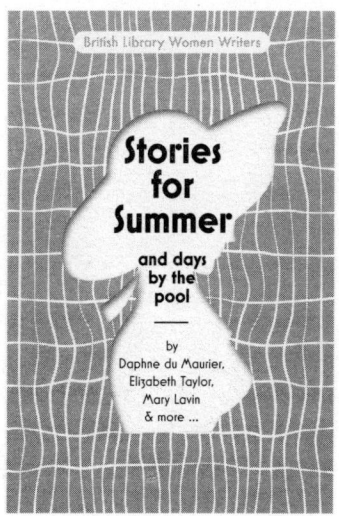

*There were fewer boats now down in the harbour. She got into bed. Her
sunburned body was fiery between the coarse sheets; she felt wonderfully lulled
and, turning her cheek at once to the pillow, she let out a long breath like a
contented sigh, and fell asleep.*

Recline on a sun lounger with *Stories for Summer,* a collection of seasonal
tales to idle away the hours of a long summer's day. This new anthology
includes the talents of Daphne du Maurier, Elizabeth Bowen, Virginia
Woolf, Muriel Spark, Elizabeth Taylor, Katherine Mansfield, Mary
Lavin, G. B. Stern, Mary Norton and Phyllis Bottome. Don't forget to
re-apply the sunscreen...